Xavion &
Sareyus

Isaiah Sleeping Turtle Johnson Bey

NEWMAN SPRINGS PUBLISHING
320 Broad Street
Red Bank, NJ 07701

First originally published by Newman Springs Publishing 2023

ISBN 978-1-63881-020-9 (Paperback)
ISBN 978-1-63881-021-6 (Hardcover)
ISBN 978-1-63881-022-3 (Digital)

Printed in the United States of America

Contents

Dear Readers,

O'siyo, may this tale uplift you as it did me. I would not be the man I am if not for Xavion and Sareyus. To my therapist, mentors, guidance counselors, teachers, and friends, thank you for your genuine support. This tale would not be told if not for your interest and encouragement.

It was Xavion and Sareyus who lead me to my heritage, my nationality, my free national name, and my higher self. It was Xavion and Sareyus who helped me rise from where I once fell. May they walk with you forward into yourself and your future. Wado. Alsalam Ealaykum.

With Love, Truth, Peace, Freedom, and Justice.

—Isaiah Johnson Bey
Sleeping Turtle

Warning

This novel contains content that may not be appropriate for readers under the age of eighteen and should be approached with caution. Although this book is fictional, it contains various realistic and mature behaviors. The depicted negative acts and beliefs are *not* promoted or celebrated. This story may contain several mental and/or emotional triggers. If you are sensitive, then please read at your own risk. Such depicted content includes the following:

- graphic violence
- adult language
- sexual references and situations
- bigotry among ethnicities
- one depicted suicide and two attempts
- references and imagery of self-harm
- referential and visual implications of rape, pedophilia, and sexual violence

No graphic sexual imagery or violence is displayed or portrayed in detail by any characters.
Reader discretion is advised!

Disclaimer

The East and West Nodin flags, stars, symbols, and seals are *not* representative of Israel, Judaism, Morocco, Islam, the Moors, or any related groups of people.

Of the Hallowed Pantheon & the Planet Earth

The gods witnessed the feuds among the mortals, and they were angered beyond imagination. The earth entered its Third Life, the reason being of the previous two Armageddons that destroyed the planet. The planet was destroyed because of the corruption, greed, and wars of mortal kind. Each time the gods rebuilt the earth, they reissued the previous inventions for the newer world timeline.

In a time during the Earth's First Life, the goddesses and gods crafted the Earth as a lush and beautiful ball of life. The planet was designed as a home for the many children of the Immortals. The mortal children and various creatures would inherit the planet and live under the deities' watch. As the deities would come into existence from time's beginning, the goddesses and gods appeared in groups. Though their exact ages are seconds apart, they share that time as a birthday.

Lyannis was the first goddess to exist. Her golden-blond hair and bright energy gave light to the void of space. Lyannis came to exist as an adult woman in her twenties.

Miolannis came second. As she began, the temperature became cold. Her sleek black hair possessed a white stripe that came down behind her head.

As the next deity came, a sense of duality existed within it. As the two halves separated, Sarue and Carune stood as fraternal twin sisters. Sarue is the older of the two. The sisters' brown hair is what distinguishes them from Lyannis and Miolannis. The other physical traits that differentiate the sisters are Sarue's hazel eyes and Carune's blue eyes. Sarue came out as the taller and leaner of the two. Carune, though not much shorter, possessed denser curvature. They both care for nature. Sarue cherished vegetation while Carune preferred the water.

The last goddess to exist is Sareyus. When Sareyus appeared, the temperature became warm. Her orange hair is her distinct trait, but she shares the green eye color with Miolannis.

For the goddesses, all are beautiful, distinct, and powerful. They created the first females. The goddesses each valued visual beauty in different ways. Each goddess created a necessary thing to contribute to the lives of the mortals. Lyannis partnered with Sareyus to create the sun, a colossal star of bright light and fire. Lyannis and Sareyus also created summer, a season of bright light and high heat.

Miolannis created winter, a season of low temperature to counter the excess heat from the sun. Winter allows the land to rest and lay dormant. Sarue created vegetation of all kinds, and these plants grow at varying times. Sarue also created spring, a season for all plant life to regrow after winter. Carune created all water; thus, she holds dominion of all bodies of it. Sareyus created fire. Fire allows warmth, the cooking of food, and acts as a light in the dark. The dominion for the season of fall was given to Sareyus. Fall acted as a prelude to winter. The coming and waning heat of spring, summer, and fall is under Sareyus's power.

Alongside the goddesses were the gods. Both groups began simultaneously. First came Jahveyis. As he appeared, a sense of negativity arose. Jahveyis's existence sparked the negative aspects of life; his being allows balance. When he appeared, Lyannis knew she represented the light while Jahveyis stood for the dark. His hair is straight and dark brown. His eyes became red. He felt no hostility upon seeing his opposite. As his nature commanded, in time he created war, crime, death, and destruction.

Next was Tovis. As Tovis came into being, a sense of levity and humor occurred. Tovis appeared with long brown hair and blue eyes. From his palms, he bore air and electricity. Tovis created the sky; and from his sky fell rain, hail, and snow. The sky housed the sun and the moon.

Bravious came after Tovis. Bravious was identified by his darker skin, brown hair, brown eyes; and he is the tallest of the Immortals. Bravious also possessed the highest form of fitness; his dense muscular body could be compared to a mountain. Bravious then created Earth in its many forms. A partnership of Bravious and Miolannis occurred. It was they who crafted the moon.

Jado is the youngest of the gods. Upon his existence, he was aware of his higher intelligence and refined self-awareness. He passed these two things onto the other Immortals. Jado's appearance is of brownish-blond hair and blue eyes, and he wears eyeglasses. Jado created speech, language, literacy, science, evolution, and education.

The Immortals gifted their creations and gave the race of humans a proper image. The deities gave their male and female creations physical traits that symbolically resembled them. The Immortals based the human anatomy off of the apes, who predate the humans.

Lyannis granted physical beauty and blond hair. Miolannis granted black hair, green eyes, and a light skin tone called Snow Skin. Sarue gave hazel eyes, brown hair, joy, and knowledge for agriculture. Carune gave mortals blue eyes and water to quench their thirst. Sareyus gave mortals orange hair, bravery, music, and instruments to make it.

The gods also granted their own gifts to mortal kind. Jahveyis gave mortals darkness, and for balance, he gave them sensitivity to feel guilty for any wrongdoing. Whenever someone would die, his spirit stood in and gave them funeral rites. Bravious gave physical strength, brown eyes, and visual art to humans. Tovis gave storms. Those storms rained water and gave life to Sarue's plants. He also gave humans hunting abilities.

Jado gave the abilities to learn and educate. Jado assisted in making syllabuses for many of the oral languages. Jado and Jahveyis are magical opposites. Jado's magic is centered around birth, life, healing, and medicine. Jahveyis's magic is rooted in hexes, poison, toxicity, and death. In time, two clergies arose to maintain balance among the magics.

The world was divided into four continents: one residing in each main direction. The northern continent is a mixture of large forests, mountains, and a massive ocean surrounded this beautiful land. In time, as the arctic poles began to develop, the north of this land became frostbitten. This is home to the humans of Snow Skin. This land is named *Nodin* and its people are called *Nodinians*. They were informally named *Nods (Nodes)*.

The southern continent is much different. This continent exceeded the north in size and is divided into six islands with five that circled each other. The sixth is in the center of those five. The five outer islands were mainly inhabited by tribal settlements. People of separate tribes all lived together on the large mainland. This continent is named *Soruth*, and its people are *Soruthians*.

Soruth is climatically diverse. It contains regions that have mountains, land plains, jungles, forests, and arid deserts. Soruth is home to the humans of Ebony, Ember, Sand, and Bark skin. The Soruthians are referred to as The Four due to the four skin colors. Each group inhabited the four directions of Soruth.

The reason for the different skin colors was not necessarily the work of the gods. Rather, the sun shined its brightest and Sareyus's heat was hottest in the other continents. Another factor are the different ape species that each group of humans are based upon. The regional traits of the people and their land varied greatly. Bravious took great pride in the diversity of the mortals.

Each of the human Soruthians have their own island. The fifth island is the smallest. It is home to a mortal race of animalistic humanoid creatures. Some of them lived in Nodin and elsewhere. These were people in ancient times who experimented with science and magic.

These people have small horns, pointed ears, and fangs with clawed nails. They could stand as tall as seven and a half feet! They share the same skin colors as their full human counterparts. They live in a tall mountain that took up most of the small Soruthian island.

These people are called the *Theranths*. Theranths are skilled blacksmiths and miners. They crafted items that the gods envied. In only two generations, the Theranth Soruthians tunneled under their small island beneath the continental plates and under the ocean floor! Soon after tunneling, many of the Theranths became modified with water-based physical traits. Their skin became blue and scaly. Their hands and feet became webbed. Fins grew in practical areas. They could swim quickly and became a nightmare to navies. These aquatic Theranths are known as "Aquranths."

The eastern continent is of several islands. It is home to a group of humans who were colored *gold*. They mostly have dark hair and varying almond-shaped eyes. The two strongest countries here are *Hongangou* and *Daichi*. The people of Hongangou are called *Hongangan*, and the people of Daichi named themselves *Daichinian*. Hongangou and Daichi are two of many countries. They are part of the continent known as *Yazjia*, and its people are generally called *Yazjian*. Hongangou is governmentally known for having many dynasties where chosen families govern the country. Daichi, on the other hand, is commonly divided into warring states. Their feudal Daimyo lords command legions of samurai warriors to fight in their name. Hongangou and Daichi are the easternmost nations in Yazjia. In the north is *Mognoa*, *Namvie* in the south, and *Napel* in the west. Napel is the crossroads between Yazjia and the Bark lands of Soruth. Soruth and Yazjia are connected by a natural land bridge from northeast to southwest.

The continent in the west holds many names across the world; it is commonly referred to as *Sönderfall*. This land is mysterious and scarce information about it exists.

In the year 3185 FL (First Life), the Nodinian people nearly destroyed their home and each other, killing for sport, mistreating the land, dehumanizing each other, and falling into addiction over man-made drugs. They boarded their ships in search of new lands and brought their troubles with them. Their search ended on the shores of Soruth.

At first, there was no tension between Nodin and Soruth. Eventually, due to the nature of humans, war was not far off. With several offensive raids on Soruthian land, the four nations of Soruth made a pact to unite under one banner in self-defense. These wars were bloody but alternatingly won by Soruth's superior fighting, numbers, and military tactics. For centuries, the Soruthians fought with each other before the Nodinian incursions. Each nation has their own unique martial arts and weapons.

During war, the Soruthian women and men fought together, carrying out Bravious's wishes of equality. The Four have a strict rule of war: take no prisoners. They also believed when an army retreats to their camp, it is not over. The Soruthians make sure they do not return or they kill them all.

The Ebonies are strong, agile, and fast. When they charged, their enemies viewed each warrior as a cavalryman. The Ebonies made a variety of weapons and the uses for them. Their most famous weapons are a short-staffed spear called an iklwa and a curved sword that doubles as a sickle. It is called a shotel. The Ebonies are ferocious, and they are heavily resistant to invaders.

The Embers mastered archery and guerilla warfare. Ember ambushes are stealthy and horrific. Embers are fond of concealing knives to deal quick executions. A small hand ax became a government issue among the Embers. The ax came to be known as a tomahawk. The tomahawk is a multitude of things: a weapon, a tool, and a symbol of culture, status, and tribal identification. The tomahawk has been a government issue to the entire Soruthian military in all three world timelines.

The Barks mastered the siege weapons—towers, catapults, and ballistas—to protect their lands and destroy their enemies. They were the first tribe of humans to use bronze. Bronze is softer than iron. Iron is softer than steel. Chain mail and other fabrics were used to increase protection. The Barks have close friendships with the Yazjians. They commonly shared technology, philosophy, and basic goods.

Barkish men at times wear cloth on their heads. Turbans, they are called. The women sometimes wear whole robes that hide their beauty from wandering eyes. Barkish weapons are the most advanced in Soruth. The Barks educated the rest of Soruth on how to smelt metal. Barkish society is also the most scientific in Soruth.

Through their trade with Yazjia, they acquired black powder that is used for explosives.

The Sands are close relatives to the Embers. The original Sands were actually Embers. Much of their culture and traditions stem from the original people. As time went on, the Sands became mixed with Ebony and Snow. The combination of Ember, Ebony, and Snow is what eventually became the tannish-brown Sand color. The Sands were notorious for ritually sacrificing people to appease the gods. Jahveyis was especially intrigued by this. The Sand people stick close to the Embers as much of their fellowship stems from common ancestry and traditions. The Sand language is close to the common tongue and the original tribal dialects are used in formal customs.

All but the Embers had a period of Ethnic Imperialism. The Sand, Bark, and Ebonies each possessed various empires within their territories. The Embers did not believe in such politics. The other three Soruthian groups neared extinction because of their inter-imperial wars. The Embers for the longest time lived as individual tribes before becoming a democratic union.

Nodin believed the goddesses to be spouses with their male counterparts. Miolannis and Jahveyis are known as the *Courtship of Obsidian Ice*. Her cold winters froze the Nodinian people into depression, and they saw little warmth. This coldness drove them underground, seeking warmth with the earth's core.

The males of Nodin grew thick facial and long hair for warmth. The women of Nodin were generally seen as having thick skin. The southern half of Nodin has a warmer and greener landscape. For thousands of years, most of the Nodinians searched for warmer climates.

In the Second Life, the gods manufactured six reptilian beasts to govern the mortals. The beasts are the most dominant of all animals. They are called the *lohikäärmeitä*. These dragons were used as a last resort to keep the peace. The six of them each have a color, ability, and domain.

The first was created in the swampy marshlands of Sönderfall. This dragon is male and named *Mustasurma*. His black scales were thick with parts of his decaying skeleton showing through. He has large horns that curved forward and down. His blaring red eyes mirrored a hellish world. He breathes acidic slime and fumes.

The next was created by Miolannis. While atop the mountain of *Vuorijää*, she created *Kuolemajää*, another male dragon whose scales are white with light hair and feathers. His eyes are green, and he breathes a frost that freezes his opponents. Kuolemajää is ridiculed as the weakest of the six.

Next came the dragon of Sareyus. Within one of her volcanoes, she created who would be known as *Ahneus*, the dragon of fire and lava. The most cunning and greedy of the six! This beast resides in the volcanic regions of the earth. Ahneus is the only female dragon, and she is second to Mustasurma.

Tovis combined his storms with a dragon of his own, a dragon to shake the earth with thunderous flapping wings and lightning to smite its foes. Tovis named him *Ukkosen*, who prefers to live upon the highest mountains of the world. Ukkosen is the first of the two blue dragons. They are representatives of the sky and sea.

Sarue's anger of her plant life being eradicated grew bitterly. Thus came *Hayat Katil*, a dragon of green scales, hornlets, and golden eyes. The guardian of the forests! He breathes acidic fumes and spits venoms. This power came from the thousands of plants he ate. What is deadly to humans is refreshing to him. Immunity to poisons and venoms is his gift. He is the only herbivore dragon. He lives in colorful green jungles and forests. He hears the call of the trees and comes to their aid!

Carune's oceans experienced many forms of pollution during war. Her dragon is wingless and has fins across his body. He is *Avgrund*, who defends the seas and its underwater passages. His powers are rooted in bending the water and its many forms.

At first the dragons obeyed their masters, until the mortals began to worship the beasts themselves. Even the Soruthians broke their bonds and greedily sought out dominance; the Nodinians and Yazjians were no different. Twice, the gods intervened and caused the Armageddons. The mortals did not learn from their mistakes.

In the year 878 of the Third Life, after millennia of their children's feuds, the gods sat in council with a grave dilemma. Should they or should they not invoke the third Armageddon?

"Where shall we begin? Shall we release the lohikäärmeitä from their prisons? Shall we let our children bicker and kill over their sins? With each morning, my light shines to only reveal more death," Lyannis said.

"In such times of death and misery, they reveal their true colors of nature. The lands of the earth have been permanently scarred with the ecocide of my plants!"

Sarue stated in a midrange voice with the softness of the wind.

"I agree with my sister. The seas have not fully recovered from the amount of pollution and carrion dumping! I will not accept this disrespect!" Carune said in anger.

"Leave it to the mortals to act more primitive than the animals," Tovis joked as Sarue chuckled.

Jado then spoke. "Despite them being our children, the birds are smarter than them! I say let them rot in Jahveyis's decaying marshlands. Let their souls be charred by Sareyus, drowned by Carune, suffer plague by Sarue, and be blinded by the sun goddess! Or unless anyone has a better solution, I am willing to hear it."

Miolannis then reached for Jahveyis's left hand. Her snow skin reddened with comfort. "I do feel responsible for some of Nodin's corruption. My winters bring much sadness that causes hysteria to find warmth." Even though Miolannis espoused Jahveyis, she is easily bereaved.

"And you think we do not notice your temptation of the mortals? Several times I have witnessed you tempting them into dilemmas! You say it is to test their consciousness? They have named you *Black Empress of White Winters*. If anyone is to blame for this issue, it is the *Moon Mistress, Miolannis*!" Bravious shouted.

Jahveyis stood up and shouted back upon Bravious, "And do you forget the mortals' natural urge to feel strong and dominant? Before you judge my wife, look at yourself first!"

Sareyus remained quiet throughout the debate. The possible solutions of having the humans suffer or live harmoniously were numerous—all of which she deemed foolish. She listened to the inane and asinine babble of her shared pantheon.

"As long as there is man there will always be death and suffering. However, there is also life! We cannot abandon our children to face further death and torment. Even we as Immortals cannot predict the ultimate outcome of the future!" stated the fire goddess with optimism. As she finished, the other eight insolently disregarded her words.

Tovis then spoke in great jest. "Maybe the solutions are not within the dragons but within man itself? The dragons only brought more destruction, but what if we were to construct a man, a human with the superior fighting techniques and intelligence of eight thousand soldiers!"

Lyannis happily added to Tovis's idea, "We should craft him with the ability to have control of our elements. Strength as great as Bravious, speed like Tovis, brave like Sareyus, free flowing as Carune's oceans, and be spiritual but emotionless!"

With the eight of them giving ideas to each other, Sareyus became disgusted with the entire debate. "I will have no part in creating this monster! Mark my words, you fools! If you create this being, he will seek your heads!"

When Sareyus departed, the eight who remained began the decade-long construction of this ultimate warrior.

In the year 888, the warrior was completed! The eight remaining gods chose this year as a reference to the eight of them.

He was sculpted to have the best mixture of Ebony, Ember, Sand, Bark, Gold, and Snow upon his skin. His hair hangs upon his shoulders; and it is thick, sleek, and dark brown! His body was uniquely shaped. For his eye color, they chose a shade of purple. He is fifteen years old but has the mind of an elder. They named him *Xavion*, weapon of the gods and decider of humanity's fate!

One night, the gods returned to their sleeping chambers. Sareyus came from her domain and stood over Xavion's dormant body. As much as she disagreed with his creation, even she was impressed when looking upon him. He is wearing a purple silk loincloth. He lay upon a marble altar with a purple pillow beneath his head. The more she examined his fair face and body, the more she desired a mate of her own. She remembered it is law for the gods to not court mortals. Sareyus stood next to him. She placed her right hand upon his stomach and her left hand upon his right cheek. She conjured light flames to her right palm and sent energy into his Sea of Chi. Her left hand was placed upon his left pectoral. While caressing his heart, she used a heated fingernail to gently carve a purple eight-point star upon him.

"You will not suffer long, Xavion. There is more to you than death. In times of great need, when weapon and hand fail, a burning chain of energy will activate this star upon thy heart. When you reach thirty years, I will come and search for you. No child should be used to start and end wars. When we meet, remember the woman who is ridiculed, ignored, and abused. I will be her," Sareyus said in Xavion's right ear.

She then rested her fiery mane upon Xavion's young chest. Tomorrow he will be unleashed into Nodin. As a man representing five minorities, his singularity among the full Nodinians will motivate him to fight.

The astrologers recorded the many signs as they began in the dusk hours of February 13. The correlation of the sun, moon, and earth became passionate. The moon danced around the Earth as the Earth danced around the sun. As three mothers and sisters, their circular prancing foretold their son. They danced around each other eight times. The other seven planets emboldened as they bloomed like violet stars in the abyss of space. From the Earth, the outer seven planets burned in purple starlight. In the east, the morning star arrived early to complete the encompassing powers. At dawn, Bravious carried Xavion in his arms like an infant. Bravious felt a special bond when he laid Xavion in the soft grass beneath a maple tree. Xavion's feet lay eastward as the sun rose over him. He awoke at 8:08. Little did they know the coming of the gods' son would change the fate of the Third Life.

Throughout the three timelines, the first divine romance was in the hearts of Miolannis and Jahveyis. Many years before Xavion, Miolannis was perceived as a temptress. She has convinced many to fornicate in love and lust. In the First Life, before the awakening of man, Jahveyis was more intrigued by the night sky, white moonlight, and cool winter air.

He once stood upon Vuorijää while gazing upon *Talvikuu*, the winter moon. He shed tears as his red eyes turned into a chocolate brown. During this time, Jahveyis played the cello. He would spend hours thinking of a proper melody. At first, they sounded happy with major tonality. Such music does not usually attract Miolannis.

Miolannis did not greet or appear to that form of music. Jahveyis sat in despair. Before he chose to leave, he serenaded his sorrow. Miolannis's green eye appeared upon the moon. After a few measures, Jahveyis put his poetic voice to use:

> *The winter moon with emerald hewn. Light upon the icy dunes. Blackened night, all but bright, pulls the strings too tight. My heart's funeral rite! Grim and bare! Pale despair. Waiting for my lover! Ebon hair, grassy stare, cold breath cools me fair! Stars above, pale and dove, lust is not enough! Where art thou, Miolannis? Hear my homage! To love you so, warm and cold, this I promise!*

As this poem ceased, a snowstorm covered the mountaintop. In its wake, Miolannis revealed herself.

"Do you really mean those words?" she asked in a teary smile.

"Yes!" he replied as his eyes remained brown.

"I accept you! I, Miolannis, do honorably swear my heart onto yours! Dark night and moonlight shall be our might!" she stated as they kissed.

At that moment, doves, bats, ravens, and crows flew to the mountain to partake in this union.

The second union was of Sarue and Tovis. Whenever his rainstorms fell upon the land, every plant is nurtured and begins the conception of life. The first time Sarue and Tovis ever made love was upon the earth. When Tovis orgasmed after Sarue finished, a thunderstorm shook the sky. They consummated in the tallest hollow tree in the southern coast of Soruth. The Sand and Ebony Soruthians especially revere this Holy Tree. After this climax, the tree was turned into a shrine. The Soruthians have many stories about the gods. They believed this storm meant *Mother Earth* and *Father Thunder* made love. The tree of this romance was named *Ma se kamer* (Mother's Room).

The next tale of love is between Carune and Bravious. In the days before the First Life, when Carune made the seas, Bravious carved the stones and soil. When he began to design the stones beneath the sea, he asked the permission and opinion of Carune.

"Why would you wish to have the stones beneath my waters?" Carune questioned.

"I wish because I desire even a pebble of mine to be within your beautiful waters. It appears to be instinctive for earth and water to meet. Think of your sea creatures who wish to hide from their predators. Open water will only suffice for a time. Earth will hide them better and prolong their lives. If nothing could shield them then all would consume into extinction," Bravious said.

"I see your point, Bravious. But tell me, do you really care for my creatures or do you care for me?" asked Carune.

Bravious knelt down as if he were bowing to his superior.

"Why do you bow to your equal, Bravious?"

"I bow to the serenity of you. Carune is to me what air is to the lungs! As large as I am, I am small and weak without you. Please be honest if there is a chance for us?" asked Bravious.

Carune stared long and hard into Bravious's earthly brown eyes. Earth and water would've come together eventually. Carune was already aware of other romances occurring among the gods. She debated with herself if she ever needed a partner. She gazed upon Bravious's large muscular body. He is 50 percent more the height of her.

"If you truly mean your words, then please give me some time to consider your request," she asked.

"I'll wait a thousand years if needed!" Bravious exclaimed.

Long did Carune swim and meditate within the seas, often wondering how earth and water could be used as one. In seven days' time, she sought out Bravious. He was carving another but lesser mountain on an Island between Nodin and Soruth.

"Bravious," Carune called.

"Yes, my lady?" he replied.

"I have thought hard and long about your request. I am willing to experiment by combining earth and water. An experiment that allows the sea to wash upon the shore, caressing your sand and dirt…"

"Yes! What a beautiful sight it shall be!" Bravious blushed. In his heart, he was happy that Carune is willing to share her element with him. They went to work on this creation. Carune raised the oceans to the surface as Bravious expanded the earthly area with an earth-quaking press. Whenever Carune raises her waters, her eyes turn into a solid, bold, and clear blue. As peaceful as she can be, may the gods forbid her tsunamis from swallowing the earth! Thus, the beaches were created! The white sandy beaches with the sky blue sea beside it. This island was nameless for the time being.

"It is beautiful!" they said together.

"Thank you, my lady," Bravious said as he went back to carving the mountain.

Carune was preparing to dive back into the sea, but her heart begged her to stay. She began to unclothe herself and started bathing between the water and shore. As Bravious turned to his side, he dropped the hammer and chisel.

"My lady?" he shouted in shock. "What are you doing?"

"I am bathing in what is half of mine," Carune stated in a humorous tone.

"This is indecency!" Bravious replied.

"Since when is love indecent? Since when do mortals only court? I know I am a goddess, but I am still a woman. Bravious, I accept your love!" she exclaimed as her sapphire eyes brightened.

Last but not least came the tale of Lyannis and Jado. There are many versions of these stories, but the truest of all is this: Jado, out of all gods, is the most knowledgeable. He often sits in his library reading tome, book, and scroll. Jado is the second hybrid-haired deity (having brownish blond). Despite knowledge being the greatest power of all, Jado suffers from overthinking. He would have searing headaches from all the information he stores in the universe of his mind.

During one of his studies, he rattled his brain thin with the science and logic of homicide: how the mortals would mercilessly inflict pain upon their peers, how empires and countries are forged by war, how the mortals waste creativity to take life. He spent years in vain to comprehend the illogical. Jado submerged himself in his library. His vast intelligence was beginning to destroy his spirit.

Lyannis was the only one concerned for his health. She slowly walked over to him. As he was speedily recording his thoughts, Lyannis sat next to him and placed her left hand upon his right. His dense focus was not fazed by the soothing infant skin of the sun goddess. The bags beneath his eyes sank lower with each word. She rested her bold golden mane against his and caressed his sore hand. Lyannis usually has this effect on people she comes in contact with.

"Jado, please calm down. Do not torture yourself over the mortals' mistakes," she said in a low and soft feminine voice.

"Why have you come to me? You have never given me such affection," he added.

"I wish to counsel you in your time of need," Lyannis stated as she turned Jado's gaze from his book into her blue eyes.

Jado lay on his bed as Lyannis sat next to him in a chair. Jado opened his thoughts. Within several months,

Jado chose Lyannis to be his spouse. Lyannis revealed to Jado that she is often accused of being a matron of lust. Long after the humans awoke, Jado instructed one of his scholars to write a theoretical tome on Lyannis. Many still believe Lyannis is promiscuous, but the majority chose to believe the scholar.

Lyannis was happy with this act of kindness. She entered Jado's library and walked over to him. "Thank you for your wisdom!" she exclaimed and laid a kiss upon his lips.

Amid the growing unions within the pantheon, Sareyus fought her envy. Each kiss she viewed lowered her self-esteem. Her thoughts flooded with desire. As fifteen years passed, her journey began.

Book 1

Divine Mortality

Chapter 1

In Narration

It has been fifteen years since Xavion was created. The gods paid no mind to him. His life among animals and nature educated him greatly. Xavion was placed within the western woodlands of Nodin.

Nodin is divided between two groups of people: those living on the surface and underground. The surface of Nodin is separated into seven countries with many individual cultures. The Seven Nations of Nodin are *Cel*, *Franc*, *Ang*, *Gern*, *Nor*, *Ital*, and the city states of *Gresha*. The underground half of Nodin is inhabited by two empires based on Nor in the west and Gern in the east.

The underground kingdoms were renamed East Nodin and West Nodin. West Nodin is a monarchy ruled by the Edling Dynasty. The East is governed by the fascist ruler Aylund Rudolf. The entrance to East Nodin is a large multilayered iron gate. The gate is straight at its sides and is rounded at the top. At the top of the gate is a blue hexagram with its points facing left and right.

Behind the East Nodin gate is a city crafted from stone, wood, and metal. Much of the city is illuminated by the light of lava pools. As one would go deeper, they would witness the citizens committing crimes out of poverty and desperation. Many people in the first half of East Nodin are poor and medically ill. The guards at the command of Aylund Rudolf built a wall that separated these people from the wealthier portion of the community. East Nodin holds the most Soruthian slaves in the continent. Aylund is a business partner with a corrupt Soruthian politician.

Toward the back of East Nodin, the homes and people became elegant and prosperous. At the very back of this place stood the palace of the *Vakuuttava*, Aylund Rudolf. In reality, he is a tyrant and driven mad with power. He is greedy and reeks with evil lust. He defiles married women, kills non-heterosexuals, and indulges in pedophilia. A common color to be seen here is blue. Much clothing is this color, and some armor parts are also blue.

West Nodin's entrance gate is the same but with an upright red pentagram at the top. West Nodin is less impoverished and wealthier. Most of the population is accustomed to having extra money. A majority of the rich population refuse to be acquainted with anyone upon lower social classes. Red is this kingdom's color. As mentioned before, West Nodin is a monarchy and has a royal family. They are the Edlings. The remaining royal member is *King Johan Edling*. Johan is almost fifty years old. He had a wife, *Queen Helga* and two children, *Prince Hakun* and *Princess Astrid*. Johan has become as bad as Aylund. For example, all men must prostitute their wives and daughters to produce soldiers and stimulate the economy.

On the dawn of February 14, 903, East and West Nodin would go to battle. The prize is a strip of underground caverns that connect the two kingdoms. The caverns are only 37.8 miles in width and diameter. This area is in possession of thousands of metal veins. One long road connects the East and West while in the center are the veins. The morning before, the goddess Sareyus sensed her time came to find Xavion. Through the years, many dead Nodinian soldiers said a Soruthian man with purple eyes was their slayer. In the late night, Sareyus stepped out of a lava pool in West Nodin.

In Sareyus's View

As I ascended out of the lava, I looked upon West Nodin in disgust. Disgusted, because for decades, I have witnessed the foul deeds of its people. This part of the city is more of the common neighborhoods. Whenever I appear out of lava, I am nude but I chose to grow snow skin. The skin takes a few seconds to form. Meanwhile, I appear as a feminine humanoid lava creature. I quietly but quickly dashed behind a building to find some type of clothing. I began rummaging through a back alley and found an old tattered white dress. When my chosen appearance grew, I have freckled light skin, bold orange hair, and green eyes. I weigh about 160 pounds.

During the night of February 13, I went in search of Xavion. I cannot imagine how he may look now. Fifteen years ago, I gazed upon his young face. I wonder how he has aged.

For several hours, I traveled throughout the streets of the city. Many times the citizens would stare at me curiously. With no luck, I asked one citizen where I could find Xavion.

"Excuse me, ma'am. Where may I find Xavion?"

She looked upon me bewildered. "I do not know any Xavion."

"He would have darker skin, dark hair, and purple eyes."

She paused for a moment to think. "Oh, you mean the Mud Monkey? I wouldn't know where to find him," she said as she went about her business.

My eyes and ears were startled upon hearing that slur. Mud Monkey, how bigoted! I proceeded to ask others of his whereabouts, and many continued to insult his name. The used derogatory terms for him like Turd Thumbs. Another slur was Bruised Eyes, referring to when bruises become purple.

I ignored their bigotry and continued my quest. As I traveled, the city has many red pentagrams with three points up and two points down. The symbolism behind it loosely stands for West Nodin's independence from Aylund Rudolf in the East. The original pentagram comes from Ang and Cel. The meaning of the original five pentagram points is spirit, air, water, earth, and fire. Speaking of Cel, I speak with their western accent.

Moments later, I heard a young and middle-aged man talking.

"Do you know where I can get my sword sharpened?" asked the young one.

"There's a blacksmith in the military outpost near the royal palace. The smith is the dark man," replied the elder.

I went to find the royal palace. King Johan is preparing his army for war. I have a hunch Xavion would be one of his soldiers. How he came into this city is unknown to me. Hopefully, it has been a more positive experience than it appears to be.

I found the royal palace! Even though it is the largest building and fully viewable, getting to it is a challenge because the rest of the city is built like a maze to confuse invaders. The front of the palace has a large wooden door with metal bracings. These people get their lumber from the surface.

The rest of the palace is decorated in red. I am amazed by how stylish these red ornamentations are. Even though my divine identity is hidden from the mortals, I still resemble the average Nodinian woman with orange hair.

The military camp is caged with many wooden fences with barbed wire. Infiltrating this area will be a challenge. I scouted the perimeter to find an opening with little guards or wire where I could climb over. As the night continued, many guards were changing shifts. Toward the northern part of the camp, there is a heavily rotted part upon the bottom of the fence. There is little light around. While I was shrouded in darkness, I gently broke the wood and crawled under it. The camp has been breached.

As I began to wander, my dress is stained with dirt. I am looking for a dwelling with smoke rising from the top. If Xavion is the smith, then his forge should be producing smoke. I have not seen any smoke, only thousands of tents containing soldiers.

"Hey, boys, we gotta whore out here!" I heard a man shout. I realized the guards are chasing after me. I sprinted through the field of tents. The guards wear armor with red fabric. On their right arms, they wear the red pentagrams.

"Stop in the name of the West! Halt!" yelled one of the guards.

I was blocked off by a guard wielding a hand ax. The two chasing guards subdued me.

"Well, well, well! Looks like one of the whores escaped from the palace brothel! Oh, and what's this? Orange hair? Just like ole' Astrid! Take her ass to the general's tent!" said a guard.

I was thinking if Xavion could be the general. The general's tent is the largest with the West Nodin insignia upon the flaps. As we approached the tent, I heard two voices shouting at each other

"If we do not leave by the crack of dawn, Aylund would surely beat us to the veins!"

"We will leave when I am damn good and ready! And besides, Aylund would order his men to battle for his amusement. The less we have to contend with, the better!"

The guard holding my right arm opened the right flap on the tent. "Excuse me, my lord and General," he said.

"Do you not see we are discussing the battle, you grunt!" the older man said. He wears a long red robe

8

with a gold chain that has five rubies at its center. He also wears a sword upon a belt that rests against his right thigh. On his head is a circlet with more rubies upon it.

"My lord, with all due respect, if we do not leave by at least 6:00 a.m., we should expect a full invasion!" the general said as he reviewed the map of the underground mines.

I am guessing the other man is King Johan Edling. There is another general staying out of the argument.

They continued to review the marching route. The guardsmen and I listened to the discussion. During the general and king's disagreement, the guards began making vulgar comments about the body I have.

"I say, Ewan, this one got a fat ass!" said the man to my right.

"And some lovely tits too! Forget the brothel, we should take her back to my tent and fuck!" said the guard on my left.

I am enraged for how they look upon women as objects; in a second, I could immolate them into smoldering ashes. I broke free and smacked Ewan across his ugly face. As I did it, my fingertips were hot and left light burn marks upon his cheek. I began to squabble in order to grab the attention of the king and general.

"What in the name of Tovis is going on?" the king exclaimed.

When the skirmish ended, I took a punch to the gut.

"Who is this bitch?" asked the quiet general.

"General Daveth, we found one of the whores trying to escape from the palace," Ewan replied.

"What is your name?" Daveth asked me.

In common Nodinian custom, parents with orange-haired daughters would name them after me.

"I am Sareyus," I answered.

"Named after the fire goddess? Talk about being hot!" the second guard said.

"Where did she come from?" Daveth asked.

"She could be one of those Easterners poking about our territory," Ewan said.

As Daveth and the guards continued to bicker, I noticed King Johan was looking at me curiously. Johan is about fifty years old with orange-blond hair and beard. He stood at six feet two with brown eyes.

"Silence, you fools!" the king exclaimed.

Johan continued to glance upon me. "Send her back to the brothel!" Johan said and spat on my feet.

I did not resist because I can crush them all! Keeping my cover is most important in order to find Xavion. The guards proceeded to take me to the brothel. I did not know it was located within the actual palace. Inside the palace, it becomes more elegant with statues that were carved from stone to honor the gods—except me. Where my shrine would have been is empty. The beauty of the palace is only a smokescreen for the oppression of the citizens.

Toward the back of the palace, it became darker. At the end of a long hallway, there is a bright light. In the middle of the hallway, there is a heavy dark spot that looks like a cell. As we walked by, I caught a glimpse of eyes that came from the abyss. Those eyes are bright; their color is brooding. Could Jahveyis be monitoring my actions? As we passed the area, the eyes continued to follow.

When we reached the end of the hallway, the light is the entrance to the brothel. Inside I could hear the screams of men, women, and young girls. The inside is not elegant or colorful. It is a dirty, garbage-laced, rat-infested shithole.

"An orange-haired woman? Who wants to trim the rose bush? Fifty Silvers!" shouted the male keeper of the brothel. What is it about my hair color that makes me a prostitute to these people?

Several men and women began auctioning me like furniture. Those who were fornicating suddenly stopped and were heckling each other. Several punches were thrown. Even the guardsmen joined the fights. Several seconds passed, and no one was paying attention to me. This is my opportunity to escape! I began to melt the locks to sneak away. *Click* I heard, the door opened! I took a dash through the door—only to catch a fist to my face!

Sometime later, I awoke with a bruise upon my left eye. I was tied down to a bed that I presumed to be in the brothel. The room around me is lit with candles and lanterns. The bed is coarse and uncomfortable.

"So who wants the first round?" asked the brothel keeper. "A hundred silvers is the starting price!"

Once more the idiots tried to auction me. Several swears, curse words, and slurs for me were said.

"Two thousand silvers!" said a young man.

"Two thousand silvers going once…twice…sold to the young man. All right, you shits, clear out!" shouted the keeper.

The people all cleared out.

In came a young man in his early thirties. "Well, my lady, I'll give you a few rounds. You will not enjoy this, I promise you!" he said.

The young man began to strip and tried to tear my dress off.

"Hold still, you feisty bitch!" he said as I spat in his face! He proceeded to smack me around. Upon the fifth slap, the candles and lanterns began to dim. As they regained their light, I see a tall figure hooded, masked, and clothed in black. The figure is wearing a sword and a utility belt. He caught the attacker's right hand.

"You?" my attacker shouted.

The figure did not reply.

"Who the hell do you think you are fucking up my hour?" the young man shouted. He threw a punch that was caught in midair.

The masked assailant proceeded to strike him down with many blows. He ended the barrage with a barbaric headbutt. As the young man fell, several other men from behind the door heard the commotion. The armed guards slammed the door open.

"What the hell is going on here? Jahvonis! You disrupt the king's brothel!" said the keeper.

Jahvonis then spoke! His voice is deep, clear, and menacing. "How is it you have not learned? Why are these people marketed like cattle? You are a bigot who spews rape and oppression upon these people."

"This whore is the property of King Johan!" As the keeper finished his sentence, Jahvonis cast a throwing star into his face. His right eye socket housed the star. Blood stained his clothes, and he is crying in pain. The other guards charged at Jahvonis.

They advanced with their weapons drawn. When I looked upon Jahvonis, I expected him to unsheathe his sword but he did not. Instead, he fought with his hands and feet. As they fought, Jahvonis wasted no sweat as he used brute force and searing speed to break bones. In two minutes, he defeated ten men. He rushed over to me and used a large Yazjian dagger to cut my binds. He ran and led me away. Whoever this man is, he has a large back! We stormed through the front room. Four other guards began to chase.

"Get in front of me," he said. Jahvonis drew thin and sharp needles, four to be exact. He cast them individually into the necks of the four guards. The other slaves already fled. To where, I do not know.

Down the long hallway, he brought me. When we passed the cell, I glanced over and the same eyes followed us. The rest of the palace is sleeping. Guard patrols are light. Jahvonis is still leading me. We fled to another less fair part of the palace. Upon a dusty wall is a hidden doorway. We came closer to it.

"Please go! Your escape is not yet done!" he said.

"Where does this passage lead?" I asked.

"It goes deeper into the earth. There's a small camp of the escaped. Go now!" he exclaimed.

I did not deny him. I ran hesitantly down this path. Jahvonis sealed the door behind me. When he did, I gazed through the eyeholes of his black mask. His eyes shined back at me. I could not see his color. The tunnel ran for five miles. At the end is a light, I came through the other side of the tunnel. There is a small camp of escaped slaves of both sexes.

In Narration

Upon the early morning of February 14, West Nodin marched the underground road to the meeting of East and West. The West men are divided into two fighting classes. First are infantry warriors with melee weapons. The second class is archers who stand behind the infantry. The archers also bear one-handed melee weapons for close combat. King Johan stands upon a man-pulled chariot. Everyone in this army wore red with their armor. As they approached the meeting point, they gazed in awe at the vast rivers of metal that decorated the stone. The walls are gray color. Lava fell into pools that illuminated these caverns.

Johan met with his highest-ranking general. Vallen is his name. He was the arguing general in the king's tent yesterday.

"Our scouts have seen no sign of the East men yet, my lord," Vallen stated.

"You know that sick Aylund possibly picked up another child!" Johan answered.

"Are you going to duel him finally?" Vallen asked.

"No, it is still too early in the war to kill kings," Johan replied.

"Then what will you do, my lord?"

"We'll send that bug Xavion out first," Johan said in disgust.

"My lord, Xavion has won us many battles, yet you continue to be ungrateful. Why is that?" Vallen asked.

Seconds later, a loud horn was blown from across the battlefield. The East came.

The East wore similar armor, but with blue fabric. They wear the fabric on their left shoulder with the hexagram. At the front of the horde is a chariot led by several men. Aylund rode upon it. He is a stout man with a dark-blond goatee. He is almost a year younger than Johan. Aylund wore fancy bright steel with six sapphires embedded upon his chest plate. His eyes are brown, and he has short hair upon his round head. The two armies stared each other down. Aylund began to ride forth. Johan instructed his men to pull his chariot. The chariots are merely ten feet away from each other.

"I could definitely make some fine arms with all this metal. I think a sword would be nice...or I could take yours?" Aylund said.

"You know damn well this about more than these metals! For the last fifteen years, you've sat your fat ass upon your throne, gloating over the murders of my family!" Johan shouted.

"Murders? Johan, there's no such thing as murder in war! War is all about death and misery! Father raised us on that logic until he was killed. Is it not interesting how our father trains the first son to best his younger brother? Even more interesting is, your brother defeats your son. Ah, young and brave Hakun! How bright and green his eyes were, how fresh and tight his skin was—until half his head became a trophy!" Aylund gloated as Johan's skin blushed with anger.

"And sweet Helga!" Aylund began as Johan breathed heavily. "Her hair was so orange. I loved her thick body. Her agonizing screams as I forced myself upon her only made the sex better! But that cunt didn't want to play nice for me!" Aylund continued to gloat.

Johan reached for a small dagger at his side. He cast it at Aylund, but he caught the handle as the blade tip poked his nose.

"I see this shall be the usual, my best versus your best…or shall it be the king versus king?"

"The usual!" Johan shouted as they both returned to their armies. When Johan closed in on his ranks, he spoke. "Men of the West, today we reclaim our mines! We shall strike down the evil of the East by all means! Prepare for battle! Send forth Xavion!" Johan commanded.

Even though Xavion won them several dozen battles, he has not once been cheered for his credibility. Before and after every battle, Xavion is incarcerated in a mobile metallic box. No light shined through except for the bars upon the door.

Four men pushed this box toward the front of the army. As they reached it, Johan stood to its left as two soldiers unsealed it. No movement was seen or heard. Across the battlefield, Aylund summoned his champion, a man standing six foot eleven inches. He has a muscular-toned body and a blond mane upon his head. He wears a steel chain mail shirt with a traditional Gernic helmet. His weapon is a two-handed greatsword. In East Nodin, this is called a *Zweihander*. His name is Bjorn

16

Adolf. Many have fallen to his sword skills, but he never has fought Xavion.

The black box did not release anyone.

"Where is he?" shouted Johan as he stepped off his chariot to look within. His eyes turned the corner. "You have a job to do!" Johan yelled.

A brown leather man exited the box. The leather top has three layers with a chain mail shirt in between the leather. On the outer layer of leather are twelve individual steel plates that are vertical rectangles with rounded corners. The same plates are also on his back. His gauntlets, knee pads, elbow pads, shoulder pads, boots, and helmet are all made from leather and steel.

He wears a Barkish-style helmet that further individualized him from the rest. He wears a shield on his back. It has a stout blade on the bottom end. On his left hip is a Barkish talwar (a curved-bladed saber that is designed for increased cutting power). In his right hand, he holds a studded Daichinian club called a "kanabo." The kanabo is made of dense oak wood and possesses many thick steel studs. Kanabos were invented by the samurai to break swords and armor. The long two-handed shaft has an octagonal cross section. In Daichinian mythology, their Oni demons use kanabos.

This warrior is Xavion. He walked closer toward Bjorn. The blade of his greatsword is resting flat against the front of his right shoulder. Xavion used his Tovis-like speed and charged upon Bjorn. Several times Bjorn missed decapitating him. Xavion, with little effort, dodged and evaded the swings.

As Bjorn missed each strike, Xavion began the offensive. He swung the kanabo at Bjorn's helm and dented it. As Bjorn was dazed, Xavion swung and crushed the mail shirt into Bjorn. He swung next at Bjorn's right shoulder.

Xavion is purposely using his kanabo to parry Bjorn's mighty blade. A loud metallic screech pierced through the air. Bjorn's blade shattered! Bjorn has never been bested in combat. He fell to the ground after a blow to the stomach. Xavion then stood over him. Bjorn's face blushed with envy. "Do your worst, Dark Man!" shouted Bjorn in anger.

Xavion's face did age, but he looks no older than twenty years old. He continued to stare into the eyes and soul of Bjorn. Inside, he saw someone like himself, a person used as a weapon and nothing more. Xavion spared Bjorn in mercy and sympathy. This shocked both sides.

"Finish him!" Johan shouted.

Xavion walked back toward his cell.

Johan continued shouting the command of slaying Bjorn. "I am your king, and you will obey me!" Johan yelled as he grabbed Xavion's right forearm.

"Do it yourself, Johan. It would be nice to see the king of the West slay the champion of the East," Xavion said in a medium-toned voice.

"Remember your place!" Johan stated.

"My place is not beside thee!" Xavion replied.

A horn from the East was blown, the battle began! Xavion heard the horn. He knew he could not disown and dishonor the other men. He charged forth with his kanabo and led the West beside him. Despite most not liking him, all admired his courage and skill.

During the battle, Xavion outshined the others by spilling the blood of hundreds. Nodinian wars are notoriously bloody and doleful. No battle was won without heavy casualties on both sides.

In Sareyus's View

As Jahvonis sealed the door behind him, I continued to sprint down this tunnel. I ran until the door was no longer in sight. I paused and rested after what I believe was the halfway point. During this escape, I used a ball of embers as a torch to light the way. I continued down the tunnel; the end is near! I rushed through the light. Part of me thought Lyannis would greet me beyond it. As Jahvonis said, there is a camp. I gazed upon men, women, and children who were slaves to forced fornication. The people who escaped sat in a circle. I approached them. They looked upon me in curiosity.

"Jahvonis freed you too, lass?" said a middle-aged man. "So what were you? Slave or a willing prostitute?"

"Neither one am I," I replied. "I was accused of escaping the brothel and they captured me. I was about to be raped until Jahvonis came."

"Aye, Jahvonis is a hero. Freeing us from oppression!" said a woman.

"I've heard he is the son of Jahveyis and Miolannis. His name is crossed between the two!" a little boy said.

"May I ask you all a question? On your dash out of the brothel, did any of you notice a pair of eyes gazing out of the darkness from your right-hand side?" I inquired.

All said no except one teenage girl. She has black hair and blue eyes. "I did see a pair of eyes. They were mystical, soothing, mysterious, and somewhat brooding. I think the eyes were purple. Something seemed inhuman about them. I was too scared to look more," she replied.

I could not unravel the riddle behind the other pair of eyes. The other escapees continued speaking. Some of it was about me.

"Why must you people continue babbling about me?" I exclaimed.

"Please calm down, milady!" said the middle-aged man.

I calmed down so I didn't torch the entire camp.

"Have you heard the laws for any woman with orange hair? Any woman with that hair color is condemned to sexual slavery," he said.

"How did that come to be?" I asked.

They hesitated to tell me until the little boy spoke.

"It's because Lady Astrid had orange hair. Orange hair is the natural color of the Edling family, even King Johan has it!"

"What did Astrid do to be shunned?" I asked.

"I heard she was in love with the purple-eyed man!" he replied.

I'm not surprised Xavion was in love. Men and women should flock around him.

"How come you all sound like they aren't together?" I asked.

"I'll tell you all the story," the middle-aged man said. "I was the guard who kept their love secret. My name is Sebastian Hagstrom." He is missing his right hand, and has a bronze one in its place. He continued speaking. "It all started fifteen years ago when my squad and I were searching for new trees to hew wood from. As we began chopping…" Sebastian fell asleep from exhaustion.

"Does anyone else know the tale?" I asked.

They nodded side to side.

"Shit!" I exclaimed.

In Narration

The battle continued for five hours after Bjorn was beaten by Xavion. Bjorn's life was spared, but his reputation has taken a large blow. Before the charge, Eastern soldiers rushed out to bring him aside. They brought Bjorn to the back. Aylund's chariot followed. "You weak grunt!" he insulted.

The East charged when Aylund blew upon his horn. His men were more than happy to die for this tyrant's greed. So far in this battle, the West has slain one thousand foes. Four hundred of them belonged to Xavion! He charged after defeating Bjorn. The kanabo broke through the first rank. He and anyone using a bludgeoning weapon have the advantage of breaking armor and edged weapons.

During the battle, Xavion would use Bravious's strength and Tovis's speed in the kanabo. A trail of broken bones lay in his wake! Xavion encountered an Eastern knight. He saw the knight wielding a two-handed longsword. The longsword is more nimble but will not puncture Xavion's armor. The kanabo damaged the knight's armor and body. The gods succeeded in their creation of this ender of lives, this killer of knights, the bane of humanity! The battle is down to two thousand men, half on each side.

One warrior stands in Xavion's way as a circle of violence surrounds them. It is Aylund's third in command, Stephan. He is not much taller than Xavion. He bears a large bearded battle-ax.

Xavion's kanabo was hooked by the ax and twisted out of his hands. Stephan was swinging wildly in a blind rage and cutting through the air. He drove Xavion back to the wall of the cavern. At the fifteenth swing, Xavion drew his talwar and he swung for Stephan's throat. He missed. Stephan hooked the talwar and forced it away from Xavion. When the armies separated, Xavion's kanabo was revealed among the corpses.

Xavion had no time to reach for his kanabo. He is, for the most part, defenseless. Xavion breathed heavily. Stephan backed away to take the killing blow! Xavion tapped into the star upon his chest. Sareyus's energy was unleashed. Power resonated through his body. He tore a rock from the wall and bashed Stephan's left knee. Stephan went down momentarily but still swung. Xavion dodged like a cheetah as Stephan's ax shattered upon the stone wall. Xavion was able to get to the kanabo. Stephan recovered to his feet and pulled a dagger out of his belt. Xavion stood up and turned around. As he was still regaining his strength, Stephan threw the dagger into Xavion's left thigh. He fell in agony.

Stephan was smart enough to remove his dagger. Xavion is bruised badly but disarmed Stephan with grappling. Both sides watched in awe at this match of two desperate men. Xavion went to kick Stephan in the stomach with his left leg. He caught it. Xavion used his martial arts and swung his right foot. He knew Stephan would dodge as he still held his left foot. Xavion's right foot is still free. He swung it back in the air and kicked Stephan's face. Xavion was released. Xavion's shield is still on his back. He removed it. Stephan was enraged. He charged at Xavion with a mace he found among the dead. Xavion realized his opportunity and launched the blade-ended shield and decapitated Stephan. The brains of this general stained the earth. Thus, the East fled. Xavion's body count sent fear to both sides.

"Chase them down! Now!" Xavion shouted.

"No!" King Johan answered. He ran up to his champion.

"We *must* finish them! We *must* maintain momentum!" Xavion said.

"Why bother? They've fled back to their homes... and we should return to ours!" stated the king.

Xavion looked in disbelief. "I have beaten their best! No one is left to rally them but Aylund."

"Look at my men! Look at what they have seen upon the ground! The widows of the dead must be informed! If you have this much blood lust, then go by yourself!" Johan insulted.

"We should at least begin mining! I did not slay these men for nothing!" Xavion answered.

"The veins will be here long enough to regroup and dispose of the casualties," the king said.

"Johan, you fool! Sending the dead to a watery grave angers Carune!"

"You will watch your tongue!" Johan said as he pulled a knife to Xavion's neck.

"I…fucking…dare you!" Xavion replied.

Johan knew it would be foolish to physically threaten Xavion, but he must assert order.

"Get back in your cell!" Johan said.

Xavion knew his words put the king in his place. He retrieved his weapons and walked back into his cell.

The West retrieved their deceased.

Chapter 2

In Sareyus's View

I exclaimed my frustration after Sebastian fell asleep. I sat in deep thought. "What was Sebastian about to say?" I asked myself. After the fire burnt out, the campers went to bed. I stood guard in case we were found. I do not know how much these souls have suffered; part of me does not want to know.

Hours later, I heard an ear-shaking horn call that rang throughout the underground. I stood up and tried to see where the horn blew. I ran to the edge of the camp and almost fell off a steep cliff! In my current sight, I see thousands of men marching from the East and West. The war continues.

At the head of each horde, the kings rode upon man-powered chariots. At the back of the western side, a large metallic box is being pushed. King Johan and who I believe is Aylund met in the center of the field. I couldn't hear their argument. Both sides called for their champions. The West wheeled out the large box. Moments after the door was opened, a soldier exited. This soldier defeated Aylund's champion but spared his life. As he walked back to the West, another horn was blown and this soldier charged again.

After seeing the blood of my children being spilled, I kept an eye out for the mystery soldier and he could be seen a mile away! At this time, a large man contested him. This Eastern soldier nearly killed his opponent, but in the end, he was slain. This winner of the battle sent the East retreating. As he recovered, I saw his face. Dark skin and dark hair, it is Xavion.

My heart jumped and beat rapidly. My skin blushed. After fifteen years, he still looks younger than his age. I saw him and Johan conversing afterward, but something seemed bitter about them. The campers awoke with the horn calls. During the hours of battle, they stayed hidden.

"The West defeated the East," I informed.

"Not like either side is better. Both sides care nothing for us slaves," the mother replied.

"We are not slaves!" I exclaimed. "We are human beings and should be treated fairly!"

As night fell we became excruciatingly hungry. No food is in the camp. Even a god in a mortal form must eat. As the rest came under tiredness, I stood guard. I would doze off from time to time. This time, as I dozed off, I lay down far from the edge. I could smell something burning…cooking actually! I woke up and looked over. There is a fire with a boiling pot of stew. On the ground is a brown blanket with loaves of bread on one plate. Next to it are cheeses, fruits, vegetables, and several canteens of water!

I turned around after hearing rocks sliding. I rushed over to the edge and saw a dark figure sliding down the cliffside.

"Jahvonis!" I yelled as he looked back up into my eyes.

"We will meet again!" he shouted as his feet hit the ground and he ran off into the underground.

"Bless the gods! Food!" said one of the campers. He proceeded to wake the others, and we all indulged in a much-deserved feast!

In Narration

For the next month, West Nodin continued to mine their hard-won veins. For eight hours a day, they mined as much metal from the rock as possible. The most common of these was iron. Many gems were found. Most were amethysts. The color of amethyst reminds the Nodinians of Xavion. During the battles, Xavion's eyes would sparkle, showing the beauty of his tortured soul as he slays. Every amethyst that was found was given to Xavion. Ever since West Nodin found him, purple has become a hated color. The bigots mock Xavion's eyes, saying they are colored like foul bruises. Throughout February, 250 amethysts were given to Xavion. He cherishes those stones more than money. To him, they represent balance.

Over the next several months, Sareyus remained with the escapees in their camp. Daily, Sareyus kept her green eyes out for Jahvonis. Every week, Jahvonis brought new food while eluding the campers. Each time

Jahvonis looked upon Sareyus, he wondered if she could hear him.

On October 1, he once again delivered food to the campers. Sareyus still looked for him with no luck. She began to despair and thought Jahvonis was caught by the guards or worse. After the week's supply of food was consumed, the campers sat down to a deadened flame. Only Sareyus could relight it with her powers, but doing that would raise suspicion.

"How do you all suppose Jahvonis is capable of bringing us this food?" asked Sebastian as he nibbled on a piece of bread.

A man replied to him. His name is Hamish. "Aye, he's most likely not human. How can he shroud himself in darkness and bright light?"

"Don't be foolish, Hamish! If he were some demon sent from hell, then he wouldn't be merciful! I tell you, he must be someone in town or perhaps from the East," said a woman while holding her son.

Sareyus stood over the ledge and watched the miners. *Where could he be? Who could he be? Whose eyes did I see all those months ago?* she thought.

"Sareyus," Sebastian called out to her: "Please come sit with us. He will come!"

Sareyus walked over and sat with them. They continued to discuss with each other.

Sareyus paid no mind to them as their words went in and out of her ears.

"Sebastian?" she asked. "You never told us how you hid the relationship between Xavion and Astrid or how you went from being a guard to a slave?"

Sebastian took a long deep breath while staring at his bronze hand.

"It began when we found Xavion on the surface. His home was in an alpine forest by the sea. We first found him by following the smoke from his campfire. At first, he was frightened for who knows what. He fled into the woods. When we attempted to pursue him, a pack of timber wolves guarded him. We had no choice but to defend ourselves. The alpha male of the pack was slain by my superior. When Xavion heard the dying cries of the wolf, he reversed his direction and charged at us on all fours like a beast."

"He ran so fast with little effort and pounced upon one of the other guards. When another guard tried to pull him off, Xavion used the man's gut as a springboard and hopped into the trees. He began to jump from tree to tree, psyching us out. *How could a boy act so animalistic?* I thought.

"He leaped down upon our patrol leader and began stoning his skull in with his elbow. He wrapped his arms around his waist and flipped him over his head. As he was slammed to the ground, the guard's weight snapped his neck. Xavion furiously began throwing strikes with great strength and accuracy. I've never seen a man or boy fight like him. I only survived that encounter. 'Please young man, I meant no harm!' I pleaded. 'You have brought death to my friends and disturbance to my peace!' Xavion shouted. I began to cower. 'I'll spare you out of my greater kindness than you have shown me,' Xavion stated. I then fled back underground and informed the king. I did not know Johan would send an entire armed patrol on a manhunt for Xavion. The numbers gain was too much for him. They were able to knock him unconscious and carried him back underground. The predatory animals in the area chased them far. Bears and wolves attacked us in waves. They were organized as if they were prepared for this kind of situation.

"Many of those beasts died in the chase. Still, I hear the animals crying. They were whimpering and mourning the kidnapping of their protector and the murder of their kind. For weeks, we tried interrogating him but he swore he just woke up in the middle of the woods. As the days went on, we struggled to restrain him but he managed to free himself and he injured several guards.

"One day we were relocating him to a new holding cell. We walked through the main palace where the king and Lady Astrid sat. Xavion looked upon her and became more docile. The more docile he became, the more we trusted him. We let him roam around the palace and city with a guard. I was that guard. At times Johan wanted to test Xavion's meekness. He issued Astrid an aide. Xavion was the aide. He would help Astrid eat, dress, and bathe. Somehow they fell in love," Sebastian stated.

"Why did Astrid need an aide?" Sareyus asked.

"Lady Astrid was blind. She lost her sight as a little girl," replied Sebastian.

Sareyus sat there, letting the story sink in. She wished she arrived earlier in Xavion's life.

"How did you get your metal hand?" asked Sareyus.

"The king caught wind of his daughter's love interest. He was informed that I withheld the information. Johan stripped me of guard duty and made me a brothel slave. He lastly crushed my right hand under a heavy mace. A doctor and blacksmith had to engineer a hand from bronze."

In those moments as the story faded, Sareyus chose to stand in the exit way of the escape tunnel. She was hoping to see Jahvonis rescue another slave. Sareyus stood staring through the darkness. Thoughts and memories came to her of Ahneus.

At midnight, while everyone else slumbered, the fire burnt out. She conjured a fireball and played with it like a doll. She broke off pieces of it and cast them down the hall to brighten it up. Firelight always made Sareyus glow. It has been almost a year since Sareyus played or sang a song. Going such a time without music bores her greatly.

In the tunnel, Sareyus tossed seven small fireballs. Moments after the seventh ball burnt out, an eighth ball arose. It was growing rapidly. Suddenly more and more came up out of the darkness, fourteen there are. She gently wandered further in and heard several voices coming from within. The guards found them!

"Shit!" Sareyus whispered loudly and fearfully. She ran over to Sebastian and woke him up. "We've been discovered!" she shouted as her voice woke the other campers. The others woke up alarmingly. The mother and child began crying and cowering. The guards reached them and immediately began beating them all, even the young child. Sebastian, Hamish, and Sareyus tried to defend the campers. They were overrun. It was a twenty-on-three fight.

This band of guards were sent by General Daveth. As the twenty-four campers were subdued, the twenty-fifth leaped from the cliff. The impact of the fall was not heard. Her name was Alva Amott. She was only sixteen years old. Her hair was ebony black and her eyes sky blue, a child of Miolannis and Carune.

In Vallen's View

Being a general in this era of Nodinian culture is pure evil. How many lives have I seen ended and ruined because of this constant struggle with our Eastern brethren? Many years ago when we lived upon the surface, we spread far and wide across this continent. At the time, we were never concerned with power, jewels, or empires. We lived simple lives in the chilling woods and fields. Many villages became towns. Towns became states and so forth. Times were much more beautiful. The old ways of Nodinian beliefs were much like our Soruthian cousins. We cherished nature, animals, and every blade of grass. I've heard stories of how the sky would light up in heavenly elegance. Our ancestors would travel to Vuorijää and pray to Miolannis.

Four hundred years ago when we learned of the Soruthians, those who participated began to slay indiscriminately to have better homes. Those in King Johan's ancestry were notorious for spreading propaganda and lies about Soruth. They stated they were demons from hell and had to be destroyed.

Thirty years ago when Johan was crowned king, he was a man of great honor and integrity. He righted

wrongs and brought justice to crime. He was profession-
ally skilled in battle. Fifteen years ago, when I was a
young adult, I was a foot soldier and fought in the *First
Encroachment of West Nodin*. Aylund fought in this battle. As stout as he is, he moves quickly, and killing is
a sport to him. Prior to this, Johan traveled many days
above the surface for a task he has not mentioned to
many. How Aylund knew of his absence has not been
discovered.

In Johan's absence, Queen Helga was hidden in her
palace. Where Astrid was, I do not know. Prince Hakun
led the defense. In front of the palace was the climac-
tic stage of the battle. Hakun made his comrades proud.
Hakun's armor was red-painted steel. He wore a helmet
version of his crown. His orange hair was bold and dark.
His eyes were green. He met with Aylund in the center of
the battlefield. I was not far from him.

"I thought your father would be here?" Aylund asked.

"Don't you speak of him! You have assailed my
home, slay my men, and insult my family for the final
time!" Hakun shouted. He bore his ax and shield. He
fought Aylund to death!

For minutes they fought with hundreds, dying
around them. In all the struggle and chaos, Aylund's men
found the queen but failed to find Astrid. Aylund issued
his men to blow a horn when they brought Helga to their
side. When the horn was blown, Aylund began laughing as he tangled with Hakun. He kicked Hakun in the
face when the prince was grounded. Hakun dropped his
weapons. He had many bruises on his face from Aylund.

In that final moment, as Aylund stood over him, Hakun struck at Aylund's knee. He stood back up with his ax, but Hakun's throat was cut from behind by an eastern soldier. Hakun knelt down again. Aylund stood up and grabbed the prince's ax. He chopped half of Hakun's head off. The West lost hope. Several of our soldiers were killed. We were outnumbered two to one. We had no choice but to retreat inside the palace. I ran to Xavion's cell, and he grabbed a mace. "We need your help!" I exclaimed. He helped without an answer.

We were able to drive back the East (mostly because of Xavion). We fought them back outside. Another horn was blown, and the east retreated. After the battle, I heard rumors that Aylund brought Helga far away and raped her. As they continued to retreat, Helga was brought to Aylund's palace where he continued to defile her.

After some time, Helga died and I would rather not tell of her passing. During the Encroachment, I lost too much and gained a high rank in the military. Johan lost his mind when he returned: a destroyed city, a slain son, and a kidnapped queen. After the battle, Astrid was guarded every day. Even though the relationship between the king and his champion is bitter, Johan chose Xavion to be Astrid's protector.

Right now, General Daveth, the king, and I are reviewing battle strategies and how much metal has been mined in the month.

"So two thousand pounds of iron, four hundred fifty pounds of nickel, and many jewels were found," I stated.

"It seems Bravious has blessed us with fine metal. I have commissioned Xavion to craft you a weapon of your choice. What shall it be?" asked Daveth.

Johan lost interest.

"My lord?" I asked.

"A hand ax," he replied.

"Guard!" Daveth called out, "Tell Turd Thumbs the king desires a hand ax!"

"Yes, General!" he replied.

I get annoyed by the ignorance of the other soldiers toward their champion. Without Xavion, there is no West Nodin! I put aside my ire to continue working.

"Many of the men's weapons and armor were damaged," I stated.

"Get the Mud Monkey to fix them!" shouted the king in quick anger.

"But, my lord, there are over two thousand pieces to be repaired! There are hundreds of other smiths who are willing to work!" I said.

"Fine, divide them but give the bruised-eyed turd the larger portion!" he replied rudely.

I had no choice but to obey.

I went to inform Xavion. In all honesty, he frightens me. I walked out of the planning room from inside the palace. Inside the main hall, near the throne room, we have large statues of the gods. Each stood at about eight feet. The statues start from Lyannis, and on her head is a golden circlet. Next came Jado. He held a tome, and we often depict him wearing glasses. Then the gender order rotates with each couple. Father Thunder, Tovis is next. We left Tovis standing plainly because we West Nods abandoned the sky long ago. Next is Sarue, who is standing with flowers covering her body and diamonds as her pupils. Then came her sister, the sea maiden Carune with sapphires in her eyes, who stood smoothly upon a small pond of still water. Bravious's statue was literally carved into the palace wall. Jahveyis is ominous when looking down upon us. Jahveyis has always been an interesting deity. He's the inventor of negativity and repentance. Jahveyis is dark, but I think true evil is in us mortals. Miolannis is next. We still pray to her for a lesser winter, but some pray to be successful in their marriage. Sadly, marriage has been loveless ever since the king issued all women to prostitute themselves for our national repopulation. Each woman has one full pregnancy a year. The statue of Sareyus was destroyed a while back. A theory I have is that the worship of Sareyus was outlawed because her orange hair reminds Johan of his family. The religious leaders were ordered to abandon the theological practice of Sareyus.

I walked down the hallway that leads to the brothel. Xavion's cell is not far. Inside his cell is a smithing station consisting of a forge, grindstone, workbench, and tanning rack. As I drew closer, I heard the hammering of metal.

Clank, clank, clank.

I turned my gaze toward his bars. A small lantern brightened the dark room. Toward the back of the cell, I saw two small purple lights. They gleamed and glittered.

"Who goes there?" Xavion said as the hammer paused.

"Xavion," I called. "The king wishes you to fix a portion of the broken arms." Fear grew within me as Xavion stood up and walked toward me. He carried nothing, but he could kill me with his bare hands. I distanced myself from the cell door.

"If he wanted this large task to be done, he should have asked me himself!" he sternly replied.

"Xavion, you don't understand."

"Johan is a paranoid man who does not recognize those who die for him!" Xavion exclaimed. He is right, of course.

"He also wishes you to smith a hand ax for him," I said hesitantly.

"He wants to be reminded of his son? Hakun would've been twice the king than his weak father."

"But... Xavion," I began to say. "You may be able to go to Astrid's room tonight."

Xavion stepped toward the bars and spoke dolefully. "I know you mean well, Vallen. I have not forgotten all of our work together. I cannot return to her room, for my heart breaks when I think of her. I will begin Johan's ax."

"I am sorry, Xavion," I replied. I walked away. I have never forgotten all he has been through. I should have known better than to mention Astrid.

In Sareyus's View

For eight months we were hidden. Our experience was not the best, but it was better than slavery. We were put in cuffs and collars. Whatever became of Jahvonis or what will become of Alva is a mystery. Gods have mercy on her tortured soul. We walked five miles down the tunnel and came into the palace. Guards stood on all sides, blocking the exits. What do they plan to do with us? Shall we return to being slaves, laborers, or slain where we stand? We continued to walk toward the throne room. When we got there, Sebastian, Hamish, and I were unchained and pulled aside. They separated us, and we were placed in different rooms. I sat in mine for around ten minutes. My thoughts ran wild of what the others could suffer. A man walked in and left the door open. He wore the standard armor of the palace guard.

"I am Guard Captain Jens. I've been issued to interrogate you."

"What information could you get from a slave girl?" I replied.

"You could tell me how you escaped and who Jahvonis is!"

"I know not who Jahvonis is! I only escaped because of him!"

"How did he get you to that camp?"

"Didn't you idiots go down that tunnel?"

He smacked me. "Talk to me like that again, slut, and I'll fill your fire cunt with my dagger! Now where did you come from? We have no record of anyone named Sareyus? How did you get here?"

"I am an orphan. I remained on the streets my entire life."

"You must have had a mother?"

"My mother died of illness when I was twelve," I said as he proceeded to question me.

During those questions, I could hear a voice calling me in my head, a voice that was neither mine nor any mortal's.

"What are you doing, Sareyus? Why do you interfere with the world?"

"What do you want, Jahveyis? Why now do you wish to check on me?" I replied.

"I only wish to see why you're hell-bent on finding Xavion? You know he has no emotion. He is only to kill and nothing more!" said the Dark Lord.

"Of course someone sick enough like you delights in mass bloodshed. Even you care little of how many people have died, not just by Xavion but by this war!" I answered.

"Answer me, bitch!" Jens said and smacked me again.

I smacked him back. He slammed me against the wall with a dagger facing my throat, and one of my hands pressed beneath his.

"Maybe you need to be filled? When last were you laid, whore?" he asked crudely.

I have not made my sexual debut yet.

He lifted my robes and slowly pulled down my undergarments. He stared deep into my eyes. He began to evilly smirk, and then a loud impact sounded. Blood began pouring from his mouth! I looked in shock, a kukri short sword pierced through his gut from behind. In his last breath, he tried to cut my throat but I quickly moved the blade aside.

"Jahvonis!" I exclaimed.

"Come, we have to go!" he yelled as he led me out of the room.

"Wait, where are the others?" I exclaimed.

"They'll be fine!" he replied.

We sprinted through the palace and passed through the throne room. Many guards were out cold. The shackles we saw were empty! After the throne room, we ran down many hallways. At last, we came to yet another tunnel.

Jahvonis led me long and far. As we journeyed on, I could feel the wind brushing upon me. A bright light came into our sight and was growing! The surface!

"Jahvonis?" I asked.

"Yes, my lady?" he said in his polite but deep tone.

"Are you taking me to the surface?"

"Yes, it is the only safe place from this hell you were in!"

"Where are the others?"

"They should be waiting for us on the other side. I will direct you to a village of the surface Nods!" Jahvonis replied.

In Sebastian's View

Thank the gods Jahvonis came! He came at the last minute before my interrogator sent word to the king. When Jahvonis saved me, I struggled to find Hamish's room. Jahvonis could not follow me because Sareyus was in need. I slammed door after door, looking for him. At the sixth door, I found the body of Hamish. He was stabbed in the center of his chest. I ran to him and cradled him in my arms. His hand was clenched, and a small chain was within. I laid his fingers back, and they revealed a pendant. It had an insignia scratched into its center, an outline of the sun, a hand shape within, and, lastly, an animal skull at the center. The further I inspected this trinket, it became more familiar.

"Halt in the name of the Red Star!" a guard shouted upon me. He lunged forward with a hand ax, swinging wildly. Being a former guard had me remembering how to fight. I countered his ax with my bronze arm, and I broke his right hand. I ended our altercation by parrying his ax and throwing a facial punch with my bronze hand. I stormed out the door and ran in the direction that Jahvonis said.

As of now, I am standing with the other escapees outside upon the surface. After being underground for so long, the sunlight nearly blinded us. Being under the sky had us feeling we were floating up into it. I only knew the area enough to get us to further safety, but we were instructed to wait for Sareyus (and hopefully Jahvonis).

To ease our eyes to the light, we used our clothes to shield our vision. Jahvonis never told us where he would take us. I wandered further within the confines of the tunnel where the darkness yielded the brightness of the outdoors. I could hear hastening footsteps, and a dark figure sprinted from the black. Jahvonis ran forth with Sareyus beside him. Before he addressed us, he pulled out a small ceramic object. It had a small string on its top. With a match from his belt, he lit the string and tossed the object inside. Moments later, an explosion collapsed the tunnel behind us.

"Everyone, reveal your eyes!" I exclaimed.

They were slightly timid.

"You have nothing to fear!" exclaimed Jahvonis.

Slowly everyone opened their eyes and looked upon our hero. I never realized how black his cowl, hood, and uniform are. His kukri is entirely black, and the utility belt matched. His mask is strapped on and efficiently covered his entire face, and a hood covered the back of the cowl. His eye sockets are shadowed with paint. His greaves are leather with kneepads; and he wore hunter-type boots with shin, calf, and foot guards.

"Everyone, please listen to me! We have escaped the tyranny of Johan for now. He will not give up until he has all of our heads. For the time being, we are safe upon the surface. I will guide you all to a village. Decades ago, when the bulk of your people fled underground from the Theranths, some refused to reject being harmonious with nature! From here, we will journey East! If some are not willing to travel, head southwest to a warmer climate!" Jahvonis stated.

"What would happen if we go southwest?" asked a young girl.

"If we journey that route, you will have less cold but little protection if a threat arrives. If we go east, you will have protection, food, and a community that cares for the oppressed. It's also closer to here," Jahvonis replied.

"How do we know these surfacers will treat us?" a man asked.

"I've made the arrangements. This is not the first time I have done this for the escaped!" Jahvonis stated.

Many of us felt conflicted on which way to go. *To warmth or safety?* we all thought.

"Please give us time?" I asked him.

"I will wait for your choice," Jahvonis replied and walked past us and off into the western distance.

Unfortunately, we came above ground at early dusk. The sun is slowly setting. His black figure is on top of the white snow. The wind is blowing his hood and a man of mourning upon a beautiful sight. A sight we have not seen in years! We gathered in a crowd.

"We must get the children to safety!" a mother stated.

"I would rather fend for myself if it meant getting out of this cold!" a man said.

"We would surely find warmth in a village of protection!" many said.

"Enough! By nightfall, we will freeze!" I stated.

After more discussion and reasoning, we unanimously decided to go East.

"Have any of you chosen?" Jahvonis asked.

"You have not faulted us yet. We will go east with you," I stated on our behalf.

A Short History Lesson of East & West Nodin

Originally, the surface nations of Nor and Gern began the underground excavations. All of the tunneling was first used for mining. The dysfunction of East and West Nodin dates back to when most of their families lived on the surface. Queen Helga as a child resided in the village that Jahvonis is marching to. Helga was the daughter of the *jarl* (chief) of the Eastern Ericson Clan. Johan was a young prince of the Western Edling Clan.

Decades before either were born, the two clans fought time and time again until both neared decimation. In 814 TL (Third Life), the two families called a truce to be bound in courtship. They signed a pact before the gods, and if either side broke the agreement, *"Miolannis would freeze them forever!"* The leaders of both families would marry into the rival clan. Before long, the blood members of both families soon ran out of options to marry. They convinced other minor clans to marry into the larger families.

There were other clans of Nods residing in the north. They were rumored to have aligned themselves with Kuolemajää. The white dragon operated from his lair beneath Vuorijää. They found him after digging beneath the mountain.

These northern clans experimented with the Theranth formula after the expulsion from Soruth. Another power struggle began. Several minor settlements of human Nods became aware of the Theranths. Rumors spread that they planned to ransack villages for man-flesh. The social ignorance and blatant racism caused the man-beasts to seek the guidance of the white dragon. The Theranths were persuaded to make war on the humans, it began on July 7, 820 TL.

The Edlings and Ericsons arranged the marriage between young Johan and Helga. At age eighteen, they wedded. In the years of their marriage, another man grew jealous and resentful of them. He is descended from Johan's immediate family, his younger brother, Aylund Rudolf Edling.

In time, Kuolemajää set his sights on the two clans who stood the best chance of challenging him, the Edlings and the Ericsons. The threat of a dragon and a man-beast army became too great. The humans assaulted Vuorijää. Jarl Leif Edling III met his end at the hands of a Snow Theranth known as *Amandus Amanuel Ambrosious.*

This Theranthic Nod was the chief lieutenant of Vuorijää, second in command to Kuolemajää. Amandus and Leif fought in the *Chamber of the Courtship of Obsidian Ice.* Jahveyis and Miolannis wept over the desecration of their wedding place. In the end, Amandus swung his broad shield and knocked the Giljotin battle-ax from Leif's hands. The ax fell into a trench that went deep into the ice. Amandus impaled the doomed king by the end of his large arming sword. While gripping the sword with both hands, he ran, spun around, and flung Leif's body off the 14,514.5-foot drop to the battlefield below. He coincidentally landed before Johan and Aylund, who were protecting each other. The day of December 11, 873 ended in great loss for the human Nodinian people.

In time, most of the Edlings went underground and a small portion remained on the surface. The Ericsons were led by Aylund and soon went underground.

"There's nothing left for us on the surface," both sides said. They could have defeated the Theranths but could not assail Kuolemajää.

Aylund used his silver tongue to persuade his people to do his bidding. They grew to hate their western kin for their "cowardice." Despite lusting for Helga, Aylund soon made a mother of another man's wife. She gave birth to a son, Bjorn Adolf Edling.

In Narration

When Jahvonis collapsed the tunnel behind him, Vallen and Daveth had to report to the king.

"My king..." Vallen said hesitantly.

"The...slaves..." Daveth continued as Johan's head rose from being slouched.

"They..." Vallen said and caught a deep breath. "They escaped," Vallen finished with regret.

Johan sat on his throne with servants on both sides. He quickly leaped up, drew his arming sword, and decapitated the male servant on his left. "And where is that imbecile guard captain?" he shouted in a roar that shook the room.

"Guard Captain Jens was...killed...by Jahvonis. Fifteen other guards were wounded," Daveth stated.

The anger in Johan's once beautiful brown eyes turned them black.

"I want him found! His head speared to the palace doors!" exclaimed Johan.

"But, my king, the vigilante is the least of your problems!" Vallen said.

"Elaborate!" Johan shouted.

"We have caught wind of a rumor that Aylund plans to move against us once again," Daveth said while showing him a map.

The map displayed the current underground routes. Those that are occupied by the East and West are colored red and blue.

"So far these routes are equal to the enemy. The tunnels and mines that we recently won continue to be a road connecting the two kingdoms. My king, so far after the metal was mined, the new territory continues to be an opening for retaliation," Daveth said.

"Is anyone guarding the path leading east?" asked the king.

"We've pulled a hundred men from the city and stationed them in the top five mines. Those halls are narrow enough to slow down a large army," Vallen stated.

"And what of the main gate on the surface? Should we expect an attack from there?" asked Johan.

"The extremities of the terrain are cold enough to kill an army! The smallest snowstorm could mean death!" Daveth replied.

"I fear we may not have the men to hold the mines and the main gate. If we are attacked, we have to sacrifice one or the other," Vallen said fearfully.

"We have beaten those fools time and time again! Be it the gate or mines or both at once. We'll defeat them all! I'll have that waste of sperm's head as a bowl for my stew!" Johan exclaimed with surety and passion.

"Milord, may I offer an option?" asked Daveth.

"Permission granted," replied the king.

"Despite all the trouble this vigilante has caused, he's left one enemy of his unchecked," stated Daveth.

"Enter!" Daveth exclaimed.

In walked the young man who paid to attempt raping Sareyus. He stood about five feet nine and is thirty years old with short dark-blond hair. His body is lean with thick leather armor and a hood. Upon his waist sat daggers on both sides. On his back is a Barkish composite bow and a quiver of arrows.

"My name is Alastair Beorler. I owe Jahvonis a token of redemption. He screwed me out of two thousand silvers, and he'll repay me with his life!" Alastair exclaimed.

"Assassination?" the king questioned.

"And for a man like Jahvonis, it will be expensive," replied Alastair.

"Name your price?" the king asked.

"Two thousand…gold," Alastair stated.

"So be it!" exclaimed the king in happiness.

In Sareyus's View

The twenty-four of us immediately journeyed east. Fall is my season, and my powers increase. I used that power to create a shield of necessary heat to help us survive the cold terrain. Jahvonis led us upfront. Sebastian stood behind him, then me and all else behind. After about four miles, we took a long rest. Jahvonis stood guard.

"Jahvonis?" Sebastian called to him.

He turned around.

"Why do you do what you do?" asked Sebastian.

"I do what is right for the people! Long I have seen the tyranny of both sides in this war. It is not the soldiers who concern me, but the innocent who must be defended!" he stated in passion.

The more I see this *Black Paladin*, I grow more allured to him.

Perhaps Xavion and I aren't meant to be together, I thought.

Several times I found myself staring upon Jahvonis like a naive girl who sees a shirtless man for the first time. I wonder about the details of this man's form.

"Arise, my friends! We have no time to lose!" Jahvonis said.

We started off again into the night. Many hours and footsteps passed.

"Look toward the heavens!" Jahvonis cried.

The sky began to light. Colors of the world painted Miolannis's black shroud and her moon is full. The colors and moonlight shined as they reflected off Jahvonis's suit. The mountains in the distance also became colorful. Sometimes even we gods forget how beautiful we made the earth!

"We will rest here tonight. Despite the cold around us, I've felt an aura of warmth upon us ever since we left," Jahvonis said.

The rest of us agreed on his examination. We have to rest our heads in the snow. When everyone slumbered, I shot a ring of heat around us to melt the snow. In mere seconds, we laid upon dormant grass. I looked into the heavens wondering if the other immortals have been watching. If any of us assumed a mortal body, if we die, our spirits return to heaven or to cosmos. It could take years for us to rebuild a clone of the previous. It also depends on how much damage our spirit endures. My Pantheon learned long ago if we're killed, we may not return to life. Only Cosmos can make that decision.

I turned my head to my left, then to my right. I sat up but Jahvonis was nowhere in sight. I stood up and walked in the distance of our resting spot. I had a feeling of bereavement and winter. A soft chilling voice is calling me from afar. I walked closer to it. The voice came from a nearby forest in the north. I stepped within the confines of it.

"You've had quite the adventure these last few months," said the voice.

"I thought you would be out here," I replied. I soon heard footsteps that softly caressed the snow. Miolannis it was. She wore a white dress that almost blended with her porcelain snow skin. Her hair is ebony black with a thin white stripe going down past the back of her head. Her eyes are so green that all become lost in her sight.

Her body is shorter than mine. We gods can morph our bodies, faces, and hairstyles to appear different. At times we change into Soruthian, Yazjian, and Theranth appearances.

"I say that Jahvonis has a beautiful name! If Jahveyis and I had a son, Jahvonis would be his name. I bet the person in that suit is sweet!" Miolannis stated as her eyes glistened and sparkled.

"Even when you're married, you still slobber and lubricate like an ignorant slut!" I insulted.

She conjured a dagger made from solid ice. I did the same but with fire.

"Watch your tongue!" she shouted. "If you think I would be unfaithful to my husband, then you're stupid," Miolannis insulted and yielded her attack.

I did the same by tossing my fire into the snow.

"You always did have a problem with envy, Sareyus. I, unlike you, know not to romance a mortal. I only came to you because Jahveyis was interrupted by that rapist

50

guardsman. If he proceeded, Jahveyis would have killed Jens himself. When Jens stood before us, we would've condemned him to hell! You should be grateful," stated the Moon Mistress. "Why would you risk so much for someone like Xavion? You know that we stripped him of any emotional expression. He feels nothing!"

"You know nothing about him! I've learned more of him in eight months than you have in fifteen years!" I replied.

"Do you find the rest of us so shortsighted? Since when do you find yourself so high and mighty? You're no more powerful than any of us! You've never met Xavion other than when he laid on his marble bed years ago!" Miolannis replied.

"Sareyus?" a voice called from afar.

Miolannis quickly faded into a shroud of snow that blew away in the wind. I turned to my left, and it was Jahvonis carrying a mound of dead firewood.

"Who were you arguing with?" he asked.

"It was no one. Where have you been?" I replied.

"I was off collecting firewood. This momentary heat we have been blessed with will only go so far."

"I agree. May I ask a question?" I inquired.

He nodded with approval.

"Have you ever fought against anyone besides Johan? Was there ever anyone else you had to stop?"

"I'll tell you on the way back to our camp," he replied.

As we stepped through the outer trees, Jahvonis began his tale.

"Around the time I began my work against the king, there was a figurehead of an assassin's guild who terrorized the underground and surface people. His name was *Mataraves*," Jahvonis said.

I began analyzing the name. It is a Sand Soruthian name.

"He was a man who was about twenty-two years old when we first met. I knew he was off on a few things. He wore black-and-white makeup upon his face."

As he told the story, I helped him gather firewood.

"My feud with Mataraves was doleful and sad. He became an assassin because he once was a slave. A failed rebellion was led by him. There were times when his employees would fail a task and he would strike them across the back with a wooden kendo sword. I was once captured by him," Jahvonis began. "My arms were chained to two walls, and I was on my knees. I still wore my mask and armor, but my weapons were discarded. When he came to parley with me, I asked, 'Why do you do this? Why do you enjoy the pain and suffering of others?' He replied with, '*Jahvonis, I don't care about which of my schemes succeed and fail. I only care about inflicting psychological damage, like when the snow-skinned scum would whip me senseless and leave scars upon my body. They would soak me within their poisonous ales. The truest way to feel the pain is to become the pain yourself! You see, Jahvonis, my wrath is not with you personally…it's the fact that you fight for the very people who represent false hope and lies. Now since you were able to make it this far, I'll give you a choice—join me in my destiny to destroy the Snow Skins...or bear the same fate as all those you've failed.'"*

I was engulfed in the story, and we reached our camp.

"Will you come help me with the fire?" he requested.

I thought of asking him to continue the story, but the other followers began to awake. I don't know why Jahvonis trusts me with his tale of Mataraves. Jahvonis put the wood in a pile. He pressed a stick in the center while rubbing another against it to cause friction.

"May I try?" I asked. When rubbing the sticks, I used my powers to dry it. I sparked the flame.

"We cannot let this burn out until morning," Jahvonis stated.

We all sat around the flames that burned brightly and boldly. I kept staring at our hero. I slickly caused the flames to grow with a gentle breath. I am trying to reveal the color of his eyes. As the lights rose, the northern lights also brightened. Jahvonis was unfazed by all of this, but the other campers were amazed by it.

Now I can see some of his eyes. They look brown.

"Must you continue to stare upon me?" he asked.

"Forgive me... I was dozing off," I replied.

After about two hours, a lot of us fell back asleep as Jahvonis guarded us. During my slumber, I separated my spirit from my physical self. I traveled into the *Gods' Hall*. This hall sits on top of the tallest mountain in heaven. As I finished my transportation, I stumbled upon Carune and Bravious conversing.

"Do you think Soruth will get any better?" asked Bravious.

"To be honest, my spouse, I do not know. So many issues are sprouting up every week. As the Soruthians continue to become a republic, the more corruption and greed will arise!" she replied.

"Several millennia of this repetition from one life to the next. The mortals never learn," Bravious replied.

"Or perhaps we shouldn't destroy the world again," I interrupted.

They looked at me in surprise.

"Should we allow the mortals all the time they need to change?" I added.

"They cannot be changed and cannot be helped!" said Carune.

"If that is true then why did you create Xavion?" I replied.

"He was made to end wars!" Bravious added.

"By killing all on both sides? I think not! There could be more than killing to that man. It is our ignorance, including mine, that leaves him without a real purpose. We should at least try to speak with him. He is the only physical bridge to the mortals that we have!" I exclaimed as the other gods overheard our debate and entered the hall.

"Do you not know our laws, Sareyus?" Lyannis asked.

"We have all watched your journey over these last few months, Sareyus. You should know better! And even picking a fight with Miolannis!" said Jahveyis with Miolannis absent.

"I only threw insult. It was she who drew the first weapon!" I replied.

"You know damn well she has never given herself to infidelity," Jahveyis said in defense of his wife. "I know envy has distorted your view of Miolannis and the rest of us. You should not be so envious of those who have found their other halves."

"Is it wrong that I desire a spouse of my own?" I questioned. "Is it my fault there weren't enough gods born at the beginning of time?" I asked. "After these last few centuries of you all enjoying each other, it's only fair that I choose a mortal like Jahvonis or Xavion!"

"Xavion feels nothing! He's an artificial being! He has no mother, father, or sibling!" Sarue shouted in frustration.

"You *are his mothers!*" I exclaimed as the goddesses' eyes widened. "*And* you *are his fathers!*" I said to the gods. I stood afar from them as they realized their ignorance and neglect of their child. I am no different in this stupidity. My spirit traveled back into my physical body upon the earth.

After three hours of traveling through heaven and back to the earth, I found myself lying comfortably on the grass. I awoke and turned to my left. I found myself once again eyeballing Jahvonis with his back turned to me. He is sitting down in a lotus position. I kept looking at his broad, thick, and wide back. Even as a goddess, I have sexual thoughts about men and women.

I can only imagine how sweaty and smooth his skin must be in that suit. How many goose bumps would he have if he was bare bodied in the cold? I can imagine him and I exploring an exotic forest in Soruth, where Sarue's trees stand tall and sturdy. A tall mountain of

Bravious would hold a waterfall leading into the roaring sea. Above us would be a cloudless sky of royal blue. Our camp would be set on a patch of grass that turned to sand as it led to a pool of crystal-clear water. Between the two would be a bed frame that is covered in the softest wool of thirty sheep with four campfires, one on each side. Upon that bed, Jahvonis and I would engage in the most vigorous, romantic, arousing, pelvic-thrusting sex!

I kept looking at this brave heroic man who makes my skin blush to match my hair. I began feeling erected by my thoughts. I unconsciously felt myself raising my dress and caressing my thighs.

I was about to pleasure myself until I saw a black pile of cloth next to Jahvonis's left leg. I then saw him raising his right hand and he scratched his head. I saw hair moving with his fingers. He is unmasked! I stopped my perverse behavior and thought with astonishment! I dare not call him, nor make any audible movements.

I got up slowly and tightly held my dress in a bunch to keep the wind from blowing and causing noise. Jahvonis is about eight feet in front of me. I crept quietly and stealthily. I was taking a step every few seconds to avoid suspicion. This is quite humorous and comical looking. I'm now only five feet from him, and many thoughts of his face flashed through my mind. Could his face be chubby or thin? Are his eyes brown, green, blue, or hazel?

I decided to try and rustle him to the ground. I'm directly behind him, and my perverse curiosity tempted me to caress his neck and try to seduce him. I thought of asking him to have sex with me. My porcelain hand is mere millimeters away from pulling his hair. He grabbed me with both arms and tossed me on the ground. He is leaning over me. I am now looking into these beautiful blue eyes upon a smoky black face. Literally, his entire face, neck, ears, and collar is actual smoke in a human shape. No skin tone is visible, and only his hair is solid.

"Do not *ever* do that again!" Jahvonis shouted at me.

For once in a long time, I am somewhat scared. I got up quickly and slowly walked away.

He stood up. "My lady," he called out.

I turned around.

"I did not intend to hurt you…but I must be protective of my identity. I'm sorry," he said as he finished strapping and lacing on his mask.

"As am I," I said and returned to my sleeping place.

Chapter 3

In King Johan's View

Things still do not grow in my favor. My evil shit of a
brother continues to gloat upon his throne in the east. Some
may be wondering how I and Aylund came to be such bitter enemies in a torn kingdom. It was not only his lust for
my wife or the murder of my son. It dates back to our early
childhoods. My father, *Leif Edling III,* had a long-standing
secret relationship with *Johanna Ericson* before finally
marrying. My father was the jarl of the Edling Clan, and
my mother was a commoner among the Ericsons.

My father fought in many of the battles between
their families. Leif never hated the Ericsons; his father
and grandfathers before him held on to that hate. The
rivalry of his ancestors was not enough to prevent his
love for Johanna.

On June 29 in the year 854, I was born in the master
bedroom of the Edling Longhouse. My father had dark-
blond hair, and my mother had orange hair. On April 30
855, Aylund was born in the same room as me.

Throughout our childhood, our father raised us to
be warriors. He trained us both from age ten. The old

Nodinian creed says, "Miolannis toughens us with her cold." My father trained us outdoors. He was a fan of the battle-ax. His ax was named *Giljotin*. He taught me to use an arming sword. With each passing year, my father delighted in seeing me grow into a proficient swordsman. Aylund grew jealous and resentful of Father and I.

My father favored me for progressing further than Aylund. When Aylund and I turned eighteen, there was a trial to decide who would first succeed our father. How it worked was the elders would stand around us as we fought. The Ericsons were invited to witness the duel.

That is when I saw Helga, so beautiful as a young adult. Her hair burned like molten lava, her cheeks were rosy from the cold, and her freckles made any boy want her. It was held at noon. The winner was decided when the other was slain or could not come to his feet before the count of ten. The fight was gripping, but in the end, I shield bashed Aylund to the ground and he could not answer the ten count. If I killed him, all of this could have been prevented.

"Hail, Young Master Johan, future jarl of the Edlings!" the elders said in unison.

"Hail!" the bystanders exclaimed.

What drove Aylund to such despair was that Father would not recognize his bravery. I disapprove of our father choosing favorites. In a way, he created the tyrannical monster that plagues the East. After my eighteenth birthday, my father arranged my marriage to Helga on August 1. The peace between the Edlings and Ericsons began to falter after my wedding. The ongoing war with the Theranths was corroding the familial truce. Before the First Encroachment of the West, I went above ground in search of help against the coming storm. I looked to our surface-dwelling kin for aid, but they replied with *"What happens beneath our feet is no business of ours. We will not fight a war that is not ours!"*

The second request fell upon the sharp ears of the Theranths. They said to me, *"Ah! One of the Little Flakes comes to us for aide? We have no debt to pay. The Theranths owe allegiance to none!"*

When I returned home, I only had my daughter left. My kingdom was in ruins, my men were dead, my wife was taken from me, and my only son was slain while fighting his uncle. As far as Xavion goes, he's only a tool to defeat my brother. Xavion is no different than an ordinary soldier standing guard! What difference does he make in this world? I'll have that bruise-eyed, turd-thumbed ape slay Aylund! He is not worthy of facing me again!

Currently, I am upon my throne. I can still smell the blood of that worthless servant.

"Daveth!" I called.

"Yes, my lord?"

"Do we have news on Alastair's search," I asked.

"No, sire, and we have no news of Aylund's forces…"

"Damnit!" I exclaimed. I proceeded to sit upon my throne. The bloodstains from the dead servant will not come out soon. Now that I remember killing him, I am reminded of Hakun. The flashing memories of the people I killed. Tears came to my eyes. My queen's throne sits to my left and is empty. My mind betrays the memories of her and Hakun.

In Alastair's View

It's about time I get payback on Jahvonis. The fire-haired bitch was mine! I paid good money, and one way or another I will get her in my bed! I'll have her suck me dry as I use Jahvonis's skin for new armor! So far, I've hustled down people he has saved. The first person I harassed was a man. He knows Jahvonis. Months ago he was being mugged by some petty thief. Jahvonis popped out of the shadows and defeated the mugger.

"Where is he?" I asked the man.

"Who?" he replied.

I grabbed his throat and pressed him against the outside wall of his home.

"Where's Jahvonis?"

He grunted and gasped for air. "I don't know!"

"When was the last time you saw or heard of him?"

"All I know is that he freed slave pack months ago!" he said as I slammed him against the wall and released his throat.

After he and twenty other people, I inspected the site where a tunnel collapsed. As I examined it, I found ordinary traces of dust and dirt. I soon found piles of ash, as if there was an explosion. The ash is familiar. I suspect the ash was caused by a ceramic-based bomb that was filled with blasting powder and a fuse. The Hand of Doom uses these to distract, dismay, and sabotage.

The man who taught me this was my former employer and mentor, a man known as the Killing Bird, or in his tongue, Mataraves. He was a fine mentor, and in a way, he was like my father. I never knew my real parents. They abandoned me when I was an infant. For years I was raised in the Hand of Doom. I was living in East Nodin, and the rule of the Vakuuttava was miserable for all people. It all changed when I met Mataraves and his group of rebels who planned to assassinate Aylund Rudolf. Our faction was named by both countries. East Nodin called us the *Black Hole Sun* and West Nodin titled us as *Hand of Doom*. Several times our attempts on Aylund's life were foiled by bad luck. Honestly, we came so damn close.

In all that time, I learned to kill and torture. Violence no longer shocks me, and I particularly enjoy harming young girls and women. My favorite whore who escaped always got me off by listening to her painful crying as I fucked her for one silver coin per round.

So far, Jahvonis's trail leads me back to the brothel. I barged my way through anyone in front of me. I could've gone for a whore, but my mission is at hand. I came into the room where I was assaulted and inspected it. I was on the bed, Jahvonis was behind me, and the door was locked.

I came across a board that was nailed to the floor. I found a hammer and took the nails out. I removed the board from its place and discovered a tunnel. My hypothesis is, Jahvonis came up through the floor and ambushed me. How the nails were removed without my knowing is most likely due to the noisy and physical struggle with the orange-haired whore. The noises in the brothel also masked Jahvonis's entry. How the candles dimmed low enough to camouflage him is beyond me. I jumped down into the tunnel and followed its direction. The tunnel was all but bright. I lit a small torch to see. The torch is held in my left and a dagger in my right. The passage is about ten feet wide and ten feet in height. These tunnels under the palace are used to flee from invaders. I came to a fork in the road that contained four other directions. One of them is unusually cold. It must lead above to the surface.

In Vallen's View

I stand in the War Council of the King, Daveth and other officers. A few hours ago, I was within the mines of the previous battle. An emissary from East Nodin crossed into our borders. Why he was not struck down is because in our culture. If you wave a yellow flag, you come in peace.

"My Vakuuttava wishes for a message to be delivered to his brother. In this sealed envelope, he offers one final challenge. I trust you will deliver it?" he asked.

I nodded my head up and down with my approval. The man left while under close watch from my guards as he returned east. I returned to the palace and delivered the message to the king. When he read it, he grew excited and wrathful.

"So it is set! On May 1 of next year, the War of West and East Nodin will conclude!"

"Vallen, where the hell is my new ax? I want as much practice with it when I cleave the fathead from Aylund's shoulders!" he gloated.

I knew he meant for me to go back to Xavion.

As a general, I cannot express fear for any man, but Xavion is no ordinary man! The way he fights with such passion…is angelic and poetic! His stature is intimidating…and I'm almost three inches taller than him!

His eyes are beautiful. I'll be honest, I find myself appreciating Xavion's looks. Yes, I am a homosexual. Xavion's body to me has several colors. His head and neck are brownish-red, and yet his shoulders and upper chest are golden brown. His stomach is brownish red, his upper thighs are gold, and his legs from the knee down are brown and red. He's not lean or overly muscular. He has body fat. I am walking toward Xavion's cell.

"Xavion!" I called to him.

No answer was given.

"Xavion!" I called through the bars. I leaned further in, he is sleeping in his bed with the blankets over him. He faced the wall. I used my keys and unlocked the door. As I walked into the room, I became so tempted to stroke his long dark hair. I turned over to the small forge and found a hand ax that gleamed with silver steel with five rubies in the shape of the Western star. I have it by my side and made my way to the door.

I made my way back to the king and presented the ax to him after kneeling.

"Finally, the ape is finished! Yes! Just like my late son's ax!" Johan gloated.

For the gods' sake, every time he spews this bigotry, I get further disgusted! Xavion has bravely fought for our country and still gets no recognition!

"Vallen! Bring me the ax man! I'll need to practice for the final battle!" he exclaimed.

In Narration

As the journeys of these characters go forward, their roads will intersect. So far, the gods began paying more attention because the planet has many more issues. Still, the whereabouts of Miolannis is unknown. Jahveyis became worried. Could the promiscuous rumors of his wife be true, or has something worse befallen her? He sat in their bed chambers. He lit several candles and burned much incense. This form of meditation is what he used to assemble the spirit, power, and body of Mustasurma. Now he uses this to find Miolannis. This is possible because thousands of years ago in their courtship, they created a ritual. To their priests and priestesses, it is seen as the *Blood Exchange*.

They collected each other's blood into gold and silver goblets. They held them to each other's mouths with their left hands. They drank their blood. This in turn would allow them to feel more of each other's presence, emotions, and heartbeat. Jahveyis sat on the bed with his back straight, hands on knees, palms up, and sealed his eyes. He then felt Miolannis's fast and rhythmic heartbeat. Her current emotion is fear. In shock, he telepathically used his mind to communicate with his wife.

"Miolannis, my love, can you hear me?" he asked.

"Yes, Jahveyis, I am here!" she answered.

"Why are you fearful? What is it?"

"See this through my eyes!" she pleaded.

Jahveyis used his power and saw through her eyes, which turned his red eyes into green. Miolannis is thousands of feet beneath Vuorijää. The temperature there is no longer cold. They looked upon the empty cage of Kuolemajää.

"Where did he go? The cages for the dragons are impenetrable and cannot be opened by them!" Jahveyis exclaimed.

"This is impossible! Not even Mustasurma could escape, but Kuolemajää could!" she replied.

"Inspect the cage! Quickly!" Jahveyis requested.

As Miolannis fiddled with the magical lock that sealed the doors, her heart began to fear for the safety of the mortals. She entered the large cell to find only feathers and fur. She walked further into the back of the cell and passed a rock formation. Still, nothing else was found. As she searched, Kuolemajää was nowhere in sight.

The earth around began to rumble. A small earthquake shook the room crazily, and the rock formation behind her collapsed. The rocks hid a large ditch in the ground, and slowly the beast raised his claws and featherless body. The immense heat made him shed them. Miolannis turned around, and through her eyes, she and Jahveyis witnessed Kuolemajää freezing her in a hundred-foot-thick block of ice. He also sprayed the entire cell in frost. He escaped through the cell doors. His ice has no damaging effect on the winter goddess, but it leaves her defenseless. One effect is her spirit is trapped within her body. The dragon then spoke in his sharp voice.

"Well, Mother. The hour of continuing my ambitions has arrived. As you hear my voice through your icy prison, remember that a novice plan granted me freedom and allowed me to reconquer this wretched snow land. As I reclaim my lordship over this continent, you are my trophy beneath your once holy mountain," the beast gloated and made his way further to the surface. It will take many months for him to return to full power. For now, he once again made Vuorijää his domain; and his creator, Miolannis, is his prisoner. When the ice froze Miolannis, Jahveyis lost his signal with his wife.

"Damn you, Kuolemajää!" Jahveyis shouted in anguish.

He called an emergency council among the remaining Immortals. All were struck with fear. Jahveyis's anger and rage grew higher upon the beast.

"This is unacceptable!" he shouted.

"Jahveyis, calm yourself!" stated Jado.

"Be relieved that the ice has no harmful effect on her! Miolannis was at least smart enough to check on Kuolemajää. If the weakest of the dragons could escape with a simple plan, then how long until the rest of them do?" Sarue said.

"It was pure luck!" Tovis replied.

"This was no mere chance of luck! He must have been planning this for a long time," Sarue replied.

"We would only waste time by trying to get Xavion to contend with him," Bravious mentioned.

"Isn't he meant to battle such things?" Carune asked.

"To my knowledge, Xavion has a war to end. Sareyus is right...we designed Xavion to act upon our sloth," Bravious stated.

"I feel so mortal," Lyannis said while pressing her hands to her face and bowing her head in shame.

All but Jahveyis agreed the Nodinian War must end before they could request Xavion to save Miolannis. Jahveyis went to bed in anger that night.

In Sebastian's View

I awoke this early morning to find Jahvonis standing guard and facing the East. I assume he gazes at the mountains far off in the distance. He stood in front of the rising sun, yet another beautiful sight to behold.

"Sebastian," I heard Jahvonis call. "What is the pedant you found on Hamish's body?"

I pulled the pedant out of my pocket and gave it to him to examine. He looked at it closely.

"Who killed Hamish?" I asked.

"They have two names. In East Nodin, they call them the Black Hole Sun, and from the West, they're called—"

"The Hand of Doom," I continued.

"I believe it was Alastair. Everyone, listen! The village is only a few more hours away. We will continue when all are rested enough," Jahvonis announced.

We walked for about two hours. We cut through a patch of woods. The trees still looked beautiful despite being adorned in snow. After about five miles through these woods, we came out back onto the valley. We can see smoke rising in the distance. With it, we saw wooden buildings. We arrived at a surface Nodinian village.

"What is the name of this village?" I asked.

"*Starkstad*," Jahvonis replied.

In Sareyus's View

Finally, we came into the village.

"Let me do all the talking," Jahvonis requested.

We then walked into the village in a huddled grouping. The men and women of this town wore thick, heavy, and furry clothing. A good amount of them have blond hair and blue eyes (which are common traits in Nodin). We are walking past a busy street that has a temple, blacksmith, mausoleum, several stores, and a longhouse (often home to the leader of this Nodinian town). We walked to the entrance of the longhouse. There are guards on duty.

"Jahvonis, once again with freed slaves?" the guard to his right asked.

"Indeed so! These people wish to reside here until the war is finished," he replied.

"All right, you may pass," the guards said.

We passed through the doors and down a long room that displayed people enjoying a feast. The merriment paused as we traveled further inward. There is a man who sits on a broad and large chair, most likely a lesser throne. Jahvonis continued to walk toward this man. He has dark-blond hair and a gruff and hairy goatee. His eyes are hazel and stands even at six feet. He has medium-thick eyebrows. He wears a coat made from bear fur. Around his neck is a pendant of bronze and shaped into the East Nodin hexagram. Upon us seeing it, we all shook in fright! Has Jahvonis sold us out!

"Jarl Kristoff Ericson," Jahvonis called.

"It's been a while since you were here last and you have company, more than last time. Heroic, you are. A symbol of hope for us Nods," Kristoff replied.

"I freed these people from Johan. They were in need of saving, and who else would do so?" Jahvonis said jokingly.

I guess he does have a sense of humor.

"Kristoff, war is approaching…a war that will consume your settlements in bloodshed. I know from a reliable source that Johan and Aylund are implying their final battle will be fought on the surface!" Jahvonis exclaimed.

"This is not the only threat which troubles us!" Kristoff replied.

"What do you mean?" Jahvonis asked.

"Our allies from northern Nodin sent us word that they have seen something out of folktales—a dragon!" Kristoff exclaimed.

Those words surprised me. Kuolemajää has escaped? Where is Miolannis in all this? When Kristoff confessed this, Jahvonis's shoulders dropped!

"They tell us it just sits on top of Vuorijää. At any time, it may grow bored and hungry! We cannot fight two feuding nations and a mystical beast!" Kristoff continued. "Jahvonis, what should we do?"

Jahvonis stood in thought for a few seconds. All in the longhouse anticipated his answer like the coming of psalms!

"Build ships!" our hero exclaimed.

"Pardon?" Kristoff asked.

"Build your ships…empty this land! Gather all who wish to flee this war and escape!"

"To where?" Kristoff asked.

"To Soruth!" Jahvonis replied as the whole room dropped their mugs and gasped.

No Nodinian has stepped upon Soruth in many centuries. Most have forgotten it exists!

"A land far to the south…far from the tyranny of kings and dictators! What other choices do you all have?" Jahvonis asked.

Kristoff sat back on his throne. "Please allow me some time to gather my council. For now, you and your companions are welcome to stay in the spare hall within the temple," he stated.

"Make haste! The longer we wait…the sooner death and carnage will surround us! Thank you!" Jahvonis said as he led us back outside and into the temple.

The temple has ten stone steps that led into a wooden doorway. When we opened it, we saw a long and wide room of several shrines, the goddesses to my left and the gods to my right. Each one had their spouse across from them, except me, of course. We are entering a spare hall. Inside I thought I saw Miolannis. This woman's black hair looks almost identical (except for the skunk stripe). When she turned around, we saw the living and breathing Alva!

"Alva!" most of us exclaimed. She came running and immediately jumped into Jahvonis's arms.

"Lucky!" I said to myself.

"How did you survive the fall!?" Sebastian asked.

"My life flashed before my eyes as I descended further down to Bravious. Instead of crashing into the rock, this beautiful, heroic, handsome man caught me in his arms!" she exclaimed with her sparkling eyes that were given to her by Carune. "There must be some way to repay such a selfless man?"

"In fact, there is one way for you *all* to repay me. To continue the rest of your lives without regret. If it were not for all of *you*, there would never be Jahvonis!" he replied.

Those words alone made us all joyful! We all eventually kissed and/or hugged Jahvonis. When my turn came, I kissed him directly where his lips should be, and when I pulled away, he winked at me! I've made up my mind: I choose Jahvonis!

In Narration

Finally, things are moving. The board is set! The coming battle is at hand, and the immigration to Soruth is in process. If this war is not concluded before Kuolemajää is at full power, all of Nodin will fall under him. Aylund however only has to sit and wait. He already has plenty of men to fight. For now, he spends his time violating the children and the women of his country.

Jahvonis left the temple in Starkstad and walked out into the white lands. After he winked at Sareyus, she is now enthralled by the *Black Paladin*. In late October, she and most of the townspeople had to briefly vacate the village and move further to the sea (which makes building ships easier). They went further west until they found a suitable place between the land and the ocean. They would cut the trees down and move them closer to the water. They also planted two trees for every one they cut down.

The chilling fall continued, but they need as much time to build as possible. With fall passing, the power bonus for Sareyus began to fade. The people's heavy clothing was enough to warm them. After a day's work, they would all rest inside small huts that were made from wood and stone.

During the construction, Kristoff remained in his longhouse to take care of other important business. He appointed Sebastian in charge of the construction. Every day since Jahvonis left, Sareyus could not stop remembering him. Each time he saves her, she grows more in love! Jahvonis went back underground; each oppressed person needed his help also.

As for Alastair's hunt for our hero, he made his way above ground and scoured Nodin in several directions, even crossing the paths of the Theranths. They knew him well because a while back, he murdered a Theranth child. Anyone to harm a child of any kind is hated, but the Theranths thought twice about tangling with the leader of the Hand of Doom. Alastair went to many settlements of humans looking for any trail of Jahvonis. His path took him to Starkstad. As he entered the village's borders, his wardrobe and weaponry attracted much attention. He began to make his way toward Kristoff's longhouse, but on the way in, he was stopped by the guards.

"Halt! What purpose do you have here?" asked one.

"I am, by the order of King Johan Edling, to find a man heavily adorned in black with a matching mask. I am told he led a small band of slaves above ground," Alastair answered.

The guards are caught in a hard place. Any word could give away their knowledge of Jahvonis.

"You may speak to our jarl if you like?"

"I shall!" Alastair said arrogantly. He barged through the doors and marched toward the throne. Kristoff sat upon it with two more guards at his sides.

"And who walks toward me, barging through my house doors?" he asked.

"I am Alastair Beorler. I have orders from King Johan Edling to find a man named Jahvonis. He wears all black and masks his face. Have you any knowledge of such a man?"

"Nay! No one I've ever known or seen wears such mournful colors! Why only Jahveyis would wear those clothes."

Alastair looked into Kristoff's eyes for honest surety. "Well then, where may an exhausted traveler take refuge?" he asked.

"There's an inn down the road. Only five coppers per night," Kristoff replied.

"Thank you for your time," Alastair replied.

Normally, Kristoff would direct the weak and exhausted to the temple, but of course, he would contain any threat to the operation of immigration.

As the assassin made his way to the inn, he once again passed by the temple. As far as his faith goes, he highly reveres Tovis for his archery and Jahveyis for the dark influence on his heart. If any remorse is present, it is in a microscopic amount. When he passed by the temple steps, Alva was praying long. She thanked the gods for their blessings to the mortals. Except during storms, the doors of the temple are open, Alva was in sight of Alastair. Before Jahvonis's rise to vigilantism, Alastair was Alva's most common customer. Luckily, she wore much clothing that concealed her charming face. Alastair now entered the inn and paid for a room.

In Alva's View

I know some are wondering how I came to Starkstad unharmed. When Jahvonis directed me to the surface, he already had a horse prepared for someone. I rode until I reached Starkstad. I was bruised and spiritually ill. The four years I spent as a prostituting slave were terrible. I am sixteen. I always heard that sexual intercourse is a gift from Miolannis, but rape is a crime too cruel. Every day, for 1,460 days, I was raped at least once. My healing is only through the gods. I wonder if they'll pardon my attempted suicide. Could they have another plan since I was saved before hitting the stone? I know my past is not my fault. My parents hid me from West Nodin's government for the first twelve years of my life and were slain for it. My parents' unfriendly neighbors sold us out for only five copper coins!

When I was encamped with my escaped companions, I was beginning to heal. If Jahvonis never caught me, I would have wept for my heart to be frozen and sent to join my parents in eternity. Because of my past, I finally understand why Jahveyis created such evil things: If there is no evil then how can there be good? If there is good, then how can there not be evil? One does not exist without the other, and if there is a god of evil, then there must be a god of good?

My past in the brothel always cursed me with nightmares. Even when I dreamt of my daytime horrors, I would awake to women and men abusing me. When I was rarely alone, I was cutting myself upon my thighs and forearms. My scars are small, and my wounds were never deep. The man who regularly hurt me, sometimes for half a day, got off on my crying and pain. I have never been pregnant from any of the men who harmed me.

In my prayers between Miolannis and Jahveyis, I question them if Jahvonis is their son. If the gods verbally reply to prayers is unknown to me. After my prayers passed, I retired to my bed. In the resting chambers of the temple, there is a window that is opened by a wooden door. This window faced north. The stars are bright on this black night with a crescent moon. I gazed out this window with my arms upon the windowsill. My mother always sang this song to me when I would go to bed.

Sleep, my child, be troubled no more!
The world above you must explore! Sky
you'll gaze and kin you'll raise. Hope
and passion will braze! Snow and grass
you'll walk. High leaves and strong
bark! A splendid sun will yield the night,
a day will rise serene and bright. Never
surrender faith to fright! When the worst
is behind you, forward you walk!

I sang this song out of my window and onto Nodin.

In Sebastian's View

We are done with some of the hull of the ship. It should be large enough for Starkstad and one more village at best. If we plan on taking more, then it will be a tight journey. We must also pack at least a year's supply of food for about 250–300 people. I don't know how long the journey will be, but Jahvonis has not steered us wrong yet. I am now directing the construction. I and thirty others took the first six-hour shift, and then Sareyus and her workers took the next six hours. I admire her courage and bravery. She gives hope and strength to our people. I know she and Alva have obviously been bewitched by Jahvonis's valor.

I no longer have much use for romance. The wear and tear that war and slavery does to a man my age is weakening. I would describe myself as being middle-aged with blond hair and a matching beard. I have blue eyes and snow skin. My body is thick skinned, and I am as tall as Xavion. I was the first guard who befriended him with an open heart and mind. My first witness of Xavion's skills in the war was during the First Encroachment of West Nodin. I was helping barricade the palace doors from the enemy. We lost the queen, but I hid the princess. Astrid was hidden in a secret room on the top floor of the palace. King Johan did not return from his journey yet. Vallen ran to Xavion's cell and released him.

He was equipped with a unique mace. It was different than the flanged maces we are used to. Xavion's mace was a big ball of steel with twelve thick one-inch pyramidal spikes extending from it.

In the battle, Xavion killed the most men. During the bloodshed, everyone else wore armor. A mace is used to break armor and the body underneath. In my opinion, a mace (and every bludgeoning weapon) is most important for armored fighting. Swords and axes are wonderful, but they are less effective against plate or chain mail.

Even though Xavion saved us, the rest of the government demanded he was to never use his mace again. The West Nodin government is biased and ignorantly prejudiced. Xavion and the other bludgeon users came through for us because they used anti-armor weapons. There was no other reason for this ban than the government's jealousy for Xavion!

My shift is now ending for today, and Sareyus is entering hers. I sat in my small hut. In my thoughts of personal time, I often look upon my artificial hand. Sometimes I become depressed. I have no feeling within it. My hand works because the fingers have adjusted tension with one large mechanism on the backside of my palm. I have them opened enough where I can grip things to a firm effect. Johan definitely knows how to scar a man's will, rendering my strong arm useless and allowing me to live. I'll kill him myself for all those he and his brother have trampled upon! My punishment was unjust! The king mutilates a guard for ensuring his daughter's happiness? Bullshit!

"Sebastian," someone called while opening my hut door. It was Sareyus.

"Shouldn't you be working?" I questioned.

"Yes, I will, but I have questions."

"Aye, you may ask."

"Thank you! Sebastian, how long have you known Jahvonis?"

"I do not know him personally, but I know of his work."

"Do you know who he could be?"

"I'm afraid I don't know, lass. Jahvonis is as much of a mystery to me as the next person," I replied as she paused and spoke again.

"Do you know anything else about Xavion?"

"Ah yes, Xavion! He's an honest man. I enjoyed sharing the battlefield with him. Even in our time alone, he taught me a few things about life. Fifteen years ago, he and I built a strong friendship. It was a friendship briefly through music! Before my injury, I loved to play the lute! I once played it for him. 'May I try,' he asked. I allowed him to play it, and he blew my ears around the world! He played with endless taste, feeling, and passion! He was in love!" I exclaimed. "Go now, there's work to be done!"

She went on her way. Minutes later, a courier delivered a letter to me. I unsealed it, and it reads:

> *Sebastian, a man came into Starkstad a short while ago looking for Jahvonis! His name is Alastair Beorler. He is resting for the night at the Inn and says he will return underground. It seems King Johan has hired an assassin to slay our liberator. So far he's being held under close surveillance until he exits. As a precaution, tell no stranger of our town or operation.*
>
> *Jarl Kristoff Ericson*

In Sareyus's View

So far, my work on the ship is tiresome. We gods haven't done so much manual labor since rebuilding the earth. I'm starting to think Sebastian knows Jahvonis's identity because he was about to tell me more until he sent me to work. Did he send me off to conceal Jahvonis's identity for safety purposes? I did begin to think about Xavion again. The memory of him lying upon the stone bed in his entire splendor is inspiring. Watching him in that battle was menacing. The other gods truly made him the ultimate warrior. Yet he was merciful and heartfelt when he spared East Nodin's champion. Jahvonis, on the other hand, is a hero.

After six hours, I returned to my hut and went to sleep. I divided my spirit from my body and returned to the Gods' Hall for the latest news. In the past, whenever a goddess or god would leave and go to the earth, we all felt their presence but not how they felt. When our spirits leave our physical bodies, they appear as projections of our current forms. When my spirit arrived in heaven, I was welcomed by Sarue.

"Welcome back, Sareyus," she said.

"It is nice to see you, Mother Nature! What is happening?" I asked curiously.

"Nothing good I'm afraid," she said. Sarue told me all that went down beneath Vuorijää and the despair that has taken Jahveyis.

"We have to save her!" I exclaimed.

"No! First of all, if you vacate your current journey, you will bring much suspicion and false hope to those whose lives you have touched! And second, our hostile presence in Nodin could cause much unintended destruction!" Sarue exclaimed.

"Then what is it you propose?"

"Come, we must summon the Immortals!" Sarue exclaimed as she guided me to the other chambers of the gods.

Our first stop was the room of Carune and Bravious. Each of our chambers can be the size of whole countries.

How Carune and Bravious share a room is that the entire area on the inside of the door is a small bay of Carune's water. She most often swims nude. To us, nudity is neither sinful nor indecent. At the back is an island with a beach along its border and a small mountain in the center. This is a copy of their first island after the first was destroyed by Avgrund. On the inside, the door floats in the air.

Sarue spoke aloud in Sandish. In translation, she said, "Great Carune...please raise thy sea so thou's eldest sister may pass!"

"Why did you speak in the Sand language?" I asked.

"Fantastic effect," she replied humorously.

We waited a few seconds with no reply. We looked in confusion. Sarue spoke once more, this time calling out to Bravious.

"Bravious! Lord of the Earth, the first Soruthian, raise the seafloor to us so we may cross this wet veil!"

Still no answer was given. A land bridge soon rose from the water, and we crossed. The water around us stood still when we landed on the beach. We searched for the mountain entrance.

As Sarue was about to open the door, she looked out at the sea and admired Carune's creation. I looked out with her. Then in front of us, at a random moment, a creature burst out from the water and gave a snarling scream that scared Sarue to the ground. The creature was of the sea, an Aquranth. The creature began to chuckle and laugh as it fell back into the water. After a few seconds, Carune rose up and laughed.

"I told you something would happen if you interrupted my love time with Bravious!" she exclaimed while continuing to jest.

"Oh, you jester!" Sarue said with laughter.

We continued to briefly laugh until my seriousness arose again.

"Please enough! Carune gather Bravious and meet us in the council hall!" I asked.

She went inside the mountain as we left to find Jahveyis.

"Sarue, you should find Tovis. I'll find Jahveyis," I offered.

Sarue left my side. Her portion of her room is all forest with a bold blue sky with white clouds that belong to Tovis. The room of Miolannis and Jahveyis begins with a black door. Behind it is a bedroom with many dark forms of art. As I opened the door, Jahveyis sat upon his bed in meditation. I saw dried tears upon his handsome face.

"Jahveyis," I called as he opened his bloody red eyes. Much anger has grasped his heart since Miolannis's capture.

"The gods have been summoned," I said politely.

He vacated his bed and made his way toward the council hall. I followed him. As I entered, Jado and Lyannis were already seated.

"So what is our plan?" Bravious asked.

"This meeting was the idea of Sareyus. She should speak first," Sarue stated.

"Kuolemajää is a threat. With Miolannis not controlling the harsh winter of Nodin, the continent may be doomed to a treacherous season. Aside from Kuolemajää; East and West Nodin are preparing for their final battle. King Johan Edling and his brother, the Vakuuttava Aylund Rudolf Edling, are going to settle this blood feud on the surface," I stated.

"Do you think the beast will enter the war?" asked Jahveyis.

"If the human Nodinians destroy each other, then they leave less resistance to face him. One village of Nods are building a ship to flee to Soruth from the coming peril. A vigilante who calls himself Jahvonis is leading us there. For the last several months, he has saved my life and the lives of the innocent many times. The people he comes in contact with are calling him the Son of Miolannis and Jahveyis," I said as Jahveyis turned to me with concern. "His identity is unknown to me, but I will join his pilgrimage to Soruth," I added.

Jado then spoke his mind. "The Soruthians will not let a group of Nodinians enter freely on their lands. Besides, Kuolemajää used the last of his power on Miolannis. He won't be a severe threat until he regains his full strength, so the Nodinians have nothing to fear from him for now. Our place in their war is to judge the dead and answer prayers. You, Lady Sareyus, your part in the war has yet to be revealed."

"Then who the hell will save my wife? Should I go myself? I'd love to make a coat out of the dragon's fur!" Jahveyis shouted.

"Calm yourself! Miolannis is in no pain. The ice has no harmful effect on her!" Carune replied to Jahveyis.

"We can't fight him without upsetting the planet. One of us should petition a warrior strong and brave enough to face the beast," Tovis said.

"It doesn't seem smart to ask Xavion. The reason being that we have no logical or intelligent way of asking him. As stated before, he is busy in the war and he does not know us. Yes, his power rivals Kuolemajää but... I don't know," Lyannis said.

"Power? What power?" I exclaimed as they all paused. "Well?" I added.

"During our construction of Xavion, we gave him a portion of our powers so he would carry us all with him. I gave him the ability to immediately hydrate himself and quench his thirst by swallowing his saliva. When drinking actual water, it replenishes and replaces lost blood while also healing wounds. He can also manipulate and control water in its forms," Carune admitted.

"I granted him the intelligence of the smartest people who have ever lived. His intelligence is gathered from doctoring, math, science, history, ethnography, music theory, martial arts, and military tactics. His first weapon masteries are the mace, sword, and shield. All of his senses are increased tenfold," Jado said.

"I gave him one-twentieth of my speed, which is superhuman to mortals but novice compared to me. During a thunderstorm, he can absorb air and electricity and blast them through his palms and feet. He can enchant any weapon with them. He can also store electricity into his bodily electrons and weaponize it," Tovis stated.

"I made him a skilled alchemist and botanist. He knows how to make about every form of medicine and poison. He is immune to natural poisons and venoms but can be harmed by their supernatural variants. He can also bend plants to his will. Whether he has realized it or not, I don't know. Xavion can telepathically communicate with all animals, including Theranths," Sarue added.

"My gift to him was with the right tools, he can mend metal into any shape. His earthly powers can also shape metal and remove rust. I gave him one-thirtieth of my strength. He climbs stone and metal walls with ease like an insect. It is possible because he excretes the iron in his blood like a paste and sticks to many surfaces. If he's wearing armor, the same ability applies. The iron bleeds through the materials and attaches him to the wall. The more he uses a weapon, the quality and damage of it increases. A special ability for him is he can conjure weapons and armor that he crafted and kept. It will take a long time until he unlocks that power." Bravious said.

"I gifted sight where he can see clearly in the dark. I thought it would come in handy when battling at night. He can also conjure light in dark places. This was given for group traveling. I do not know if he has unlocked it," Lyannis added.

"I believe Miolannis gave him the talent of controlling the low-temperature air around him. He could make it cool or ice cold. He cannot overheat in the hottest desert or freeze to death in the coldest tundra. He can cast and breathe frost," Jahveyis spoke.

"Tell Sareyus what you gave Xavion," Jado requested of Jahveyis.

Jahveyis chose his words carefully. "I made him a talented poet. I gave him 10 percent of my ability. Consequently, I gave him a high susceptibility to negative thoughts. His ways of killing and fighting are inhumane. Every time he commits those acts, he hides his shame and gives into his guilt," Jahveyis finished.

I spoke again. "You fools! You made him a false god! If the mortals witness his full power, then they will worship him like they did the dragons! If they do not pray to us, then we will die by fading into time and space... forgotten!" I exclaimed.

They all bowed their heads in fright, realizing how their past ignorance may have changed and sealed the fate of the third world!

"Also if you want Xavion to fight the beast, and if he wins, then think of his increase in power! Please tell me that is not possible!" I asked.

They all looked at each other in surprise. I'm guessing the answer is yes!

"Un-fucking-believable!" I said in anger. "How is that possible?"

They were timid to answer.

"Xavion's powers increase by drinking dragon blood. The more he ingests, the better he becomes. How we implanted his powers within him was by injecting a portion of our blood into his body. This caused his eye color to be changeable at will, but his default color is purple," Jado said.

"Sareyus, have you ever witnessed Xavion in battle?" Tovis questioned.

I told them my experience during the recent battle underground, how their weapon slew four hundred people! All their eyes widened. Never has one person ever killed so many in one day, single-handedly!

"I don't know how we can save Miolannis other than doing it ourselves. She will have to wait until we elect a solid plan that will not upset the earth!" I stated.

Jahveyis grew more upset, not with us but with the fact there's nothing he can do that will have no dire consequences. He held his anger within.

"I must leave now. Thank you all for your time. Please for our sake, do not do anything drastic!" I said and departed back to the earth.

Chapter 4

In Alastair's View

My experience in this town seems nothing but ordinary. I have noticed people eyeing me. It's understandable because I'm carrying several deadly weapons, but otherwise, it does not surprise me. At night, I strolled around town. The person posing as Jahvonis could be a citizen here. Most likely he would operate at night. I questioned several people, and something tells me they're hiding him. I moved into the temple. As I passed the nine shrines, I stared long and hard at Lyannis. It's too bad that she's not mortal, I would be the first to ravage her. There weren't many people as I walked further in. Nine others exited.

I am now moving toward Jahveyis. My master Mataraves took the beliefs and reverence of Jahveyis and trained me with them. I learned how to fire a bow and soon became the deadliest shot in our organization. Here beneath the shrines, I knelt before Lord Jahveyis.

"Great Evil One! King of Sin! Monarch of Murder! Saint of Suicide! Reverend of Rape! Grant me thy blessing so my journey to slay the hero, Jahvonis will be successful!" I whispered aloud. As I stood up, I removed my hood to expose my hair. I heard a cup drop, and a woman then ran. I investigated this odd occurrence.

This woman ran fast into a room and slammed the door behind her. I heard the door lock. In retaliation, I pulled out a lockpick and a small knife. Unfortunately, I'm not too good at picking locks but this one seems doable. After a few moments, I finally unlocked the door. I gently opened and closed it behind me. Inside, a teenage girl is cowering in the corner. I know this girl. She was my favorite whore back in the palace brothel. I never cared to learn her name. She has black hair and blue eyes.

"Stay away!" she shouted.

"So this is where that black-masked bastard brought you!" I replied.

"Murderer! Don't dare touch me again! I'm not your whore anymore!"

I grabbed her by the arms. The cunt slapped me in retaliation. I punched her in the face, which sent her to the ground. I proceeded to rapidly kick her head and stomp on her like the cheap seed garden she is. I always liked striking women; it's empowering. I stood her up again with my forearm against her throat and pressing her hands together against the wall.

"Since I found you, it means this stupid town has been hiding Jahvonis from me! Look at you now, still so beautiful. Now, whore, I'll give you a choice—you either tell me where Jahvonis is or I will rape you in this temple!" I said in a calm tone.

"I swear after Jahvonis lead me here, he returned back underground!" she shouted while crying her bruised eyes out.

"Where are the other slaves?" I asked.

"They scattered all across the land. Jahvonis spread us out to avoid a group roundup!" she exclaimed.

I didn't believe her. I headbutt her and continued to beat her. I threw her down in front of me. I heard her nose break on the floor. Blood flowed from her. I was scared it might seep beneath the door. I tore her clothes off and piled them beneath the door frame. I decided to rape her anyway.

After my amused insemination of that bitch, I have to escape from this town immediately. I waited until I couldn't hear anyone on the other side of the door. I bolted back to the inn to pack my luggage and return underground. King Johan will be delighted with the news!

In King Johan's View

My training with the new ax is certainly different than using a sword. During sparring sessions, I have to use a wooden ax for safety reasons. I wore my real one on my left thigh. So far in these sparrings, I have won three out of five. The flaws that cost me the last two were that I swung recklessly and I neglected my shield. I must learn to have enough control but give enough force to land a successful hit. We switched to using real axes. Over the next seven spars, I continued to be defeated.

"Damn this!" I shouted in frustration.

"My king, you're not paying attention. You cannot swing wildly. You'll need as much precision as possible. Also, correct your stance. Hold your shield closely!" the trainer said.

"I give the orders!" I swung my real ax into his head. As he fell down, I continued to chop him wildly. This moment took place in the throne room. This correction of my trainer was witnessed by Daveth, Vallen, my servants, and other guards.

"Johan!" Vallen shouted. "You just murdered the Ax Master!"

I walked over to him in anger. I began to sweat. "He was weak and expendable!" I replied.

"You don't see it, do you? Ever since Helga and Hakun died, you've become your brother!"

I glared back at him. "I am not like Aylund!" I yelled as I held the ax toward Vallen. He grasped his ax in retaliation.

"Your father would be ashamed of you both! How evil, ignorant, and immature the great king and Vakuuttava have become!" Vallen said.

I swung my ax at him, but it was hooked by his own. We were then exchanging blows. The guards didn't come to my aid because I did not command it. If I can kill Vallen on my own, then I can kill Aylund with no problem! As our battle ensued, I saw Daveth frantically run down a hallway with his keys in hand.

Our fight erupted the palace in shock. I held my weapon in my left hand as Vallen gripped his in his right. I swung horizontally, but once again I was hooked by Vallen. I struck him in his face. He swung and lightly slashed my chest. Nine struggles happened when our axes collided. Upon the tenth swing, Vallen struck me three times with his fist. I punched his throat and kicked his knee. He fell beneath me in a bowing position. Such treason is punishable by death! I raised my ax like the hand of Jahveyis and prepared to smite him. My hand was grabbed in midair. I turned to my left, and there was Xavion. He clenched my wrist so firmly that I dropped my ax. Vallen looked up with blood on his lip.

"Should you strike him down, Aylund will have already won. You say you're not like him…prove it!" he said.

I gazed into his purple eyes, thinking of his logic.

"All right…as king, I command you to kill him!"

Vallen glared at us. Xavion grabbed the ax from the floor. I backed away and sat on my throne.

"Xavion… I'm sorry…for everything. You deserve better," Vallen mournfully said as his words echoed throughout my hall.

The turd then raised his arm but repositioned himself on Vallen's left side. He raised his hand again…and tossed the ax toward me! It spun three times through the air. I dove off my throne as it embedded itself in the Red Star insignia on top of the throne.

"Guards! Seize them! To prison, they'll stay until May 1!" I shouted.

They dragged Vallen and escorted Xavion to the holding cells. I removed the ax from the star and sat clenching it in my hand.

"I am the king!" I shouted in aggression.

In Narration

After Alastair committed the vicious rape and assault of Alva Amott, he fled Starkstad by using his stealth and escaped into the night. The next morning Alva was found naked and battered. She was physically, mentally, emotionally, and spiritually broken. The other priestesses discovered her. She lives and is physically healable. As for her spirit, heart, and mind, only her inner strength can cure her. She will never be rid of the memories, but without them to motivate her, she's truly lost.

A written message was sent to Sebastian. As he read it, he grew angry because Alva is a daughter figure to him. Sareyus learned of this tyranny that defiled the holy walls of the temple. A crime in a temple is a crime against the gods themselves! That night she telepathically communed with her fellow Immortals. Jado secretly pledged to himself that Alastair will not get away with this. An agent of his is years at work.

For two weeks, Vallen has been imprisoned. He is allowed to attend war councils but is to return to his cell afterward. So far he has refused to attend. Vallen is Johan's cousin from his father's side. His cell resides in the northern end of the palace. Daveth however seems out of touch also. So far, he's been a mystery. He and Daveth were drafted many years ago. It was also Daveth who released Xavion to stop the fight between Vallen and Johan.

The construction of the ship is progressing. The construction crew has finished the overall shape of the vessel. They're anticipating the towns of *Starkstad, Coldhill,* and *Steelburrow* to accompany them. At the moment, they are looking at about four hundred people.

It took Alastair days to return to King Johan.

"What is the status of your mission?" Johan asked.

"Jahvonis's trail led me above ground to the town of Starkstad. Kristoff Ericson lied to me about Jahvonis going there. I had to interrogate a temple maid. She told me Jahvonis returned underground," Alastair replied.

"Find him and kill him already!" the king shouted.

Alastair hates Johan. Then again, Alastair hates everyone.

Alva at the moment is being doctored on. Her nose is broken and until further notice, she must wear a special metal brace that will hold her nose in place. Hopefully, it will heal and permit her to breathe easily enough.

In Vallen's View

Damn that foolish king! Murdering his trainer and raising his weapon upon his most trusted general! Some family I was born into where siblings start wars and kill each other! After many years of Johan's mind deteriorating, he is unchangeable!

"He is no longer capable of being king. What disaster and oppression he has brought to our people. He has dishonored the name of the Edlings," I said out loud.

"Now you choose to realize this?" interrupted a voice. "Now the best general since Leif Edling chooses to open his once blind eyes?" it replied.

"Where are you?" I exclaimed.

As I sat at the bottom of the cell wall from the door's right side, Jahvonis dropped from the ceiling. He stood up in front of me.

"Vallen Fredrik Edling, have you finally realized your family's treachery?" he asked.

"Yes!" I exclaimed.

"Johan must be stopped!"

"What makes you think I can do anything at this point?"

"One of your other relatives despises the way their father asserts power. I was able to free him from Nodin's corruption. He's making his way to the surface. I can release you now, or you can finish your sentence and go to war. Which is it?" he asked.

I entered deep thought. If I leave now, I can build a new life above ground. If I stay, then the rest of my life is wasted. "I will go," I replied.

"In return for this, all I ask is, should the war cross through Starkstad, you will general the people. Encourage them to defend all that is good!" he requested.

"I will!" I said enthusiastically.

Jahvonis pulled out a key from his pouch. He reached through the cell bars and unlocked the door. He secretly led me to the surface.

In Sebastian's View

Poor Alva! After all she's overcome, victimizers still find their way to her! What man is evil enough to assault and violate a temple maid in the gods' holy house? If I ever find her attacker, I will castrate him! Alva is daughterly to me. When she and I were brothel slaves, I impregnated women against my will. Alva needed someone to back her up when she needed it. I stuck up for her when she was exhausted. She was convinced I was in love with her. I said to her, "Alva, I'm not the right man for you. Please understand I'm not looking for anyone. You're still a young woman, Alva. Always remember, even darkness must pass!"

I still do my work on the ship. Ten of the rooms are in progress, and we're scheduled to fit many more.

One week later, a messenger came from Starkstad. They delivered thirty more volunteers from Steelburrow and Coldhill. He also gave me a written message from who I presume was Kristoff. I opened the letter and read it to myself.

> *Dear Sebastian, it is an old friend who composed this message. I was smuggled from West Nodin by our mutual friend. I revoke my service to King Johan. I am on my way to see you now. I come in peace and hope we can bury the hatchet.*
>
> *Sincerely,*
> *Vallen Edling*

Vallen left the service? I wonder what caused him to do that. Our "mutual friend" must be Jahvonis. If Starkstad is to be engulfed by the war, the people must fight!

In Sareyus's View

It is not the first time a crime has been committed within temple walls. There have been murders, thefts, rapes, assaults, arsons, and many other crimes. Regardless of how many times this has happened before, it is *not* acceptable! Poor Alva, so many times this has happened to her, but within holy walls, it should destroy her faith. If only there was some way to track down and slay this rapist.

Otherwise, I have finished my shift and I am settling down in my hut. I speak for all the gods that we witnessed evil humans and Theranths. There were many who we wanted to smite to prevent them from committing more heinous deeds. If we did, then the mortals would be fearful of us. Fear is no way to lead!

The memory of Jahvonis's smoky face has not left me. His eyes were so bright, beautiful, and blue. The way he winked at me gave me pleasant dreams that night. The war is scaring me. I've become attached to these people. I feel terrible that my last encounter with Miolannis ended so abruptly. None of us have ever been imprisoned by the dragons before. However, we are grateful that only one of them escaped. Kuolemajää always struggled to prove he was as strong as the rest of his brethren. Kuolemajää will forever be remembered as the first dragon to escape from prison.

Speaking of dragons, I am cursed and haunted by the creation of Ahneus. The Second Life of the Earth went terribly. It became worse when the mortals worshipped the dragons. Our creation of the dragons was the second largest crime we have ever committed. My relationship with Ahneus is bitter. She is second behind Mustasurma in the dragon hierarchy. Ahneus is the only female dragon. In my short sight, I made her strong enough to challenge me. If she is ever bold enough to duel me, I must do it alone. I have never feared any of the dragons.

After the Second Life, I sealed Ahneus on a volcanic isle to the northeast of Soruth. The actual cell is fathoms beneath the volcano. Ahneus can be harmed by my fire and lava. I created a curse that if Ahneus ever left the inside of the volcano, her power would be stripped. I created a special ruby to control and monitor her. The ruby is called the *Firegem*. The Firegem can safely release her if it is cracked through an energetic charge from within the prison.

We deities created the *Stormgem, Icegem, Watergem, Naturegem*, and *Darkgem*. We use them to link our minds with the dragons to issue commands and restrain them. At the time, Ahneus was the most cunning. After the Second Life, I carved the core of the Firegem into a ring. I have worn it every day since.

Ahneus once said to the Ember Soruthians, "*I blessed you with fiery skin. You were formed in my color. I spawned flame and purged your once pale skin in time before life began!*"

Thus the Embers worshipped Ahneus in my stead. This was the first nail in the coffin of our relationship. We rued the dragons when they assumed the forms of mortals. Many times Ahneus took the fair guise of a orange-haired, porcelain-skinned woman. When among the Embers, she turned into a woman of theirs. Her golden eyes are easily distinguishable.

As I have been living among humans, our children have been teaching me how to do my job as a goddess. They share stories of bravery and what they see in the gods. It is ironic if you ask me. The ship is coming along at a moderate pace. Sebastian is on his shift now. I lay down and slept. I dreamt tonight. I saw a man engulfed upon a large pyre where the flames cremated his body. The flames grew tall. Then through the flames, I saw a group of people masked in war paint who set the body aflame. All around them, thousands of mourners wept. I could see this man's soul being sent by smoke into the Gods' Hall. His face I never saw.

In Alastair's View

My search underground continued. I have trotted around this kingdom with no luck, then a thought came to me. *A trap must be placed.* Surely, with the right coin, any of these simpletons would help. I staged a fake mugging: one man would play the victim and the other would be the thief. I would stand watch from the nearest rooftop. When Jahvonis comes to the rescue, I'll fire an arrow through his skull!

"Help! Someone! Help!" the victim screamed.

"Shut the fuck up and gimme the coin!" the mugger yelled.

They looked around to see if it was working. Bystanders paid no attention. The crook then proceeded to rough up the victim. As he raised his fist again, a senbon needle pinned his right hand to the wall.

"Low the Hand of Doom has fallen. Pathetic bait those men are, and yet Mataraves trained you?" Jahvonis said aloud.

I turned my head in rage and fired, but he caught the arrow in midair. Jahvonis stood away to my left side. I did not see or hear him at all! He must have been watching this whole time!

"After all your progress, you never learned to keep your temper controlled!" he mocked.

I fired at will. Jahvonis closed in on me. I swung my bow like a club but the arrogant prick has to show me up!

"Your bow skills are potent, but your melee combat still falls short to your master!" Jahvonis said.

"Shut up!" I grunted as I kept swinging, but his evading technique was well executed. He struck me nine times in my face and body. I dropped my bow during his strikes. Mataraves never prepared me for this man, damn him! I went for a punch that was caught in his palm. He was gripping so hard and knelt me to the ground!

I struck his left knee with my remaining strength. Finally, he's grounded! I stumbled up to keep beating his left leg. Now I know his weakness. With every stomp on his knee, Jahvonis clutched his leg in pain. I stood up long enough to grab my dagger. He rolled away to his right. I felt his right foot sweep my feet from under me, and I hit my head on the roof. I was knocked out. Later, I awoke. Jahvonis is long gone.

In Sareyus's View

After my current shift, I went off into the woods to collect firewood. Sometimes I feel bad that I'm killing Sarue's plants because they're living beings also. When my pantheon was creating the earth, our creations all have logical effects on each other. Things like this have a purpose. It is our duty as users of her gift to not abuse, waste, or be ungrateful for it. I went on my errand and journeyed into the forest that is north of our construction site. Instead of cutting down trees, I prefer to use deadwood.

I've been out here for about an hour, and night is upon me. I do worry about Miolannis. If she is saved and Kuolemajää is defeated, I will apologize for my offense to her. I will try to be her friend. By my calculations, I have about ten pounds of firewood, ranging from maple, oak, ash, and alder. It became darker, and I lit a torch from a branch. I began my way back to camp. I started to hear a male cardinal chirping to me. As a goddess, I can understand its dialogue. Most animals recognize us when they see us.

"Lady Sareyus! You must follow me!" he said and flew through the trees.

I am behind him. I jogged through the forest to keep pace with the bird. He led me to a rock formation near the northwest corner of the woods. I could hear a man screaming in agony.

"Down here, milady!" the bird exclaimed. It took a dip over a small hill that came to a snow patch.

The man had his right leg flat and his left leg arched in the air. As I looked at his left leg, I saw a large bump where his kneecap is. In fact, it is dislocated. The man wears black.

"Jahvonis!" I exclaimed in surprise.

He is screaming in a voice that is not his standard menacing tone.

"Jahvonis, hold on! Stay still!" I shouted.

"Sareyus?" he questioned. He is next to a small cave that housed a Kermode bear. It growled at me for possibly thinking I was inflicting harm. "Yield, Spirit!" Jahvonis yelled in a rebuttal. The bear did yield, but it still monitored me.

"Jahvonis, the only way for me to fix your knee is to remove the clothing from it!" I shouted.

"Only my knee and nothing more!" he screamed in pain while still clutching his knee.

He won't like this next part because I have to completely straighten his leg in order to push his kneecap back in place.

"Okay, hold still, clench your hands together, and try not to fight back," I requested.

He gripped his hands hard, but he still fought back. The bear stood up and stepped upon his hands. I made my attempt to straighten his leg.

"Fuck!" he shouted. Three times I struggled to do it slowly to no avail. Jahvonis continued his agonizing profanity.

"Hold on! I'm almost done!" I shouted as I made a continuous movement, bringing his leg down to a flat horizontal position. His screaming grew louder and more intense. The bear looked on and growled in anger. I gripped his kneecap with my hands and gently pushed it back in place. He cried in relief that the damage was neutralized. The healing will begin. I am in disbelief how Jahvonis was hurt! Hearing him scream in what I believe was his real voice still rings in my ears! He took ten deep breaths to calm himself.

"Thank you, my lady… I could not take any more of that pain. How can I repay you?" he said once again in his deep menacing voice.

"Show me your real voice, Jahvonis," I requested.

He looked at me with some disapproval in his eyes. He looked at the ground and prepared his words.

"I don't know what to say." he said in his real voice.

"How is your leg? Do you need anything?" I asked.

"Could you spare some wood so I can craft a brace?"

"By all means," I replied as I gave him three maple branches from my firewood.

He pulled several bandages out of his pack. "Can you hold the branches on my leg while I tie?" Jahvonis asked.

I did as he asked, but he remained wary of me. He lightly gasped in pain while he doctored himself. Jahvonis then whistled to the bear to move back. I gently helped slide him back into the cave. The cave is warmer than outside. The bear lay on its stomach while Jahvonis sat next to it. He is caressing its reddish-blond fur. It once again growled at me when I entered.

"Easy, girl. She means no harm," Jahvonis said.

"I am here if you need me," the Lady Spirit Bear said.

Jahvonis took a sighing breath.

"Sareyus, why are you here?" he asked.

"I was collecting firewood until I followed the cardinal here and heard your screams…"

"Is Starkstad finished with the ship?" he asked.

"No, but we are picking up the pace."

"Good, that's good." Jahvonis rested his head against the cave wall. "Remember what I said about touching my mask?"

"Yes?" I answered.

"Good," he replied.

This could be the only time I'll have him alone, I thought. I decided to light a fire. I sat there staring at him. He is looking off into space.

"Jahvonis?"

He looked back upon me.

"I wanted to personally thank you for all you've done for me. You put yourself at risk for the safety of others. Why?"

He took a slow deep breath while still keeping his leg movements at a minimum.

"I do it…because the gods lost hope in their children. The people need a symbol of hope and justice! I victimize the victimizers. Terrorize the terrorizers! I work against the evil in this world. A black shadow who darkens the blinding light of corruption!" he softly exclaimed.

"Why do you feel the gods lost hope in us?" I asked.

"The gods are mysterious beings. How or why they let war and crime plague our beautiful world is beyond me. I feel they lost hope because we take all their gifts for granted."

"Not all gods have lost hope in us. Yes, they do work mysteriously, and sometimes they let things happen they may not like. It is a part of the laws they set among life. You see, Jahvonis, sometimes the gods are as mortal as you and I. Sometimes they want someone to understand them, to see their jobs are never easy. Sometimes they look to their children for guidance. Even they are not perfect or have all the answers," I replied.

"You seem to be very insightful, Sareyus. Are you religious?" he asked.

"I prefer to be spiritual. How did you domesticate this bear, and how did that cardinal know to find help?"

"Any animal can be trained when you put in enough understanding and effort. I named this female bear *Spirit*, and she's been my friend for more recent times. The bird who found you is named *Cardalen*. I am most fortunate you understood he was leading you to someone."

Cardalen is beside him with Spirit.

"How did you dislocate your knee?"

He sighed as he began to speak.

"An assassin is hunting me down. He staged a fake mugging to lure me in. I knew because he is not the best at hiding. The mugger and victim weren't good actors. I got cocky, and he targeted my knee in our skirmish. When we meet again, I will not underestimate him or any other opponent."

"Why is he after you?" I asked.

"A man like me is naturally riddled with enemies. Some people would pay a hefty price to see me dead. This assassin has a much deeper vendetta against me than most. He is the leader of the notorious Hand of Doom, a group of rebels who sought to murder Aylund Rudolf. I would've joined if things didn't go ill for them after several failed attempts. The leader I spoke of is named Alastair Beorler, the man who paid to try molesting you and who murdered Hamish. His vendetta against me is that his master, Mataraves, requested my assistance in his merciful fate. Would you like to know my origin?" he offered.

I nodded with approval.

"I owe you more," he said. He started to untie his mask! I am finally going to know my protector's identity! Numerous images of his face are scorching my mind. Everything is untied. His hands gripped both sides and slowly pulled up. The result nearly gave me a heart attack.

"My name is Xavion Mourningstar."

My heart, my eyes, and my skin are warm and blushing. Xavion was Jahvonis the whole time! How could I not put two and two together? It's been fifteen years since I was this close to him. His eyes are purple, his skin is colorful, and his dark hair is worn in a tail. He looks so handsome and attractive in his armor.

"So you're the Xavion I have heard about. You don't look very Nodinian?"

"I am one-sixth. The other percentages are the four general nations of Soruth and the gold of Yazjia. I am most noticeable when my face is revealed," Xavion replied.

"You're the soldier who spared Aylund's champion? You're the one who slew those four hundred men in battle. The Xavion who is both feared and loved?" I asked.

"*Loved* is a strong word. A word I haven't known in many years. This land would surely change their views of Jahvonis if they saw my face. To them, I'm just a Mud Monkey weapon. Jahvonis is really a mask to hide my taint," he stated.

Xavion speaks pessimism and self-hate. The society he was placed in truly is bigoted.

"You are *not* tainted! After all you have done for these people, they will regret it! What about Sebastian? He speaks highly of you," I stated.

"Sebastian is one in a million. He stood up for me when I had no power to do it myself. These people have an ill will to any and all who are different. Humans, a race of people who despise each other over skin complexions, tribes, nations, and creeds. Humans, who despise the Theranths because of their mixed blood. Mortals have no place in this world but to worship," Xavion replied.

I did not speak. In a way he is right. The Immortals needed our life force to be potent through prayers. His admittance shames me. A void in my heart opened. My ignorance of his youth has tarnished my involvement. Lowly are we deities to our children.

"I often question why this Jahvonis character came to me? As if the identity or spirit of him passes from man to man. I will begin my origins with this alias."

Book 2

Knowledge of the Past

Chapter 5

In Xavion's View

Today I woke up in my bed without the intention of getting up. This town and this whole damn country are beyond simple crime rates. In the last month, I've witnessed the people being stripped of their rights and freedom by the government, the same government who swore to abide by the conceived laws and to defend their citizens from crime. It seems that war is more important than the oppression within these borders.

I got up anyway and decided to walk about the city. I am a slave, and a guard is ordered to supervise me. His name is Sebastian Hagstrom. I met Sebastian when I was captured a few weeks ago. He was the only guard I spared in the first attack. The next time, the guards were on a manhunt, and sadly, I was defeated. Since then, Sebastian and I have come to an understanding that our meeting was a matter of poor communication. So far he is the only good-willed guard I know.

When we are walking about the town, I'm allowed to take part in standard community activities. The only things these people call fun are mostly drinking and indulging in the palace bordello. I choose not to drink because I've seen what it does to people. Alcohol is a man-made poison. Nothing good comes from it, nor anything that intoxicates. As far as the bordello goes, my first job was as a guard for the prostitutes.

I have seen many sexually disturbing things there, and they haunt me. When I was issued to enforce safety in the brothel, I was tempted to slay everyone and escape. I stayed because I felt someone had to stand up to the troublemakers.

As a guard, you can indulge in the prostitutes for a discount. I did not have the option because King Johan does not want his people "tainted." When on duty, I admit many of the women are attractive. I always remember they are forced into it by law. I say because I used to harshly judge them. I believed they enjoyed being sex workers. My views changed when I saw children in their early teens in the profession. A child should have zero business in a bordello. Adult women and men partook in the legal pedophilia. The workers I felt awful for. Children who are not much different than my age are subjected to being sexually objectified.

There were few standards for the people. Women who showed signs of pregnancy were laid off for six months after birth. Female customers also paid male workers for insemination; it was not always done through sex. Male customers jumped from woman to woman as long as their seeds were planted.

My cell is down the hall, and I can always hear when someone is getting it on. I admit my misandry. As much as I resent men, not all female customers accept refusal.

I remember certain men who were mauled by women; their sperm was shared after a sorrowful release. I myself have been pursued by the female clientele. I understand the exotic context of my appearance, but being crudely complimented by these predatory women sickened me.

Eventually, I became a blacksmith because I was able to fix most of the broken furniture and cells, including my own. It is bewildering for many to say I'm the best blacksmith and warrior Nodin has seen in years.

I remember my first battle in the military. In late February, Johan traveled above ground. Three days into his trip, West Nodin was under siege by East Nodin. I could hear the mass panic in the palace. I prepared to defend myself when I crafted my first weapon, the spiked ball-headed mace, also called the Morningstar.

This particular mace was crafted entirely of steel. The overall length is twenty-four inches long. It has a four-inch diameter ball. The ball is adorned with twelve thick two-inch pyramidal spikes. The octagonal tube above the handle is hollowed to reduce overall weight. This also puts more forward balance into the mace head, which is also called a crown.

General Vallen was a foot soldier at the time. During the Encroachment, he requested that I fight. I was scared and somewhat happy. I had a chance to prove my worth and skill. I entered the battle when the Westerners were forced to retreat inside the palace. About fifteen of them held the gate shut. Another four hundred stood behind and prepared to charge.

When I came into the entrance hall, I looted a round shield off a dead soldier. Immediately, I was grabbed and pushed to the front like a pawn on the board. I still was behind the gatemen. East Nodin had at least 2,500 men with a few dozen using a hexagonal battering ram. Twenty-five times the East hit the door. When it flew open, a vessel in my brain burst. I lost my mind when the Blue Sleeves entered. I only had a weapon, a shield, and no armor. I sprinted and jumped high over the gatemen and began bashing bones, spilling blood and slaying any warrior in blue. I saw this as a great exercise. The adrenaline rushed through me. Unfortunately, I relished in the bloodshed. One thing about all mortals is that, no matter what we look like, we all bleed red.

I never had so much fun! It felt like a child's game with sticks and stones. Seeing the mace denting bodies and having the enemies' blood on me was exhilarating. In those few moments, I took the lives of seventy-three men ranging from the age of eighteen through forty-five.

A horn was blown, and East Nodin fled. Our battle was not won but drawn out until the enemy retreated. In the aftermath, as I came to my senses, all the remaining West men gazed upon me in astonishment. Seldom has any person slain several dozens of people in one day. I looked ahead, and many stood around the body of Prince Hakun, with whom I had a steady acquaintance beginning.

I gently walked over to him. The men stepped back in fear. I stood over what was left of Hakun. I was still grasping my mace. People looked upon a slave who went from being a brothel guard to a blacksmith to a warrior. People wept at the sight of my mace, which was still covered in blood, skin, chipped bones, and organic tissue.

I placed the mace in my holster and saw a gleaming helm in the dirt. It was a royal crown helmet. After using a piece of my shirt to wipe it clean, I returned it to the burning mane of its prince. I hoisted Hakun into my arms and bore him into the palace. The soldiers marched behind me in five vertical rows. Their shields were held to their chests and weapons hoisted in the air. Vallen marched behind me. He sang his sorrow into the stone.

Deep in Nodin in the rock, a mighty Prince once walked. Fell in battle in the dirt, to leave him, we will not desert! Under siege, the gate is breached, blood is leached! The snow is away from us. Young Hakun—Prince of Snows— you fought bravely, to leave us now is strange. Failing you we regret gravely. Gone you are, lost you're not, our honor you've left hot. Long live the Prince! Long live the Victorious Dead! Hail! Hail! Hail! Hail! Hail!

That battle mourned me in guilt. I killed men I never knew, and some may have had a lot in common with me. I lost myself in the bloodshed, the rush of adrenaline, the puddles of sweat, and streams of blood. The next day, my mace was named by the public as the *Mourningstar*, and I took the name onto me as punishment for my wicked deeds. It did not end there. For several days, I had terrible nightmares of the dead faces looking at me, staring through my soul, cursing my name and the air I breathe.

I could see their last hours and each following dream was ten times worse than the last. I often do not sleep because they're staring, glaring, upon me with the gods at their hinds.

That day I said I would never fight again; but sadly, after my participation, the men won't march without me. They say they hate me but won't be brave unless I stand beside them? To honor the fallen, I retired the Mourningstar mace. I did not smelt it because I needed a reminder of why I don't enjoy hurting people. I forget who I am when in battle. The human instinct to survive takes over, and I am forced to fight.

King Johan returned from his travels, I could see his pure rage, failure, depression, anxiety, and anger. He came back to see the final image of Hakun. To lessen the damage, I bandaged what was left of his head.

Hakun's funeral was depressing. His uncle invaded his home, slew his men, and kidnapped his mother. We chose to cremate Hakun in lava so the goddess Sareyus would be the first to welcome him above. I was given minimum credit, but I was banned from using my mace again.

For killing the most people, I was appointed to be Princess Astrid's personal bodyguard and assistant. Sebastian is to advise me. Today is my first day as the princess's aide. Sebastian woke me at about 8:08 in the morning.

"Xavion, wake up. It's time for work," he said politely.

When I woke up, he was next to me sitting upon my smithing stool. I turned to my left to see him.

"Is today the day?" I asked.

"Yes, King Johan calls for you to protect and assist Princess Astrid. Get dressed and clean up as much as possible."

"No matter how much I clean, I won't be full snow…"

"You know that's not what I meant," he replied.

"Yes, Sebastian," I replied as I used the last of my drinking water to wipe my face. The only change of clothes I have left is a tan shirt and pants. The only form of footwear I have is my boots.

"Princess Astrid lives on the fourth floor in her chambers," Sebastian informed.

"Surely she's an ordinary young lady," I inquired.

"Not exactly. When she was about thirteen years old, she developed blindness in both eyes and never recovered. Still to this day she remains visionless. She needs someone to be her eyes, to help her dress, bathe, and anything else."

We found the nearest staircase and climbed up to the fourth floor.

"Where does the king lay his head?" I asked.

"The king has more than enough rooms. Prince Hakun's room remains vacant and sealed. The king and queen's original room is now a shrine to his wife. The room he sleeps in most is hidden. Only he and General Vallen know. Johan is faithful we can retrieve Helga. Rumor says we're planning a counterstrike to occupy East Nodin and kill Aylund. We also hear Aylund has had a son for a while now," Sebastian said.

"What is the name of Aylund's son?"

"He is named Bjorn Adolf Edling," Sebastian replied as we entered the fourth floor.

This floor is not as large as the others, perhaps to keep it more convenient. We walked from hallway to hallway until we found Astrid's room. On the door is a West Nodin Pentagram. Sebastian pulled out a key and unlocked it. Inside is somewhat of an elegant room with a feminine feeling to it.

"Princess Astrid, it is Sebastian. Your new aide is here," he stated.

"Oh yes, come in! Come in!" she called back.

Sebastian escorted me through the room to where he heard her voice. On the far right side, Astrid sat in a chair while wearing a dress made from red cotton. On her head is a gold circlet with five rubies across its band. She wore red slippers. She has bold orange hair like her brother's.

"And who is this helper?" she asked.

I did not immediately reply because I felt intimidated and yet interested in her. I say intimidated because she could have me killed on the spot. Sebastian turned to me.

"I am Xavion," I said.

"Do you have a last name?" she asked.

"Mourningstar is my last name…"

"Morningstar referring to Lyannis?"

"No, my lady, Mourningstar in reference to my mace. The 'mourning' portion is referring to grieving."

"Are you a soldier?" Astrid inquired.

"I am, but I am also your bodyguard," I replied.

"Sebastian, does he know what exact work he will do?" she asked.

"I made him aware," he replied.

"I am to bathe, redress, and then dine on breakfast," she said.

The breakfast part would be no problem, but I am most concerned that I have to clean her in the nude. Wouldn't another woman be better suited when helping a princess?

"I'll watch you both from across the room, Princess. You need not worry. I swore to protect you if any problems arise. Xavion, I trust you to do your job and be professional, understand?" Sebastian stated.

"Yes, Sebastian," I replied.

He began to draw up a bath, and I still trembled with nervousness that I'm somewhat engaging in an intimate act by undressing this woman. At the same time, I'm learning how Nodinian gowns are put on and taken off.

Astrid's tub is bowl shaped. I am blushing as I view her nudity, as if my Ember blood rises like flames of the sacred fire. Her circlet was placed on her bed with her clothes. Her shoes are at the foot of the bed. Astrid is about five feet six in height and about 145 pounds. Astrid is also nervous, most likely because it's a boy bathing her? I then helped her into the tub.

"Watch your step, Princess," I said.

She felt around for the rim of the tub. She gently sat down and submerged herself in the water. The water went up as far as her diaphragm, and she bent forward to have her knees cover her private areas. I started to scrub her back with a clean lathered cloth. I continued to move further down her back. She proceeded to wash her full-frontal areas. It was an interesting experience to see the female body in a cleaner way than at my first job.

After cleaning and drying her, I redressed her in another red gown. Next, I brushed her hair. I think it's nice how Helga and Johan passed the orange hair gene to Hakun and Astrid. Hakun had nice hair. Astrid's is thicker while his was finer and smoother.

"May we eat now, Xavion?" she asked.

I turned over to Sebastian.

"Yes, Princess, we'll be eating in your family's dining room on the second floor."

We helped Astrid down the stairs. The dining room is heavily decorated in red. The table was set with many platters of cakes, pastries, beef, and chicken.

"Xavion, feel free to eat," Sebastian said.

I was hungry, and the food the slaves have is of poor quality, but the food of the palace is great! The next few hours were uneventful. As the three of us sat in Astrid's room, Sebastian grabbed a lute that was in the corner. He tuned it and started playing melodies that soothed the ears of Astrid. My head was also happy with his music. Sebastian offered me the lute. Upon receiving it, I felt my mind audiate music. I played it as it was heard. The combination of chords and arpeggios came out in ambient bliss.

As my third week of being Astrid's bodyguard came, I started to feel more optimistic, possibly because Astrid does not know what I look like. Astrid does look a lot like her mother. I remember one moment that occurred between the king and queen. The moment was a conversation they had about their youth. I was in the throne room cleaning the floor one week before Johan left on his trip.

*****

"My love, do you remember when we first met?" Johan asked.

"I do. We were young when my father brought me to your duel. I saw how you looked at me. Your eyes were bold. I bet you fought harder from me being there," Helga joked.

"I admired your orange hair, possibly because my mother had it," Johan replied.

"I remember Johanna. Back then people thought I was her daughter. Do you remember our consummation?" Helga asked.

"As if it was a moment ago. To think it has been many years since. Seeing you in all your splendor and glory puts the gods to shame!" he complimented as they kissed.

I looked in delight for Johan's happiness.

"Do you think Aylund is all right in the East? My side of the family welcomed him after he stood against the Theranths with my father."

"Aylund proved he is charismatic. Indeed he can fight and lead. Before I took our people down here, Aylund and I met to say our goodbyes. When I saw him, he verbally lashed out at me, saying I was a 'cowardice excuse for a king.' Those who I led had enough death from the battle with Amandus and the Theranths. We continued to argue, and I left after I had enough. He pursued the war against the Theranths. I heard a rumor that Aylund fought Amandus one on one. Since Aylund is across the rock, I suspect he lost," the king replied.

"Johan, where did the Theranths come from?" the queen asked.

The king took a deep breath and spoke. "The first of the Theranths were the product of when Nodin fought Soruth several hundred years ago. The Soruthian military, from the stories I heard, are bloodthirsty. They took no prisoners. They banished or slew every Nodinian who stepped on their shores."

When Johan mentioned the name "Soruth," he immediately caught my attention.

"Soruth is possibly the largest continent in the world. Its people vary greatly in appearance. It is made up of five outer islands and mainland in the center. Each major direction of Soruth is home to many tribes of indigenous people. To the north, is a group of Ember, reddish-brown-skinned humans. Many have similar traits like high cheekbones, straight triangular noses, and straight dark hair. They wear feathers in their hair, and much of their clothing is leather. They lived off the land and lived for its preservation.

"To the west are a group of more tannish-brown sand-colored people. They made pyramids that were supposedly made from gold. Most of the men in that group were soldiers at least once. The Sands are closely related to the Embers. Their traditions have many commonalities. The Sands were heavily militaristic. Their religion was bloody. They practiced human sacrifice to appease the gods.

"The south of Soruth has people of the darkest color, ebony brown. They normally wore light or little clothing due to the heat. Seeing a bare-chested woman was not sexual or provocative to them. They have dark hair with varying curls.

"The east is home to more brown bark-skinned people. They wore more fabrics and robes. The men sometimes wore bounds of cloth on their heads. The women (depending on which culture) covered their entire bodies. The Barks usually have more scientific progress than the other nations. The Barkish were the first in Soruth to use bronze, iron, and steel. The Theranths came into reality because the Sands were experimental with science. Many said magic was a part of it.

"The Theranths are compiled from traits that included humans, apes, and other predatory animals. They have the same human anatomy. With all the combined traits, they became tall beasts solely built for war. The Sands eventually passed the knowledge onto their allies on the other islands. When Nodin battled Soruth for the final time, the Theranths numbered about ten thousand with approximately one hundred thousand human Soruthians. Nodin was dwindled down to only thirty thousand. Only six hundred survived because we fled back north. Thus Soruth became the greatest military force in the world. They have so many soldiers because they united against a common enemy and their women fought alongside their men until the end."

"When our ancestors returned home, we took the Theranth formula with us and made our own. Our Theranths fought against us before we could launch a counterstrike against Soruth. At first, things were going smoothly, but someone or something turned the Theranths against us," Johan finished.

The queen spoke. "Why did Nodin attack Soruth?"

"We started as friends. When traveling to foreign places, the traveler has no idea how to adapt to a new place. To put it simply, we wanted a new home. The Embers were the first to befriend us. Some time passed for Nodin to expand and find their place. Generations passed, and in all honesty, Nodin forgot who their friends were. When the war became so intense, any Nodinian was killed or banished. If you take a look at the young man cleaning, he's very much Soruthian," Johan stated.

In the middle of my service with Astrid, all in town were gathered in front of the palace. The news was being given. I was moved to the crowd for some reason. That contradicts my job, protect and serve the heir to the throne, except during a large town gathering? Some people who didn't attend were beaten in the middle of the street for their "disobedience."

The oppressive imagery of these people depresses me. Unfortunately, I'm one of them. I don't recall much of my parents. Whoever they are, I hope they loved me. The public event was held by the king. He sat upon his balcony in the company of Astrid. Her father decreed a town crier to issue news and laws.

"People of the West, your king brings you the news that I am honored to deliver! First, the king issues all females upon first menstruation must submit to insemination in order to produce soldiers for the war. Second, all fertile women must contribute to repopulation through sexual reproduction. All able men are to be drafted into the military. Third, anyone refusing to engage in said laws will forfeit their freedom of choice and will be arrested with immediate punishment. Men who disobey the law will be jailed. Women who break these laws will be forcefully inseminated to bear a child. Female volunteers in these said laws will be paid for their services. Fourth, all weapon trainers will sacrifice ten hours of every day to train soldiers and our great king! Fifth, all men and women are available for service except for our royal king, the princess, and the Mud Monkey."

As the shepherd herded the sheep, I grew more disgusted and disturbed at the people who make the king what he is. To have to listen to the verbal assault upon their rights as citizens and as human beings! My disgust for the Nodinian government grows with its greed and selfishness. They forgot their roots were embedded in honor and respect. They gave it up for invading and pillaging foreign lands because theirs is dying! I brooded with the thoughts of the chaos and harm these people will cause.

Later that day, Astrid had me comb and brush her hair. She conversed with me.

"Xavion, is this really happening?"

"I'm afraid so, my lady. At least you'll be safe with me," I answered while gently stroking her irresistible fiery locks.

"That's nice to hear," she stated, which put me in slight tranquility. I was crushed when she asked, "Who is the Mud Monkey?"

"It is a derogatory term for people with dark skin," I replied.

"But everyone is dark to me," she stated.

I thought about her statement and laughed because she made a blind joke! The moment became a laughing spasm between Astrid, Sebastian, and me. The princess's laugh made my day!

Soon I returned to my cell. I would spend my free time reading books, tomes on history, art, music, and self-defense. One time I found a smithing book on Yazjian weaponry. I have always been interested in foreign weapons and culture. I do have a smithing set because I am one of at least a hundred who craft the weapons and armors for the military. I always wondered if we could learn anything by adapting to use Yazjian, Soruthian, and Theranthic weapons. We could use more knowledge of other people in the world.

I read until my brain fatigued. With each passing word, my intellect became potent. My brain capacity increased incrementally. I then turned my attention to the *Hallowed Holds of Goddesses & Gods*. This book tells of the beginning of time and space. It says the entire first documents were carved into the stone by Jado. These acted as testaments for humans to use the earth's resources caringly.

The stories began with the event known as the *Cosmos Commencement*. Jado notes it as, *"A large explosion that created the Gods. The Gods then created the planets and all life among them. The Cosmos Commencement is the parent of the Gods. The creators, Cosmos, are all. The Ladylord and Lordlady."*

Jado, the Lord of Knowledge, is the intellect of the Cosmos and best knows their will. Each goddess and god is an aspect of Cosmos's psyche. Each of them is no greater than the other, for Cosmos is all existence.

The book displayed the gods and what they rule over. Their gifts and commandments are among these pages. The final pages were composed with what I believe are metaphoric stories that represented the best and worst of mortal people. As I turned upon the fifth fraction of the book, my eyes came unto the fire goddess known by many names. Universally, she is known as *Sareyus*.

The page presented a charming image of her. Her hair is a nice fiery orange and her eyes are green. In my opinion, her eyes are most appealing. As I read on, I am more interested in her than the other deities. Each deity in this book has several ethnic appearances. All of them have several general images as Nodinians, Soruthians, Yazjians, and Theranths of each demographic. Carune has an extra image as a blue-skinned Aquranth. Upon finishing the book, I sat in deep thought and reviewed the messages in the Holds. I reread, documented, and read again.

Once more, I reread the Hallowed Holds for answers. I read the Holds of Jahveyis, Jado, and Bravious.

> *Whoever uses sin for power must repent or thy be damned! (Jahveyis)*

> *Should you use thine anger for thy cause, remember to forgive yourself and those who have been harmed! (Jado)*

> *People must be equal on all terms. Equality must be a part of mortal nature by all means! (Bravious)*

In my doubt, I turned to the hold of Sareyus.

In the face of doubt, my fires of faith shall engulf you! Bravery shall always prevail over cowardice and Justice over crime!

I sat down and remembered those verses. I went to my smithing station to catch up on my work. I had spare pieces of steel lying around. I recalled two odd medium-range weapons from a Yazjian smithing manual called shuriken (sher-ric-kin) stars and senbon needles. I read the directions for these weapons and tested them out by throwing them against a wooden plank. I am amazed and fascinated with how well they came out on my first try. If I wanted to use these, I should practice them on something human-like. I used a burlap dummy that was anatomically shaped like a human body. I remembered a book I own that holds records of human anatomy. In that particular tome, it tells me the vital and nonvital areas, nerve endings, and bone joints.

For three days, I practiced these Daichinian-throwing weapons and have become proficient. After my practice session, I looked into the Holds again. This time I read through the stories depicted within Jahveyis's hold. It described a man from thousands of years ago who came from harsh life lessons. His name was *Adrian Erik*, and much death surrounded him. On one foul day, his husband was taken from him. During a skirmish between the Nodinians and Soruthians, Adrian's husband sacrificed himself to protect him. One early fall night, he traveled and sat in *Sönderfall, the land of Mustasurmu*. Adrian was visited by Jahveyis and Miolannis that night. In their conversation, Jahveyis said, *"My child, many ill fates have assailed you, but I propose to you a new life! Fight for my wife and I. Become our Black Paladin! Fight for the victimized. Castrate corruption from your home, and for this, I will grant you one wish within my power!"*

"Should I do this, and if I fulfill this role, all I ask is that you bring my beloved back to me!" Adrian replied.

"It shall be so!" replied the god. He then stood above Adrian and raised his flanged mace. *"Starting tonight, you are our herald and bridge to the mortal world. From this night until the end, I dub thee... Jahvonis!"* announced Jahveyis.

After reading that passage, my path is now shown to me. I could rekindle the legend of this hero! I could bring the evil and corrupt to my feet and have them beg for mercy from those they've preyed upon! A paladin shall rise from the grave to continue the master's work! I will inspire hope to the weak and instill fear to the predatory! The common people will once again claim what is rightfully theirs! As I turn the page, there is a picture of Jahvonis's suit, weapons, and armor. It appears the suit and weapons are all Yazjian inspired, but how did Jahvonis get a hold of the suit? Did he craft it? Did Jahveyis gift it? In the description of the suit, I noticed some strange things than what I'm used to. It was originally designed for speed and agility and therefore is lighter.

As far as weapons go, I cannot use the same ones for the army and they can't weigh me down too much. The shuriken and senbon are perfect, but I'll need something for close-range combat. A sword will work, but if it's too big, then I can't conceal it, but if it's too small, then I'll risk getting too close. I looked through another book of Yazjian weapons. I came across many different weapons from *Daichi, Hongangou, Napel, Mognoa,* and *Namvie.* My favorite of these are Napel's kukri and Hongangou's ringed dagger. When crafting this suit, I must hide it somewhere safe but close by. No one can ever know who I really am.

I was able to finish my version of the suit in about one week. The whole suit is black. It has a steel cowl that is also a mask. The entire upper body and thighs are a thick leather top with strong chain mail and then silk underneath it. This combination of silk and leather is used by Mognoan warriors because it prevents most arrows from piercing flesh. Arrows spin as they fly. When they puncture the leather, they get tied up in the silk. The silk also gently mutes the chain mail. The gauntlets and boots are made of leather. I also added hard padding for my knees, elbows, and shoulders.

All the leather and silk components are dyed black. For the mask and weapons, I dipped them in a black coating. The main weapon is a kukri, and the side arm is a large ringed dagger. The kukri is a sixteen-inch forward-curved blade that is four millimeters thick. It has a styled steel hand guard that is shaped like knuckle dusters. I use those for punching. The hand guard has a long curved quillon on the back of the handle. It has a pyramidal pommel that I'll use for bludgeoning. This feels more like a Greshan kopis sword than a traditional kukri knife. I still prefer to call it a kukri.

The ringed dagger is sixteen and one-fourth inches in overall length. It has a broad ten-inch, double-edged leaf-shaped blade with a six-and-one-fourth-inch handle. The pommel is ring-shaped (hence the name). The ring is useful for reverse grip techniques.

All the senbon and shuriken are black as well. It's not always about what I wanted them to be. I have to test everything out. West Nodin is underground. There is no sunlight to reveal where I'll hide. The light from the lava pits stretched far, but I cannot control where they shine.

Down here, the armors are not too heavy because it is hot. Heavy armor will only tire you out from heat exhaustion while also slowing you down. I hid my suit beneath my bed. After a while, I dug a hole with my bare hands. The stones and dirt moved like sand.

One morning, after digging the hole, Sebastian caught me! We engaged in a quiet argument.

"What the hell is this?" Sebastian said.

"Oh, Sebastian…you…"

"Think I must report this!" he stated.

"You can't!" I exclaimed.

"I could be killed if someone found out about this!" Sebastian replied.

"You don't understand! I have to help these people. You know all the terror we've seen!"

"How can you help by dressing up and killing people?"

"I want to fight corruption!" I replied.

"Give me a good reason why I shouldn't toss this in the forge?" he asked.

I thought hard for a reason to justify myself.

"Think about how many crimes the guards don't handle. Wouldn't people feel safe knowing there's someone helping them?" I asked.

Sebastian thought and replied, "The princess is waiting. We'll talk about this later. Hide your crafts."

During our shift, Astrid took a nap, leaving Sebastian and I to speak.

"Sebastian, about what you saw..."

"How did you make that without anyone else knowing...and what odd designs were you using?"

"I made them because I want to help people. Johan has lost his mind since the Encroachment. What sick man passes a law where all citizens, married or not, young and old, must produce children who are meant to die in battle?"

"Johan does this for our people!"

"And what will stop him from harming his own men. What will stop him from condemning all priests and priestesses to death or worse? Gods forbid he tries to have Astrid provide an incestuous heir for him," I exclaimed.

"What he does is for the people of Nodin!"

"*West* Nodin!" I interrupted. "Johan does this because he plays directly into Aylund's hands. Underground Nodin would be whole if we had a suitable person on a single throne instead of two brothers fighting over this land like a toy!" I said as Sebastian sat in silence. "Sebastian, I'm asking you, nay, begging you to allow me to help the guards catch the crooks who get away. If you want justice to come to the unjust, allow me to become an agent for it!"

He sat for a few moments and responded, "You'll have my answer in the morning. Now excuse me, I must fetch more water for the princess's next bath."

I continued to stay put in a state of alert.

"You are right, Xavion," Astrid said calmly and sadly.

I got up and knelt down on her left side of the bed where she faced.

"My father's mind is failing him. Aylund's tyranny has infected my family and all of Nodin. My brother, Hakun…" she said and cried profusely. "I cannot remember when I last saw his charming face. I am cursed with this blindness, and I couldn't even see him depart from home. Why? Why would Aylund murder my brother and kidnap my mother? Now he's slowly taking my father down to his level!" Astrid continued to sob. "That's what we Nodinians do. I worry myself sick thinking of what my mother is suffering from!" Astrid then cried the following in Noric: "Mother! Brother! Why is this happening to our family? *What could we have done to deserve violence like this?*"

"Astrid, what your father and uncle have done is not nor ever will be your fault. Your brother fought his best to protect you and he did," I said to reassure her. I grabbed a piece of cloth to wipe her face.

In Noric, I replied to her: "I would take an axe to my neck before they touch you!"

Astrid continued to look in my direction. Her increased senses of hearing and feeling compensated enough to pinpoint me.

"Astrid, it's time for your bath," Sebastian said.

"Okay," we replied. I stood up to walk away. Astrid grasped my right hand with her right. I halted my pace, and she stroked my arm. She gently pulled me back onto my knees. Her tiredness failed to keep her from coming to my kneeling position. Astrid is feeling my face and held her finger beneath my nostrils. She is looking for something. Then she started touching my lips.

"Sebastian, turn your back, please?" she asked.

Sebastian did not turn. He clicked his boots on the floor to mimic turning. Astrid pressed her lips against mine with a kiss. It was magnificent! I always wondered what a kiss felt like. The closest I've had were animals licking me. Something odd occurred with the kiss. When our eyes met, I felt my vision becoming strange. I could see white smoke flowing from my pores. It is vague. It sunk into her eye sockets and tear ducts. Astrid pulled herself away as her lips plucked from our separation. "Thank you, my protector."

"The honor is mine, my lady. *Aquene*," I said to her. I gave Astrid her bath, and I swear she was teasing me.

After, she lay back down and fell asleep.

Sebastian walked me downstairs and spoke. "That was unexpected."

"Are you going to kill me?" I asked in serious curiosity.

"No, but I will say she finds solace with you around her."

"And what of it?" I asked.

"She has not been happy as of late. Consider it a privilege to be her source of it…"

"Quite odd that a guard would allow a slave to lock lips with a royal woman…"

"Quite odd that you've been the only man to do such a thing," he replied.

We didn't speak until we reached my cell.

"Xavion," he said.

I faced him when he called.

"I have faith that one day you will be a free man. Pay no mind to the stupidity of kings and empires. West Nodin is sick and ripe with disease. If its own people cannot save it, then perhaps a stranger from above can aid us," he stated.

I continued to listen.

"Don the suit and dress your face behind the mask. Tomorrow night after our shift, you may help us," he said.

As I entered my cell, he closed and locked the door. "I cannot say what kind of people you'll find. Know this, none of their crimes are your fault. Catching them will be our responsibility. Good luck!" Sebastian said.

That night as I slept, I couldn't stop staring into the bright forge light.

Chapter 6

<u>In Xavion's View</u>

My dreams became smoky and gray with stars and twilight around me. Time clocked ever forward as we people roamed the earth. In my dream, I sat with both legs crossed and my arms rested upon them. I feel that the suit beneath my bed is fusing with me. Within my dream, Jahvonis sits before me. There is a pint-sized ceramic jar to his left. His black suit is ethereal, and a transparent black mist gently danced about him. The mask's eye holes are blank. The hood shadowed his already gloomy appearance. This place is gray with fog and mist. He spoke.

"Are you certain you wish to resurrect me?" he asked.

"That depends. I assume you are Adrian Erik?" I inquired.

"He was me…but I am what my parents made me. You want to help these people, and you are aware of who I am?"

"I know you are the child of the Courtship, and that you were ordained to purge the evil from our world."

"And what would evil be to the beholder? Would it be a God who creates negativity from the beginning of time? Or the people who become what he created? The weapon or the wielder?" Jahvonis asked.

I remained still. Though this is a dream, I will not risk provoking him. "Could the answer be within the viewer themselves? What could be bad to one may be good to another. How would you know where to draw the line?" I replied.

"Only the one who becomes me can decide that. Of course, it depends if they are good enough and deemed worthy. I, myself, once answered to the Courtship. I still must fulfill my duty as I was born to complete it," Jahvonis said.

"As long as life exists, there will always be evil."

"But there will always be good! It is my job to extinguish the issues that are too dangerous for the average people."

"And what would 'too dangerous' be?" I asked.

"That is for us to decide," he stated as he pulled out a small knife from his utility belt. The hilt is a pale bone, and the blade is black obsidian. I do not believe he intends to harm me offensively. However, I have no comprehension of what dark powers Jahveyis gave him.

"With this knife, I require a sample of blood from your feet, legs, torso, arms, hands, and head. When you wake up, the wounds will be healed and your body scarred. The blood is used to bind your soul with my spirit, as when my parents wedded. I will be able to telepathically communicate with you. When you wear my mask, you will be able to switch between our voices at will. You will have an increase in any fighting skills you possess. I must warn you, Xavion Mourningstar, once this ritual is complete, you are Jahvonis until the day you die. When you do, our souls are separated. My parents will judge you not just as a person but how well you did as me. If you choose not to participate in this, you will wake up refreshed but your memory will be erased. The suit you crafted will be in my care. What say you?" Jahvonis asked.

I contemplated the pros of becoming Jahvonis. The amalgamation of us could be what the earth needs. Every now and then I would look back at him. While looking through the blank eye holes, I imagined what he had done with Jahveyis. He is still and holding the knife in his right hand. I'll say he is truly menacing. Is he a shapeless wraith who is only visible within the suit? The dark force that made him seems anxious to return to the world. Can I be sure to trust him?

"Explain how my blood will fuse with you? How will you do this?" I questioned.

"I will have to remove my gauntlets so we can join hands. I am, in a sense, invisible to the eyes of mortals. Your blood will act as a beacon of control. To put it bluntly, I will be in the suit with you and your enemies will be fighting two men instead of one."

"How much blood are you requiring?"

"About half a pint all together…"

"Tell me, Jahvonis, do you want to return to the earth? Not much good has happened."

"And that is why I want to return. I must rise again because my job is not complete! Fighting these things is what I was born to do!"

"Do you serve the Courtship so willingly without question? If you are the son of the gods, then are you not a god yourself? Shouldn't you try to wean humanity's anger and not incite it?"

"Do not speak to me of humanity's anger and the reckless short sight of the gods! I have witnessed the wrath of the dragons! I have seen the ground shatter like glass. Fire razed the sky, lighting struck thousands. Sunlight bleached and ascended the good as the evil were condemned to die. The air dropped to freezing temperatures as famine destroyed all vegetation! I have seen death and slayings on scales that would make your soldiering look like a boy stomping upon ants!" he exclaimed while leaning forward. The mask remained eyeless, but his point was made. He slowed his pace and calmed his tone.

"Forgive that outburst. I try not to remember those terrible days. The gods, their wrathful arrogance, asinine behavior, and irresponsibility are why the dragons took the world hostage. It's the gods' fault why Mustasurma, Ahneus, Ukkosen, Hyatt Katil, Avgrund, and Kuolemajää betrayed their trust. They were made to be governors and law enforcers to the mortals. Still, both of my parents are dumb enough to create me to do the same with a never-ending job. They feed off of our prayers like bread and our blood like wine! Tell me this, Xavion, do you feel the guilt of every life you take? Have the hellish nightmares sunk in?" Jahvonis asked calmly.

"I am haunted by the young men and adults I have killed. I was chosen to participate in that battle against my will! When my mace hit its first target, I couldn't stop the rampant slayings I committed. When it was over, I was traumatized by my homicidal psychopathy. What Sönderfall is to you is what the battlefield is to me. I named myself Mourningstar as punishment for my crimes," I explained.

"We both understand the concept of self-punishment. Self-forgiveness is alien to people like us. Xavion, it's my job to fight criminals, politicians, and religious leaders. I try to protect and save as many innocent people as possible. I can only do that with a host, and you can protect your loved ones better as me than yourself. Think of me as a mask to protect the ones you love," he stated profoundly.

He is wise in his theory of aliases. "All right, I will give you my blood as long as we work together. Can I trust you?"

"Yes." He scooted closer to me and rested the knife upon the ground. I removed my shirt and left my pants on. Jahvonis picked up his knife and knelt on his knees above me as I lay on my back.

"You can still refuse, but when the first drop wets the blade, I must continue without hesitation or interruption. This will hurt, I warn you…"

"I choose a new life," I replied.

Jahvonis made his first incision on the top of my right foot. He made individual incisions on his way up to my head where he slit a wound upon my front hairline. He pulled me back to a seated position. He used the ceramic jar to collect the half-pint of blood. While my hands still bled, he put the blade to his palms. His right palm bled white and his left palm bled yellow.

My eyes did not deceive me, for my blood began to change color. My right hand is black and my left hand bled red. My partner held my hands. Our chakras and chi from various areas of the body fused together in a bright colorful aura that circled and swirled around us. It shifted between a wheel divided in quarters, an octagon, and then an octagram divided in eighths. Each shape would rotate around us. I realize the colors are of an Ember medicine wheel.

With the shape-shifts, I am obliged to stare within his eyeholes. The shapes, rotations, and colors are animated. I felt my vision distort and change. As it happened, my eyesight allowed me to see my muscle tissues, bones, blood flow, heartbeat, chakras, chi, nerve endings, and tendons as well as my standard sight. What sorcery is this? The four colors blinded me until the gray abyss began its deglutition. I was cast from the moon down through the sky. I fell into a stormy fog where thunder and lightning bashed on the air like drums and cymbals.

My falling paused. I hovered in the air. The power and energy of the Sky Spirit surged through me like a match on black powder. My breathing became one with electricity. Day and night unified in a solar eclipse. Minutes felt like years. The seasonal weather blended to forge a super season. Leaves changed color at will. The temperature shifted dramatically. The snow kept falling as my body crash-landed into the earth. Boulders buried me within a tomb. I felt the realm of the dead pull me into the catacombs. The spirits of my executions escorted me. The dreadful dead lynched me in their gallows. No matter how many times my breath left me, my heart and organs worked to stressful and deadly paces. On each face, I saw the orphans, widows, and grieving parents of the slain until the sun rose again.

I frantically awoke in my cell. I realized the dream was over. For a moment I thought it was only a dream until I examined the scars upon my body. Jahvonis now has my blood. I felt stressed but relieved the illusions are over. I agreed to be him until death. An alliance between the hero and the soldier was made. I have to honor it. The Courtships' son? I hope I didn't make a pact with the devil.

"Are you all right?" Sebastian asked as he approached my cell.

"Mostly," I replied.

"It's time," he stated as he walked in.

I sat up to collect my thoughts.

"Are you prepared for tonight?" he asked.

The horror of the dream struck me again.

"You can back out if you wish?" he offered.

"No! I can do it and I will," I replied.

Sebastian nodded with approval.

I stood up and began stretching my limbs. As we walked to Astrid's room, I can still feel my eyes shifting between many visions, nine to be exact. We reached the fourth floor and continued down toward the princess's room. I began to sweat, and my heart raced. It could be that I'm smitten with her. Sebastian gently opened the door and entered.

"Princess! Xavion and I are here."

"Good morning! Please send Xavion over." the lady requested.

Sebastian tilted his head over for me to obey Astrid's request.

"Yes, Princess?" I said as she sat still on her bed.

Her light nightgown looked stately. The women of the royal houses notably have glamorous clothes even on bad days. Her hair…my gods, her hair.

"Can you sit and talk for a moment?" she asked.

Sebastian closed the door.

"I want to ask your opinion of my family, mainly my father."

I held my breath and turned to Sebastian. He crossed his arms with a stern and curious look.

"What is said by the princess in her own room will stay in her room by my command," she said aloud and was directed at Sebastian.

He obeyed and responded without objection. "So it will be," he replied.

"What do you want to know?" I asked.

"Tell me what you know, starting with my brother, then mother and father," she asked.

"I remember meeting Hakun some time before the Encroachment. He showed an interest in me and who I am. Very polite, he was. Somewhat naive to the struggles of Nodin but he still knew of them. I would watch him train with his ax while under instruction. He could've used a better one. He spoke out against your father. It was about his total disregard for the surfacers, Theranths, and the Ericsons. He called your father a *blasphemous hypocrite whose arrogance stains the North.*

"I learned later that he said those things because Johan would not allow him to renounce his royalty.

Hakun loved a surface Ericson woman. Hakun wanted a more simple and common life. Despite your mother's approval of his choice, Hakun was banned from going above ground or to be married without your father's consent. I don't think he ever forgave Johan for that moment," I stated.

"And yet another family affair of which I have no say or knowledge of. What do you think of my mother?" she asked.

"Well, I found your mother to be a strong-willed woman who was held down by the patriarchy of Nodin. Her appearance in comparison to her age is most deceiving. She would mention you from time to time, how unfairly you are treated by Johan for your exclusion. Helga is incredibly beautiful. Hence, why you both delight people's eyes," I replied as she blushed and felt for my arm.

"What about my father?" she asked.

I felt my vision distort and divide. I could see the heartbeats of the three of us. All is black before me except the red heartbeats pumping before me. At a most inconvenient time, I could feel the grim presence of Jahvonis boiling within me. Then still as our hearts beat, I could see and feel the chakras from my crown, third eye, throat, and heart. They channeled into Astrid. Is this the smoke from before?

"Johan is losing all honor and hope. His loss of wife and son, and the betrayal of his brother are destroying his mind. In all of that, I do not see any room for you," I said.

Astrid's heartbeat slowed down, and her temperature lowered. Sebastian looked on with shock. The white smoke from me is now visible enough for him to witness it.

"If he is to die in this war, there is no one to lead. I cannot become queen due to my blindness, nor do I have a son," Astrid mourned.

"I am your aide as long as time allows. Should you ever be queen, I will be here with you as your eyes, your sword, your shield, and your friend," I comforted as I stroked her hair.

"Would you ever be my king?" she questioned.

I stayed silent, not knowing what to answer. The two of us as Nodin's next royal family? Sebastian was intrigued with piqued interest.

"I do not know if I qualify for that position, Astrid."

"As princess and last heir to the Western kingdom, I can choose whomever I wish to lead at my side!" she lightly exclaimed.

Sebastian remained silent. Perhaps caught in the drama?

"What are you saying, Astrid?"

She took her time to choose the correct words.

"I am asking if the time ever came..." She suavely sighed. "Would you take me as your wife?"

Sebastian's jaw hit the floor. My body gave me both pain and pleasure. Jahvonis immediately gave me a jolt of his mysterious power. My eyes became their normal sight, and the smoke ceased. Astrid stroked my arm softly while caressing my hair.

"Shall I run your bath, my lady?" Sebastian asked.

"Yes!" Astrid replied. She continued to feel me, and I looked at her. Her eyes are less dull. As her aide, I must wash her, but this time seemed…intimate due to Astrid's erected chest. What is this feeling I sense between my hips? I believe she's trying to arouse me. Why?

Her bath finished, and her dress was strapped on. The rest of my shift was dominated by the thought of tonight.

"Good night, my lady," I said.

"And to you!" she replied.

Sebastian and I returned to my cell. He and I communicated by small notes about how he can get me out of here unnoticed. We decided I would gather the suit in a sack and he would escort me out of the palace and to a hidden place for me to change. This carried on into the late night. If anyone asked, he would say, "The bag contains weapon orders to be delivered."

"Are you sure?" he asked.

"Yes. Please give me a moment?"

"Indeed," he replied.

I'm about to leave my home to engage in vigilantism. Before that, I knelt down in prayer.

"Immortals above me, you have given me a path that could lead me to many good deeds…or my doom. No matter which, I ask for your guidance and forgiveness for the harm that is brought upon the evildoers. Should I die in the process, I gladly welcome and honor your judgment upon my soul. This prayer, I ask in all of your names. Amen."

I left my cell while carrying the suit in a large heavy bag. Sebastian and I used shortcuts to travel more privately. When we made it into the city, we used darker alleyways and small tunnels to get around. The area we chose is a building whose rooftop is high above the lava pits. The lava light is out of range. Sebastian only went halfway above the building.

"For the rest of this night, you are on your own," he stated.

"Thank you for your help, my friend," I replied.

"Good luck," he said and left.

The suit is on, and I have to apply the mask. I strapped and laced it upon my head. My hair is in a ponytail. My body is hidden by the suit. I stood in the darkness of the rooftop. Jahvonis lives once more! His blood ritual mixed with the suit made me faster. All I must do now is stand lookout. A bloodcurdling scream may catch my ear. It is now my job to investigate the reason for the scream. I began speaking in Jahvonis's voice. I started to think like him and move like him. The menace of his vocals is hellish! I waited for about a half hour. As I stand on the roof, it is rare for West Nodin to be quiet. Suddenly, I heard rushed and heavy footsteps coming to the roof. I hid within the shadows. In front of me, I hear and see two men in a struggle.

"Where's my coin, you little shit! You owe me two months' rent!" said the dominant man while holding a knife.

"Please stop. I'll pay you double! I just need more time!" the victim cried.

"You'll pay with your blood!" he screamed.

I reached into my right pouch that held my shuriken, I aimed it properly. With a throw of the arm, its cold touch brushed my fingertips and flew forward. The star spun rapidly across the air. I didn't want my first day on the job to start with death. The star knocked the knife from his hand. I still hid in the darkness and used his confusion to my advantage.

"You have one chance to run," I growled.

The man turned in curiosity. "Show yourself, you sodomite! I can take ya!" he gloated.

I stepped slowly from hiding. My black suit still camouflaged me but to a lesser state.

"Oh shit!" he exclaimed as he took a swing.

I grabbed his fist in a countering maneuver that consisted of me kicking his gut and then stomping his left knee. This forced him to the ground. The man threw another punch but with his left hand. I caught it within my right.

"Who...who are you?" he gasped.

"Jahvonis," I said as I headbutted and knocked him unconscious.

His tenant was frightened.

"Do not cower...you're not the criminal here," I said as I knelt down to the attacker, took his coin purse, and tossed it to the tenant.

"Thank you! My son can eat tonight!" he said in relieving glee.

"You're welcome!" I replied.

In the past few weeks, I've foiled several crimes ranging from theft to assault. During my dreams, Jahvonis would train me in combat. One fighting style called *ninjutsu* is a Daichinian martial art of combative trickery.

He would show me multiple ways to counter other weapons, to manipulate my opponent's actions against them, and methods to escape from a fight.

When I slept, he used my subconscious and imagination as his own. He staged fake missions to test my skills that strengthened our physical and spiritual bond. Each time, the experience transferred to my physical self. When sparring, my blood still acts as his beacon of visibility. He would alternate between wearing and not wearing his suit. My blood within him made a red figure connected by dots. He also said if or when someone else takes up the role, the skills of the previous wearer would transfer, making them even stronger. I'll admit fighting Jahvonis is fun.

Sebastian would speak to me in private about Jahvonis's reputation, from praise and criticisms to what the guards and Johan are thinking. Astrid gets suspicious when I do not attend to her. She refuses Sebastian's help with bathing and dressing. Today is June 2. Astrid's birthday is July 13. She will be fifteen.

I can tell she likes me more than a friend or aide. She still wishes me to rule at her side as husband and king, but I cannot. If I know anything about being Jahvonis is whenever someone falls in love and has an enemy, they use your lover against you. I must try to put my oath to Jahvonis before others, including romances. I still do my work helping Astrid, but I cannot let someone weigh me down. It sounds selfish, I know, but it is not my intention. Rather it is the protection of a third and first person. Since then, I've overheard many people tell of their rescue. Some refer to me as a demon, and some call me a hero. Since Jahvonis's resurgence, people have ventured into the Hallowed Holds. In other copies of the Hallowed Holds, I see no mention of Jahvonis.

I'm on patrol now. Things were fine until this suspicious man caught my eye. He wore brown leather clothing and a hood. I stalked him because usually hooded people mean trouble, including me. He was doing simple daily work, but something else caught my attention. He went into a mead hall and sat down for a drink. I was able to sneak into the mead hall unnoticed. I crept from afar with patient curiosity.

Another man is sitting down to his right for a mug of ale. As he turned his head, the hooded man slipped a powdery substance into his mug. The powder is white. It could be poisonous! The hooded one walked away from the counter. The drinker was about to sip. I couldn't risk him dying, so I threw a shuriken and shattered his mug. All were alarmed with the glass breaking at loud volume. I leaped into the crowd and chased the hooded man as he ran through the streets. After about a half mile, he took a left into an ally. He rested and huffed in exhaustion. I crept up behind him.

"Big cut, here I come," he gloated.

I threw a shuriken at his back. He knelt down in pain. I kicked him in the head to ground him.

"Why did you try to kill him?" I yelled.

"He's dead!" he replied.

"I shattered his mug before he drank!" I replied.

"You fucked up my contract!"

"Your contract is terminated! Who do you work for?"

"I ain't tellin' you shit!" he exclaimed.

I punched him out cold with my right hand.

Ten minutes later he awoke with his legs in my hands as he dangled about forty feet above a lava pool. He began panicking and squirming like a worm.

"Who's your boss? Who hired you?" I growled.

"Please…put me down!" he begged.

I dropped him close enough to the lava. I couldn't kill him because I need information, so I tied a thin but strong rope around his ankle. His searing screams on his way down were entertaining to me. I ceased his fall above the lava. It began to bubble.

"Are you warm enough?" I said as I pulled him back up.

"Fuck you!" he screamed.

I loosened my grip on the thread, which sent him screaming back down below. To be honest, I was struggling to hide my laughter. I stopped the fall before he was decimated.

"Okay, okay! I'll talk!" he said as I pulled him back up and grabbed his left ankle.

"Who hired you?!" I shouted.

"The contract came from a client in the mead hall. The owner said the target is a violent drunk who starts brawls on short notice. The job was simple…poison the drunk and collect the coin!" he exclaimed.

"Give me a name!"

He continued to sweat with trepidation.

"My arms are getting tired," I said.

"Don't! Please don't let go!" he cowered.

"Then give me a name!"

"His name is McIntyre, one of our regular customers!"

"Now who's your boss?"

"I don't know his actual name. He's some man wearing makeup. I'm new. This was my first mission. All I know is, on this side of Nodin, we're called Hand of Doom and East Nodin named us Black Hole Sun. Please, that's all I know!" he exclaimed.

After the interrogation, I bound his hands and legs and left him in front of the guards' barracks. They've been issued to arrest any and every member of the organization. The next day I searched for the person named McIntyre. Luckily, when I tied up the assassin, I looted his clothing for any tip of the contract. I found a note with an address on it, I suppose it could be McIntyre's, but I'll have to see first. I, unfortunately, had to break into the home and wait for the owner to return. I hid in a nearby closet. Real original, right? Two minutes later a door opened, and I heard a man ranting.

"Why is that drunk still breathing? I paid good money for that hit, so why the hell is he alive!" he shouted.

Another voice replied, "I told you someone foiled the hit! And we don't give refunds!"

I'm assuming the other man talking is an assassin.

"If you don't give me my coins' worth, then I'll have to kill him myself!" the first voice exclaimed.

He began walking toward the closet that I hid in. As he grabbed the door handle, I kicked the door at him. In the heat of the moment, the assassin drew a dagger. I threw a shuriken at his dagger, and he fled. I turned my attention to McIntyre by jamming my forearm into his neck.

"Why did you hire someone to slay the drunk?" I asked.

"That bastard alcoholic owed me a hundred coppers, and every day he gets into a fight with anyone around him!"

"That's no excuse to have someone murdered! How did you contact the Hand of Doom?" I asked.

"I'm no rat!" he exclaimed.

"Your first assassin is recovering in prison. If you don't want to be opened from your mouth to your crotch, then you tell me all I wish to know!" I said.

"All right! There's a hidden stone door built behind the meadery. They use a pendant to open it!"

"How do you use it?" I asked.

"The keyhole has the design on the pendant. You place the pendant in the hole and fit the designs together! Now please don't hurt me!" he begged.

"Sweet dreams!" I said as I punched him out cold and bound him. Now I just need one of their pendants and to find the door. I could go to the mead hall and wait for the door to open, but it may take too long. Who knows what kind of trouble could happen in the meantime? I'll have to wait for another assassin to appear. After these two incidents, they may turn their attention to me.

Three days later I was on patrol. So far things are calm enough for it to be a quiet day. Times are slowly changing in Nodin. Crime is minimally down, and the people are starting to have hope. Where I am at the moment is on a building near the royal palace. It is quite a charming sight, but unfortunately, it is not all that safe.

The soldiers continue to train. They are still recovering from the First Encroachment. I've been patrolling the town for many hours now, and it's about time to call it a day. I felt myself sweating, and my heart beat quickly. This normally isn't a good sign. I turned around, and there is someone hiding in the shadows. I went to pursue this person, but I was shot by an arrow in the right side of my stomach. This bodes ill because if I continued to chase, the minor wound will quicken the blood loss. The armor I'm wearing prevented most of the arrow, but the smallest part of the tip punctured my stomach. It feels like a needle puncture.

I must take their pendant! I thought.

I sprinted toward the shooter before they could escape. Another arrow was fired, and I was quick to dodge. When I made it to their location, I fought them closer to the edge. As this person knelt over, I grasped their head under my left arm and used my weight to force their head into the floor. As they lay on the ground, I turned them over to see their face. It is a man. I took away his weapons and destroyed his bow.

I tore open his body armor and found his pendant. It has a skull, sun, and a hand carved into it. I tried to remove it, but he gained his wits, and I was forced to knock him out. I bound his hands and legs and dropped him off at the guard barracks. Now to find the door!

I sprinted to the mead hall as quickly as possible. When I searched its rear side, it was dusty. One thing about Nodinian stone doors is that they can blend into the rock and are nearly invisible. One technique I learned in the military is if you come to a dead end, try tapping the walls. If any of the tones are hollow and resonant, then it could be a hidden door or tunnel. Tapping the stone with your hands does hurt because you have to do it hard enough to generate a resonant tone.

After thirty minutes of tapping this wall, I suspect either the door is not here or McIntyre led me on a wild chase. I stamped my foot on the ground in frustration, and something wasn't right. Even though I'm light-footed, I heard a drumlike sound. The door must be on the ground! I knelt down on one knee and brushed the garbage and dust aside. I found a small hole.

Does the pendant fit in here? I thought. I placed the pendant inside the hole. I expected something to happen, but nothing did. I tried four more times, and still, nothing occurred.

At my fifth attempt, I placed it in as an idea came to mind. What if I spin it as the carvings match? Alas, it worked! The effect of the pendant caused the ground to move. A large circular shape formed around me. The circular door descended deeper into the earth. As I stood on it, the door reached the bottom of its destination. There is a torch before a tunnel. I chose to follow it. Instead of walking upright, I crouched closer to the ground. This tunnel must be at least eighty to a hundred feet in length. I'm reaching the end. There's another door; this one seems more complex.

It has a symbol in the center. It is a circle with many interwoven lines within it. It looks like a web. Under the symbol are four feathers. They are red, black, yellow, and white. The feathers are attached to pins. There are four holes on the outer rim of the symbol that seem large enough for the feather stems. In what order do they align? I doubt these feathers go in the order I found them. Normally, if these puzzles are answered incorrectly, then the price is death. I was hesitant but placed the yellow on the right, red on the bottom, black on the left, and white on top. When applying the final feather, I hurried back to avoid any traps. I then witnessed the wall being divided into four sides, and at last, it opened. The other side held another hall, but I could hear people grunting and wood clashing. It sounds like a fight!

A large room is at the end. This tunnel is not lit, and the darkness hid me. It looks like an arena. I could see several people sitting in aisles of benches. They are all adorned in matching uniforms of this organization. In front of me, there is a man with long dark-brown hair; it reached his back. He sits in a stone chair. He wears black leather. His face is painted with a white base and a black design.

Obviously, this man is devoted to the Courtship of Obsidian Ice. In my history books, people around the world wear this type of makeup to frighten their enemies in battle. This style of makeup is Soruthian. He could be from Soruth, but why would he be here?

In the arena below, two teenage boys are dueling with wooden swords. They are different heights. The shorter one is losing badly. This ended when the shorter boy was kicked in the head. He fell to the ground. The shorter boy has dark-blond hair. The man in black stood from his seat.

"Stop! This is finished!" He then turned to the winner. "You've won this fight. A fine swordsman you're becoming. Master Kane has taught you well. You are dismissed."

"Thank you, my lord!" the teen replied.

As the winner left the arena, the losing opponent then stood.

"Alastair!" the lord shouted as the boy looked upward. "You need more work! Your swordsmanship is becoming weak. Your bow will not do much in close combat!"

"And what would you like me to do? These heavy-handed weapons are used by the mindless brutes that this faction is riddled with!" said Alastair.

"When you chose me as your sensei, you bent to my teachings. These 'mindless brutes' are your companions! It is the hatred of Nodin's corruption that spawned the Black Hole Sun. The hatred that has forced the Hand of Doom upon Aylund Rudolf," he replied to Alastair.

"Why should I continue obeying you? By now you've taught me everything you know. What we need is a leader who has a face. Not some feminine make-up-wearing queer who's a long away from Soruth!" Alastair insulted.

"Such arrogance will be your downfall, you snot-nosed brat!" His master removed his weapons and stepped into the arena. Alastair swung with forceful precision. The master dodged his swings. He slapped Alastair whenever possible.

"Now let's see how your taijutsu is!" he stated.

They engaged in precise fighting. The maneuvers are from Yazjia. When there was some distance between them, Alastair went for a roundhouse kick but the master caught his leg in the air, lifted him up, and slammed him to the ground. After these past two skirmishes, Alastair is bleeding and bruised. When on the ground, I saw him reach for a knife out of his boot. The master went to grab him with his right hand. Alastair sliced at his palm. The master's hand was cut, but it didn't seem to faze him. This gave Alastair some time to stand. When he did, the master tossed a shuriken and knocked the knife from his hand. He slapped Alastair with his bloody palm. This man could be a problem in the near future. They are speaking, I hear their words clearly.

"It seems the student still has much to learn. You know damn well I taught you to carry an emergency knife in your boot. Your bow skills are potent, but your melee combat still falls short to your master!" he commented.

"One of these days, Mataraves, you will meet your match. And then I will take my seat as jonin!" Alastair said.

Mataraves then kicked him in the sternum. As Alastair restored himself, he retired from the arena. Mataraves returned to his seat. I dare not show myself with him around. I felt a blunt force striking me in the back that sent me into the light.

"Intruder!" I heard being shouted. I suspect one of the assassins came through the hidden door and found me. I will have trouble engaging up to two dozen of these people! Most of the members vacated the stands, and only ten remained, including Mataraves. When I was found, I was thrown into the center of the room. When I looked up, I caught the dreadful gaze of Mataraves. His war paint is intimidating. It looks like a turtle shell. I say this because the black streaks heavily divided his face into very square sections.

The remaining ten assassins soon surrounded me like wolves on an elk. The strokes of their blades came one after another at high speed. I dodged many of them, but four blades cut me. Challenging this many swordsmen is exhilarating and scary at once. Eventually, the numbers of these men took their toll. In the military, I've engaged more than this but I've had soldiers watching my back.

"Stop!" a voice called.

The men halted and kept their distance at the command. Mataraves reentered the arena.

"This one is mine!" he stated.

If these men are this difficult with their greater numbers, then what could their master accomplish alone?

Mataraves spoke again. "It seems this is the Jahvonis who has foiled our missions. Anyone who can make my men cower should present thyself to me!"

His weapons included a metallic bo staff, shuriken, senbon, and a Daichinian short sword. He reminds me of myself. Mataraves drew his bo. His hand-based combat is like mine, but I fear he may be better. I felt a large clunk on the back of my head, which knocked me out. I think it may have been a club.

Awhile later, I awoke. I am kneeling with my wrists in chains that are bolted into the walls. With my vision returning to me, I found someone sitting with their legs crossed upon the ground.

"And you wake," he said.

Indeed, it is Mataraves.

"So you're the one who cost us many coins? The one who tried to incinerate one of my men in the holy lava?" he asked.

I remained silent.

"The silent treatment, eh? Well then, I'll speak. My name I take it is known to you. It was my opportunistic apprentice who knocked you out. A fine learner he is, but well-mannered he is not. Quite an obnoxious child," he stated. "It seems you admire Yazjian weaponry as much as I do? Your shuriken and senbon are well made. What say you? Criminal? Assassin? Vigilante? Or some of each?"

"What matter is it to you?" I replied.

"It matters because you've caused quite a bit of trouble in the public. The Hand of Doom keeps all eyes and ears on the streets."

"You've been watching me?"

"And your work on the battlefield. You're quite the slayer," he said.

I felt as if I defecated in my trousers. Does he know who I am?

"Now I have questions for you. What do you know of Johan Edling? He's the other half of Nodin's troubles. Once his brother is taken care of, we'll turn our attention to him. Now tell me or be punished…"

I came to an odd thought in my brain. I did make it a goal to revoke Johan from the throne. Could killing him be more appropriate? If these men do the deed, who knows who will take charge?

"However, I'm in no hurry for your information. I have my own contracts to fulfill. When I return, you best have an answer. Any attempt of escape will have you turned into a pincushion," he said as his archers monitored our movements from above the room.

For one day I was a prisoner. I hope Sebastian found some excuse as to why I am not there and is taking care of Astrid. From beyond the walls, I could hear people screaming in pain. During my imprisonment, I was not able to feed. Even if I could, I dare not remove my mask, not even for food. A few times I questioned if Jahvonis is necessary. Is he needed or not at all? How would Adrian deal with a situation like this? Three more hours went by, and Mataraves returned. His face is still made up and his bloodlust is quenched. He used his bo like a walking staff when he entered the room. As he came in, he called off his archers and once again sat before me. He carried a burlap bag.

"Tell me who are you? Why do you wish to dispatch Nodin's lords?" I asked.

"Why? It was Nodin who created us! It was Aylund's men who came to Soruth and hauled me away from mi familia. The *Cabron* subjected me to years of backbreaking labor in his mines. By his own hand, he forced me to drink Nodin's fire-water—might as well call it bison piss!" he exclaimed. He continued to speak. "Aylund and all of his bloodline, all of the Snow Skins who try to rule the earth. Their colorless pale skin, the same paleness of death! Years of their foul, ugly, fat whorish women forcing themselves upon me and subjecting me to things that only a monster would commit. I may lead a group of ninja, but I will return to Soruth. My brothers and I will see the snow melted. A justified genocide!" he exclaimed.

This young man is mad. He is truly hateful of not just Nodin but anyone who bears snow skin!

"I will give you visuals of my rage and hate!" he said as he unlaced his bag and tipped it upside down.

Falling upon the floor was the head of McIntyre!

"As long as the Snows die, that's all that matters! Jahvonis, I don't care about which of my schemes succeed and fail. I only care about inflicting psychological damage, like when the Snow scum would whip me senseless and left scars on my body, soaking me within their poisonous ales. The only way to truly feel the pain is to become the pain yourself! You see, Jahvonis, my wrath is not with you personally. It's the fact you fight for the people who represent false hope and lies. But since you were able to make it this far, I'll give you a choice—join me in my destiny to destroy the Snow Skins…or bear the same fate as all those you've failed."

I spoke in my normal voice but used the Sand language: "You give us Soruthians a bad name. I know of the wars and terror that our people have done to each other. You may be a devout worshipper to Jahveyis, but before my days are done… I will kill you. When you stand before Jahveyis with all your hatred and bitterness, he will send you to hell! And if I am to join you, I will show you the meaning of true hate!"

Mataraves stood up and drew his bo staff. "Killing you would be too easy. Your punishment will be more grievous!" he said as he began to brutally bludgeon me with his bo for about five minutes. He grew blazingly angry. Yes, it hurt, but showing any amount of pain will only please him. In that enraged beating, he was not only hitting me but striking the chains and loosening them. He struck ten more times. He became uncoordinated. The left chain fell out of the wall. The right is nearly broken.

"Thank you, sir! May I have another?" I shouted in my growl.

Upon his final stroke, I used what strength I had left and tore the right chain from the wall. I caught the staff in my left hand. I stood up and began the offensive! My objective is to escape and regroup. Our skirmish intensified. He tried to ground me with his staff.

Mataraves is so skilled in combat. Where his training came from is unknown to me. He was smart enough to aim for my legs because if I can't stand, then I can't fight. The only weapons I have are the chains on my wrists. Our bout ceased when I grabbed the staff. I headbutted him and began a barrage of elbows to the face. In the end, I flipped him over my head as we both grasped the staff.

I bolted from the room. Mataraves called his guards. I must find my weapons before leaving! I opened every door I could. The guards are not near yet. After five rooms, I found a small dresser with three drawers. There is a chest on the other side of the room. I found nothing in all the drawers.

A thought came to me. *What if I'm supposed to think the drawers are empty?* I tried to dig beneath the corners of the drawers because sometimes there's a hidden compartment. The third drawer had a key. I hastily unlocked the chest. My weapons and tools are all here. I used one of my senbon as a lockpick to unhook my wrists. I then strapped on my equipment.

"I think he might be in here!" someone shouted.

I hid beside the door with one of the chains clenched in my hand. Someone walked in and was not smart enough to check behind the door or the space beside it. Three men appeared in the room, armed and dangerous. I leaped from the side and punched them with the chain. I must defeat them quick before I have a small army upon me. I finished them off by disarming and knocking them out.

I ran with fear to not find an exit. This place could have miles within it, and I don't have time for a lengthy search! I ran through the hall with all guards looking for me. After ten minutes of running scared, I am back at the arena. Hopefully, the entrance I came in will be the exit to go out! On the other side of the arena, there is a staircase.

I entered the arena and ran up the staircase toward the tunnel. The assassins entered the room and began firing their arrows at me in a reckless fashion. Among them is Alastair. After realizing they missed, I sprinted through the dark tunnel.

On my way to the puzzle door, another person came through it from the other side. He wore a fully brass-colored mask and wore a short ko katana on his waist. I was choiceless and had to force my way through. Hopefully, I can reach the ground door before it's too late. I did come to it finally, but there does not seem to be a way through. I began to remember my last good moments even if they weren't perfect. I tried to see if I could open it. What I found was the same insignia pattern that was on the top floor. I prayed on my soul that they didn't take the pendant I looted from them. "Yes!" I exclaimed as it is in my pouch. With no time to gaze at it, I shoved it in the hole and rotated it. I must wait for the door to descend.

"There he is!" Alastair shouted.

I turned and began throwing shuriken as fast as possible. I hope I can delay them long enough! My shuriken did harm them enough to buy me time. The door lowered, and I hopped back on for it to rise, but it was slow. When I could reach my arms to the rim of the hole, I tried hard to propel myself to the top. When I did, the door sealed shut and I made my way home as quickly as possible. I escaped the Hand of Doom…for now.

Chapter 7

In Xavion's View

I couldn't reach my cell fast enough to take off my suit and rest. What Mataraves said echoed in my ears: "The Hand of Doom keeps all eyes and ears on the streets."

He complimented me for my skills on the battlefield. How long have they been watching me? Do they know about my job? Does he know who I am? My eyes grew too heavy to hold. I strayed into a slumber.

"It appears we have a new enemy," Jahvonis said.

"How does he know who I am?" I replied.

"The both of you are presumably the only Soruthians in Nodin. How he learned of you can vary between thousands of possibilities."

"He sounds like he has plans. The man with the brass mask and that Alastair child. Their techniques are ninjutsu. The same you teach me. How does it come so far from Daichi?"

"There are many ways that Ninjutsu could expand."

"There's something you're not telling me, isn't there?"

"You will know more in time. We will earn each other's trust along the way. Yes, there are many things I will tell you, but time has not decreed it," he stated.

"I hope your secrecy will not go in vain! I must rest now. If you sense any danger, wake me!" I said.

Jahvonis faded back into my subconscious.

Morning came, and I awoke to see another day. My breathing is calm, and the temperature cooled. In my absence, the flames of my forge died. My books are neatly shelved and my weapons are on their stands. Jahvonis's armor is under my bed. For several hours, I lay in bed to regain my strength and wits. I hope Sebastian will visit me.

The wounds I was given by the Hand of Doom are still in their potent state. The arrow wound is on my stomach. The four sword wounds are on my right thigh, left bicep, right calf, and left hip. I have several bruises from Mataraves's bo. I still have the knot on the back of my head from Alastair. My cut marks will have to be cauterized closed. Thankfully, Jahvonis's armor shielded most of the full impact and lessened my injuries.

I looked into another of my books. I was drawn to these gauntlets with four blades on each one. They're used to block swords by catching them between two of the forearm blades. They can break narrow-width swords. If you stack your forearms on each other and a blade comes down the middle, when you horizontally pull your forearms apart, the pressure from both sides can break the blade.

"Xavion? Thank heavens!" Sebastian exclaimed while rushing to unlock the door.

"Yes, I am here. I am safe but wounded," I replied.

"You were gone for a long time. What have you learned?" he asked.

"I learned terrible things…" I proceeded to tell Sebastian of Mataraves and his revolution.

"Gods, have mercy! We must inform the king and the guards!" Sebastian exclaimed.

"Wait, Sebastian! Johan will only get suspicious if I tell him," I said as I retrieved the pendant.

"You tell Johan what I told you and give him this pendant as evidence."

We got ready to inform the king and the rest of the guards. Sebastian allowed me to continue up to Astrid's room. I assume Sebastian will compose a story to explain the pendant. I'm also curious about the guards' perception of Jahvonis. I knocked on Astrid's door.

"Who's there?" she asked.

"It is Xavion, Lady Astrid."

"Oh, please come in, dear!"

Dear? I thought.

"Where have you been, Xavion?" she said aloud while facing the wall toward the foot of her bed.

I walked over to sit beside the princess.

"I was doing important business for Nodin," I replied.

"Oh goodness, it's so wonderful to have you back. Sebastian and I were worried." She embraced me with a hug and laid a kiss upon my cheek. My thirst is rising. My wounds sting. The lady had a container of drinking water at her feet.

"May I have a drink of your water, Miss Astrid?"

"You need not be so formal with me, Xavion. And yes, the water is yours."

"Is it being formal or having manners? And thank you," I replied.

She smiled and blushed.

I reached for the water and drank it all in one sip. Afterward I felt a strange and relieving feeling where my wounds are. Like a storybook, the scarred and open tissue in my flesh closed and healed. Is this some power of Jahvonis? What water is capable of such action?

"Quite tasteful water, milady," I said calmly.

"Xavion, I am ready for my day," Astrid said.

Hours after her proper care, Sebastian returned and asked to speak to me in private.

"You can trust me, Sebastian," the princess said.

"I think it is best for Xavion and I speak alone. It is of military concern."

"Normally, I would insist that I hear this affair, but the tone in your voice seems quite stern. Do not take too long," Astrid replied.

Sebastian took me out into a more remote part of this floor. We still kept close enough to Astrid's room.

"Johan is rallying the men to move on East Nodin. We leave in two days," he stated.

"What of Astrid and the Hand of Doom?" I asked.

"Astrid will have a stand-in aide. His name is Hamish. We do not have men to spare in the investigation of the Hand of Doom."

"You're telling me I'm on my own?" I lightly exclaimed.

"I'm afraid so," Sebastian replied.

"Dammit! At least tell me Johan has a proper plan of attack?"

"He wishes to muscle on through Aylund's forces with the element of surprise," Sebastian informed.

"You think with what few men survived the last attack, we can force our way to Aylund? What Johan arranged is a suicide mission!" I exclaimed. "And what 'surprise' does the fool have now?"

"The king says, and I quote, 'What better surprise than walking through the front door?'"

"His grief will cost the lives of thousands! He is ungrateful to the soldiers who fought and died defending your country! If Johan were not looking for the Theranths, then we would be safer in our own borders. Helga would be here, and Hakun would still be alive!" I said in frustration.

"West Nodin is not just 'my' country, it is the only true home we people have! I would love nothing more than to be above in the wilderness instead of being down here with the moles! I dream of a day where we are no longer at war with our own people! To gather around and feast with ourselves and our Theranth cousins. Hell, I would love to have a wife and children and that's not impossible. We survived the First Encroachment because you helped us, slave or not! You, a Soruthian man, born and raised in the wilderness of our cold land. You carried our fallen prince in your arms. Each surviving soldier marched behind you like you were our king! I understand your disdain for West Nodin's political idiocy. If you don't care about our struggles"—Sebastian lowered his voice—"then why are you jumping across rooftops and having criminals and guards think twice about every step they take?" He added, "And if there's someone who threatens to take or destroy my home, I will be first in line to die for it!"

"It's worse than ever out there, isn't it?" Astrid cried as we turned in dismay to see her standing in her doorway.

"My lady?" Sebastian asked.

"Astrid," I spoke aloud.

She faced the wall before her, looking into an endless fade of her lost sight.

"My father is all that is left, only he can atone for my family's sins. He hastens the death of our people. I cannot provide an heir to our throne. My father will not take a second wife if my mother is gone. I fear when you leave for battle, my father will die by the sword or from his guilt. That guilt will cast him into a realm of relentless malice like Aylund's. The name Edling would be forever tainted," Astrid lamented.

Later that night as I slept, Jahvonis interrupted, "You'll need more training if you're going to survive the next attack…"

"An attack that is not of my concern," I said.

"It will be if Aylund swarms the West and attacks Astrid! You are their best hope of any victory."

"It is not my war!" I replied.

"You're right, Xavion. It was made your war. I realize you are out of place here, but as Sebastian stated earlier, the soldiers will not march without you. You are a far better warrior and person than I was centuries before. My job is not finished, and I need you to help me. Your destiny is not known to you yet. Only you can make Nodin whole again," Jahvonis said.

I chose to end our conversation and continued to sleep.

*****

The two days passed. I am suiting up in a set of armor that I built in the past few months. It is composed of an undersuit of brown leather and steel plating. The entire suit is the standard cuirass, gauntlets, boots, greaves, and helmet setup. The cuirass has twenty-four individual plates in front and back (twelve on each side with four rows of three). My helmet has a spire that goes from my nose to about four inches above my forehead. The entire helmet covers my head except for the two eye and mouth openings. My weapons begin with a long studded club called a *kanabo*, which is a Daichinian weapon that is used for breaking swords and bludgeoning armor. I would wear my shield on my back while I carry the club in hand with the studded part resting on my shoulder.

My sword is a hybrid Barkish saber. It is a combination of a talwar hilt and a kilij (kill-lidge) blade. The talwar comes from *Nidia*. Nidia is one of the four Barkish nations in Eastern Soruth. The other three nations are *Paseri*, *Abaria*, and *Kemei*. The kilij comes from the Abarian province named *Tur*.

What makes my sword a hybrid is the blade has the weighted tip of the kilij and also has a false edge. The blade is thirty inches long with a standard backward curve. It has a dense brass crossbar handguard and matching hilt. The guard has langettes to trap opposing blades. My talwar hilt is seven inches long with a disk-shaped pommel. The bulbous handle with the guard and pommel force me to hold it differently. I hold the sword like a hammer; and its cutting power is generated by my hips, shoulder, tricep, bicep, and forearm—never the wrist. The scabbard is made from oak that is bound in brown leather with brass fittings.

I also made a Barkish *jambiya*. The jambiya is a double-edged curved dagger that is a scaled-down version of my saber. The blade is twelve inches long. I will publically wear the jambiya as a symbol of my Barkish lineage and for self-defense.

Sabers and many curved swords specialize in cutting, chopping, and slashing. Contrary to common belief, certain curved blades can thrust straight. My sword favors curved thrusts as long as I follow the curve.

I also engraved Ember symbols on the blades of the talwar and jambiya. The first is a *turtle* for adaptability. Next are two *arrows* facing opposite directions for war. Next is a wheel divided in quarters to symbolize the *Four Ages*: infancy, youth, adult, and elder. The final is a *hawk* that represents the Ember equivalent of angels. Birds bear the word of the gods and deliver the dead to their hall. The symbols are doubled on the opposite sides of the blades.

"You look terrifying," Sebastian said as he opened my door. He stood with another guard who looked at me in controlled fright.

"Xavion, this is Hamish. He will be aiding Astrid while we are away," Sebastian stated.

I walked over to Hamish. I saw him take a half step back.

"I trust you will take care of the princess?" I asked.

"Y-y-yes," Hamish stuttered unintentionally.

"I will hear from her if anything goes wrong. I keep track of my belongings. Should any go missing, I'll know who to begin my search with. Astrid will tell the truth about any man who hurts her."

"Yes, Xavion, the lady and your things will be safe," Hamish replied.

"We must go, Xavion," said Sebastian.

As we walked our way to the yard of Johan's palace, the other soldiers, like Hamish, felt intimidated by my armor and weaponry. As I continued my way, I saw a large metal box with a door and cell bars.

"Are you kidding me? Fucking mook," I said, referring to Johan. I know damn well he wants me in that box. So I don't intimidate the other men, I stepped inside and slammed the door behind me. Sebastian also was surprised and turned to the other men with disdain. I saw him walk toward the approaching general, Johan's cousin, Vallen Edling.

"General Vallen!" Sebastian called.

"Yes, soldier?" he replied.

"What is the meaning of that…that box?" Sebastian asked.

"The king prefers all possible threats to be detained when on campaign."

"You're the one who set this man loose on our enemies! In so little time, Xavion slew more men while wearing rags than all of us could in armor!" Sebastian exclaimed.

"First off, soldier, he is a child."

"And next you'll tell me the seventy men he killed was beginner's luck?" Sebastian rebutted.

"You'll be pulling the king's chariot today," Vallen said.

Sebastian turned back to me. I bowed my head to show thanks for standing up for me. I stood alone at the back of the box, sinking into the dim light. I sat down and crossed my legs. I am meditating to banish anger from my mind. When the fighting starts, I cannot lose my judgment or distort my technique. I hope Jahvonis does not interrupt me. This is not a time for some lecture on fighting or some philosophical debate.

"How about a history lesson?" he asked.

"What is it now?" I replied.

"Before I begin, that is fine armor. Soruth would be proud," he complimented.

I continued to stare.

"This is not the first time that Nodin has been divided. It was happening even before my creation," Jahvonis said.

"Elaborate?" I requested.

"Before my father cast me onto Adrian Erik, Nodin incited a clash with Soruth at a trading port that was run by a Hongangan shipping company. The island housed a volcanic mount. Adrian and his Ember husband were there as vacationing civilians. They were caught in the crossfire of raining arrows. A massive arms deal went wrong and the products were put to use. Adrian's lover, *Black Leaf*, was caught in the explosion of a black pow-der bomb. He shielded Adrian by lying on top of the bomb. After the fighting ended, the dragon Ahneus rose from the volcano and laid waste to the land. Adrian was able to make it to the sea and lost consciousness. Nearly drowning, he was rescued by a Hongangan fisherman and taken back to Hongangou. There, in Adrian's grief, the Hongangan and Daichinian people pitied him."

Jahvonis continued, "To live with his despair, he learned many martial arts from the locals. He learned because the next time he was in danger, he will not be defenseless. For ten years, he trained day and night, remembering how both the nations of he and Black Leaf tore them apart. The pettiness and greed of both he condemned guilty.

"At age twenty-eight he left the people he loved in search of himself. He felt they had nothing more to offer. For they did more than he could ask. For months, Adrian sailed the seas. He returned to Soruth and Nodin, only to drown his heavy heart in the cold snow and hot sand. From there, he traveled to a more obscure place in the world. In time it would be named Sönderfall. When he journeyed further in, the fall forest showered him in black leaves. The breath of autumn respirated him. He spoke out into the land. *'I would give my sight to watch you sleep. I would give my voice to hear you call. I would give my legs to see you stand. I would die to see you live. I would say goodbye to hear hello. Black Leaf, I love you so!'*"

Jahvonis quoted as my eyes teared. He continued to tell the tale.

*****

Adrian then grasped a dagger and called out once more, "Jahveyis! Miolannis! Hear me, please! My world is damned and void. Why place me in this plane where love is a fantasy? Grant Black Leaf the mercy I cannot have! I cast aside thy gift of life for it no longer has meaning or purpose for me!" Adrian raised the dagger in the air to thrust it into his heart. As the blade came down, the soft, cold hand of Miolannis caught his. Jahveyis appeared in the next obsidian leaf-laden breeze. Adrian turned his sight to this person and asked, "Who are you?"

The goddess replied with "I am Miolannis, and this is Jahveyis."

"What fool do you take me for?" Adrian asked.

"A sad and bereaved young man, not a fool," the Dark Lord said. "Adrian, we have heard your pleas and watched your journey. I can assure you Black Leaf did not suffer then or now. Because of his sacrifice, he was permitted into our hall."

"Then please strike me down, allow me at his side!" Adrian begged.

"No…" Miolannis answered.

"I will not kill you," Jahveyis said.

"Then what can you do?" Adrian asked.

"All I can suggest is that you become a priest to our court," Miolannis stated.

"No, my lady, and forgive my refusal. But my life was ruined because two corrupt governments became greedy through the common people. Death would be my wish, for the longer I live, I suffer!"

"Adrian, do you hear thyself? You wish to die before us?" Miolannis asked.

"Yes! Jahveyis, crush my skull with thine mace and send me to death! I beg thee!" Adrian exclaimed.

"Please, child, do not request such things!" Miolannis said.

"What I request is mercy! Only with death can I have this!" Adrian said.

"Dammit no! Adrian, I will not slay you and surely not upon my feet nor in front of my wife! Can we make an arrangement?" Jahveyis asked.

"Such as what, my love?" Miolannis questioned.

Night fell, and a waning crescent moon rose. Jahveyis spoke once more.

"My child, many ill fates have assailed you, but I propose to you a new life! Fight for my wife and I. Become our Black Paladin! Fight for the victimized and castrate corruption from your home—and for this, I will grant you one wish within my power."

Adrian went to his knees looking at his palms and the nightly woods around him and the gods. He looked upon Miolannis as her moon shined bright off her white gown. A tear dripped from her left bright-green eye. He turned to Jahveyis as the Dark Lord's eyes changed from red to warm brown. Cold air blew all their hairs in the south wind.

"Should I do this, and if I fulfill this role, all I ask is that you bring my beloved back to me!" Adrian replied.

More tears came from the Moon Mistress, and Jahveyis searched deep within if his powers of necromancy were a fair trade."

"It shall be so!" replied the god.

He then stood above Adrian and lifted his mace, the mighty *Hellhammer*. "Starting tonight, you are our herald and bridge to the mortal world. From this day until the end, I dub thee... Jahvonis!" The Dark Lord knighted him. It went further than that. Since then, Adrian has been the adopted son of the Courtship of Obsidian Ice. Jahvonis was the first demigod!

*****

I listened intently with astonishment as well as some suspicion.

"You...a demigod? I don't know if I should be honored or frightened?" I replied.

"Someone like you, Xavion, shouldn't be frightened," he stated.

I felt more bumps in the road as the wheels rolled over them. The connection with Jahvonis was paused. I thought of Astrid once again, and I already miss her. I do hope Hamish is nice to her. The loud clunking and booming footsteps of the army became earthquaking. Hours passed until we came to a halt. A mob of confusion and distraught soldiers formed. Hearing the commotion inspired me to stand and look through the bars. I see a reddish mount upon a wall in front of the crowd. Johan's screams and shouts rose above our heads. The men moved aside as the king's chariot was pulled quickly to my cell.

"You!" Johan called to me. "Come out of there and clean up that mess! And be gentle!"

My pulse rang loudly in my ears, sweat dripped heavily. I walked slowly after leaving my kanabo in the mobile box. The mound of red grew larger in my vision.

"Xavion! Turn back!" Jahvonis shouted at me.

"Go back, Xavion!" Sebastian shouted from away.

What I see is an idol of heinous violence, mind games, and morbid psychopathy: the dismembered body of a woman. Cut into six pieces and arranged in the shape of the East Nodin hexagram. This woman is…

"Queen Helga," I said while trembling in my boots. Even though I've killed many men, never have I had to remove an innocent woman from the field. In war, a queen is as much of a target as any soldier. The level of hate and the extremity of East Nodin's warfare now changed the situation entirely. I started with each piece from head to legs. Johan called out for a large quilt of red cloth. The cloth was brought in case Johan was slain.

I placed each part to make Helga as whole as I could. I carefully wrapped her in the cloth. Silence fell upon the crowd as most tried to keep their stomachs intact. The stench of decay is the worst I have smelled. I was never sickened by violence before—but this is beyond violence. If Hakun's death was evil, then the destruction of his mother is unholy. How am I going to explain this to Astrid?

"Turn back, men. We are done here," Johan said aloud in tears. He stepped from his chariot, held his wife, and then laid her gently on the rails in front of him. I reentered my cell. The next few hours were grueling, but the worst has yet to come. I do not know if Johan will inform his daughter of her mother's passing; I surely do not want to. My cell held me within. The trauma of my mind is slicing deeper into my brain. Helga, that poor, defenseless woman, turned into a graven idol of the East. Why did I have to clean the mess? Why am I the scapegoat and excuse?

When I returned to my room, I changed into my clothes.

"Xavion," Sebastian said. "Astrid requests you in her room."

"What for?" I replied.

"She does not believe her father's words about her mother."

"First, Johan makes me pick up the pieces and then his daughter wants me to confirm it?" I sighed.

"I cannot make you go, but someone else may," Sebastian stated.

I stood up, and he escorted me to the princess's room. The royal guards and the king stood by awkwardly:

"Xavion, please tell my daughter what we found during our march to East Nodin," commanded the king.

Sebastian stood at my side. The king and his men stood to our right as Astrid remained standing with the face of dismay upon her. My nose started to run, and my eyes watered. My first few attempts to speak were delayed by stuttering. My imagination of Astrid's reaction is torturous.

"Astrid, as we made way to battle, our path was delayed by a body we found," I began as Johan's face melted with tears of his own. "When the face of the person was revealed to us. The body was…your mother's."

Astrid screamed at the tops of her lungs in a dramatic act of horror. I did not say how the body was arranged out of mercy. Johan and his men left the room, leaving the princess, Sebastian, Hamish, and myself. Minutes passed, Sebastian sat in a chair. At that time, I held Astrid close to me in a sideways hug upon her bed. Her tears dried upon my shoulder where her head lay.

"Sebastian, do you know where my mother is being kept?" asked Astrid.

"She is being prepared for her last rites. She will be placed in lava as Hakun was before. If I'm not mistaken, she is with a priest of the Courtship of Obsidian Ice, giving her the blessings of Miolannis and Jahveyis," Sebastian said.

"Can you three escort me down to the temple? I would like to say my farewell," Astrid requested.

"Yes, my lady," Sebastian replied.

We helped Astrid up and held her hands all the way downstairs. Short moments passed until we were crossing through the statued shrines of the Nine. All were kept tidy except for the shrine of Sareyus. When we passed the Shrine of the Courtship, Jahvonis's presence was especially potent. My head turned, and I heard him utter, "Mother, Father," under my breath. We came to the morgue. The undertakers were polite and loyal enough to allow Astrid to see her mother. Helga lay on a stone tablet and still wrapped in the red cloth she was placed in. What would be the normal rotting smell of carrion was covered up by the scent of flowers, but not enough.

"Here she is, Your Highness," the priest said.

Astrid began to reach for the cloth. I hoped she would not unwrap the queen. Her delicate fingers rested on the shoulder area of her mother.

"Mother," Astrid said as she wept, "I know I cannot see you, but I hope you can see me. I am here to see you before you depart to the hall of the gods. Give Hakun a big kiss and warm hug for me," Astrid mourned.

The following morning, Queen Helga Anastasia Edling was laid into the lava, which consumed her body. The king and princess sat on a small platform not far from the pit. The lava pit is one hundred yards to the left of the temple. West Nodin and all its noble families attended.

Those who could afford it wore a ruby necklace and red raiments. I remained at the sides of Astrid, Sebastian, and Johan. The king sat to my right, and Astrid sat to her father's left. There are five staves in front of the crowd which bore the Western Pentagram on top. Johan sat in his chair stiffly and silently. Astrid still cried hard, not just for the rites of her mother, but that she could not see the beautiful vigil before her. As I looked on, I saw Johan arise from his chair and spoke aloud to all around us.

"Everyone, please turn your gaze to me! In these past few months, we have all been wronged, pillaged, and harmed by those whom we once called friend. East Nodin reminded us that they are our enemy and why they hate us so. Some wonder where I was on the day East Nodin invaded our home. I and a company of guards traveled to the surface. We attempted to enlist the help of the Theranths. Now most of us remember the old wars that drove us underground. From our quest, we came home empty-handed. East and West have not been the best of allies and rightly so, but that does not justify them to slay our people! Starting today anyone affiliated with East Nodin will be put to the sword. Taxes will have a 5 percent increase to pay the stonemasons to rebuild our kingdom.

"The age of military service will be lowered from eighteen to sixteen. Prices of goods will be decreased by a quarter. Anyone who has enough space to house two soldiers will be compensated. The laws surrounding prostitution still stand as we need more men to defend this kingdom. The hours of the smiths will be increased."

As he continued his speech, I heard a "pinging" sound of something hitting the floor beneath me. It was a small needle with a piece of parchment wrapped around it. I grasped it in my hand and unraveled the parchment. Within is a note written in Sandish and signed by an *M*.

I translated and read it to myself, "When west is weak, long are the blood streaks." This "M"? Mataraves!

"And when we are fully recuperated, we will show East Nodin the meaning of wrath!" Johan finished. He gained some applause with his final statement.

I looked hastily around us. Where could he strike from? Are his men hiding among the crowd? Are they guards? My ears heard rushing footsteps. I turned my head around and saw a sword-wielding, brown-leathered ninja rushing toward me!

"Look out!" I shouted as I traded blows with the attacker. "Sebastian, get Astrid and Johan to safety!" I yelled as the crowd went into a mass panic. I dodged a sword strike that put the ninja close to the platform edge. I kicked him off and he landed on the ground. His sword flew from his grip into the air. I looked out to the panicking crowd, all but several dozen remained calm, and those same dozens tore off their red garments and revealed their uniform for the Hand of Doom, so far I'm counting sixty-six.

Sebastian, Astrid, and Johan fled. I hope they are safe. I am not wearing armor. The Jahvonis suit is in the palace. My only weapon is my jambiya. By my calculations, the odds are in my favor as far as the number's gain. The guards are not familiar with the Hand of Doom's combative trickery. A war horn was blown to alert any available guard or soldier to battle the enemy. Within seconds, I was engulfed in a combative mob.

I felt adrenaline and anger pumping my blood at high speeds. I was covered in blood before I knew it. From an opening in the crowd, I saw a rather muscular man outfitted with the Hand's brown leather. He wore a brass-colored mask. It is the swordsman whom I pushed aside during my previous escape. When he entered the mob, he exercised brute force with poetic finesse. He wielded his ko katana and slashed his way through the resistance. The guards and I were pushed into retreating. If I make it back to the palace, I can hopefully adorn the suit. The guards in their heavier armor could not outrun these attackers. Only half of what we started with made it to the palace. Any others were left defending themselves and the citizens. Oddly enough, I saw none of the Hand harming civilians. Forty of the nobles were slaughtered in the initial clash.

"They're only here for the nobles, soldiers, and Johan. Astrid!" I said to myself as I broke from the crowd.

I ran to my cell, and at the end of the hall, I saw pools of blood spilling from the brothel. The Hand is slaughtering the guards but let the civilians free. I don't have time, and it wouldn't be smart to put the suit on. I went inside my cell, and I grabbed the Mourningstar mace. I am still wearing my jambiya.

I burst down the hall and stormed the brothel. Five ninja slew their eighth guard. When I entered the house of promiscuity, I bludgeoned the ninja to death. I have a dilemma. Should I make haste to my suit? No, because it would take too much time. Should I aid the men in this battle? Should I make sure for the safety of King Johan, my friend Sebastian, and my beloved Astrid?

"I must protect those who need protecting!" I said to myself.

The staircase to the upper chambers is two halls away from here. The throne room is past the temple, but another hallway bridges all of them. That must be where most of the fighting is. I know not of a shortcut to Astrid's room, if she is there. If I can reach the staircase undetected, this would be easier. I do not know how many of the Hand are here. "No more thinking, I must act!"

I walked gently around the corner to the connection hallway, one ninja is standing guard with his back to me. My jambiya is useful for sneak attacks; my mace is tucked into my belt. Jahvonis taught me how to walk with stealth. I covered his mouth and used the jambiya to sever his throat. For good measure, I pierced the right side of his head. Blood has once more been painted on my face.

With no time to lose, I ran. This one hallway also connects several other rooms. The sounds of fighting still raged and masked any sound of my movements. In one room to my left, I see five guards who are outnumbered. The Hand is capturing several rooms at a time. Our numbers are decreasing by the minute.

The West Nodin military may outnumber the Hand of Doom, but West Nodin is outmatched. The training of these assassins is not conventional. In comparison, Nodinian armies march in ranks and charge at once. The way Mataraves has trained the Hand is called guerrilla warfare, or to put it bluntly, "Fight dirty, hit, and run."

I ran inside with my mace. I swung at one of the Hand to cause an opening for the men to turn the tide. One enemy swung his sword toward me which was blocked by a guard. It was Hamish. In the clash, I outmaneuvered the enemy. With grappling, I used their weapons against them. For example, one enemy failed to lock my arms in a hold. I reversed it. When face-to-face, I grabbed his knife and stabbed him twice in the bronchial region of the chest. Hamish spoke to me.

"Xavion, thank heavens you came!"

"Hamish, have you seen Sebastian, Astrid, or the king?" I asked.

"No, none of us have. We were only changing shifts when these fools barged in."

"How you fight these men is to corner or overpower them. You will all come with me. If we can clear the throne room and the front gate, we can hold the palace," I ordered.

"What are they after?" Hamish questioned.

"They're the assassins guild that Sebastian told you of. They're after the royal family!"

The guards and I proceeded to travel between rooms. I pursued this not by chance. If the greater threat is extinguished, then the king and princess are in less danger. Should Astrid and I both live, I am going to lay a kiss upon her red lips and be her "king."

With each rescued guard, our posse grew. Our numbers together are enough to overpower the lesser Hand members. If we come across Mataraves, I fear only I can stop him.

"The thirty of you split in two. Half watches the gate, the other half search for survivors. The rest of you come with me to secure the throne room!" I said aloud.

"Yessir!" most shouted aloud.

"Why are you barking orders?" one guard asked.

Another guard answered him with, "Because he saved our asses twice!"

We ran to the throne room. Each sprinted step and drop of sweat was heavily fatigued. Adrenaline seems to be our motivation, other than desiring to live. In an instant, the Hand began to retreat into the throne room, but what for? As we entered, a small host of guards failed to hold the room. Their slayer was, once again, the brass-masked man. He and his men turned and stood still in our direction.

Without warning, my host and I charged the room in fury. My eyes caught the attention of the brass-masked man. He spoke to me clearly as the mob of fighting surrounded us.

"You are stupid enough to fight without your suit?" he asked in a Gernic accent. I say this because he said "without" with a *v* sound. His voice is low, salty, and clear.

They must know who Jahvonis is, or at least he and Mataraves. I took a guess with my next sentence.

"I don't need a suit to stop you—Kane!" I uttered as his eyes narrowed.

The conflict became more intense as strength and speed once more did battle with and against each other.

Kane's sword expertise is amazing. If he was not trying to kill me, he would be a great sparring partner. In his eyes, I see the pleasure and frustration. Kane seems more than a man: he's too short for a Theranth but he fights like one without losing control. I was forced to use my mace to shatter one of his swords. He has a shorter katana on his waist, it is called a wakizashi.

"You fight full of bravery and desperation, though your skills are trivial!" Kane mocked as the battle momentarily ceased. He and his surviving men moved to a vacant part of the room. Kane shouted, "Fire!" From four entrances of the room, the Hand shot arrows into our crowd, wounding and killing several of us. I had an arrow embedded in my left thigh.

I lay on the floor, looking upward at the ceiling. I heard more footsteps in my area. Kane stood over me. He gripped his short sword in a thrusting position toward my head.

"I am sorry, Xavion. A worthy opponent you are, but this ends the only way it could," Kane stated as he thrust his blade. I moved quick enough for the short sword to miss my head; it pierced into my right shoulder.

I felt an abnormal sense of heat. The heat sparked one last reserve of adrenaline. I was able to kick Kane in the knee area, and I stood back up. My thigh wound still partially immobilizes me. I can't take on this many of the Hand and live. A blast of shuriken then found their mark onto my body. One struck me in the stomach. I turned toward the direction of their casting. The throne of the king is occupied by their caster, the Killing Bird, Mataraves. In front of him are three people. They are kneeling while bound and gagged. From left to right they are Sebastian, Astrid, and Johan. Only Astrid is not bruised or battered. Johan is the worst of all.

"Ah, yes, the Mourningstar! Valiant and brave! Xavion, the Soruthian who fights for his slavers," he said as he removed the gag from Johan's mouth.

"You turd-skinned son of a bitch! You think you can attack my home and get away with it? You're a dead man, dead!" Johan shouted.

Mataraves drew a tomahawk from his backside. Behind the blade is a pipe bowl. He bludgeoned the back of Johan's head. Mataraves kicked him down the stairs in front of the throne. A slow trail of blood formed a puddle on the floor. I spoke Sandish to Mataraves.

In the common tongue, I shouted: "Mataraves, stop! This madness must end! Whatever crimes Johan and his brother have done to us, the princess and these men have none! The lady is blind! Do not let her final moments be spent without seeing those before her. She and her guard are of no threat to you. Spare their lives and slay me! I have challenged your revolution! Should you harm my friends, I will unleash upon you tenfold! Let them go now!"

Mataraves looked at me in minor astonishment. He unsheathed his dagger and gripped a handful of Astrid's orange mane. He sliced her hair and kicked her down the stairs. She butted heads with her father. She is unconscious. Mataraves stuffed her hair in his pouch. I stayed knelt from the shuriken wounds to see my beloved lie on the ground. A massive roar was heard. The other half of my posse then stormed the room with what reinforcements they acquired. A frontal wall of shields blocked a wave of projectiles. In that opening, Sebastian thrust toward Mataraves, knocking him down. The battle resumed. Mataraves began beating Sebastian with the pipe bowl of the tomahawk. In the skirmish, one of the guards dropped a water pouch. If water healed me before, hopefully, it will again. First, I pulled the arrow and shuriken from my body. When the water dripped down my esophagus, my wounds healed enough for me to fight. Mataraves must die!

I fought my way toward Sebastian. Kane did as well. Another guard jumped in front to delay Kane. I ran toward Mataraves and ended his assault on Sebastian by tackling him. In my anger, Mataraves used my techniques against me. My mace fell and lay on the floor. My jambiya is in my right hand. This man is toying with me, humiliating me in front of the people I protect! I tried my hardest to slash him.

At the most unfortunate time, Kane broke free from the fighting and kicked me across the face. Next, he struck me with my mace. A large gash bled on my forehead. Once again, I am out cold. I live but I am defeated.

Chapter 8

In Xavion's View

I began to come to my senses and awoke from unconsciousness. I am in my bed. I hear no sounds of conflict. I do not feel in danger.

"I'm glad you're awake!" Sebastian said. He is not as hurt. He has bruises from his beating. He has purplish welts on his left cheek. He is sitting next to my forge.

"Sebastian, what happened? The Hand of Doom? Where's Astrid?"

"Slow down, Xavion. One answer at a time. General Vallen told me after you and I were defeated, a larger band of guards charged in but most of the Hand of Doom escaped. The king and Astrid's wounds are being tended to."

"How did they infiltrate the crowd without being seen?" I asked.

"The guards believe the Hand stole the raiments which concealed their armor. No one would've known who they were."

"How did they escape?"

"From what I was told, they used these small pellets that released smoke. In their hidden whereabouts, they rushed their way out. We are trying to determine where they went," Sebastian informed.

"They were here to kill the king and princess," I stated.

"I doubt that. If they wanted to kill Johan and Astrid, they wouldn't have fled. They must have had another goal?"

"Like what?"

"To get to Jahvonis?" Sebastian suggested.

"Why would Mataraves go through all that trouble to get to Jahvonis? Why would he not kill Astrid and Johan while he had the chance?"

"I don't know, Xavion. I must go now. Rest easy."

"Good day," I replied. I turned to my books to pass some time.

"Xavion," Jahvonis called.

"What do you have for me now?" I questioned.

"To check on your well-being," Jahvonis stated.

Within my mind, I continued to look upon him in a scornful gaze. I am expecting a lesson from him. "And to also offer…a confession."

"What confession do you have?" I asked.

He began to speak; and his voice became less deep, more understandable, and clear.

"When the Courtship gave me my mission, I spent several years scouring the lands to fight crime. I inspired women and men of all kinds to do the same. I gathered all who would follow. They asked and pleaded that I train them. All across the world, they were organized. Not just in combat but in ritual.

"With many of these practices, we set out to police the world by all necessary means. We used assassinations to rid any and all corrupt world leaders, politicians mostly."

Jahvonis's words are curious. What he is implying angered and dumbfounded me.

"Xavion, in my lifetime, I created and led the Hand of Doom."

My ears rang loud like sticks upon the medicine drum. My anger and confusion are stupefying.

"That makes no sense! That can't be true!" I shouted.

"I assure you I am telling the truth," Jahvonis replied.

"How could the Hand of Doom survive? You said you perished in the Second Armageddon. If you died, then how could *your* organization survive?"

"My father does mysterious things, some to balance the good in the world and others for his personal gain. Out of all the policing in the world, perhaps Jahveyis preferred one guild of assassins?" Jahvonis said.

"If the Hand has regained their international status, then the earth is at risk! Wait, if they're your guild, why are we fighting them?"

"When I created the Hand of Doom, they followed my words as law. Each chapter bent to my will out of respect. Seldom did I ever use my powers to discipline. Those who knew Jahvonis is the son of the Dark Lord thought twice before challenging me. I admit I sought to create the perfect world without crime or war, but the only way to have a perfect world is to control it. I doubt this incarnation of the Hand knows of their previous existence. Perhaps things I took part in were also reincarnated? I hope not. Jado and my father would only know," he stated.

"There's still a hole in all of this. I learned from you in a book. If you died so long ago, why do modern people know you?"

"To clear that up, I must reveal Jado's secret. The Lord of Knowledge in some way is the most powerful of the Immortals. Politically, he is a single party. With each of the Armageddons that passed, Jado indiscriminately notes all world events and truthfully documents them. He is also in charge of writing the Hallowed Holds (which have been rewritten twice). Whenever the earth is rebuilt, Jado passes the knowledge forward and hopes the mortals will learn from their mistakes. The gods wipe out mortals as the earth continues from where it left. This is a mystery where we need the help of each other."

I took my turn to reply, "Why not ask your father for the answers we seek? With you being his son, would he oblige to help?"

"I died along with the Second Life. Who do you think condemned me?" Jahvonis struck me once more with the curiosity of his divine family.

"After all I accomplished, Jahveyis and my negligent mother chose to betray me. It was they who chose me to purge crime from the world! With the Hand of Doom, I was doing that. We had the continents cower at our name. All crimes that were committed by civilians, service personnel, and politicians were punished. They saw my methods as 'questionable.' They chose to destroy the world instead of having their emissary govern it. It was the Hand and I who were warring with the six dragons who bewitched people to their will. As you can imagine, Mustasurma was a great enemy of mine," Jahvonis spoke clearer than earlier.

I can hear a normal man's voice in the overtones. He has a Noric accent.

This is maddening! The being before me accomplished so much in his life. I did not know the full extent of what I swore an oath to. The human ignorance of which we are destined to feel has drawn a large point on the wall. Jahvonis implies he wants to lead once again. His stories go deeper than blood feuds; it is a spiritual rivalry of heaven and earth!

"I did more good in a day than they have in a year of their eternal lives! They chose double genocide of their children instead of me governing. Jahveyis spared Mustasurma because he thought he deserved mercy. I remember my failure to this day.

"Hell was my home then, far from the gods and heaven. In hell, I became 'royalty' for being the heir to the Dark Throne. Adrian Erik died on the earth, but the spirit of Jahvonis lives as long as the name exists. My life force can die like the gods if our names are not remembered. My name in the Hallowed Holds keeps me alive, and when you reforged the suit, I lived once more in a physical sense. I chose you, Xavion, as my second chance to atone for my past sins and prevent them from destroying the future! That is why the Hand of Doom must be repealed. Only you and I can do this!"

"You cannot believe I alone can help you save an entire planet. I am just a young man, not even twenty," I replied.

"Do you really think you're just a man? How you can kill so many at a time and come out close to woundless? No average man has more than one vision or can climb walls without equipment. You are far more than 'just a man,' you are the next breed of humanity! It is who you are to protect and serve those you love. Sebastian is your dearest friend and Princess Astrid is the love of your life."

"Jahvonis, you are right on several points. I did not know the disdain for your parents was so deep and lasted multiple lifetimes. I am sorry for the losses of yours. What more can we do as far as the Hand of Doom are concerned?"

"Mataraves. He leads this chapter of the Hand. Without him rallying them, they should disperse. Mataraves is deadly, and he'll be hunted by West Nodin now. If we can prevent his future, West Nodin will have one less threat. By the way, there's a visitor at your cell," Jahvonis said as the trance within my brain broke to see General Vallen and Guardsman Hamish.

"Sir Xavion," Vallen said.

"Princess Astrid is awake, and she is calling for you," Hamish added.

"Do you wish to answer?" Vallen asked.

"I will go to her," I replied as I stood up for them to escort me out.

"I am glad to see you live, Hamish. I recall an arrow struck you?" I asked.

"Yes, I am alive, Xavion. Indeed an arrow struck me in the shoulder. When I fell, I was knocked unconscious from my helmet hitting the floor. Thank you once more for serving us," Hamish stated.

"I and reinforcements were the ones who grouped with the rest of your posse and charged the room. That was when the Hand of Doom escaped," Vallen admitted.

"Well, I am in your debt, General," I said.

"No, Xavion, I am to you. You saved us during the Encroachment, you taught Hamish and the guards how to fight the Hand, and you held them off long enough for help to arrive. If only the king understood that," Vallen complimented.

I did not speak again until we came to the room of the princess. "Princess!" I exclaimed as she lay bandaged and under her blankets.

"Xavion? Oh, Xavion, thank heavens you're alive!" she said aloud.

I knelt down at her side to hold her delicate hand.

"What is going on?" I heard Sebastian's voice ask. He came from behind.

"General, is there a problem?" Sebastian questioned.

"No, Sebastian. The princess wished for her aide," Vallen replied.

"If you permit, may I take over here?" Sebastian requested.

"Permission granted, Sebastian," Vallen stated.

"Sebastian, may I join you in your watch?" Hamish asked.

"What for?"

"I would rather be closer to our savior. I can also help with the lady," Hamish said.

"Very well, Hamish, your permission is granted," Astrid said.

Over the next few hours, the guards and I watched over the princess. I had thoughts that another attack could happen at any time. The more times my life is in danger, the more I value Astrid's and care less for my own. Other than Sebastian, Astrid is what motivates me to survive. I can never truly be with Astrid as long as these negative familial and political strains are linked to her.

If she has Hakun's dream of common life, then I am happy to share it. In these few months, I confess to myself that I am in love with the princess of West Nodin. While mixed relationships are nothing new, they are beautiful every time. In the moments when I bathe Astrid, I find it more artistic and less erotic. I enjoy the contrasts between us. My multi-colored skin with her snow complexion. My dark hair next to her orange locks. I wish she could see. I also worry she would disown me for my Soruthian appearance. Thoughts like that are common when someone is a part of a minority. It's one more thing Mataraves and I have in common.

After all this, I bear no hatred toward him but he sparked my anger when he cut Astrid's hair. I don't know what sick plan he has for it, but he will not get away with it. The next time we battle, I will slay him, with or without Jahvonis's consent. While looking at Mataraves's past, I understand it is tragic but I will not let it cloud my judgment. I do not understand why he did not kill me? I was defeated by him and Kane, yet he spared me. Kane is not an average man. He's too good to be second-in-command. When we fought, his maneuvers were similar to mine. He hits hard and moves fast, more than Mataraves in my opinion. If he is better, then why is he not the Hand's leader? When I fought him, my vision distorted once more and I could see his blood flow. To my calculations, 40 percent of it was human. I saw the remaining sixty as Theranth blood.

I assume this is a Soruthian method of enhancement. Kane must have lost enough blood that some of it had to be replaced. My theory of how this happened is that Kane was a soldier in the Theranth Wars. He must have been greatly wounded, and the doctors had no choice but to replace his lost blood with Theranth blood. Over time as he healed, the Theranth blood became dominant.

Theranth blood acts as a super enhancement when injected into humans. Since Theranths were designed to be powerhouses from the start, putting blood from one Theranth into another offers no enhancement. For humans, this comes at a risk. The Theranth blood has to be the same blood type as the receiver. I learned through my "blood vision" that each blood type reacts differently from person to person. The doctors got lucky, I guess.

I have to start taking the fight to the Hand of Doom, but I'll need the guards' help. I thought it would help if the guards arranged a meeting with Jahvonis. If Sebastian could get a few dozen guards to follow him to a rendezvous point, I'll be there wearing the suit so we can plan to wipe out the Hand of Doom. It will have to wait until we are permitted to leave Astrid.

The princess fell into a slumber.

"Hamish, can you stay by the princess for a moment?" Sebastian asked.

"Yes, sir," replied Hamish.

"Xavion, a word please?" Sebastian requested.

I followed him to a remote place on the floor. We both checked we were not being followed.

"What are we going to do about the Hand?" he asked.

"I thought you could arrange a meeting between the guards and Jahvonis. From there, we can plan to fight the Hand more appropriately," I replied.

"Did you not see how the Hand nearly wiped us all out? Even with the advice you gave the men, we were hilariously outmatched! Those ninja kicked our asses!"

"If they wanted to kill us all, they would have. After Kane (the masked man) said I needed my suit, he confirmed that my identity is no secret to them. After their barrage of arrows, Mataraves heard me out when I spoke to him. He could be trying to draw Jahvonis out, but the question is why?" I stated.

"What could Mataraves gain by attracting Jahvonis? If he wants to die, then he's made enough enemies!"

"I don't know what the true intent of the attack was. If all I've learned of the Hand is true, they will never stop and next time they won't retreat."

Sebastian heeded my warning. "All right, I suggest you have it on the roof of the meadery. From there, you can use the door from the last time that goes to the Hand. I'll try to get Hamish stationed to a group of men. How will you get to the meadery?" he asked.

"I'll find a way. With what I've learned from Jahvonis, sneaking onto a rooftop is child's play."

"All right, I'll grab Hamish and assemble guards to discuss it. With both Johan and Astrid out of commission, General Vallen has been chosen as a caretaker to the royal house. While we are doing this, you must stay with the princess," Sebastian said and departed.

When we returned to Astrid's room, Sebastian called Hamish away so they can consult Vallen. I sat down in a chair to the side of Astrid's bed. As she turned in my direction, she breathed softly. She looks so warm and comfortable in her bed. Her delicate eyelashes and thin orange eyebrows kept me in a trance. I continued to watch her sleep. A warm ticklish feeling arose in my stomach. As I gazed upon this fair and gorgeous woman, I began to perspire. My sweat caused the strange white smoke to surface once more. For a half hour, Astrid was engulfed in a warm and sweet-scented cloud. I noticed a slight smile coming onto her face. She must be in a pleasant dream. She woke suddenly and voiced an offer to me.

"Xavion, would you join me in my bed? You have worked hard, and I feel you deserve some refreshment. I ask only that you rest comfortably."

"My lady, I feel it may not be appropriate for a slave to join a princess in the same bed," I replied.

"When you are with me, you are a person, not property. I ask this not for a sexual matter, but to share what I have plenty of," she replied.

"If you wish it, then I am honored to oblige."

Astrid moved over. I lay on top of her blankets.

"Please go under, the blanket won't move with you on top of it," Astrid stated.

As I climbed under, I could see her smirk enlarging. The smoke from my body thickened. The room is hidden within itself. I am trying to not gaze at Astrid.

The hormones of my youth are overwhelming. It became worse when she laid her orange scalp on my chest and her hand over my stomach. With her head on my chest, my heart danced. I breathe heavily. Despite her words, she is clearly trying to seduce me. My body accepts, and my brain is refusing. If I sexually slept with the princess, I run the risk of having an ax to our throats or to impregnate her. I hate to say it, but I cannot allow this to happen.

Astrid continued to caress me and moved on to kissing me upon my face and body. When I looked at her, I noticed a clearer and greener reflection of myself in her irises. Somehow she can pinpoint where she is kissing. I am consumed in my heart's desire for this forbidden fruit. I joined Astrid's kiss with my own. As the moment became romanticized, it grew in intensity. I gently fondled Astrid's stomach. As wrong as this is, I feel no shame or regret.

"Xavion, thank you for everything. Thank you for your compassion, care, honor, and gratitude. You are the best man I have ever known, and I will always love you!" she said.

That was the greatest compliment I could've heard.

"I love you more," I replied.

I know I should refuse but the conflict of my conscience is damnable. This is a woman who shares a mutual affection and is willing to risk her life to have me. For the next hour, we remained kissing and softly talking. The topics were, if she and I led West Nodin, what we would name our children, and how we could better the people. We fell asleep. When she faced the wall, I placed my arm around her abdomen and breathing lightly down her neck and ear.

The next morning, I awoke while still holding onto Astrid. It is still early. Dawn, I believe. I could not stay much longer; a guard could come in at any moment. I cannot leave unless another guard takes my place. I returned to my chair. I am watching the room. I looked under the bed for intruders. Four more hours went, and I heard a knock on the door.

"Who is it?" I asked.

"It is Guardsman Hamish, may I enter?" he said.

I got up and opened the door. It is truly him.

"Yes, what is it, Hamish?" I said.

"General Vallen is finished meeting with the guards. He also has relieved you of your duty for now, and he trusts you will return to your room. I will watch over the princess until then," Hamish informed.

"All right, good luck, Hamish. You've been a good help, and I appreciate it," I complimented.

"It is the least I can do for the man who has saved my life more than once!" he said. Hamish and I shook hands.

I began my journey back to my cell. For once, I am free to go unattended. I drew a few eyes because I do not have a guard beside me. It feels that I am walking home after a hard day's work. I entered my cell and sat on my bed.

"Xavion... Xavion are you in there? May I come in?" I heard Sebastian whisper.

"Yes," I replied as he unlocked it.

"The Caretaker has supported meeting with Jahvonis, but he doesn't know how to contact him," Sebastian said.

"Tell the Caretaker that Jahvonis will meet him on top of the meadery tonight," I said.

"I will, but he will not go himself. He must watch the throne, and I've been placed with Astrid. Hamish has been put with the group to accompany Jahvonis," Sebastian informed.

"So be it," I said as Sebastian left.

Sebastian returned a short while later. After my daily routine with Astrid and Sebastian, I dressed in the suit and made my way to the meadery. How I got there is too long and complicated to note. I stood in the center of the rooftop in the direction of the door. The hood covered the cowl.

"Jahvonis, can you hear me?" I said.

"What is it?" he replied.

"You know someone like Mataraves won't stop unless he dies, nor will the rest of the Hand," I replied.

"I realize that now, Xavion. I wish they could be persuaded to change, but with men of this caliber, putting them down is merciful for the innocent. Tonight, Jahvonis slays once more!" he stated.

"I have a question, why is the Hand of Doom also called Black Hole Sun?" I asked.

"The Black Hole Sun is a magical spell that I created in the Second Life. The original Hand of Doom of the four continents would use magic to conjure a black vortex that blotted out the sun. This was going to trap the dragons in an empty void. Thus, the spell was named the Black Hole Sun. It was never cast. I only know how to safely cast it," Jahvonis said.

I heard a knock at the door. As it opened slowly, I picked my head up and gazed at Hamish. He is with a host of guards.

"By the gods!" he said.

They each came through the door, twenty in total. I glared at each one as they stood in a crescent formation.

"Is this all Vallen Edling could spare?" I asked in a deep tone.

"Yes. The Caretaker found us expendable. Please try to understand," Hamish said.

"Gentleman, welcome to our convocation. I assume you all know of me?"

"You're the Vigilante, the Son of the Courtship," a spectacle guard said on my left.

"We have a common enemy. The Hand of Doom has assailed your home and held your palace under siege. Even that Soruthian boy could not help you," I stated.

"Watch your mouth! Xavion is not just some Soruthian boy. If it weren't for him, we wouldn't be having this 'convocation'! And where the hell were you anyhow? If you're the vigilante, why didn't you help us?" Hamish exclaimed.

The guards agreed with him.

"It is no offense to say what someone is when the proof is physically evident. I was not there on time. Consider this meeting and my plan as repentance. There's a door beneath this building. I have a key that will open the lair of the Hand. I need your help to destroy their leader," I replied.

"You all saw how they manhandled us last time. It's suicide!" a frightened guard exclaimed.

"You have survived worse attacks. It's not the size of the army, it's how you command it," I said.

"All right. We'll follow your orders. Please grant us a prayer on behalf of the Courtship. We ask them to allow us to live past this day," Hamish requested.

They knelt to the floor. I unsheathed my kukri and held it straight into the air. I spoke a suitable prayer in the West Nodin language.

In translation, I said, "*Lord Jahveyis! Hear the plea of these brave men as they near the journey into battle. Please spare their lives, delay their end and show them not to fear death, for we will face you in the end. Amen.*"

When I finished the prayer, I waved my kukri from left to right and sheathed it. "Follow me," I stated.

The guards and I lined in single file and traveled back to ground level. We startled a few people on our way out. When we entered the back alley, I looked down and the keyhole is gone.

"Damn it!" I whispered. I returned to my deep tone and spoke. "The keyhole is gone!" I said.

"What happened to it?" Hamish exclaimed.

I looked back at the keyhole. It is filled with smelted ore and sealed closed.

"I don't know of another way to find them," I said.

"We'll have to travel the tunnels then. There's a pair of them by the gate. One of them runs underneath here," Hamish said.

It's our only bet, and we followed through. I chose one tunnel that went in a loop beneath us and continued straight. After about a mile, we were under the meadery. This tunnel began to darken. The few torches the guards brought are dimming. After one burnt out, Hamish lit another. I can see fine, but the guards cannot. For another hour, the torch illuminated the dark. Minutes later, I saw a small person. They are clothed in brown leather. They threw a shuriken at me. I caught it between my fingers. I realize they are no ordinary short person but a child. I know this child, it is Alastair!

Alastair ran as I chased after him. The guards pursued me. Alastair ran faster. From his body language, he does not seem scared; he's leading us! I debated if we should stop, but this is our only lead to Mataraves. We continued to chase after Alastair in a prolonged track. I've never had to pursue a child before. Running through these dark tunnels is dangerous: if the torches fail us, the guards will be trapped down here. At least with my strange sight, we can survive.

After several yards, Alastair jumped across a small ravine. I lunged forward and gripped onto his hood. He was quick enough to grab a dagger from his boot and tried to stab me. The blade did not pierce my cuirass but gave him time to run.

"You won't get me, you geezer," he shouted as he sprinted further into the darkness.

I could not follow him yet because the other guards need to cross the ravine. They may need help.

"All of you, be brave! The ravine is very narrow, you must jump!" I said to motivate them.

It only took a few minutes for each one to hop across. After that, we resumed our search. Ten more yards went by until we came to a dead end. I felt around for a clue. Maybe there's a keyhole. After a few moments, I found another keyhole, one of the same pendant design as before.

"Men, I do not know what awaits us beyond this door. I thank you all for coming this far," I said as I placed the pendant in the hole and turned it.

Dust and dirt fell in front of me as the wall shaped into a vertical rectangle and opened backward and up. On the other side is our goal. A host of twenty-five of the Hand of Doom was waiting for us. In the back are Mataraves, Kane, and that runt, Alastair.

"Jahvonis, welcome!" Mataraves said aloud.

As I glare through the cowl, he wears a choker made from Astrid's hair.

"The vigilante is forced to find help? From the law no less? How humorous!" Kane mocked.

"Mataraves, you have much to answer for!" Hamish shouted. The ninja drew their weapons and awaited orders.

"Hold it! We have a rare opportunity," Kane began. "The last time Jahvonis was here, he shoved me aside in his escape. I want to know how one man, an amateur no less, escaped all of you? Let's make this interesting. Jahvonis, if you can beat me, your men will be spared and you will fight Mataraves with no interference," Kane stated.

Mataraves's eyes turned to Kane. Something feels off about this.

"Why the tournament-style delays? If you wanted to complete your mission, then you would've killed Johan and his daughter at the palace," I said.

"You're right, we could have killed him, but why rush it? Right now Johan believes his closest allies are plotting against him. After every tragedy from his brother's invasion, his son's death, and his wife's fleshy gallery, it was ideal to strike when he's mentally unstable and vulnerable. Johan, El Rey de la basura, his paranoia will bring his kingdom low. Consider this tournament as a sport," Mataraves stated.

"This room is too small for us. I bet this is another route to the arena where Alastair was beaten. If so, it will be a suitable place for our duel."

"So be it! Men, let them pass," Mataraves commanded.

The ninja moved aside to allow us through. My hunch was right, the goose chase Alastair lead us on was an alternate route to the arena from before. As we walked in, Mataraves sat on his stone seat and Kane stepped into the arena.

The Hand stood on the side of Mataraves; the guards stood with me on the opposite side. Kane wears armor like mine. Instead of all black, his is brown leather with a brass-colored mask. Why does he wear it? I assume the metal is painted steel. He has no hood and wears a belt with six pouches. On his left hip, he wears a ko katana. On the right side of his lower back, I see a tanto dagger.

To recap, my weapons are my kukri, shuriken stars, senbon needles, and my ringed dagger. Kane's sword has a reach advantage. To slow him down, I must get in close. The shorter blades I use have a speed advantage. Though Kane's sword is designed for slashing, my kukri is intended for piercing and chopping. His sword needs two hands to be wielded correctly while my kukri is single-handed.

Kane and I circled each other while studying our movements. He threw a punch as I caught his arm. We began a grappling bout with techniques from judo, jiu-jitsu, and freestyle wrestling. Kane is taller than me; his leverage is an advantage with grapple-based martial arts.

After ten minutes of Kane's technical expertise, he dropkicked me with so much force and fluidity that I groaned in pain. The blunt impact of my chain mail against my chest felt like a mace. Kane landed on his feet after the dropkick. Round one is his victory.

"You're well trained for a young man," Kane stated as I resurfaced into a guard stance.

Kane drew his tanto in a reverse grip. He lunged forth and tried to cut my throat. I evaded the slash and kneed his groin. I gripped his right hand to try and disarm him. Kane struck with his left to break the grapple. He then landed a 360-degree spin kick that dazed me.

This is very difficult. Up close, he can out grapple me, and at a distance, his kicks are near lethal. In a split second, Kane went for a barrage of slashes. I used my forearm blades to bind his tanto and punched his throat. From the impact, I disarmed him and broke the tanto blade after casting it at the stone wall. Kane headbutted me. I hand chopped his throat, banged his head on the wall, and finally roundhouse kicked his ribcage.

Kane quickly drew his ko katana and began using techniques from Daichinian kenjutsu. I quickly tossed a shuriken to buy time. He went for a decapitation. I countered with my forearm blades, drew my dagger, and sliced in the pit of his left elbow. I grounded him, and nonfatally pierced his mask with my dagger. He reversed our positions after a groin strike. He bashed me with the pommel cap of his sword. I rolled over and drew my kukri. My dagger is still stuck in his mask. He removed it and tossed it away.

Our masks are almost blade proof. My dagger nearly broke in his mask. Kane's swordsmanship with the ko katana is impressive. I wonder if he has ever seen a kukri before. My kukri is possibly the same weight as his sword. We are now in a conflict of clashing blades. Kane has much more reach while I am able to hook his sword out of the way. This allows me to close the distance and prevent Kane from winding up his strikes.

For three minutes, our blades clashed. Kane is proficient in kenjutsu. Where did he learn it? My eyes once more cycled through the different visions while I underwent an energy boost. In seconds, I am now outmaneuvering Kane. He is struggling to keep up. He is getting angry, and it weighs his technique down. Our sword fight encompassed the arena.

Kane swung. I caught his sword in my forearm blades and broke it. I punched him with the kukri knuckle dusters and repeatedly bludgeoned his mask with my pommel. He went for a punch. I dodged it and hip tossed him to the ground. I climbed on top of him with the edge of my kukri angled at his throat.

"Yield!" I growled.

Kane lay with his leg arched. He is bleeding minorly.

In the stands, I heard Alastair shout, "You bastard Ponce!"

A guard began screaming in pain. Kane saw this opening and stabbed me on the right side of my gluteus maximus. Our battle brought us near my dagger. Kane threw me off him.

"Kill them all!" Hamish shouted as the guards rushed into combat with the Hand of Doom.

As the fighting ignited in the stands above, Mataraves rushed down and moved Kane to safety. As I bled from my backside, I tried to capture one of them. My limp running up the arena stairs was met with a shuriken grazing my mask, which caused me to fall to the floor. The unarmored parts of my arms and thighs were pierced by sharp pins. I read about them before. They're called *makibishi* spikes, a type of caltrop used to floor opponents when they are stepped on. As I looked up, the Hand of Doom were retreating. Those who escaped made their way down a hall to the far left of the stone seat. The guards went to aid me instead of chasing after the Hand. "No, get them!" I shouted gutturally.

When they chased after them, I rolled and tumbled back down the stairs. Some of the makibishi went deeper inside me. I had no choice but to pull each one out. I drank the emergency water pouch to heal my wounds. I went into a fetal position to cover my face along with my hood. I reached for the pouch, loosened the cowl, and quickly downed the water. My wounds closed enough for me to join in the chase. I frantically bolted down the hall and passed several rooms. I could see the mob of guards still chasing the Hand.

The hallway went into a tunnel. The guards lit their remaining torches as they ran. The Hand are many feet ahead of us. I see a large horn built into the earth. Mataraves is blowing into it. A cavernous bass note rang through the rock, causing it to quake. The archers from the Hand rained arrows upon us to buy Mataraves time. The guards who had shields formed a wall to block the projectiles. My haste is in vain. The area between Mataraves and the guards collapsed and created a canyon between us. When I made it to the edge, Mataraves looked at me from across and ran back to the assassins. We failed again to capture the Hand of Doom.

I stood on the edge of the canyon that Mataraves created. The guards held their shield wall still. Once more I failed West Nodin and to avenge Astrid's harm.

"What the fuck was that?" Hamish exclaimed.

"It was an old stone horn from our ancestors. The damn thing made me shit my trousers! It has probably been here since the first excavations," another guard yelled.

I never knew that a bass note could crack stone. More importantly, how could they have designed this? The horn must have built into a resonant area of the rock that would vibrate to the floor and crack it. This must have been an emergency escape plan, but now their hideout is revealed. Could there be clues to where they went? As we reentered their domain, I questioned the guards on how the commotion started.

"What happened? How did the battle begin?"

"The child threw one of those star things and slew the new recruit," Hamish hastily informed.

"Everyone, go into their lair. Search it for any clues," I said.

The hideout is grim and vast in size. The memory of my first escape repeated in my head. Each guard searched a room. When I chose mine, I noticed two specific door decorations. They are the skulls of a raven and a crow.

"This must be his room," I said in reference to Mataraves.

I resisted my hesitation and forced the door open. The home of my enemy is adorned with several weapons. There are many ceramics of Sandish and Ember design. His name is labeled as the artist. His armory contains many Yazjian weapons. Most of the inventory are of the bo staff. He has more metallic staves than the traditional wooden ones.

I see an unlocked chest in the corner. I chose to look into it. Inside are several scrap papers with avian symbols on them. At the bottom of the chest are two books. The first book has a name on the first page. It reads, "*Santiago Mataraves Salvador*."

This is his diary! I thought in glee, but the next book caused me to shiver and sweat. The next book is a black grimoire. It is bound in leather and without a label. Inside on the parchment is a horrific face drawn in black ink. The face is reptilian with forward-facing, down-curved horns. Jahvonis spoke the name of this image: "Mustasurma."

My search for once gave interesting results. The grimoire felt evil. I couldn't help but feel like a child tasting their first sugary piece of fried dough. I still felt timid, but I know this can't be left in the wrong hands.

"Xavion, when we get back to the palace, make sure these books don't go missing," Jahvonis said.

After our search in the hideout, the guards and I returned home. We gently carried the deceased with the intention of a proper funeral. Most of the evidence they found were weapons, progress reports, and employer documents. I retrieved my dagger during our exit. When we reached West Nodin, the guards reported back to Vallen and sent another patrol to garrison the hideout. I remained in the caves until I was alone and free to go back to my cell.

My cell is dark. I entered, shut the door, unsuited, and sat in silence. My legs are crossed upon my bed. The books are at my sides. I wore my jambiya on my sash belt. The brothel at the end of the hall is silent. There are no horrid screams or obnoxious parties. My eyes soon graced the pages of the Killing Bird's diary. The first date was twelve years ago, around the time he was stolen from Soruth. He is the firstborn of a Sand father and Ember mother (a common mixed union).

He has two younger brothers. The middle child is *Matando*, and the youngest is *Draven*. Mataraves goes to explain the Soruthian slave trade. The person behind it is a Barkish man named *Laden Awad*, who has an arrangement with Aylund.

Mataraves briefly mentions the *Allied Sand Nations of Soruth*. From north to south, they are the *Mexic*, *Ayam*, and *Inco*. "Mexic" is pronounced "Mesheek." Matando and Draven were being trained early to be jaguar and eagle warriors. Mataraves then describes how his father's Mexic and mother's Cherok lineages represented drastic differences among philosophy. Yet his parents were happily married and in love.

Mataraves talks more of his father. The father, to my astonishment, is Emperor Montzu, the king of the Mexic Nation! Mataraves was next in line to the throne!

His mother is named Red Tail Spirit Woman, which was simplified to Red Tail. She was not of noble blood. She was a commoner who immigrated from the Ember Isle.

Mataraves admits he had no original intention to be a warrior for his nation. That path was removed when he was kidnapped by Barkish slavers while in the jungle. He sacrificed his freedom to protect his brothers when their game of tag went wrong. His last image was of his brothers retreating to gather help for his rescue; they came too late.

Next Mataraves explains how he met Master Kane and became an assassin. I suppose Kane must have trained Mataraves and then allowed him to lead the Hand. He briefly alludes to a chance meeting with Mustasurma. It was through a spiritual emissary.

One log is of despair and grief.

Even though my past as a slave is not my fault, I've been a terrible person because of it. Each time my tomahawk lifts someone's hair, I pull a thread off my soul. While my middle name is my identity to the beast, my name to the gods is Santiago. I have become one of the most feared men in Nodin but it gives me no purpose nor reason to live. I see each battle scar from my missions as a reminder that I am damned to join the Dragon in Hell. The first time Kane took me under his wing, I knew I would die at the hands of another Assassin. When you pledge yourself to the Hand of Doom, you live and die with it.

June 18: Recently during Alastair's duel, I began to wonder if I can live up to Kane's leadership. Alastair is arrogant, short-tempered, and immature (even for a child). All these months I have never been so depressed, the memories of mi familia and how heavily I wanted to kill Aylund those years ago. Kane is motivated by his late wife to kill people. His sadness goes deeper than that.

As Alastair was defeated, he chose to yell out and insult me. I had to discipline him as if I was his father. My wallowing ended when this man in a Ninja-style wardrobe fell into the arena. I knew he was the Jahvonis from the grimoire. He was captured and held for some time. Through his interrogation, I learned he is not an assassin. I falsely projected myself as an anti-Nod bigot to anger him. He swore he would kill me.

I no longer wish to live but I will not subject myself to suicide. If this man is not in league with the Hand then he must slay me in order to free me. I will put up a fight but he must willingly kill me. When I received his death threat, I beat him with my Bo but I was aiming at the chains that restrained him. He eventually made his escape and yet I never caught the name of the man behind the mask. Jahvonis spoke my modern native dialect quite fluently. Could he be one of the other Soruthian slaves who accompanied me? This will require further investigation.

We escaped, battered the king, slew his men, and struck terror into the people. The best however was when I confirmed Jahvonis' identity. I figured he is Soruthian and a soldier. He loves the princess. His reaction when I cut her hair and kicked her to the ground was priceless! He'll find his way to me for sure. If I can fight him alone then my death will be granted and I will be free from the Hand. I care not if my soul is damned, no life is worth living if it's full of death.

I suspect the law will find us if Jahvonis helps. Xavion Mourningstar, a modern legend, is the Jahvonis from eons ago. He would be a perfect assassin, but he's too light-hearted and car-

ing. Should things go wrong and the
hideout is compromised, we will retreat
to the surface. We will find refuge in the
mountains to the southeast. We hoarded
our entire treasury from our contracts.
From there we can journey further out
of the region if needed.

That was the final log of Mataraves. I will relay the information to Sebastian. I should try to read the grimoire.

"Xavion, place your hand on the grimoire and come see me," Jahvonis said. With an open palm, I grasped at the inner image of Mustasurma. I sensed a dreadful force accompany me into my subconscious. I am with Jahvonis and the grimoire is in his hands. The Son of the Courtship spoke.

"You must be careful. This book is evil and must be protected."

"Jahvonis, have you been aware of these tomes?"

"No. This kind of book should be in Jado's library. Any knowledge of such craft should be kept from mortals."

"Then how does it exist? Did it travel from eons ago through space?"

"I do not know for sure. If there's any useful information on Mustasurma, then we must read it," he replied.

"Where do we begin?"

Jahvonis looked through the several spells that were encased within. Some of these seemed more fictional. I hope none of these are real, including the Black Hole Sun spell, which was mentioned before.

"It tells of the original Hand of Doom, including me. These words sound more like propaganda against me and my father. So far there's nothing on an exact location or other information. There are more spells and rituals that Mustasurma designed," Jahvonis said.

"So the dairy is useful, unlike the grimoire?" I replied.

"Unfortunately. However, Mustasurma is no immediate threat for now. As they say, '*One at a time.*'"

"I can hide these among the other books. Besides, no one ever searches this room," I wittily remarked.

As Jahvonis and I parted ways, I began to sleep. Before my slumber was whole, I could see faces in the dark. I saw what I believed was my imagination. People clad in black with creatures and imagery from the grimoire. These are cinematic in a way, a theater of my thoughts. There are six people, three men and three women. First is an Ember man with three black feathers behind his head. Second is a Barkish woman with a black turban. Third is an Ebony man with a feathered headband and silver forehead piece. Fourth is a Sand Theranth man with a panther-shaped helmet. The last two women are fraternal Nodinian twins. One is a blond with a black hood and gold circlet. The other is a brunette with a black hood and silver circlet.

The star mark on my chest began to send strange energy through me. I am not scared. Instead, I am curious. The traumatic memories from my battles will never leave me. It is the soldier's curse to always remember those they have fought and slain. Even the memory of the blood ritual with Jahvonis plagues me. It is a soldier's oath and a good person's ethic to uphold their promise as best they can.

I awoke later in the night and relit my forge. Out of the weapons I own, most are Barkish or Yazjian. I have not built an Ember, Sand, or Ebony weapon. The image of Mataraves's tomahawk bashing into Johan was not just politically motivated violence. It was a forceful blow delivered by our fire-skinned heritage to our snow-laden enemy. In an impulse, I forged three of my own. The first has an ax blade and peace pipe joined in a tool of symbolism. It has an eight-and-three-fourth-inch head length with an anti-reflective finish. The primary edge is three inches. The bowl is hollowed out. It includes a solid ovoid-shaped, nineteen-inch handle. The other two tomahawks are identical, except one has a solid hammer-head while the third has a thick V-shaped spike.

The next morning, I relayed the information of the Hand to Sebastian.

"At least we have an idea of where the bastards are going. I'll report to the Caretaker. Also, Astrid wishes for you to escort her to her throne."

He and I made our way to the lady's room. Astrid is sitting upright.

"Good morning, Astrid!" I said cheerfully.

"Xavion! Sebastian! Good morning!" she said glee-fully. "I would like to sit on my throne today," she added.

I am to bathe her next. Without trying to sound per-verse, I cannot stop gazing upon the blissful and sinless nudity of Astrid.

Aside from the obvious sexual overtones, I see this as the artistic secret of Lyannis. The sun goddess has given Nodin a rare treasure in Astrid. The princess still blatantly teases me as I wash her. I don't doubt that Sebastian has realized the flirting between us. A man his age can see these things before us youths. As I was putting her gown on, Astrid kissed me quite passionately. I could not gently separate us because I did not want to cause an issue. Neither could Sebastian because Astrid is royalty and her wishes are seldom questioned. He watched in surprise. The walk downstairs had Astrid joyously smiling and laughing. As she sat beside Vallen, she greeted her relative pleasantly. I stood to her side while Sebastian and Hamish knelt before Vallen and proceeded with their report.

"My lady Astrid and caretaker Vallen, in the wake of the investigation of the Hand of Doom, the guards have acquired evidence," Hamish said as other guards came.

"We have acquired mostly weapons but also various reports and business letters. We have arrested the assassin's contacts, and they are awaiting your judgment. The vigilante known as Jahvonis did not accompany us back home, but he remained in the caves," Hamish added. He also told the tale of Jahvonis leading the guards against the Hand of Doom.

"We have reason to believe they will be retreating to the mountains in the southeast. I propose that a small army march in their direction and ultimately destroy them," Hamish said.

"No!" Astrid said as I turned to her in shock.

"If the Hand of Doom are going above ground, then they are crossing into lands that we have no authority over. When we came underground, we forsook our ancestral homes from the Theranth Wars. The Nodinians who rule those lands have governments of their own. Regardless of our quarrel with the Hand of Doom, we cannot cross foreign land without causing suspicion," Astrid stated.

"Well, what about this Jahvonis character? Is it possible to hire him as a mercenary? Surely for the right price, he can be bought. Never mind vigilantism, he would be doing a public service!" Vallen suggested.

"Unfortunately, it is not easy to contact them. They are one of these 'ninja.' Jahvonis is almost untraceable," Hamish said.

"Sebastian," Vallen called, "it was you who told Hamish where to meet Jahvonis before the investigation, and you personally have been harmed by Mataraves. How is it you've come in contact with the vigilante more than anyone?"

"I was the guard who found the first criminal captured by Jahvonis. His gravitation toward me is a mystery. I fear for my life if I should tell more than I know. I only know he has criminals thinking twice," Sebastian said.

"Until Mataraves and his captains are executed, I forbid anyone going to the surface. If Jahvonis wishes to legally pursue these assassins, then he is to meet me first. If any of the guards come into contact with him, then please send him hither. I will not spare soldiers. We need them in case Aylund pays us another visit," Vallen stated.

"Do we know the identities of Mataraves's captains?" Astrid asked.

"It is our assumption the man in the brass mask is the second in command. We know his name is simply Kane," Hamish replied to the princess.

"Hamish, let me see the sword you carry," Vallen requested.

Hamish handed him a ko katana sword that he recovered.

"Where in the world are these made?" Vallen asked aloud.

"We do not know, but its design is clearly foreign. No sword in Nodinian history has ever looked like this. Several of the assassins carried these," Hamish said.

"Add it to the evidence with the other weapons. Until we contact Jahvonis, I see this meeting adjourned," Vallen said as all the guards left the throne room. I assume they are going to devise a plan to get Jahvonis's attention.

That night when all were in bed, Astrid begged me to join her again.

"You know you want to, Xavion!" she said cheerfully.

Internally, I feel many conflicting emotions and thoughts. They ranged from lust to anger to depression. I am sad that Mataraves has done all of this to die. He freed me from captivity and allowed me to escape. I am positive he allowed me to find his diary and the grimoire! The memory of him kicking Astrid to the floor and cutting her hair was really an elaborate taunt to enrage me!

"You know you want to feel my stomach again!" Astrid playfully said.

"My lady, I can't right now. There's too much on my mind," I replied.

"What is wrong, my love?" she asked.

"The memory of how Mataraves hurt you. I failed to avenge your harm in that battle. How can I possibly be together with you if I cannot protect you from harm? How can I be in love with you when we have these social classes that forbid two people from being together?" I sadly exclaimed.

"Xavion, I am royalty. When anyone is involved with politics or has government affiliation, they are a target. If I could not be a princess, I would not be one. Hakun and I had that in common. A monarchy is defined by those who bow to them. Without the working and common classes, monarchs are nothing. Soldiers win wars while the royals sit safely in their castles. The royals must die for their subjects just as their subjects die for them," Astrid stated wisely. She would make an excellent queen.

"Astrid, with the gods as my witnesses, I love you. I love doing anything for you. If it weren't for you, Sebastian and Hamish, I would not be able to wake. I love waiting on you hand and foot. I love your personality. I love your hair, I love your freckles, voice, face, and body. I will be damned if I let another person hurt you!" I said as I began to cry.

Astrid's expression is similar. She is satisfied with my admittance of loving her.

"I don't want to be involved in these wars, always fighting for the cowards and never given equal rights. I make a wageless living on making tools for death and going to sleep in a prison that I call home. I want to live outdoors and play the lute for Mother Nature. To watch the sun and moon rise and set. To wrap you in my arms without fearing harm to us!" I stated as I sobbed.

Astrid crawled from her bedside to hug me as she stood, my sobbing face resting against her stomach as I sat in a chair. She hooked my underarms to pull me up. She used a cloth to wipe my face. She's getting good at finding my limbs.

"The wrongdoings of our people will not be forgotten. When you and I rule this kingdom, they will beg forgiveness!" Astrid softly gloated.

"I cannot be king because they're *not* my people. They're your people. I'm not one of your snow-skinned kindred. I'm the Mud Monkey whom your father belittles. I'm the bruise-eyed, turd-thumbed Soruthian who is not allowed to have children. I am treated like dirt, but I am always needed when there's a battle!" I exclaimed loudly.

The confession of my heritage surprised the lady. She chose her words carefully and spoke.

"I don't care what complexion you are! Anyone disgusted by our mixed love can sodomize themselves with a sword! Love is both colorful and colorless. I love you as you love me! What is 'forbidden' about that?" Astrid inquired. "My father cannot and will not dictate who I love, whether it is a Soruthian or no one at all. You, Xavion Mourningstar, are who I want to have children with. You carried my brother from the battlefield, you put my mother back together, and you saved my home time and time again! And I want you to be *my* husband and my king!" Astrid said as the white smoke flowed from my pores.

In Astrid's eyes, I see more green and shining light. My tears dried, and I slowly tightened my grip upon her.

The confessions and support of each other brought us closer until we were kissing and caressing upon her bed. We went no further than that. As we lay under the blankets and my head rested upon her right breast, Astrid massaged my back and put me to sleep.

Chapter 9

In Xavion's View

The next night as Vallen slept in his room, I stood in the shadows wearing the Jahvonis uniform. Before he fell asleep entirely, I spoke in the deep tone, which startled him.

"Caretaker, may I have a word, please?"

"You're him! What do you want?" Vallen replied.

"Safe passage to Mataraves. Can you grant me that?"

"He's going above ground. If you can find him, then he's yours! Name your price!"

"What I ask in return is large and may take several years to fulfill."

"What would that be?"

"If West Nodin defeats the East, then I ask for any form of slavery to be abolished and everyone is given an equal opportunity."

"You ask something that may not be possible in our lifetime. I cannot grant you that and uphold it," Vallen replied truthfully.

"However, during this, I can guarantee no one in the kingdom will interfere in your mission. Leave no survivors among the Hand if you want. If you do this, the king and his subjects will be in your debt," Vallen added.

"A fair trade. I'm leaving tonight. If I do not return by November 11, then assume I have failed," I said.

"Good luck to you," Vallen replied.

"When you sleep, I will be gone." Vallen returned to his rest, and I departed. I went to see Sebastian before my journey began.

"Vallen is giving you leave. I will watch over Astrid, but what should I say of Xavion?" Sebastian asked.

"Tell her Xavion escaped. She'll believe that more than he went missing."

"It's risky. Good luck, my friend. The guards know to open the front gates for you. What message should I give Astrid?"

I was hoping to avoid that question. "Tell her Xavion says, 'I will always love you. We will be together again someday.' If I never return, tell her Xavion died by the sword for deserting the army."

"Until next time, Jahvonis. It will always be a pleasure," Sebastian said as he shook my hand.

My journey to the front gate was strangely met with a few people applauding me. Most of them are people who I previously saved. One of them is a woman named *Isolde Amott*. As I passed through the gates, I saw the nightly land of surface Nodin. I turned to the southeast and began my march toward Mataraves.

In Sebastian's View

I looked from afar as my friend began his mission and passed through the gates. I fear he may not return. This rivalry with Mataraves became a blood feud when he harmed Astrid and I. I am restless. I hope Xavion does not march to his end. I will bear this lie until I'm certain Jahvonis will not return.

As October came, Astrid questioned every day about Xavion's absence. On the fifth of October, she had a fit upon me about Xavion. If I am to keep my word for Jahvonis, I bring endless grief to the princess.

"What aren't you telling me about him? Where is he? I am the princess, and I command you to tell me where my beloved rests his head!" Astrid shouted upon me.

In the trial of my honor, I was forced to lie to the lady to keep Xavion's cover.

"My lady, back in July, the guards were alerted of a deserter. I went to his cell and saw Xavion was gone. He left me a note that read, *'Sebastian, thank you for your friendship. I refuse to fight for a land that does not treat me as a person. Please tell Astrid, "I will always love her. We will be together again someday."'* This past September, the guards found Xavion. He…" I hesitated to finish.

"He what, Sebastian?"

"He…was put to the sword."

Astrid went into an angry and saddened tantrum. I tried to restrain her with a hug, but she shouted, "Let go of me! He was our friend! He loved me! We were going to be married, and you let him be taken from me! How could you, Sebastian?"

I cried also and left her room. I lied in order to protect another friend. If I must bear Astrid's resentment, then so be it. Jahvonis has a little more than a month to return. I feel I may lose two friends instead of one. Jahvonis, please hurry!

In Xavion's View

My search of the wilderness has lasted almost three months. I have not reached the mountains yet. I've been using the memory of Astrid and Sebastian as motivation. While I hope they are okay, I'm not concerned about my safety. I understand if Astrid does not move on, but I couldn't promise my return. At this time, my communication with the animals is reuniting. I can hear their thoughts and speak to them. I've been using birds as spies to watch for the Hand. In my travels, I ran into three men from one of the towns.

"We are soldiers from Starkstad. Jarl Kristoff Ericson claims this patch of trees to be cut. Who are you?" one of them asked.

I spoke in the deep tone. "My name is Jahvonis. I am hired to undo the Hand of Doom, an assassin's guild who attacked Johan and Astrid Edling."

"You refer to King Johan Edling of the Underground West Nodin?" the second asked.

"Yes. His cousin gave me this mission," I replied.

"Aye, we know of the Hand of Doom. They killed our lord's nephew some years past. The assassin was captured and slain," the third informed.

"If it is possible, I propose an arrangement—if I rid this land of the Hand's leader, could Kristoff spare some food on my return journey?" I requested.

"We'll have to send a messenger bird. We cannot guarantee it, but we're sure he will be in your debt if you complete your quest," the first guard replied.

"Thank you. Will you permit me to pass?"

They moved aside, and I continued southeast.

It is the thirty-first of October. The nights are longer, and the days wither in a crisp chill. The orange and red leaves of the forest remind me of Astrid. A sad beauty how trees change color only to foreshadow dormancy. The time of the fire goddess is coming to an end while the Woman of Winter prepares to cast longer nights. I've always admired how the goddesses take pride in making the earth beautiful. Despite their trivial bickering, they make a wonderful decorating team. I wonder how I will be judged when I die.

I came to the feet of the mountains in southeastern Gern. Mist and snow are on the peaks. I am afraid I'll have to search each mount for Mataraves. Many hours passed, and it is before noon. The wind is soft and slow. Upon the first mountain is a staircase that climbed high. There is a fortress built into these hills. The blue drapes and banners bear tattered horizontal hexagrams.

"These must have been used during the Ericsons's last stand with the Theranths," I said.

Each step became weighted, and I began to rest. I sat on the steps and thought about how this could go. *Is Mataraves alone here? Is he going to change his mind? Is this a charade?*

I continued stepping. Another half hour passed until I reached the halfway point on the mount. I can see some-one in the distance. My following steps became hesitant. Twenty more steps passed. I realize who it is. I am only five feet away from them.

"He is waiting for you within the stone."

"After our last battle, Kane, I thought you would attack me on sight?" I replied to the Master.

"I have my reasons for not killing you now, but you owe me a rematch. So far it's one to one. Mataraves will not let me kill you. To fulfill both agendas, you will have to fight us both. I hoped it wouldn't be so, but Mataraves is the jonin. My time passed. Follow me," Kane said as he climbed the stairs.

I followed and continued to speak. "Where are the rest of you?"

"The other recruits are doing missions. Mataraves prefers himself and his elder to fight you alone. I trained him to succeed me, the Grandmaster commanded me to resign," Kane replied.

The "Grandmaster" is most likely Mustasurma.

"What is your reason for this life?" I asked.

"I had a wife when I fought in the Theranth Wars. I was struck with a torch that set my face aflame. The mask protects what is left. I lost much blood that day. While I was recovering from the implanted blood, my wife was raped and became pregnant—with Aylund's child. She chose to dance upon the gallows after the boy was born. Aylund named him Bjorn Adolf. He is the younger half brother to my Alastair. I will not stop until Aylund and his relatives are dead. You guard Johan and his daughter from that."

All is silent. Through the air, I hear a sorrowful tune blown on a flute. The melody sounds familiar. When I pieced the notes together, I realized it is an Ember morning song. Its title is *"Wendeyaho."* The song is five notes played in different melodies.

After eight repeats of "Wendeyaho," Kane and I entered the fortress where Mataraves sat on a stone stool with a cedar flute in playing position. His eyes are closed. For the first time he looks peaceful. His sword is on his left hip. His bo stands to his right against the wall. His tomahawk sits on his right hip. In his lap is an Ember smoke pipe. The bowl released tobacco smoke. In the Ember culture, tobacco is a ceremonial herb that is used for prayer. Tobacco and other medicinal herbs should not be used for recreation.

Mataraves wears all buckskin clothing. In many areas, the leather is fringed. He wears brown knee-high moccasin boots. Upon his head is a red-and-gold Ember turban. Tucked in back of his turban are two female red-tailed hawk feathers. They are on the left side. His war paint is present; for now, it is elegant. It is a white base with lightly blackened eyes and black lips. This is his regalia, and he wears it into battle. If he falls, he is properly dressed for the gods.

On the floor is a hollowed turtle shell where sage, cedar, sweetgrass, and tobacco burned. This is also an Ember custom. The combination of these ingredients is believed to heal and ward off evil spirits. He must be trying to lessen the dragon's grip and preparing for someone to die. When Mataraves opened his brown eyes, I can see his goal is unimpeded. I stopped in the doorway as Kane continued. As the master and student stand with each other, a deafening silence is at hand.

"Xavion, you have faced armies and painted the underground red, be careful with these two," Jahvonis said from within.

"Santiago!" I said in my normal voice. "It does not have to be this way! You have a family who misses you. I know being a slave is horrific. Please do not throw your life away! You can still redeem yourself. Cast aside the Hand of Doom and return to Soruth!" I pleaded.

"Xavion, you do not understand! I became an assassin to stop the slave trade of our people!"

"So you sell your soul to someone who wants to enslave the whole world? If Mustasurma returns to power, he will invoke the wrath of the gods! Then what good is your goal?" I said, which shook him gently. "Kane! What good would avenging your wife be if you are enticed to someone worse than Aylund?"

Kane refused to budge. Mataraves gazed in an emotionless glance through his war paint. He is unwilling to hear reason or show remorse.

"Your kind banter is futile. I broke you out of our prison so we could fight without the other ninja interfering. This moment in time is perfect for one of three great warriors to die. Just when the Jahvonis out of legend returns to Nodin, a man worthy of killing me falls into our arena. The knowledge that the Mourningstar and the Black Paladin are the same made it better. You will fight me, or I will take more than Astrid's hair next time," Mataraves threatened.

Aside from his main weapons, Mataraves has a utility belt and a dagger in each boot. Kane has a ko katana and a wakizashi on his left and right hips. Kane also has a utility belt and two daggers in his boots.

My weapons are my kukri, the hammer tomahawk, the ringed dagger, and my supply of shuriken and senbon. My bonus tools are the forearm blades. Mataraves and I drew our tomahawks and held them horizontal to each other. As in the Ember warrior tradition, we rotated the blades up, signaling war!

Kane pounced forth with his wakizashi in hand. Mataraves is on his left with the bo. I moved to the defensive. This is difficult because I have two masters of separate martial arts. Mataraves gripped his bo with both hands and swung for my feet while Kane aimed to decapitate me. Whenever I caught Kane's sword in my gauntlets, Mataraves would issue a short barrage of staff strikes to straggle me. The next time I caught Kane's blade, I had the bo in my right hand. In the short tension, Mataraves kicked my hamstring. I prevented Kane from a killing blow by once again catching his sword in my gauntlet, but this distracted me from Mataraves's bo bashing my cowl.

I have an advantage over their swords, but I've never encountered a staff weapon other than a spear. Kane threw a spin kick, which sent me flying toward the center of the room. With no time to be groggy, I drew my kukri and aimed my chopping at limbs and vital spots.

Mataraves's technique to counter bladed weapons with the staff is called *jojutsu*, which is a pain because he is taller than me and the staff is his height. This gives him a greater distance of offense while increasing his defense. This is how I'm being fought: Kane attacks upfront while the bo attacks from away. If I can get the bo away from Mataraves, then I have him!

Kane greatly used his enhanced physiology to his effect. His swordsmanship is on par with my own. When my kukri parried Kane's wakizashi, the bind was broken by Mataraves. Kane quickly sliced my right bicep. The cut is not deep, but any wound in battle is a disadvantage. I kicked his knee, lifted, and slammed him to the ground.

With Mataraves away, I threw two shuriken, one of them he deflected but another punctured his left hand. I ran and tackled him. I tried to stab him on the ground, but we struggled for the bo. He still grasped the staff as I pushed it further down to his neck. The shuriken bled his hand until he could not resist me.

I could hear Kane assembling from behind. "Xavion, duck!" Jahvonis shouted as Kane's wakizashi missed my head and broke on the wall. Mataraves saw an opening to reverse the pressure and pushed upward. The shuriken is cutting into my cowl. I let go and punched him in the face. Kane kicked me off Mataraves. I grabbed my kukri and dueled Kane with his ko katana.

The rush of energy from the Star Mark began as I fought harder and swung faster. Both times that I've fought Kane gave me pleasure as a warrior. During one of the sword bouts, I used a free hand to grab four senbon and stabbed Kane's forearm. Mataraves struck my cowl, which freed Kane, but I turned and struck at the torso of Mataraves.

He struggled to create distance as his bo was unhanded. I grabbed and tossed it at him like a lance. The rounded end bounced off his skull like a ball. The sound of it was unpleasant. Kane regained his stance and continued his onslaught. I caught his sword in my left gauntlet and pummeled his mask with my right forearm. The scrapes I am creating are weakening his facial protection. That's it! If I can get his mask off, then his bare face will be his weakness!

I broke his ko katana with my gauntlets, but he is not defenseless. He kicked me in the thigh and drove his dagger into my leg. The overpowering adrenaline from the mark acted as an anesthetic. I pulled the dagger out and pierced Kane's fleshy part of his thigh.

I began to chop into his mask with my kukri. The inhuman strength I felt had the mask looking like a worn shield. Mataraves belted a treble-heavy shriek and began to defend his master. As Kane laid down bruised, I am able to battle Mataraves for a time. He is using his anger and sorrow as motivation. He wants a warrior's death. The Killing Bird and I locked swords. We traded counters with our blades.

"Behind you!" Jahvonis yelled again. Kane had his student's bo in hand and went to attack. I kicked Mataraves in the gut and returned to fight Kane. His time with the bo was short. In the moment of his shock, I bludgeoned his armored hand. When he dropped the bo, I kicked his right knee and threw a frightening right hook with the knuckle guard of my kukri. My punch sent Kane flying back against the wall. With the dented wall behind him, the mask fell in pieces off his face, revealing severe degree burns on 60 percent of his face. His blue eyes stared at me in a trance of shock. Kane met his match. He is awake. I ran and stomped his head, which knocked him unconscious. Mataraves is now alone!

Mataraves came with his sword in a rageful array of swings. On his tenth swing, I grounded him with his sword in one hand. He was able to reach his bo and he bashed my cowl. I kneed his head, which dazed him. He dropped his sword. I swung my kukri and slashed his right cheek as he fell over. He came to his senses and used his bo in both hands to block. My kukri continuously chopped into his bo. The friction and tension, the bo felt were like wood. After ten swings, the bo snapped in half!

As I went for the final blow, Mataraves used the two halves like escrima sticks and battled back to his feet. His blows went from my arms to my face. He is pummeling me with all his might. With my left hand, I punched him, gripped his hair and turban, and punched him eight times with my kukri knuckle dusters. His eyes blackened as he bled from the nose, cheek, and mouth. In his last effort, he trapped my right arm in a hold and disarmed me. We grabbed our tomahawks and were soon caught in odd hooking struggles. Mataraves used all his strength in a missed stoke. In return, I drove my tomahawk into the left side of his left collarbone. The Killing Bird began to cough blood and fell to the ground. The red life force is a pool upon the stone. I breathe heavily for my quest is ending.

"Please"—*cough, cough*—"come…here…" he requested.

I walked to him to hear his final words.

"Xavion, please"—*cough, cough*—"stop the slave trade. Our people, show them they can go home. I know you found my diary. Please find my brothers. Tell them I am gone," Mataraves spoke as his coughing became worse.

"Mataraves, you were a worthy foe. I'm sorry we couldn't be friends. I'm sorry it came to this!" I lamented in tears. I took off my mask and knelt at his side. I held his head in my arm.

"Do not weep for me! You have given me peace! My soul is free from the Hand of Doom. Only a friend would grant me that. I hope Kane will understand. There's a raven-foot pendant in my pocket. My brothers will know I am gone once you show them it. Astrid's hair is with the pendant," he said as I retrieved them.

"Please, Santiago, be still your words!" I replied.

"Xavion, it's him," Jahvonis said in a clean melancholic voice. I turned to my left where Jahvonis stood in a black ghostly manner.

"Only Jahvonis is worthy to slay me. Mustasurma knew I would find you, Adrian. I am sorry for all I have done," Mataraves said shockingly to me.

"Black Leaf! Don't leave me again! How are you alive?" Jahvonis cried.

"Jahveyis brought me back as promised, but the dragon got to me before you. Please…finish me!" Mataraves said.

"Xavion, don't! We can help him!" Jahvonis pleaded.

"It's too late! He's lost too much blood. He's suffering!" I replied.

"I will not lose him again!" Jahvonis yelled back as Mataraves went into a coughing spasm.

"Adrian, please!" Mataraves cried back. "My boot…" he said.

I looked into his boot, and I found a knife. In fact, it is near identical to the one that was used in my blood ritual. I grabbed the blade and placed it to Mataraves's throat.

"I love you, Black Leaf!" Jahvonis bereaved.

"I love you more!" Mataraves said.

"Goodbye…my friend," I stated as I quickly pushed the blade into Mataraves's neck. He gripped my hand like a first handshake.

On October 31 of the year 888, Santiago Salvador, known by many names, passed from our world. He lived two lives because of his love. The tale of Mataraves began and ended…with death.

"The shores of the Southern Gate will mourn him. He will join the dead in the Gods' Hall, but his memory will never be forgotten. Mother Earth will welcome his body home, the blackbirds will cry his name, and the sky will carry him beyond," I said as the last testament to my foe and friend.

Jahvonis knelt down to close the lightless eyes of his late husband. The man who he sought to resurrect was the man who terrorized the North.

"What do we do about Kane? He's alive," Jahvonis asked.

"Leave him. He is defeated, and we accomplished our mission," I replied.

"He will never let this go. Kane will track us down."

"I will spare him. The loss of his student is bad enough."

The journey back down the mountain was hard for both of us. Out of all the men I have killed, Mataraves was the worst. The wind blew as the sun and moon began to shift. As the shinobi travels through the Tall People, a rare albino raven soared overhead. I thought Mataraves hated me for protecting the Edlings, inside he was a man looking for salvation. I acknowledge that Kane and I will battle again. As Alastair grows, he will also become an enemy of mine. Only the gods know if this will pass. I kept Mataraves's knife to remind myself of our relationship. I drank some of my water to heal my wounds.

With the dysfunctional relationship of Jahvonis and Jahveyis deepening, I question my faith in the Immortals. Why do they allow us mortals to war and harm our brethren? Why do they allow these wealthy and pitiful politicians to abuse their power and bring the undoing of peace? There are too many complaints for us mortals to give. Do the gods even exist? If so, are they worthy of prayer? I couldn't believe that I heard Jahvonis's true voice, the deep vocals were an act on his part. He has a softer midrange tone with a Noric accent. The melody of "Wendeyaho" still echoed. Nightfall came as we stood beneath the full harvest moon of Miolannis. The energy of the star mark did not repeal. I could feel the presence of Jahvonis slowly growing more powerful and angry.

My breathing quickened as it became cold and white. The moon grew brighter and dreadful. I am taking longer and deeper breaths. The violent power of my mark flashed into my eyes. I see a white ethereal Jahvonis. He glared with disdain into the night and the moon. With a clear rageful roar, he shouted into the heavens, "Father! You dare mock my faith again? You curse me with an unending quest to conquer what you need to survive! You cruelly bring my husband back only to have him bewitched by Mustasurma! Heed my words, you selfish coward, this will not go unchallenged!"

As the Black Paladin finished his divine scream, green and black rings formed upon the moon. I realize it is the great eye of Miolannis. I looked in fear of this holy event. She stared down upon her son while he engulfed her in his vision of disdain. I removed my mask. I must see this with my own eyes! My jaw remained dropped as the lady's eye opened wider in a shocked manner upon me, and in a split second, the eye vanished. This is proof that the gods exist. I began to believe that becoming Jahvonis was a grave mistake!

We traveled on into the night and watched the sunrise over the forest. We sat and rested. The light of Lyannis is so beautiful; it deserves to be welcomed. For if the light ever faded away, all life would perish. Jahvonis cared not for the sun; all that mattered was our mission and nothing more. He is still in his ethereal form. He cannot sustain this much longer. He will have to return inside me soon. I began to welcome the morning in song.

Wendayaho, wendayaho,
Wen day ya, wen day ya, ho hohoho
Hey ya ho, hey ya ho, ya, ya, ya!

The first verse was done by me in Ember vocables. Jahvonis sang next.

> *Wendayaho, wendayaho,*
> *Wen day ya, wen day ya, ho hohoho*
> *Hey ya ho, hey ya ho, ya, ya, ya!*

The sun rose in full motion with us in musical bliss. Jahvonis and I sang the last two verses in unison.

> *Wendayaho, wendayaho,*
> *Wen day ya, wen day ya, ho hohoho*
> *Hey ya ho, hey ya ho, ya, ya, ya!*
> *Wendayaho, wendayaho,*
> *Wen day ya, wen day ya, ho hohoho*
> *Hey ya ho, hey ya ho, ya, ya, ya!*

An ensemble of birdsong occurred after us. Jahvonis spoke in his natural voice. "I first heard that song when I met Black Leaf. He had such a heavenly voice. My family immigrated to Soruth during the peaceful years. I met Black Leaf when I was twelve. It's always been hard for two men to be together. That's why when we were old enough we left on an unofficial honeymoon to the island of *Tuánjié*. It's Hongangan for 'unity.' That's where I lost him. He gave his life for mine…and I'll never be able to repay him. I thought Mataraves was familiar. He was my man!" Jahvonis sobbed.

I held him in a hug with my left arm over him.

"Come, Xavion, there's a friend and princess waiting for you. We'll be able to move faster because we know the way back," Jahvonis stated.

"Most of the caves in this area lead underground. I can feel the vibrations of the kingdom beneath my feet, but we have to find one first!" I added.

We continued walking until we came to the patch of woods that was occupied by Starkstad. The same soldiers were there to greet me.

"Aye, welcome back! Did you find who you sought?" the first said.

I returned to the deep voice with a reply, "The leader of the Hand of Doom is dead. I bare his pendant and ritual knife as evidence."

"You have fulfilled your part of the bargain. Our Lord had us acquire any spare resources. In this pack, there's a blanket, three days' worth of food, and this canteen of water. It is not enough to repay you, but feel free to visit our town sometime," the soldier said.

I shook their hands and retrieved the supplies.

"Jahvonis, there's a tunnel behind that rock formation that travels under. It's en route to West Nodin. It's much quicker, and you'll be there in less time. We'll inform Jarl Kristoff of your triumph. We look forward to working with you," the soldier added.

"Thank you," I replied.

The tunnel is about fifty yards northwest from here. The tunnel went down and westward.

It is now November 5, and I'm almost in the kingdom. I owe the soldiers for their care of my quest. It took me months to find Mataraves. While underground, I used Jahvonis's power to enhance my running. I'm coming home, Astrid!

In Narration

While Xavion hastens toward the palace, danger lurks within it. King Johan came back into his health on the night Sebastian lied to Astrid. He demanded that Jahvonis be the second most wanted man behind Aylund. Xavion reached West Nodin on November 10 and raced to Vallen, still thinking the Caretaker is in power. That afternoon, General Daveth, at the command of Johan, listened in on Astrid crying out loud for Xavion. She added how she and Sebastian miss their friend and that she would do anything to be his wife. Johan heard how his daughter shared a bed with a Soruthian slave and made Sebastian keep the secret. Thus the king had Sebastian arrested for "endangering the princess" and breaking the law on mixed relationships. After a gang assault on Sebastian, he was dragged into Xavion's cell and restrained. Johan entered next and spoke to him.

In King Johan's View

"Guardsman Hagstrom! When you took the oath to enforce our laws and protect the royal house, you also pledged honesty to your king. Now tell me why I heard my whore daughter crying about how she loved the Mud Monkey?"

"His name is Xavion Mourningstar! Astrid has every right to love whoever she wants!" Sebastian shouted back.

"You allowed the Turd to rape my daughter? She's been tainted by the magic of those apes of the south! She is cast out of my family and must be erased!" I yelled upon the traitor. I could feel my flesh blush with rage. I have not been so hateful since Aylund assailed my kingdom.

Sebastian spoke with heeded words. "If you harm Astrid, Xavion will kill all of you!"

"We'll see," I replied.

Daveth slammed Sebastian's right arm on the Mud Monkey's anvil. I grasped the dreaded Mourningstar mace in my left hand. Five times I bashed the hand of Sebastian. The mace spikes punctured his arm and hand. The weight of the mace crown demolished his dominant arm. Next, I dealt one massive blow to his face. Daveth and the guards then trashed the cell.

"Enjoy being a brothel slave, traitor!" I stated.

We left the cell with Sebastian screaming and crying in pain. He lay under many of the turd's possessions.

I dispersed the guards, and I journeyed to confront my traitorous heretic of a daughter. As I gently climbed the stairs, the memory of my beheaded son and dismembered wife flashed through my vision. I remember all that has led to this day. I noticed on the day the Mourningstar boy was brought here. I felt the air change. I remember hearing stories of those wretched Soruthians with their non-snow skin! How those savages slaughtered my ancestors with their curved swords. The menace of their feathered and towel-wrapped heads! I have never seen any of those barbarians until that blood-lusting Xavion came to my palace!

I could hear Astrid crying in her room. With haste, I kicked the fucking door down, which shocked her into a scream. "Who's there?"

"Astrid! What the fuck has the vile dark man done to you?"

"Father, Xavion has done nothing to me!"

"General Daveth overheard your weeping of how you missed Xavion. Daveth told me you shared your bed with that…that warmonger!"

"Father, you do not understand! Xavion has never hurt me! He and I never made love, and I did not ever give myself to him nor anyone. Yes, I love Xavion. He is the best young man I could ever hope for. I know of his appearance and his rainbow of skin tones has me eagerly awaiting him. You call him a warmonger? Tell me, Father, which of our House has fought in the Theranth Wars? Whose brother has corrupted you to his level to which you dishonor your wife and son? For you to torment the man I love to the point of desertion is unjust! Not only have you taken him from me, but you took away every chance I had to see his beauty with my own eyes. Johan Edling, *I dub thee unforgiven*, and I curse the day my grandfather released you from his root!" Astrid screamed at me with tears in her eyes as she stood.

I could see greenness in her eyes. "For you to admit loving that monster, there is no hope for the continuation of our House." I struck the right side of her head and face with the Mourningstar mace. The cracking of her skull worsened as she hit the floor. Her circlet rolled off her head, and its rubies fell from it.

"Farewell, daughter, and be gone with your love of color. Face damnation for every Snow to bare mongrel children who further replace the master color and the only color of *people*."

She looked up at me with her crying beating upon my ears. I cast the mace beside her, and I left her room.

In Xavion's View

I finally was able to sneak into the palace. I sprinted to my cell with the intention of hastily removing the suit and rushing to see my beloved Astrid. I cannot wait to eagerly hug her and kiss her lips. I blushed with the thought of gently running my hand through her irresistible orange hair. As I came upon my cell, the door is open. Immediately, I grabbed my tomahawk. When I looked through the door, I broke down in shambles. I saw my room destroyed. Sebastian lays on the floor bleeding and battered. I could hear his painful crying. His right hand is swollen and broken.

"Sebastian? Sebastian, what happened?"

"Daveth told Johan of you and Astrid! Johan attacked me and is going after her!" Sebastian replied frantically.

"You need help!" I exclaimed.

"Go find the princess, *now*!" Sebastian yelled.

I quickly removed the Jahvonis suit and ran frantically to find Astrid with my hammer-headed tomahawk in hand. My immediate confusion and disarray clouded my mind. Sebastian needs medical attention; his arm being so damaged will have to come off.

"Astrid! Astrid!" I screamed repeatedly up the stairs. My sprinting matched a horse herd. As I reached the top, I see her door is open and all is quiet. I peered from outside and saw Princess Astrid Edling lying on the floor with a large gash on the right side of her head and face. Blood greased her orange hair as she wept.

"No, no, no, no! Astrid? Astrid!" I said as I knelt and shook her awake. The white smoke poured from my body and seeped into her immediately.

"You're alive?"—*cough, cough*—"But Sebastian said—" Astrid began.

"I was on a mission. He lied to protect me!" I confessed as I rambled in hindsight. "I should have told you! I shouldn't have gone! I should've stayed to protect you!" I went on and on about what I should have done. The spirit of Jahvonis stood next to me. He saw the parallel of Mataraves's passing and wept.

"Xavion... Xavion," Astrid softly and repeatedly said.

Through my tears, I see her eyes. They are clearer and greener than ever. I sobbed as she kept calling my name.

"Xavion. Xavion... Xavion!" she said loudly as I paused to hear her. "I love your eyes..." Astrid said as the greenness of her eyes forever lost their light. I paused with tears and mucus running down my face. I realized Astrid Edling regained her sight, and her final vision was of the Soruthian boy with the amethyst eyes. I cradled her head in my elbow pocket.

"I love you, Astrid. Then, now...forever!" I said aloud and cried in arcane grief. I gently rocked her back and forth like an infant. Her blood continued to seep into my clothes and skin. I closed her emerald eyes for the final time. I looked to the side and saw my mace laying there covered in the blood of my best friends. I held on to

Astrid for many hours. Jahvonis sat next to me sobbing. I could not bear to leave her. My mace will never forget the blood of my dearest friends. My mind replayed our happiest times together.

Farewell, my first love. In a better world, we were meant to be.

Book 3

Change & Progression

Chapter 10

In Sareyus's View

The soulful beauty of this man is apparent. Goodness, I am crying and have been weeping for thirty minutes. Poor Astrid, Sebastian, Mataraves. And every event Xavion has told me is insane! His tale carried on into the next morning. Jahveyis has much to explain about his adopted son.

"In the fifteen years that I have been Jahvonis, I have led many slave liberations and have repeatedly traded blows with Johan and the Hand of Doom. What began with Mataraves passed on to Kane and now Alastair. As Alastair aged, he has made it his destiny to best Mataraves and destroy me," Xavion stated.

"What about Sebastian's arm and Astrid's body?" I asked.

"A doctor heard Sebastian screaming. He brought Sebastian to the infirmary. It was there that the doctor amputated the damaged portion of his arm. Before that happened, Hamish was going to see Astrid. He saw me cradling her and panicked. He thought I killed her, and I was arrested. He did not judge my fate because he had not heard the whole story. That changed when he saw Sebastian, who told him the tale.

"Hamish was brave enough to heckle the king when Johan told the kingdom of Astrid's passing. He shouted from the crowd, 'Johan killed the princess and assaulted one of his own men!' Hamish's words were in vain. He was arrested, beaten, and stripped of his duty. Johan and his men were not brave enough to target me. My military career never changed, but the king continued to belittle me with his bigoted remarks and Soruthian propaganda. That's when he passed the law for no newborns to be named after his family and for orange-haired women to be wageless prostitutes. That's how you ended up in all of this. Astrid's body was secretly placed in lava. I saw from afar as I hid in the shadows," he said.

"Why didn't you liberate Sebastian, Hamish, and Alva earlier?" I asked.

"Sebastian and Hamish were not sentenced to the brothel right away. Johan had them imprisoned. I did not see them again for eleven years. They and Alva were sentenced to the brothel on the same day. During that four year period, the guards were ordered to slay the brothel workers if Jahvonis tried to liberate them. It was consistently too dangerous to risk all those people's lives. I had to wait to make my move, no matter how awful I felt idling by." Xavion replied.

"Before you cut my binds in the brothel, the other slaves fled. They seemed prepared for their escape. Was that part of your plan?" I asked.

"I spent weeks preparing for that escape. Luckily, I found the hidden passages within and beneath the palace. They also are near the new mines. I already decided to infiltrate the brothel from beneath the bedroom you were in. One week beforehand, after midnight when the violent orgies ended, I snuck in as Jahvonis to collaborate with Sebastian and Hamish. In seven days, the condemned brothel slaves were prepared for my entry. The first ten guards I defeated were important. The slaves outran the final four, I finished them off after we escaped. It was never a mere chance, only proactive organizing."

"Why do you tell me all of this?" I asked.

"Because you cared enough to listen and you relocated my kneecap. I say you deserved to know this. When I saw you being dragged past my cell, I had enough. I refused to see another woman be objectified. You are so beautiful. I had to save you because I could not save Astrid! The humor of the time when you tried to unmask me. The time we shared when collecting firewood. The day you kissed me gave me hope!" Xavion confessed as his voice began to whimper.

He likes me! Never has anyone admitted to liking me, but Xavion does!

"Thank you so much…for everything!" I said as I crawled over to him with a hug. "Please come back to our camp, you must heal!"

"I can't go until I am able to walk and besides my suit must be hidden," he replied.

"I can go back! I'll bring Sebastian and a horse! I'll be fast!" I quickly said.

"First, grab me a hunk of snow so I can slow the pain. Hurry back! Also, bring a blanket and a sack so we can carry the suit in secret!" Xavion replied as I grabbed the snow and made haste back to our camp.

*****

"Sebastian, I found Xavion! He's hurt, and we must retrieve him!" I exclaimed.

He did not question. He must have figured that I know about Jahvonis and the jig is up. We grabbed an available horse and a large burlap bag. We rode fast to the cave that is still guarded by the bear. Cardalen stood within.

"Xavion, by the gods, how did you get here?" Sebastian asked.

"Alastair got one over on me. I managed to escape and Jahvonis used some spell to get me all the way here," Xavion said.

"For a moment, I thought you and Kane fought again. Let's get you out of that suit." Sebastian began to remove the armor from Xavion's body.

Because of Sebastian's handicap, I did more of the removal. Goodness, Xavion is a handsome man under that suit! He wore only his undergarments. We held on to the leg brace while keeping Xavion's leg straight (if we bent it, his kneecap would pop back out). When we braced his leg, we had an easier time hoisting him onto the horse. I wrapped the blanket around Xavion while Sebastian placed the Jahvonis armor in the sack.

"Sebastian, I'll take that. You walk alongside the horse."

"Sareyus, do be careful with the sack," Xavion added.

I was not just being nice. I wanted to feel for myself if the presence of Jahvonis is truly in the armor. There is a supernatural aura in the sack. I feel Jahveyis and Miolannis's energy among the armor. When we get back to camp, I am returning to the Gods' Hall so Jahveyis can explain before the rest of us. As we crossed into the camp, people turned and saw Xavion.

"It's the Mourningstar!" one man said.

"The Knight Killer is among us!" a woman shouted.

"The Liberator of the Tompkinians has returned! Hail, Xavion!" a young mother cheered.

One guard of the camp approached us and spoke. "Who is this?" he said as if he had never seen a non-Snow person before.

"My name is Xavion. I have pressing matters with the construction site. Starkstad, Coldhill, and Steelburrow are fleeing to Soruth to escape the war of the Underground Kingdoms. The Soruthians will attack you as soon as you set foot on their shores. I wish to act as an intermediary between the two groups if possible," he replied.

"While you make perfect sense, that is not my call to make," the guard said.

"Then will you send a message to Jarl Kristoff Ericson?" Sebastian requested.

"Aye, we can. By the way, there's a man who wishes to speak with you, Sebastian," the guard replied.

We went further into the camp to get Xavion situated in my hut. I placed the sack at his side. Sebastian left to see the man who wanted to meet him. As I sit next to Xavion, I feel his powerful aura. It is extravagant. I rested my head against his shoulder and closed my eyes. After a moment, I asked Xavion, "Why do they call you the Knight Killer?"

Xavion breathed before he spoke. "It is because I destroyed a portion of the *Eastern Knights Order*. Vallen sent me on a long-term secret mission to remove the knights from the Nodinian Kingdoms in the east. East Nodin was allied with the Kingdom of *Gern*. Aylund as a lord chose an army to be raised into knighthood. I had to infiltrate the headquarters and leave no survivors among the knights. Some escaped, and the knights were greatly weakened. There were only fifty among the casualties. The incident was titled '*the Eastern Knights Massacre*.' There were other foes I had besides Johan, the Hand of Doom, and the Eastern Knights Order. One of them was the Angish *Witchfinder General*."

In Sebastian's View

I hope Sareyus does not know too much of Jahvonis, but that is not my call. I act only as an assistant to Xavion and I trust his judgment. Before I left to meet the other man, I greased the fingers on my bronze hand. After my real arm was amputated, it was Xavion who built my bronze arm. It is detachable. The only time I do not wear it is during sleep. Xavion gave it to the doctor who was able to attach it before I was imprisoned.

In the four years beforehand, I believe I have about ten children from eight women. It's impossible to know because of how many...nonconsensual partners have chosen me. Yes, I admit that I, Sebastian Hagstrom, am a survivor of rape. It is possible for women to target men. In one instance, I was threatened to be denied my food if I did not yield to a woman's lust. I've never been paid, but I have been forced to penetrate and often inseminate the female customers. I hope to never meet my children.

Many of us slaves could not take anymore. After much time, Hamish, Alva, and I sunk into despair. Gods! It must have been Alastair! He always picked Alva! That snot-nosed motherfucker better hope he doesn't fight Xavion again! It makes sense that he would track us up here. After Mataraves, Alastair and Kane have been after Jahvonis for years. Kane, where is he in all of this?

I walked into the barracks of the guards. "So you did leave, Vallen?" I said.

"Yes. After all these years, I've finally seen the faults of my family," Vallen replied.

"What have you learned?" I asked.

"It's grim. Johan and Aylund are preparing for the final battle. It will be where their feud began, on the surface," Vallen said, which took the breath of the guards.

"They're from Starkstad," Vallen added. "Johan also hired Alastair Beorler to kill Jahvonis. We have until May 1 to get as many people away from here as possible. If either side wins, we all lose! Jahvonis said he freed someone from East Nodin. Has anyone matched that description?" Vallen asked.

"A messenger bird arrived when you came back, Sebastian. It's addressed to Jahvonis. If by chance would you give this to him?" a guard said.

"Yes. Vallen, come with me, please." I brought him to the hut where Xavion and Sareyus sat in an embrace.

"Holy shit! Xavion, oh Xavion, you're here! This couldn't be any better," Vallen said with glee.

"Vallen! It's about time you got here. I knew after our last incident you would come!" Xavion said.

"Indeed. You're the young lady from the king's tent that day! Sareyus, am I correct?"

"Yes," Sareyus replied.

"I should've said before, I love your hair! But, Xavion, business first," Vallen added. He told Xavion everything that Johan planned for the war.

"Sebastian, close the door," Xavion requested.

I closed the door and hoped no trouble would start.

"Vallen, it was you who brought me into the military. It was you who represented the better of your House. You were the Caretaker to the throne. You fought Johan in my defense when no one else would. It was you who hired Jahvonis to kill Mataraves. Vallen, you have earned my respect, and you have proven your honor and valor," Xavion said as he began to unravel the sack. He signaled us to keep silent.

Sareyus gripped unto Xavion. She loves him. Xavion with his right hand pulled out the hooded cowl of Jahvonis!

"Vallen, you and I have met and worked together before. Can I trust you to keep your faith and keep this moment in this hut?" Xavion said without speaking the name of our hero.

Vallen could not hold his shock and excitement forever. As the puzzle was finally solved, Vallen had a tremendous idea.

"You, Xavion, should lead us! We should prepare a militia if we do not finish the ship in time! Now that we have you here, there's no way Johan or Aylund could stop us. Show them both that their feud will not take hold of the free surface people!" Vallen exclaimed.

"Leading an army of my own was not on the agenda. I hoped the ship would finish so we could flee south," Xavion replied.

Sareyus sat quietly still holding on to him. Her head rested on his left shoulder.

"Xavion, I agree with Vallen. We need a backup plan in case the ship is not done. The neighboring towns of Cold Hill and Steelburrow have contributed to the construction. Starkstad has military allies to the south and west. The towns of Natur, Hav, Stentran, Vindtra, and Miolan would be willing to amass a force to defend their independence. Up north is Theranth territory, but they have their hands full with Kuolemajää. No news of conflict is known," I said.

With Xavion's absence, I have been appointed as a representative of freed slaves. Kristoff gave me this role after Jahvonis left.

"When Jahvonis freed me, I turned to Starkstad to find shelter. I told Lord Kristoff of my identity, and he was ahead of me with amassing an army," Vallen added.

"The surface knows of your military deeds, Xavion. Having you among the Independent force would ease the tension and increase hope," I stated.

Sareyus felt the left leg of Xavion. She reached for a canteen of water to which Xavion drank.

"While you both make valid statements, I will not take charge unless it is officially given to me. Sareyus, what do you think I should do?" Xavion asked of the lady.

She hesitated but gave her opinion. "I have seen your bravery and willingness to find peace. You told me everything you thought I should know about your journey. I could not have asked for anyone better to lead us. I respect you, Xavion," Lady Sareyus said.

"I will have to meet Kristoff to discuss this matter. I'll take a horse tomorrow to meet him. I call this meeting adjourned," Xavion said.

"Thank you for everything, Xavion!" Vallen replied.

"Where will you be staying?" I asked Xavion.

"He can stay here if he wants," Sareyus said as she turned to him.

"Sure," he replied.

"Be safe, you two. Get well soon, Xavion," I stated as I went my way and closed the door behind me.

In Sareyus's View

I still held on to Xavion. I can feel his powerful energy resonating within his beautiful body. I started to caress him. For a half hour I was touching him from his feet to his shoulders. He's very ticklish. I could sense the heat of romance in him. He entered a state of tranquility. He allowed me to massage him.

"Xavion, do you feel the same way that I feel for you?" I asked.

"When I saw you that day, I fell into a flush of action. Your appearance reminded me of the princess. You became the initiation of my second chance. My time to act came. My tale last night with your attention opened me. Those first few months were my worst, but fifteen years of patient development is paying off. I admire you, Sareyus."

I kissed his left cheek. As the night began, Xavion and I slept in the same bedroll. We were up talking about whatever we could. He is shirtless. The star on his chest is alluring on him. Damn it, I want to mount him. He looks irresistible! I lifted up my nightgown, and he played with my stomach. All the cuddling put me to sleep. Xavion's breath upon my neck wetted my desires. He is caressing and gripping my torso folds. It tickles as he traces my stretch marks. He also circles his right index finger around my navel.

"Xavion, is your octagram a tattoo?"

"I am not sure. My earliest memory is waking up with it. I thought it was a tattoo because of the purple color. However, the skin beneath it shows signs of scarring and burns, somewhat like a branding."

I am retracing it with my right index finger. His skin is almost infant smooth. His broad chest and shoulders pulse my estrogen. Upon him, I see the occasional open and closed comedones. Parts of his body have keloid bumps, most likely over healing from acne. He also has battle scars and stretch marks on his torso. He has attractive body fat. He's somewhat voluptuous for a man.

"I like your octagram! It makes your Soruthian blood bloom. It accurately matches your eyes. The most exotic man I have seen." I smiled among our mutual blush. Our first time sleeping next to each other is polite. The gentle caressing raised my goose bumps. I have never been affectionately caressed before. I hope we stay together.

The next day after work, I returned to my hut. When I went to sleep, I divided my body and spirit. I traveled through the cosmos to the Gods' Hall. I felt a strange feeling as I journeyed. When I arrived, I called an emergency meeting. It is time for Jahveyis to explain this Jahvonis character. I projected my current form there. As the others sat in their chairs, I stood before them and spoke.

"Gods and goddesses, I, Sareyus, have called this council with new information. In my time among the mortals, I have learned many things that have crossed over from the Second Life. I have befriended your son, Xavion, and the stories he has told me include all of us. I have seen his work on the battlefield, and you succeeded in your goal. Xavion is the ultimate warrior. What I am about to say concerns you, most of all, Jahveyis."

The Dark Lord's eyes reddened with curiosity.

"Xavion for most of his life has been aligned with—"

"My son," Jahveyis interrupted.

The gods turned upon him as he took a deep breath.

"What son?" Lyannis exclaimed.

"In the Second Life, Miolannis and I came across a suicidal man in Sönderfall. This was a week before Mustasurma was created. The man was Adrian Erik. He begged me to smite him with Hellhammer, but I dared not. After talking with him, Miolannis and I persuaded him to keep his life. I offered him an occupation as a prophet to my wife and I. A bargain was struck. If he wiped crime from the world, I would resurrect his husband from the grave. As the deal was made, I titled him 'Jahvonis' after my wife and I."

"Tell them what else happened!" I commanded.

Jahveyis scowled upon me as the others returned the glare upon him.

"As the Second Life ended and the earth was near implosion, I betrayed the trust of my son and allowed him to die. I asked him to fight crime, not rule the lands with an iron fist. As he died, I damned him to hell until his job is done correctly. Miolannis and I have known about the fellowship of our sons for years now," Jahveyis admitted.

This threw the room into a frenzy.

"How dare you choose a prophet without our consent!" Carune shouted.

"We have rules against this shit!" Tovis yelled.

"Why should you have your own child?" Bravious added.

"Everyone, quiet! I have something to say!" Jado exclaimed.

"I may as well come clean. I have been providing Xavion with books. He is the only one who possesses a copy of the Hallowed Holds that include Jahvonis. When Xavion is asleep, I go to his room and place books there for him to learn from. I did not know that Jahveyis's son would latch onto him!" Jado explained, which brought shock to Lyannis.

Now the metaphorical fingers were pointed at Lord of Knowledge.

"There is more. The reason why most of you did not know of Jahvonis is because… Cosmos carefully hid him from our attention. They came to me after the Second Armageddon. It was they who wanted Jahvonis's name in the new Holds. Each banner of the original Hand of Doom displayed Jahveyis's helmet and mace. At the time, we all thought it was Jahveyis who marshaled people against the dragons. Jahvonis was well hidden and operated from the background," Jado said. "Cosmos had another secret task for me. I was ordered to maintain the health of Kane Beorler during his comatose state. I imbued his brain and body with the martial arts that are needed to be in the Hand of Doom. Kane was still formally trained by his superior. Cosmos intended Kane to have a recurring role in Xavion's story. I could not deny them. I assume Kane has a higher purpose."

Jado and Jahveyis bowed their heads in shame.

"Damn you, people! Is there anyone else who knows about this?" Sarue asked in anger.

"I will add this, Xavion forged the suit, Jahvonis is much more skilled and powerful within Xavion's body. He grows stronger by feeding off of Xavion's energy. I am convinced that Jahvonis sees the error in his ways and uses Xavion as a way to repent. He has saved me from harm many times," I said.

"Jahveyis, what power does Jahvonis have on his own?" Jado asked.

"Jahvonis is in tune with the energy of my wife and I. He has no powers in necromancy or frost magic. We stripped him of those long ago. He is a leech, and he feeds off of Xavion. Jahvonis is not one to abuse his abilities, but because of Jado, Jahvonis found the perfect vessel. His grudge is with me most of all," Jahveyis stated.

"Can we trust him not to reveal us to Xavion?" Bravious questioned.

"I cannot guarantee it," Jahveyis replied.

"This is a problem! If Jahvonis turns Xavion against us, then we are in danger!" Lyannis exclaimed.

"Sareyus, why would Xavion reveal this to you? Are you sleeping with him?" Sarue accused.

"He told me because he trusts me. He admitted that he's in love with me, and what we do is none of your damn business!" I said back at Mother Nature.

"It is our business, Sareyus! Since Miolannis created the reproductive act, we made the law for any of us to *not* bed a mortal!" Jahveyis said.

"You all made Xavion as a man with powers! How 'mortal' is that? I've seen him kill armies, climb walls bare handed, and will eventually see him cast lightning! You think a mere human being can do anything like that? Xavion is not mortal by any means! He's a demigod if anything else!" I exclaimed.

"But he's our son, Sareyus! He's a child in comparison to you!" Carune insulted.

"Your son is in love with me! He was caressing me last night!" I said back at the Lady of the Sea.

We began to argue among ourselves. I defended my right to love Xavion and take him as a mate. I shouted my right to have a husband if the other goddesses could.

"You are all unworthy to be worshipped!" a loud voice screamed from behind me.

My projected form turned with the Gods' eyes watching me. From the shadows, we saw the ethereal form of Jahvonis!

"You fools! Time and time again you prove why you can't be trusted!" Jahvonis shouted upon us.

After a brief shock, the Dark Lord stood in defiance.

"Begone, demon!" Jahveyis yelled as he conjured the dreaded Hellhammer mace into his right hand.

The other gods leaped from the table in fright. Bravious and Tovis stood in front of Carune and Sarue. Lyannis prepared a spell of light to banish the darkness of Hellhammer if it is used. She pushed Jado behind her. I stood only a few feet away from Jahvonis.

"It is good to see you, Lady Sareyus. I wondered when we would have our time," he said.

"You will not touch her, cursed child!" Jahveyis yelled.

"And who will stop me if do?" Jahvonis joked.

"Touch any of us, and I will banish you to the sun!" Lyannis threatened.

"Cast your spell, sun goddess, and Xavion will come with me!" Jahvonis threatened back.

"Damned soul of Sönderfall, what have you done to our son?" Bravious questioned in anger.

"I have given him a life and friends! I aide him to discover his destiny! It is because of me that Xavion and Sareyus are in love. But because of you, Father, I am cursed to fight forever. And thanks to Jado's assistance, Xavion chose to resurrect me. Where you all chose to neglect him and push all of your problems on Xavion, I am helping him find his way in life. All eight of your shortened sights have made me more powerful than ever! Your cowardice and demented sense of honor are the reasons why the dragons still wish to usurp you! It is all your fault why Miolannis is a prisoner to Kuolemajää!" Jahvonis said to us as he turned to Jahveyis.

"And how dare you raise Black Leaf from beyond!" Jahvonis grunted at his father. "You made a promise to *me* if I wiped crime and corruption from your world that I would have my husband back! Instead, you bring him back after I am long dead, and your bastard Mustasurma recruits him into the new Hand of Doom? I *am* the Hand of Doom! I created the Black Hole Sun to slay Mustasurma, and you spare him over me? Now with Xavion, you want to use him as a way to repent for all of your sins!" Jahvonis screamed at us.

"I am guilty of creating Ahneus, but I had nothing to do with Xavion. The rest of us had nothing to do with you, Adrian Erik. Your parents adopted you and made you, Jahvonis. Whatever familial problems you have are between you and the Courtship!" I replied to him.

"This is not your problem, Sareyus. But for the rest of you, Xavion came to me. I trained Xavion. I showed him the way of the ninja. I am his sensei. Xavion was there for me when Black Leaf died again, and I was there when his first love was taken from him! Xavion is *mine!*" Jahvonis menaced.

"Heretic! We created Xavion. He bares our blood in his veins!" Sarue said.

"And I bare his blood in mine!" Jahvonis added. "I am a part of the parents, and therefore, I cannot be touched without harm being brought to Xavion!" Jahvonis gloated.

Jahveyis lost his calmness. His eyes flared red, and he cast Hellhammer through the air. Lyannis panicked and tossed her ball of light. The light shined upon the mace as Jahvonis caught it by the handle in his right hand. A mass of darkness and light resonated in the hand of the Black Paladin. The eyes of Jahvonis sparked and turned purple. Multiple pupils formulated in his eyes, and he cast the mace back to Jahveyis. The bright light tainted Hellhammer, and the mace struck the face of the Dark Lord and sent him to the floor!

The other seven of us reeled in terror as Carune and Sarue screamed. Bravious and Tovis charged to attack. Bravious ran and wound up an earthquaking punch as Tovis threw a lightning bolt. Jahvonis grasped the fist of Bravious while catching the bolt and casting it to the ceiling. The Black Paladin kicked Bravious far across the room into the arms of Tovis. They both crashed through the table and knocked a hole in the wall!

"This is how the mighty gods choose to treat their child? I've learned all I need to know. Good luck getting Miolannis back on your own!" Jahvonis said as he backed into the darkness and the shadows faded to light.

Tovis and Bravious are unconscious. Jahveyis lies bleeding with Hellhammer tainted by the light. The goddesses cower in fear as two of their husbands were defeated. I returned to the earth.

"Sareyus, Sareyus, wake up, beautiful," Xavion said as I awoke with his arm wrapped around my stomach. "You looked troubled while you slept. Is all well?"

"Only a dream. I am safe now that you're here," I replied. I turned over to the sack and saw a piece of Jahvonis's black fabric poking through. I was startled.

"Easy, my lady. It's only clothes," Xavion said to comfort me.

I could not tell anything about my dream. I fear Jahvonis may tell Xavion that he shares a bed with a goddess. If he tells him, all of my work could be undone.

"I should get going. Kristoff and I must meet," Xavion said.

As I crawled away from him, he firmly clasped my stock.

"It's big, huh?" I joked as he smiled.

He spanked my right cheek. It stung.

In Xavion's View

I gathered my things and prepared to leave for Starkstad. After handling Sareyus, I grabbed the sack and soon stuffed it into another. I have a small utility knife sheathed on my waist. Before I left, I opened and read the letter addressed to Jahvonis.

Dear Jahvonis,

> *Thank you once more for freeing me. My life was at a turning point to which you guided me in the right direction. I will serve the Independent Party of Nodin. We will unite our land and banish the two empires. I owe you my life and will serve*

you as a friend and ally. As planned, I
will come to the construction site to wait
for you. The time of one Nodin has come!

Sincerely,
Bjorn Adolf Edling

All according to plan! I knew Bjorn hated his father enough to join Kristoff. All these years of hard work are paying off. In the past fifteen years, I have been planting the seeds of a free Independent Party for all people in Nodin. While I am freeing slaves, I inspire some to join our cause. Kristoff and the other willing towns have been encouraging peace with their Theranth neighbors to the north. About forty-five of the Theranth tribes have signed treaties and pledged to serve the Independent Party. They joined to defend their freedom and their land from any threat. Although I did not intend to lead their forces, I admit it would be a fine story for a Soruthian to lead a Nodinian Army. It's an hour's ride to Starkstad. I brought the suit with me. I kissed Sareyus before I left. As I rode, I spoke to the horse, "Do you mind carrying me?"

"It is an honor to carry you, Lord Xavion. My father told me you healed his sore hoof when he was young. My master named me Aapo," he replied.

From behind, I heard the loud chirping of a bird. It landed on my left forearm.

"What have you learned, Cardalen?" I asked.

"East Nodin has begun building camps outside their gate. I managed to fly inside to watch Aylund train. He's become proficient with a sword," Cardalen said.

"What else?" I replied.

"I overheard that Aylund sent a party of men to acquire Theranth help. Amandus slaughtered the party and impaled their heads outside of his village," Cardalen said.

"After what Amandus did to Leif Edling, he will not join either of his sons. The Independent Party has aid from the Theranths but not Amandus's tribe," I replied.

"Will you be fighting, my lord?" Cardalen asked.

"Fighting is a last resort. If we cannot get enough of the civilians out in time, I will join the battle to unite Nodin," I said.

"Xavion, you are a friend to the animal kingdom. We will fight if you need us," Cardalen said.

We crossed into the forest. Cardalen rested upon my left shoulder. I've always enjoyed being beneath the trees, more than any other environment. The trees are still lightly dressed in snow. Except for my utility knife, the weapons I use as Jahvonis are hidden in the sack.

All of my other weapons are back in my cell. I have no way to retrieve them yet. I do miss my talwar, jambiya, and books most of all. Cardalen began to whistle a tune to pass the time. The air is cool. A strange mist appeared from the snow.

"Someone is watching us," Jahvonis said.

Cardalen and Aapo turned their heads to the southeast. Upon the branches of a tall alder tree is a congress of ravens. They are led by a rare albino.

The birds of Miolannis looked down upon us in frozen silence. Aapo stood still.

"In the trees," Aapo said.

I looked up and nothing but dormant leafless branches were above.

"What do you mean, Aapo?" I asked.

"Someone is following us," he replied.

The white raven croaked at us.

"She wants to speak," Cardalen said in reference to the white bird.

I signaled the raven to fly down from her perch. She flew with grace through the autumn air. The soft flaps of her wings carried her onto my right forearm.

"Thank you for your time," she said in a melancholic Noric accent.

"What is it, white raven of the woods?" I replied.

"My name is Valkoinen. I have seen you many years ago in the mountains to the southeast. My congress and I know who you are, Xavion. We are here to deliver news. Our world is in danger. The dragon Kuolemajää is in possession of something powerful. He threatens all that is living. He has tried to enlist us as spies. This congress refused, and we have been exiled from the mountain. Xavion, all the people of the north are in danger. Human, Theranth, beast, and bird alike. Will you battle Kuolemajää?"

"I am aware of Kuolemajää's status, but I'm not sure of what I can do. There is a war looming among the kingdoms and towns. I'm afraid I have priorities," I replied.

"I did not know you are overextended. May I ask if this war resolves in your favor, would you consider our request?"

"I will," I replied.

"Xavion, there has been a strange masked man lurking in these woods. Be mindful of your surroundings," Valkoinen warned.

"Thank you for your warning," I replied.

Aapo strutted on.

The congress of ravens disbanded and flew in all directions.

An hour passed, and I gave permission to Cardalen to depart.

I can hear another horse trotting from ahead. The steps became louder as the horse entered my vision. An armored man is upon a husky bronco. He wears a helmet and an arming sword on his left hip. He looked at me through the eyeholes of the helm and stopped his horse in front of mine.

"I wondered when we would meet again," he said.

"Hello, Bjorn, how are you?" I asked.

"I am grateful to have my life thanks to you. That was the best fight I've ever had."

"Thank you, I'm sorry that I broke your sword. I wasn't expecting my kanabo to be that strong. How is the new blade?"

"This one is more portable. On a battlefield, I feel more comfortable with a zweihander."

"If you're going to the camp down the road, I can possibly make you a new one?"

"If possible, it would be nice. I'm cleared to join the Independent Party. Kristoff had me swear an oath to which I'm happy to help. Are you on your way to the jarl?"

"I am. I can't promise that I'll be accepted."

"As popular as you are up here, I think they would love to enlist you."

"I hope," I stated as Aapo trotted closer. "It's nice to see you again, Bjorn," I politely said, and shook his hand.

"I am sorry for the slur I called you. I was wrong. I was not myself."

"Apology accepted," I replied.

Bjorn and I continued on our ways. Another five minutes passed until I was within Starkstad. The town looked the same. As usual, I drew eyes because I stood out like a sore thumb. Even though I've put up with it for years, it still irritates me. I don't think of them as bigoted; they clearly haven't seen too many Soruthians before. Aapo trotted past the temple. I will make an effort to see Alva. I will have put my suit on so I don't confuse her. Before I left the construction site, I overheard someone speak of a temple maid being attacked by the Hand of Doom. I know in my heart it must have been Alastair who tracked Alva above. She was his favorite. If any harm was brought onto her, Alastair will not get away with it.

My memories of Master Kane also came to mind. I do not hate him. What happened with Mataraves years ago was hard for both of us. Kane was defeated twice by me, and he lost his finest student. At one time Kane admitted he bears no hate toward me; instead, he respects me. Every time we fought afterward, he gave me the option to stand aside and I would not be harmed. His only goal in life is to dethrone Aylund. I doubt he cares anything for Alastair.

I came to the stable of the longhouse. I carried the sack with me.

"Halt. State your business here, young man," one guard said.

"My name is Xavion Mourningstar. I have come to offer the Jarl Soruthian assistance with the journey southward. I have also come to show my support for the Independent Party," I replied.

"So you're the famous soldier from below? Permission granted!" the guard said.

I passed through the doors and entered upon a feast of food and drink.

Kristoff sat in his seat in a proper position. As I came to his front, he looked upon me in curiosity. "State your business, sir," he requested.

"Lord Kristoff Ericson, jarl of the village of Starkstad. My name is Xavion Mourningstar. I am a former soldier of underground West Nodin. I am here to make a request if you allow me?" I said.

"Your name carries weight in Nodin, Mister Xavion. You may make your request," Kristoff permitted.

"First, may I ask that we speak in private?"

"All right then," Kristoff replied. He stood up, and he walked me to a backroom in the longhouse. He took me in and closed the door behind him. "What did you bring that for?" he asked in reference to the suit. He didn't say what because he never knew who may be listening.

"It's a long story. Kristoff, if you plan on going to Soruth, you'll need a Soruthian to intermediate between the two groups," I replied.

"The ship is only a last resort. Johan and Aylund will selfishly have their battle in or near Starkstad. We must show them that the surface people will have no part in their feud. The Independent Party must prove its might by being willing to fight!" Kristoff stated.

"That's the other thing. I want to enlist in your army."

"No, you're going to lead it. You are an army within yourself, and with you, we cannot lose!"

"All right, but we will have to fight them my way. I know Johan and Aylund's armies better than they do."

"Agreed! Welcome to the Independent Nation of Nodin, Commander Mourningstar!" Kristoff happily said with a handshake.

At night, I suited up to find Alva. I checked the inn, but no sign of her is near.

"She's most likely in the temple. The Maidens of the Courtship often gather at night," Jahvonis said.

When I entered the temple, I see many women dancing in bright white gowns. They are dancing beneath the moonlight that shined through the open stone. One of them played a hand drum with a rhythm of nine beats with accents. The rhythm is counted as 2+3+2+2. The nine beats symbolize the nine months of pregnancy. The maidens are eight in number. This is due to the original eight Moon Mothers. When Miolannis formed the moon, she wanted each shape to represent the menstrual cycle of women. The ladies danced in a cold embrace; their power in femininity is grand. I walked slowly and quietly. Their song ended as I stood among them. They are all beautiful and diverse in age. I spoke in the deep voice.

"I am seeking Miss Alva Amott. Is she here?"

"She is recovering in the infirmary down the hall, first door on the right," one lady said.

"Thank you," I replied. As I walked away, some of the women looked on in mystique. When I came into the room of Alva, she is sleeping with a brace upon her nose. She is beneath a brown blanket. There is a chair and a pail of water by her. A dresser is on her right side.

"Alva… Alva… Alva… Alva!" I said while ruffling her awake.

She began screaming frantically while trying to fight me.

"It's Jahvonis!" I said securely.

She then gripped me in a hug while crying.

"What happened to you?" I asked.

She continued to cry. "It was Alastair. He followed us up here. He found me. He beat me, and he raped me!" Alva said.

I grew angry. I pulled the blanket off her and lifted her robe to examine her stomach.

"Stay still and breathe. I will not harm you," I said to comfort her. I entered my blood vision. As I saw the blood being pumped through her body, I checked her heartbeat. Everything looked normal…until I looked at her stomach near her waist. I saw a mass of blood. It is as I feared—fertilization and implantation is complete. "Oh no!" I said to myself.

Alva is breathing heavily. She is pregnant with Alastair's child. She will not want to have a rape baby. I pondered through my mind for an idea. If my blood with Jahvonis's is partially godlike, perhaps it can heal Alva?

With his blood, I learned how to defend myself better. I looked within the drawer and found a syringe among other tools.

"Alva, you're badly hurt. I can give you back all the blood you have lost. It might heal you. If you are willing to take my blood, I will give it to you," I offered.

Alva cried more and began to speak. "Take this pain from me, once and for all!" she exclaimed.

"Help her, Xavion," Jahvonis said.

I turned around, removed a gauntlet, and stuck the needle in my arm. After eight ounces, I withdrew the needle and submerged the tip in water. I helped Alva out of her gown. I will inject the blood into four points. I chose the space above her left breast, her stomach, a space between her stomach and vagina, and lastly into her left wrist vein. The white smoke again secreted from my body.

Within the smoke, I see a white figure forming beside Alva. It looks like a white Jahvonis. For eighty minutes, Alva groaned and twitched. Her bones grew and contorted. My blood aged the fertilized egg backward. Once the egg and sperm cell were divided, the sperm cell was expelled from the birth canal. The egg returned to its original ovary. Somehow my blood detects sources of pain, be they emotional, physical, mental, or spiritual. The child was conceived from sexual violence, which inflicted pain on all four.

Her muscle tissue flexed and tightened. Her nose straightened. Several more brain stems and cells formed. She grew four inches and aged four years. I saw her blue eyes become purple. When Alva stopped, she returned to a calm breath. As she opens her eyes, she is twenty years old and five foot ten. After many deep and slow breaths, she spoke. "Take me from here."

That night Alva bid farewell to her eight sisters. She rode with me upon Aapo. Alva was not a full lady of the moon. There are only eight at a time for each temple, no more, no less. She sat in front of me on Aapo, my arms wrapped around her to reach the reins to steer. She is wrapped in a coat while wearing her black hair down her shoulders.

I can feel Jahvonis's power inside her. There is also a deep-frozen sadness.

"It's my fault. It's my fault why he attacked me," Alva dolefully said.

"It was *never* your fault! He will not get away with this, I promise you!" I replied powerfully.

The night is cold. I heard the croaking of Valkoinen. Alva looked into the eyes of the white raven, and she was entranced in her gaze. The moon is full. Its radiant light shined upon the white bird and Alva.

I know in the days to come, Alva will become more in tune with my energy, both as Xavion and Jahvonis. What was the white ethereal being in the smoke? The form had breasts. After an hour, Alva rested her head upon my chest and slept. She is charming and has much potential to be something great. On the outskirts of the construction site, I woke Alva up and spoke. "Alva, you must continue on without me."

"Please don't go! I need you to protect me!" she whimpered.

"I can't protect you forever. Soon you will learn to fight, but I have to go. Here, take this knife. The site is down the road. Please be brave," I said.

She is still hesitant. After grabbing the sack, I tapped Aapo, and he ran all the way to the site. Under the cover of darkness, I changed back into my clothes and returned to Sareyus's hut.

Chapter 11

In Sareyus's View

This morning, I awoke to find Xavion sleeping next to me with his arm wrapped around my stomach. I can feel his morning erection touching my behind. I nearly burst into flames from the ecstasy I felt. I have never been in contact with a man like that, and I thought heavy with fantasies.

He prepared breakfast for us with fruit, bread, and milk. Afterward, Xavion helped with the ship. In another three months, we should be done. We have nearly two hundred people working daily. They come from many towns. When Xavion and I were carving a large beam of wood, we conversed.

"Xavion, do you miss Astrid?" I asked.

"I miss her as much as I loved her. She was my first love, and I will never forget her. I am yours now, Sareyus. Let's not discuss our past interests."

"What is your favorite kind of sword?"

"I greatly prefer Barkish swords. The talwar I told you about is my favorite. I find the curved single-edged blades to be ingenious in design. I admire the aesthet-

287

ics of Nodinian broadswords. Personally, Soruthian and certain Yazjian blades satisfy me. Have you ever used a sword before, beautiful?"

"I have sparred with sticks, but I have no formal training. I am an admirer of the Ewart Park sword. The neighboring Cels and Angish used it extensively when they feuded. My accent identifies me as Celic," I replied.

"I have wondered which of the Nodinian nations you are descended from. What more can you tell me?"

"I am of the Western Cels. Our flag is green, white, and orange. The Eastern Cels' flag is blue and white. For a long time, all of Nodin was under the Italese Empire. When the empire fell, the other nations tried taking the ruling spot. Ang became the nearest successor but the Cels and Frankish fought the Angish at once. It was an era of Independent Wars, hence why Nodinians are often xenophobic. Nodin and Yazjia are notorious for having warring states. Soruth, at minimum, is a continental union."

"You are well educated, Sareyus." Xavion smiled with a violet sparkle in his eyes.

As we kept carving, I see a woman in white walking toward us. For a moment I thought it was Miolannis.

"Hello, Sareyus," the woman said.

I realize it is Alva, but she is…older. She is taller than me and looks about twenty years old. Within her, I sense the energy of the gods…and Xavion. What happened?

"Alva, thank the gods, you're okay!" I said as we hugged.

I cannot understand how she became an adult overnight. She looks like a cross of Carune and Miolannis.

Alva's eyes are blue and calm, but she looks energeti-
cally enhanced. Did Xavion do this? I cannot help but be
paranoid that this is his doing. Damnit, I can't ask him
without raising suspicion.

"Who is this?" Alva questioned.

"My name is Xavion, milady."

"Oh yes, you're the blacksmith. How could I forget?" Alva stated.

"Are you here to help with the ship?" I asked her.

"I was wondering if either of you knows where
Jahvonis is?" Alva questioned.

"I haven't seen Jahvonis since he brought us above,"
I replied.

"But I can sense him. He must be somewhere around
here," Alva stated.

"Alva, you should speak to the guards. They can
help you more than we can. I bet Sebastian would be
happy to see you," Xavion politely said.

"Are you two a couple?" she questioned.

"We share a hut," I replied.

"How lucky you are, Sareyus. Good day," Alva said.

After Xavion and I finished carving, we hoisted the
beam on our shoulders and placed it in its spot in the ship
frame.

That night, Xavion and I ate dinner in our hut. He
made soup with noodles, chicken, and many spices. With
it, we had a loaf of bread with cow milk and cheese. The
joys I have when eating are great. In heaven, we gods
have no use for food and drink because we are immortal.
We develop no sense of hunger or appetite.

This soup is delicious! Goodness, Xavion is a fine cook! I had two bowls. I feel beautiful being heavier. Xavion finds my numerous stretch marks to be delightful. The folds on my torso are many handles for him. Goodness, I feel blessed with how tender and firm he treats me. It was Lyannis who designed the human anatomy. Lyannis is bold and weighted, Miolannis is petite, Carune is mildly stout, and Sarue is tall and fit. In the Hallowed Holds within the book of Lyannis, it states, *"Love and Beauty are everywhere. Both have no single form."*

After dinner, Xavion and I went to bed. Even though I am the goddess of fire, I burn with warmth when I'm next to him. What I love about Xavion is his intellect, manners, altruism, genuineness, sense of formality, and kindness. I admire his eyes and smile. His eyes and face light up like the dawn sky where the moon and starlight gives way to the sun and its rainbow entrance. His body is mildly toned. I like a man with less muscle. I felt his hand firmly grip my bottom. I had no idea that my behind is so fat. I love it! As I began to sleep, I kept seeing faint purple lights across from me. The left eye hole of the Jahvonis cowl gleamed purple. He is watching us.

In Alva's View

I keep seeing Alastair in my dreams. I can't accept that I've had to let him hurt me for years in order to eat. The night he raped me in the temple was when the Eight Moon Sisters were elsewhere in Starkstad. They returned later to find me still lying on the floor with Alastair's semen dripping out of me. I can still feel him beating me and my head bouncing off the floor. All of my partners were flowers compared to him. He would always harm me during sex, and no one told him to stop! The dreams and nightmares of those dark days still cut into my soul. I hate every one of those men and women who hurt me! Yes, some of my customers were women! Human beings should never be allowed to have power, just look at all the atrocities that have happened!

Jahvonis is different. He is brave enough to fight against those who abuse their power and caught me in his arms as I fell from the cliff. He nursed me back to health and brought me to this camp. I share a small hut with Sebastian. I am wrapped in a blanket. I kept the knife Jahvonis gave me within reach. I feel so different after Jahvonis put his blood into me. I trusted him enough to see me without my gown, and he did not harm me. I'm in love with Jahvonis. He has protected me so much that I feel affection for him.

I heard someone say, "Wake up." My eyes gently crept open, and I saw Jahvonis standing in the darkness above me.

"Stay quiet. I have some work for you," he said.

I stood up and got dressed. The time approaches midnight. I followed Jahvonis thirty minutes deep into the forest. I trust he is not taking me into danger. Strangely, I see clearly though it is night. The darkness did not blind me. I can see insects on the ground. We came to a crescent rock formation near the sea.

"Why have you brought me here?" I asked.

"Alva, for years you have been a victim of men and women. You are a former brothel slave and a survivor of rape. When I came to you that night, I saw a fertilized egg in your womb. When I injected my blood into you, the fertilized egg was painlessly disassembled and your injuries were healed. I watched you toss and turn as you grew into an adult. I would not allow you to bear Alastair's child, so I freed you from a forced and unfair pregnancy," Jahvonis admitted. "I will not always be there to protect you. Your attackers made you an objectified victim. A portion of that is because you do not know how to defend yourself."

The moon shined upon me and waves bashed against the rocks.

"I have a story for you. In the land of Daichi, far to the east, a ronin samurai disobeyed his master and fled for his life. The samurai disagreed with the oppressive methods of his shogun. As he traveled across Yazjia, he crossed paths with a monk from Hongangou. As they spoke, the monk offered the ronin a way to increase his skill as a martial artist and to aid the oppressed people. This was the birth of ninjutsu, the way of the ninja. The ninja in many cases fought against high society and protected the common people. Alva, you must learn to protect yourself, for if Alastair attacks you again, he will eventually kill you. I can teach you a variety of fighting styles. As your sensei, I can turn you into the most dangerous woman alive. All I need is your trust, effort, and respect. Will you have me?" Jahvonis asked.

I looked into the eyes of Jahvonis and was entangled in hope and romance. He can save me by teaching me! "I choose you, Jahvonis Sensei," I said happily and bowed.

He stood me up, and I smiled with the light of my teeth shining off his cowl.

"First, you will learn to use this," he said while tapping my forehead. "Then you will learn to use these." He held my hands. "Then you will learn to use one of these." He unsheathed a dagger from his hip.

I nodded my approval.

The moon is centered in the southern sky. Midnight came. My training began with basic forms of defense and novice strikes. We did them slowly. Immediately, I felt like a warrior. We stood facing the ocean and let nature be our audience. I feel more sensitive to my surroundings. My senses are clearer and more defined.

"Take in the world around you. Breathe it deep into your lungs, and slowly push out the darkness. Good. Visualize your goals and make way to them. Excellent. Keep going," Jahvonis instructed.

After four hours of practicing his forms, he gave one more exercise.

"Follow me to the stone over yonder. There we will meditate above the water. A shinobi and kunoichi must be one with the world around them. As you meditate, you will straighten your back, soften your gaze, and slowly count your breath on the exhale. After ten breaths, restart from one. With each thought, I want you to release it and return to an empty mind. We are going to do this until dawn," Jahvonis said as we sat with our crossed legs toward the ocean.

While following his instructions, I keep seeing Alastair's face and each face of my attackers.

"Think of each person as an unwelcome house guest and send them out," Jahvonis stated. "The spirit, heart, body, and mind need to work as one machine, Alva. Your four aspects need healing."

For two hours, I sat with my sensei and I grew deeply romanticized with him. The silence became all I heard, and as I felt the sunshine upon my back. I stopped counting and opened my eyes. Jahvonis is gone. I returned to camp. With each soft and delicate footstep, I felt the power of the earth resonating into my body. I entered the guards' barracks to use the lavatory. There is a long vertical mirror that stands at my height. The door is locked behind me. I looked in the mirror, and my level of shock is alarming.

I looked no longer like a child. I reached a level of physical maturity that would deem me full grown. My nose is entirely straight. My hair is longer, and the light reflected off it.

"What…did he do to me? I'm beautiful!" The muscles on my arms and legs are harder and tighter. Whatever Jahvonis did caused my teenage years to be skipped and I entered adulthood. He dispelled my predator's baby, healed me, turned me into a woman, and is now teaching me the fighting arts.

In Narration

The night after Alva's first training session, Xavion suited up and met Bjorn in his hut. Bjorn told Jahvonis all he learned of Aylund's plans. Jahvonis told Bjorn to relay the information to Xavion. During autumn's passing, Sareyus's powers returned to their normal state.

On the twenty-first of December, the winter solstice occurred. Nodin's worst and coldest days have come. This is troubling due to Kuolemajää's capture of Miolannis. The goddess controls the winter every year, but her immobilization will either allow the dragon to command it or the season will rule itself. The people of the North will have to be brave during this time until spring comes in March.

Alva's training with Jahvonis transferred from the physical world to her dreams, just as Xavion did years before. With Xavion's blood within Alva, she learns quickly and advances in rank with speed.

Starkstad began smuggling operations to and from West Nodin. In time, Xavion was reunited with his military armor and weapons. The weapons included his talwar, tomahawks, the Mourningstar mace, the kanabo, the jambiya, and his shield. He also was reunited with his books and a chest with eight hundred amethyst stones. Xavion was also given his own business house. He could smith in peace while housing Sareyus, Sebastian, and Alva. Xavion hid the Jahvonis suit and weapons in a locked chest.

Alastair's search for Jahvonis continues to fail. His leadership of the Hand of Doom has lessened in quality and wisdom. Many times he has crossed Master Kane and ignored his advice, thus causing division, confusion, and turmoil among the recruits. With the knowledge of the Independent Party, Kane's mind and ideals began to shift toward a better future. He only works with the Hand in order to stop Aylund. Now there is a full nation that challenges both Aylund and Johan for independence. Kane now sees an army marching on instead of a small underground band of assassins. Where Kane was during these past few months is a mystery; thus, Alastair had no help from his father.

Back in November, King Johan sent Daveth to retrieve Xavion. When Daveth saw the empty cell, he panicked and frantically ran to inform Johan. The king's mind spun out of control with paranoia and fear. He knew he could not win the war without Xavion. Every day the guards go on a manhunt to find their weapon. They hung wanted posters of Xavion with a more ape-like appearance.

Since the altercation with Jahvonis, the gods are still timid and afraid of him. Jahveyis's past once again came back to haunt him. His firstborn son has been raising the youngest born as his own. Despite Xavion and Jahvonis being stepbrothers, they are technically also siblings with the dragons. Not all of the dragons are siblings with each other. Mustasurma and Kuolemajää are brothers. Ukkosen and Hayat Katil are brothers, and Avgrund is their cousin. Ahneus is an only child. Each problem of the gods is related to their children. Xavion may be the latest.

Sareyus feels because she is Xavion's partner that Jahvonis will leave her be. Xavion sees Sareyus as the largest ray of light since Astrid. Xavion's interest in orange-haired women is great, and it often excites him beyond belief. Jahvonis cannot tell Xavion that he caresses a goddess; it would confuse him. Jahvonis needs Xavion's trust as a partner in order to do his job. Each night, Xavion goes to rest with Sareyus. Jahvonis tunes out and blocks them to give their privacy. He envies their mixed relationship. The combination is a reminder of him and Black Leaf. He grieves because Black Leaf was a tool and once more is dead, his soul free while Jahvonis is cursed.

Sareyus now understands why Miolannis created temptation and procreation. They test your commitment and patience. Xavion is tamer. To indulge in the flesh is foreign to him. Sareyus does want to marry him, but she has not thought far ahead. How can she be a goddess and have a relationship with a mortal without conflict? Sareyus is hopeful that fate will put them together for eternity. Each time Xavion and Sareyus kiss, their powers and spiritual essence enter each other.

If they made love, they would acquire their powers. This is also possible by sharing blood. The gods did not tell her that Xavion can have multiple orgasms and ejaculations. He produces many times more sperm than any human or Theranth. It was the gods' idea for Xavion to have as many children as possible. When the Immortals are on the earth in physical form, the gods produce sperm and the goddesses menstruate and produce eggs.

In Xavion's View

I am here crafting a greatsword for Bjorn. I know he'll love it. I don't make many two-handed weapons, so this is a learning experience. Through the alliance with the Theranths, Bjorn was able to acquire a large ingot of theranthium (which I've never worked with before).

Bjorn is six feet eleven and roughly 260 pounds. I believe he can handle the size and balance. Bjorn wants a thirty-eight-inch blade with a straight horizontal crossguard, a twenty-inch handle, and a six-lobed pommel. He also wants two brown leather grips (one on the handle and the other on the blade). There is a second crossguard above the upper grip; this is used for different handling.

He also wants letters engraved on both sides of the bottom crossguard. He wants the word *Mellanöstern*, which is a Noric word for "Middle Eastern." After two weeks, the sword is complete. The sheath is wood covered in brown leather.

A sword this large is intended *only* for the battlefield, *not* for civilian use. It is intended to dismount cavalry opponents and break pike formations (hence the reason for the long blade). When marching to battle, the user of this sword will hold it with the blade resting flat against the shoulder.

Later one afternoon, I delivered Mellanöstern to Bjorn (who is head of the infantry). "By the gods!" many said as Bjorn unsheathed the greatsword. The sunlight and snow gleamed off the blade, and the letters resonated in the light. The sword glowed with bright clear silver, and Bjorn stood tall above us. His presence and stature harnessed the energy of the mighty Nodinian kings of old. I saw a tear come to the giant's eye. Never has anyone made a gift for him so beautiful.

Alva is greatly improving with her training. She'll be a fine ninja. I want her to be my partner in crime fighting. I have gotten a rise out of her to defend those who have been victimized. The image of the white female figure in the smoke still comes to mind. I call her the *White Kunoichi of Nodin*. "Kunoichi" is the Daichinian name for a female ninja.

When the time came to design an independent flag, I sat with Kristoff to plan. We chose a purple flag with a star on it.

"Hmmm. Why not a dodecagram, a twelve-point star, and color it white?" Kristoff said.

"Five plus six would be eleven, but twelve is fuller, and purple for the red and blue mixed. Thus, the two warring kingdoms are one among the surface people!" I added.

Within time, I had a flag mounted on my wall along with many purple drapes on the inner walls of my home.

Each allied town and tribe raised the Independent Flag when the design was finished. Near Starkstad is an old mountain fortress that overlooks a field. We can house the innocents deep within the stone while being walled up with an army on the ground. This fortress was used during the Theranth Wars. It is named *Amon Brav*.

My relationship with Sareyus has become serious. At first, I thought she was only using me. The more we stay up late and talk, the more I want to never be away from her. I want to marry her and give her children.

Right now, I am taking a bath with mild temperature water. I kept my jambiya on the tub rim. I lay with my head back upon two pillows with soap in hand. My breathing is calm, and I dozed off. I sense someone nearby and hear soft deep breaths.

"You may join me, Sareyus," I said calmly and smoothly.

She gently walked over from behind me with her feet patting the floor. Her white dress touched the floor. She stood in front of me and began to slowly undress. She blushed red and smiled. The subtlety of her undressing is driving my imagination wild. My wet body hairs rose in the water. My attention submitted to her visual dominance. The straps of her dress fell from her shoulders.

Next, she gripped her underwear by the hips. She inched them down. Seeing her breasts hang in her brazier flushed me red. She took her underwear off the ground and gently cast them to me. She stood authoritative as she paused her seduction. The width of her lower undergarments made my boyish grin fan between my ears. Her devious glare stood with her right hand clenching her dense hip. "Breathe me into you," she demanded softly.

I gently pressed her pair to my face. My cavernous estrogenal inhalations nearly intoxicated me. Her clean odor coursed through my nostrils as it coated my brain cells.

"Good boy."

Sareyus then gently stepped into the tub. Seeing all of her motherly and voluptuous features made the white smoke release from my pores. As she sat, the water began to bubble with heat. Warm moist steam mixed with my smoke.

Her confidence brought a boyish grin that fanned between my ears. Her emerald bug eyes twinkled in starlight. The blushing of her skin contrasts with her freckles and orange hair. To see her womanly neck revealed a feminine tenderness with equal submission and dominance.

Her body language is inviting, like a loved one who visits their beloved's home for a freshly prepared dinner. Sareyus began to flirt with me:

"How are you, handsome? You're blushing."

"I am well, now that you're here. I've never been this close to a woman before."

She looked deep into my eyes. How her emeralds gazed into my amethysts and opened a portal to an experience that further invoked my curiosity.

"You're the only man to see me this way."

I smiled as I looked her in the eye. "The milk and honey drip off you. Am I the first man you've seen this way?"

"The best man I have seen. How you emit a fatherly confidence where infant souls sing to come into life."

Sareyus' seduction awaits us to test the waters. Without intercourse, we took turns pleasuring and satisfying each other. The meeting of our physical and higher selves bloomed and blossomed. Joy, comfort, affection, communication, patience, and passion brought laughter, sighs, and wholeness. A foreshadow where a fertilized garden bears fruit.

That night I suited up and trained Alva in her mind again. I showed her combinations of striking and grappling techniques. I will not teach her everything I know because you can never be too careful with a student's loyalty. I know Jahvonis has not shown me all he learned, and I understand why.

Due to my blood within Alva, she is promoted from one rank to another in quick time. I predict by April, her basic training will be complete. The process is also quicker in her dreams because the experience is added to her physicality while not losing sleep. When the time is right, I will reveal to her that Xavion is Jahvonis while also teaching her to smith.

In the dream world, I send Alva on missions to test her progress. The people and obstacles are built off her imagination. The missions I send her on are primarily reconnaissance, espionage, stealth, combat, and assassination. Her greatest skill is espionage because most people don't suspect a woman to be a spy.

Her second-best skill is hand-to-hand combat. I teach Alva a hybrid system of techniques that come from traditional international styles. These include *wushu, karate, judo, jiu-jitsu, taekwondo, Nodinian martial arts, Shastar Vidya,* and an Ember art called *Okitchitaw.* The first weapon she will learn to use is the knife (which can be applied to daggers).

She is much more flexible and acrobatic than I am. That will add to her skill and agility. Her intuition with countering and evading involves her flexibility. She has not yet unlocked her visual powers (or the *Mourneyes* as I've begun to call them). Jahvonis has commended

Alva's dedication. He feels her energy and power growing. Jahvonis is the sort of man who encourages females
to learn martial arts but he does not discourage males
either.

Over time, I showed her how to use a knife. This
included techniques on slashing, hacking, thrusting,
parrying, and throwing. She started throwing shuriken
along with knives. I suggested that Alva request Xavion
to craft her a sword. When she spoke to Xavion at the
house forge, they were deciding on what kind of sword
would meet her needs most. Alva wanted a Nodinian
broadsword that is emphasized on cutting but is proficient with piercing. We decided on a Frankish arming
word. This sword is quite ordinary in appearance, except
that it has a more forward and blade-heavy balance.
The blade has a thick center spine that gently tapers to a
thrusting point. The blade is double edged.

Even though Nodin is one-sixth of my gene pool,
living here with its people is bittersweet as this tale is
told. To be fair, I have never lived in Soruth or Yazjia.
It's possible that the same social and political problems
happen there as well.

One thing that is trendy in Nodin is for a warrior to
name their weapons (as Bjorn and I have done). The only
named weapon I possess is the Mourningstar mace. I hope
to not use it in this war because of my view on it. I look
at it now resting ominously on its stand. It was the first
weapon I bore in the military and it has taken the lives of
friend and foe. It reminds me of when Jahveyis ordained
Jahvonis with Hellhammer. I consider Hellhammer and

the Mourningstar to be the same terrible weapon in two separate realms.

I still remember the images of the Edling family's demise. I bore the Mourningstar when I carried Hakun from the battlefield. My mace was used to maim Sebastian and murder Astrid, my first love. I stood and walked over to the mace. As I held it in my hands, I felt the grim energy resonating from within itself. After fifteen years, it still looks brand new, just as beautiful as I envisioned it.

"Xavion, what troubles you, beloved?" Sareyus said from behind as she opened the door.

"Sareyus, what do you see in me to love? A man like me is right to be feared, and yet these people treat me like family? They knew me when I never knew them, and they trust me to lead them. If we win this war, they will want me to be a king of some sort. I am not wholly Nodininan, and I am less Snow than anything else," I stated as the lady graced me with her close company.

She gently held my hands and looked up at me. "I see a man who laments all he defeats. I see a man with a conscience with the will to inspire a world to hope and not fear itself. I see you, Xavion, as someone the gods should bow to. I know you don't like fighting, and you did not want this life. It wanted you. You are a sensitive, talented, sincere, and genuinely good person that any man or woman would want. You have many great things ahead of you in both our world and the afterlife. You matter, Xavion," Sareyus truthfully said in a soft tone.

We embraced in a kiss that raised the room temperature. I held her firmly.

From behind, I could feel a secondary embrace. It is…feminine, sad, and affectionate. In my mind, I heard a woman's voice.

"It was never our fault, Xavion."

The presence of the mace changed.

"Sareyus, did you hear something?"

"Only your heart beating against me."

When night fell, I sat in another room of my house while meditating. The white smoke flowed again and surrounded the hearth. The Mourneyes activated, and the black ethereal form of Jahvonis appeared. My master sat down before me, and we spoke. He used his natural voice.

"Tell me how you feel, my apprentice?"

"Master, I am conflicted and haunted."

"Is it the mace again?"

"Partially…"

"Xavion, your mace is only a tool. It has no malicious quality. A warrior and smith should not fear their own creation."

"My tool maimed my friend and killed my first love. How does one keep the tool that hurts the ones he loves?"

"That's how I felt about my father's mace. That's how I felt about the knife we used on Mataraves. In the Second Life, Black Leaf made me that knife, the same knife I used in our ritual. Just as you keep the Mourningstar, I keep the knife to remember my husband."

"Master, how do you feel about Sareyus and I?"

Jahvonis's eyes narrowed. I sense he does not approve.

"You and Sareyus remind me of my marriage. I love how you are a mixed couple. I will advise that war can destroy love and take it away. I know the lady loves you, but I encourage you to learn more of Sareyus before you give yourself to her."

"Do you know something about her that I do not?"

"Only that she desires you more than you desire her. She carries a heavy lust for you, and you prove your strength by making her earn it."

I believe his words and will question him no more on the matter.

"How do you feel about my student Alva?"

"I feel you are adept enough to take an apprentice. Remember, even a master never stops learning. With Alva's enhanced blood, she proves her worth by passing the same schooling I gave you. In the old Hand of Doom, I trained many women to become kunoichi. My second and third in command were women."

"The white figure in the temple that night, what do you think it was?"

"It is possible that our blood with your smoke caused a spirit to enter the room. White is the color of Miolannis, and Alva was a pending Lady of the Moon. We may have spawned a new entity. We may have more company as Alva grows. We will have to make sure this spirit is friendly," Jahvonis said.

"Do you think we did the right thing to help Alva?"

"I think we did the best we could. Alva did not want to be a helpless victim forever. Her enhancements, although unnatural, were the only way to disassemble Alastair's child in her womb. When we saved her, she'll be safe for a short while, but if we teach her, she can save herself for as long as possible."

"How do you feel about me as your apprentice?"

"Xavion, you are a special student. While I have trained hundreds and have lead armies, you hold a unique place in my existence. I could not redeem myself without you. I could not have asked for a finer student," Jahvonis complimented.

As the night went on, we were bonding not just as professionals but as friends.

"Xavion, I believe your talwar is worthy of being named."

"What do you have in mind?"

"I think a Nidian name would work. Your sword has a natural beauty, and it feels feminine to me. It protects the people you love while dealing death to your foes. A natural duality for all weapons. The brass hilt blazes with sunlight, and the steel crescent blade shines with moonlight," Jahvonis added.

I walked over and grabbed my talwar from its stand. I pondered in thought as I unsheathed it. Indeed it has duality in it. A weapon of violence and empowering feminine beauty. I stood facing Jahvonis.

"*Parvati Kali,*" I said.

Jahvonis nodded with approval. As I went to bed, I heard another woman's voice as I cuddled with Sareyus.

"Thank you, Xavion."

The voice had a heavy but charming accent.

Chapter 12

In Alva's View

I have participated in the construction since Jahvonis began training me in my dreams. After my shift with the construction, I went to the secluded area where Jahvonis took me. From the early evening into the late night, I was practicing my martial arts techniques. The blood of my master has me learning quickly. The missions in my dreams are challenging.

It is December 25. A new moon is in the south of the black sky. White fog covered the area. The moon moved and bent the waves of the ocean. I began to sweat as anger began to shroud my mind. Each time I struck the air, I saw Alastair. I returned to being calm as I am taught. My instincts detected someone nearby. I hope it is Jahvonis. I stopped my training and turned to the night sky. I stood in the fog as it began to formulate and take shape in front of me. I held on to my knife. The mist first formed from two feet up to a head. This shape is womanly. She is wholly white and ghostly. Her eyes have black scleras, white irises, and black pupils. She stood at five feet seven.

"Who are you?" I asked.

"I am the Lady of the New Moon. The First Moon Mother of Miolannis," she said in a huskier woman's voice.

"My lady!" I said and knelt on one knee.

"Please stand, Alva. You need not bow before me."

"Why have you come to visit me at this hour?"

"I have come to make a request for thee. There are events in motion that cannot be undone. The blood of my brother will not be enough for you to defend those you love. I can bind my spirit to your soul and make you more powerful than you could imagine. I need assistance to rescue someone important. Her absence is dangerous to your world," said the spirit.

"Jahvonis is your brother?"

"He is my younger stepbrother. I am the first virgin birth that my mother gave. This predates the Courtship of Obsidian Ice."

"What is your birth name, Spirit?"

"My name is Mioleyis. I cannot train you to be a warrior, but I can teach you to bend the moon to your will. I do not offer this with any underhanded agenda, only that you help me."

"Help you with what?"

"Have you heard of the dragon of Vuorijää?"

"I have."

"He has committed a heinous crime against the gods. He has taken my mother hostage while amassing his power in the north."

I froze with fright. One of the gods is a prisoner, and her daughter is requesting my help.

"I will not force you, but if you help me, I can guide you to cleanse your soul."

"If I help you, I only ask one thing in return—for you to tell me who is posing as Jahvonis," I requested.

"You already know the person who masquerades as my brother. Please you are the only one who can help me and the pantheon. I need you to trust me. Alva Amott, will you have me?"

I thought about it. She speaks sincerely, if both Jahvonis and Mioleyis wish me as a student, then I would be foolish to refuse. This is the next step toward cleansing my body and soul. "I will have thee," I replied.

We placed our hands on each other's shoulders. Mioleyis caused a white eclipse-like ring around the new moon. Her eyes turned bold and bright. She broke down into vapor and mixed within the present fog. The fog danced and swirled around me like a tornado. I opened my arms and allowed myself to be engulfed. For eight minutes, a white circle formed beneath me with the power of the new moon energizing me.

"Now we are Mioleyis," she stated from within me.

In Alastair's View

The search for Jahvonis has not gone according to plan. After our last confrontation, he seemed to have disappeared. He must be healing up somewhere, but where? When I find him, I'm going to put an arrow in him. Then I'll pay that temple slut another visit and then that fire-haired girl on the rebound!

Master Kane still challenges my authority in the Hand. I don't know why the recruits look up to him and Mataraves as the best shinobi in Nodin's history. They both were defeated by Jahvonis while I came closest to killing him! Mataraves followed Kane's view of honor and look at what happened! That foolish, senile old man, why is his authority is higher than mine? No wonder he has no wife or children!

After our original hideout was occupied by the West Nodin government, we relocated to another underground area between the East and West Nodin. So far it remains hidden. In the arena, I am sitting upon a stone seat. I am watching a graduation exam for one of Kane's students. In ninjutsu, we do not have belt ranks like other martial arts, instead, we have class rankings. The foot soldiers are called genin. The genin are tasked with the actual missions (but any ninja can do missions). Genin answer to the chunin. Chunin are in charge of giving out contracts and negotiating with the ninja's employer. The ninja work in clans or guilds. The figurehead of the group is called the jonin. Master Kane stepped down and placed Mataraves as jonin. When Mataraves died, Kane resumed the position until I was of age to replace him.

The apprentice will duel his sensei, and in order to succeed, he must get Kane to yield while avoiding a fatal blow. When Kane duels any of his students, he goes easy on them because he knows he'll destroy them with full effort. To the students, Kane represented a dangerous opponent and demanded full effort to achieve results.

Kane uses many forms of sword-based martial arts and combines them into his own style. On his left hip, he wears a Hongangan *dadao* sword.

He does not teach a student all he knows for his own reasons. When in these duels, Kane and the student use bokken wooden swords for obvious safety reasons. Even though Kane and I are at odds, we respect each other's skill in the sword and bow. The duel became entertaining; it reminded me of Kane's duel with Jahvonis. I can tell the student is not fighting with the intention to kill. Kane will use his mercy against him.

After minutes of precise swordplay, the student lost his focus within Kane's intensity. The master swung his bokken against the student's stomach. The student fell to the ground without any injury. I broke out into obnoxious laughter as Kane looked above in a hostile stare.

"Oh, this is hysterical! The boy got annihilated!" I exclaimed in laughter.

The student looked back at me in embarrassment. The audience on the opposite side of the room scolded me with their gaze. Those on my side joined in the laughter.

"Lest you forget that you, Alastair, lost a duel against one of my students and your sensei! You also suffered a humiliating beating!" Kane insulted.

His side of the room agreed with shouting.

"Just as you lost *twice* to Jahvonis in which the second resulted in the death of Mataraves!" I insulted back.

My side of the room shouted in agreement.

"Just as you got a thrashing from Jahvonis at the palace brothel! Just as you continue to fail in killing or locating Jahvonis!" Kane stated as the student fled. Kane tossed the second bokken sword to me.

I'm going to put him in his place!

I went down into the arena and attacked first. I remembered my mistakes with my first duel as a child. The whacking and smacking of the wood is piercing to the ears. When we locked blades, Kane spoke.

"You are a poor shinobi, Alastair! Mataraves would be ashamed of who you have become!"

After five more blade clashes, I replied, "Just as you were a poor soldier and failed husband to your wife!"

Kane's intensity increased, and I lost tempo with his rhythm. I went for a swing, but Kane caught my bokken in his left palm and snapped the blade in his grip. He next performed a stunning spin kick to my temple.

"My wife was *your* mother!" he stated as he slowly walked closer with the tip of the bokken toward me.

I flew into a mood of immense confusion and shock. For these many years, I was not alone. Kane, my father, has been with me ever since. Now the bastard chooses now to reveal himself?

"Kill him!" I shouted aloud. The heat of the moment sent the crowd into a frenzy. The ninja on my side charged forth. Those on Kane's side rushed to the aide of their master. Kane drew his dadao and chased after me. With most of us wearing the same armor, friendly fire is inevitable. The bloodshed began, and I panicked until I reached my bow. Before I could draw an arrow, Kane ran and kicked me back into my seat.

"With your death, my son, I will begin to right my wrongs!" Kane said in a salty growl.

Before Kane landed a killing blow, he was apprehended by one of my ninja. As they fought, I quickly shot an arrow into his right shoulder blade. The impact sent them both into the arena. I blew a horn to call reinforcements. A host of archers soon ran inside.

"Those with Master Kane retreat!" Kane shouted as he pulled the arrow out.

An intense chase began as about fifty of Kane's students fled with their master into the caves.

"Let them run! They are no threat!" I gloated.

Hours later, after collecting and disposing of the dead, I became curious about Kane. He never allowed anyone to enter his room. I chose to enter his domain.

In Kane's room are many of his weapons. He has several duplicates of his mask and armor. I rummaged through his room, perhaps there's something of use. After a thorough search, I came across his diary. Within the pages are accounts of his 314 completed contracts. There is one entry that mentioned Jahvonis. This may be the information I need.

> *I remember the morning when I awoke to find Mataraves dead. Blood leaked from his throat wound with his war paint faded on his Ember-Sand skin. I crawled over to him on my hands and knees. I cried instantly and held his deceased youth in my arms. His staff was broken and dented. I gathered his body and the weapons that were used in the battle with Jahvonis. In an outdoor grave of soil and stone, I laid*

Mataraves on his back with his feet facing the east. I cleaned his face of the makeup, combed his hair, and applied his turban. I put all the used weapons at his feet. I placed his Tomahawk in his right hand and one half of the Bo in his left. As I piled the soil on his body, I hoped Bravious and Sarue would welcome him into their kingdom. The grave is beneath a maple tree. I placed stones around and upon the grave to mark it. The Early Sun was still in the east, even in death, Mataraves would watch the dawn. This is one form of an Ember burial.

I know Mataraves preferred one of his kin to slay him. When he learned that Xavion Mourningstar saved West Nodin and is the Jahvonis from legend, he planned his death. I was not going to let him get killed, so I insisted that I fight beside him. I do not hate Xavion for killing him. I feel Mataraves has a divine role to play in our world history. After all of this, if anyone is worthy to be my student, it is Xavion.

"Xavion Mourningstar!" I shouted in dismay. Now it all makes sense why Jahvonis is so skilled! I now fear for my life. I am contracted to assassinate the Mourningstar! I'll need the whole Hand of Doom to bring him down! I regret chasing Kane off and dividing us.

In Xavion's View

December went and January came. The New Year ushered in many snowstorms. Those who stayed in huts were housed in the neighboring towns, except for Sareyus, Sebastian, and Alva, who all lived with me. We all sat around the hearth conversing about the weather. Sareyus is the quietest. Alva is retelling "The Legend of Winter's Birth."

"Miolannis, during the shaping of the Earth, feuded with Lyannis. Lyannis formed the sun from light and the heat of the fire goddess. Miolannis crafted the moon from Bravious's stone and combined it with her cold and dim light. When Lyannis created the hot summer, Miolannis created the cold winter. Miolannis wanted her creations to contrast with her sisters."

Sebastian then spoke. "The Nodinian myth of winter is that the cold made us strong. We fought to find warmth."

"That's what Soruthians hate about the far north. The past wars made them believe that Nodin's bitter weather forced them southwards. They were willing to commit genocide to find a new home," I added.

Alva then spoke. "In Nodin, the old belief is, to enter the Gods' Hall, you must die in battle. Our original tribes were nomadic and traveled extensively. They made the grave mistake to assail Soruth. I've heard the stories from the slaves about your fighting, Xavion. When you enter the field, you strike utter terror into the soldiers."

Sareyus looked deep into the fire as it emboldened.

"Sareyus, sweetheart, are you all right?" I asked.

"I never liked winter. It always made me depressed. I prefer summer and fall," she replied.

Later that day, the snow stopped falling. I shoveled a walkway before the front door while everyone else slept. Afterward, I sharpened all of my edged weapons. It is both pleasure and work. After I finished my pipe hawk, I heard a knock at my door. I kept my tomahawk in hand. As I opened the door, I was surprised. Master Kane stood tall and firm in the doorway. He is armed and alone. As he looked through the eyeholes of his mask, he spoke.

"We must talk. Do you trust me to come in? I mean you no harm…and I'm cold." Honesty is in his voice. I was cautious, but I took him in. We went into a locked room.

"What is it, Kane?" I asked curiously.

He took a deep breath and replied, "I and about fifty ninja have defected from the Hand of Doom. Alastair ordered my loyalists and I to be killed. We fled. There is only one group who could put us to use, the Independent Party."

"While I can sympathize with your current situation, the Hand of Doom have made enemies on all sides."

"The majority of the enemies we have made are the Underground East and West kingdoms. On the surface, after you and I dealt with the Witchfinder General, I felt the Independents could use more boots on the ground. You're a neutral party who is fighting for their freedom. Why not put fifty assassins to use?" Kane suggested.

"It's not that we don't want you, it's the public perception if we take you," I stated.

"We have been used by politicians and civilians alike. This is our chance to fight for the greater good of Nodin. Allow me to speak with your leader. If I can explain, then he may see us of some use," Kane replied.

"Why did you defect?"

"You know the idea of family has been corrupted for many years now. Alastair has been a poor leader. On many occasions, he has ignored my advice, which has brought us trouble. I forced Alastair to duel me to prove himself. He insulted my wife and I. He forced me to reveal my parentage over him. His first response was to have me killed. My host and I fled, and here I am."

"How do I know this is not an elaborate scheme to seize control of the party? We have fought before. How do I know I can trust you?" I asked sternly.

Kane took a deep breath. He removed his mask, revealing his burned and scarred face. He has patches of brittle blond hair, and he looked at me with shiny blue eyes. "This is my best opportunity to stop Aylund and avenge my wife. With you commanding the defense of the Independent people, we cannot lose. I have seen and felt your skill in battle. You are charismatic and inspirational. You save civilians, and you lead soldiers to victory. Your honor and valor have changed me, Xavion. While I have been a recurring foe, I ask for my chance to redeem my soul. I plead on the behalf of my wife and Mataraves. If you accept us, we will be at your command," Kane pleaded with a sincere voice. A single tear fell from his left eye.

"I believe your words, Master Kane, but I cannot entirely make that decision. If you accompany me to meet Kristoff, I'm sure he'll consider your offer and place you at my command."

"The sooner we meet him, the better. Thank you very much, Xavion. I and my host will be resting in a nearby cave," Kane said.

I escorted him outside after he put his mask back on. I returned to my bed and placed my arm around Sareyus. Jahvonis has felt another form of energy emitting from Alva. He wants us to meet Alva in her dreams in order to investigate.

In Alva's View

I went into a dream as I slept in Xavion's home. Mioleyis sat with me in my dream. It is a gray void with a moon in the sky. Mioleyis appeared in her white ghostly form. Her skin is albino white with her celestial form still potent. Her hair is dark. She is teaching me the old Nodinian rituals of the moon. We were there only a short time when we viewed a mass of black smoke rising. Mioleyis moved me behind her. Out of the smoke stepped forth Jahvonis with a hardened glare. He spoke to Mioleyis in a natural voice with a Noric accent.

"The Mother of the New Moon reveals herself to the world beneath her. Why dost my eldest sister come to the mortals' center world? What say you, Mioleyis of the Lunar Realm?"

I am tingling as I viewed these two full bodied. Simultaneously, I bask in awe and shiver with fright.

Mioleyis replied, "I have come to seek assistance for our mother. Kuolemajää has taken her hostage in Vuorijää. She must be saved!"

"So you came to take my student from me?" Jahvonis questioned.

"She bears the blood of you and the Mourningstar. With you training her in combat and me teaching her the moon's power, she can slay the beast!" Mioleyis replied.

"Dragon slaying requires more than a person with divine accompaniment. You need an army to do such a thing," said Jahvonis.

"He is right, Mioleyis, Kuolemajää is a great threat," a voice said. The speaker stepped out of the smoke. It is Commander Xavion.

"An army we do have, but our war is not yet won. Whatever agreement you and Alva have made, she is not yet strong enough for your goal to be achieved. Even I would be at a disadvantage for Kuolemajää."

"We must see the outcome of this war before Kuolemajää is dealt with. My lady, the Moon Mistress, will have to wait," I said to Mioleyis.

"I will wait. But our father, Jahveyis, may not. He is growing restless and wishes to contest with the dragon by himself," Mioleyis said.

She, Jahvonis, and Xavion faded away.

I awoke sometime later. In those hours, Xavion and I looked at each other with different viewpoints. I see him the same way Sareyus does. It is Xavion who has been saving me. It is him who I now love. He and I are both former slaves. Now we are being guided by sibling spirits.

We talked minimally, for we did not know what to say. He broke the silence when he said he is going to teach me smithing.

"I want a suit of armor like yours…but in white," I requested.

He replied with, "And you shall. As I have made mine, you will make yours."

To save time and materials, we took the design of the Jahvonis suit but changed the color from black to white. My suit is not more feminine looking because the enemy cannot know what gender I am.

We worked long into the night. The first weapons Xavion taught me to make are star and dart shaped shuriken. The darts are known as "Bo Shuriken." Next are senbon throwing needles and small throwing knives. I impressed him for a beginner, but I will get better.

Xavion gave me a Nodinian dagger as a gift. The dagger looks like a miniature version of my sword. It has a thirteen-inch double-edged blade with six-and-a-quarter-inch handle. The look and the scabbard are identical to my sword. I also crafted a targe shield.

By morning, we took a break.

Xavion spoke. "Alva, I have business to attend to in Starkstad. While I am gone, I want you to practice your aim on that wooden plank. You have built fifty star shuriken, bo shuriken, senbon, and throwing knives. You will throw one of each until all two hundred are thrown. You must make them all stick in the target to progress."

When he left, I began throwing the items with both hands and at different angles. I began decently, but I was not motivated. I took a quill and ink to the plank and drew a person. On their chest I wrote, "Alastair," and my aim improved greatly!

In Xavion's View

Kane and I are on our way to see Kristoff. We are on horseback as we entered the town. The guards are watching us, more so Kane than me.

"I assume you use the dadao because someone snapped too many of your katanas?" I asked Kane.

"Indeed. While the katana is a fantastic sword, one opponent knows too well how to counter it. Fifteen years ago, I thoroughly used the katana but the dadao uses the skills of the sword but incorporates more forward balance. The dadao on the surface is great because of the open space. Also, the wider blade prevents it from being broken by Jahvonis's gauntlets," Kane said.

"Kane, I can't guarantee that Kristoff will hire you. He may have you arrested and interrogated."

"I'm prepared for the worst, Xavion. I've committed crimes against Nodin as a whole, but your party could greatly benefit from my host and I," Kane replied.

The meeting with Kristoff was mildly unsettling.

"Commander Xavion, tell me why you have brought this assassin to my town?" Kristoff raised his voice.

We all sat at a table in the same private room as before. We surrendered our weapons, and Kane removed his mask.

"My name is Kane Beorler, son of Abdon and Ingrid Beorler. My lord Kristoff, I have come on behalf of myself and my followers. King Johan hired the Hand of Doom to kill Jahvonis. My host and I defected from the Hand not long ago. I come to you to offer our services as bodyguards, soldiers, spies, and assassins. I fought in the Ericson Army during the Theranth Wars. I know Aylund's tactics better than he does. With Xavion, myself, and a host of ninja, we have more of an advantage over the other two kingdoms," Kane stated truthfully and confidently.

"Tell me how you could be used during open combat?" Kristoff asked.

"I'm trained to battle many opponents on my own. Jahvonis and I know all the same techniques but better," Kane said as Kristoff turned his eyes toward me and back at Kane.

"I have seen Jahvonis fight about fifteen men when he saved my life years ago. I guess that explains why the Ninja are so good. Very well, you have won me over but I must counsel the other generals to have this approved. Please bear with me until then," Kristoff said.

"Kristoff, if Kane and his men are accepted into our ranks and something does go amiss, I will take full responsibility," I said.

"Fair enough, Xavion, I may have to hold you to it. Master Kane, you are lucky that the ninja who slew my nephew is dead. Otherwise, I would have you and your host rounded up and slain," Kristoff said as we departed.

Kane left before me while I stayed behind. I did so because a Theranth chief requested to speak with me. I don't know who it is, but he wants to meet in the field outside of Starkstad.

As I sat on Aapo, the air became colder. From the northeast, I saw ten tall men in armor come over the horizon. They waved the Independent flag to signal me to come over. I rode to them. The closer I got, the men grew taller and taller. I notice their flag has purple drawings of animals outside the dodecagram.

They stand at equal height as me on horseback. They are all armed. The center Theranth has a helmet similar to Bjorn's. On his back is a shield. A large arming sword is on his left hip. He removed his helm. Underneath is a knife-eared, snow-skinned, hazel-eyed Theranth man. He has fanged teeth and six small horns on his head. His white fur is shined. He has a Gernic accent. His *W* words were said with *V*s.

"Do you know who I am, sir?" he asked.

"Pardon my ignorance, my lord, I do not know," I replied.

"My name is Amandus Amanuel Ambrosius," he said as I fell silent at this most famous of Theranths. The man who destroyed the legacy of the Edlings and Ericsons.

"Are you now an ally to the Independent Nation?" I asked him and his guards.

"We are the last Theranth tribe to join your numbers. I assume you are Xavion Mourningstar?"

"I am he."

He walked closer and stood three inches taller than Bjorn. Looking up at him is intimidating.

"You are the commander of our forces. As a precautionary warning, we Theranths will not tolerate the racism of you humans to our people. You humans created us to fight, regardless of the opponent. You as a Soruthian know how it feels to be discriminated against. I hope you will maintain the unity in this army. You know how human Nodinians can be," Amandus said.

"Even the Soruthians discriminated against their Theranths. Your people prove your social superiority by sticking together as one race. I am not one to promote bigotry, but I will do my best to see that humans and Theranths are treated equally in arms. A new Nodin is coming, and all people indigenous or not will be treated equally," I stated.

"I respect your kind words, Commander Xavion, I hope we can accomplish a great victory for all people," Amandus said as he and his men shook my hand.

When we parted ways, Jahvonis spoke to me telepathically. "I hope you haven't forgotten who Amandus's master was during the Theranth Wars."

"I haven't forgotten that Kuolemajää was the hidden hand behind the Theranth Rebellion. The Theranths needed someone to rally them and show them they did not bend to humanity. In a way, I respect Kuolemajää for encouraging them to fight for their rights as people and not property," I replied.

"But Kuolemajää is not one to allow his power to be shared. It's possible that Amandus and the tribes are living on their own. With the dragon free and regaining his strength, Amandus may be called back to his master."

"Kristoff and the rest of the party trust the Theranth people, and Amandus is a powerful ally. Theranths are more honor bound than us humans. A handshake is a physical and moral bond. Theranths of all nations are culturally bound to their word. Should any of our Theranth allies break this alliance, they bring shame to their people. Who knows, perhaps Amandus sees our cause as beneficial for all people? Kuolemajää would surely enslave us all and the Theranths refuse to be slaves to anyone."

"Your wisdom has grown, Xavion. You are most worthy to bear my name," Jahvonis said.

Chapter 13

In Sareyus's View

Xavion and I have become more intimate as a couple. We talk more about our lives. Xavion tells me his stories of when he lived in the wilds. He is a grand storyteller, and his word choice is *Jahveyan*, ripe with detail and imagery. When he asks me about myself, I tell him memories of the gods but refer to them as my friends.

I admit my sexual desires for him, and he blushes. He enjoys my thicker stomach, wider hips, dense behind, and thick thighs. Somehow he gets aroused by watching me eat. I control how much I weigh, and he loves me the way I am. I now weigh two hundred pounds.

Xavion considers women to be more powerful than men. He views men as those who factually have committed more crimes against the world than women. He says, "*Men misunderstand their existence. With the exception of our seeds, women create life. They are the gatekeepers to our world. All conceived children are first female. Otherwise, they become male. Each child is nurtured in their mother's garden. For nine months, children moor the womb from the navel. The birth canal is their portal for life. Women have the greatest spiritual connection to the earth. The earth gives life and birth to all life. Thus, the earth is our mother and the sky is our father.*"

His wisdom dumbfounds me. His personality has the best attributes of the gods. I want to marry him. I want our first time to be special.

I sensed some dysfunction up above. I chose to investigate. When my spirit traveled, I projected my current image. Luckily, I succeeded. When I arrived, I came upon an argument among Lyannis, Jado, Carune, and Sarue.

"We must destroy Xavion! Jahvonis cannot be allowed to live!" Sarue shouted.

"Our husbands were injured by that scourge from hell! He dare assault the Immortals!" Carune stated angrily.

"He wouldn't have had a reason to come here if Jahveyis did not betray him," Jado replied.

"And Jahvonis wouldn't have Xavion's body if *you* did not give Xavion a revised edition of the Hallowed Holds!" Lyannis shouted back at her husband.

"What is going on?" I said.

"Your goddamn boyfriend's master assaulted three of the gods," Lyannis said.

"Jahveyis wronged him many times! Jahveyis and Miolannis made him their prophet without our knowledge, and Jahveyis betrayed his son during the Second Armageddon! Jahvonis sees we are flawed and have abused our power since the dawn of time!" I replied.

"You're taking his side?" Sarue shouted.

"No, I'm being honest because I am as guilty as the rest of you. We have committed genocide of the mortal races on *two* occasions! Jahvonis has every right to be angry and to rebel against us all!" I shouted back.

"Then why has he not harmed you? You share a bed with the carrier of his spirit!" Lyannis asked.

"Because he knows Xavion loves me more than himself! I am the light in Xavion's war-torn travels. He shows me more love and appreciation than any of you have ever given me! Jahvonis loves Xavion and cherishes him as a student, brother, and sonly figure. Jahvonis and Xavion can be as powerful as any of us. They have gained more approval, admiration, and respect than any of us," I said truthfully with passion.

"Sareyus, you do not fully understand how dangerous Jahvonis is to us! When Jahveyis threw Hellhammer, my spell tainted the power of the mace. Hellhammer is powered by Jahveyis's black magic. When Jahvonis threw the mace at Jahveyis, the light entered through his wounds. Jahveyis is infected and weakened by my powers. His mace could have killed us if Jahvonis attacked. Jahveyis's magic is poisonous to all of us all except Miolannis. Yes, my magic corrupted the mace and protected us. I did not intend it to harm Jahveyis!" Lyannis lamented.

"Sareyus, with the blood of eight gods and Xavion, Jahvonis has enough power to resurrect himself and build a body!" Jado stated, which silenced the room. He continued to speak. "I analyzed Hellhammer, and indeed, it is tainted by the light. The mace still has a trace of Jahvonis's power. It also has some of Xavion's. With the mace tainted, it cannot be used at full power by Jahveyis. Jahvonis is powerful enough to cause physical and spiritual damage to any of the eight," Jado said.

"When Bravious's punch was caught, Jahvonis absorbed his strength as well the electricity of Tovis's lightning. When Jahvonis struck Bravious, he kicked him with his own power. Jahvonis mildly absorbed the lightning and passed it into Bravious. When Bravious was forced into Tovis, he was electrocuted and crushed by Bravious's weight," Jado informed.

"He has us in a corner. What have we done?" Carune said as she and Sarue wept for their husbands.

"Where is Hellhammer now?" I asked.

"I placed it in Jahveyis's room," Jado said.

A Short Narration

Jahveyis, Tovis, and Bravious lay in their rooms unconscious. Bravious and Tovis have been treated for electric shock while they and Jahveyis suffered blunt force trauma.

In the room of the Dark Lord, Hellhammer is on a stand. Its once blackened form and grim aura is conflicted by white magic. Jahveyis's face is scarred and bandaged, blood still stains the wrappings. Another black figure walks the room. Jahvonis yet again infiltrated heaven. He bears Hellhammer in hand and stands above the Dark Lord. The Mourneyes raged within his head. Jahveyis is defenseless and trapped by a comatose state. Jahvonis raised Hellhammer and prepared to smite his father!

"Master Jahvonis, I call to thee!" Xavion's voice called from within.

Jahvonis departed and took Hellhammer with him.

In Sareyus's View

"What makes Hellhammer's affliction so vital?" I asked.

"You may have forgotten the story. Hellhammer was crafted in the First Life by Bravious and gifted to Jahveyis. Bravious crafted the physical weapons we all possess. Hellhammer draws power from black magic and the violent nature of war. Jahveyis is the Dark Lord, and negativity is his nutrient. Hellhammer was used in Jahvonis's ordainment and demise. With Xavion and Jahvonis fused together, Hellhammer gorged on their shared power, despite being tainted by Lyannis. When the mace hit Jahveyis, it poisoned him with light and thrashed him with Jahvonis and Xavion's energy. Jahvonis acquired a visionary form of magic that transformed his irises. They were purple, and his pupils multiplied into nine per eye," Jado added.

"*Oh no!*" I shouted. "The star on Xavion's chest! Through the years, he must have harnessed my power and amplified it into an ability. He's ten times more dangerous than we planned!" I panicked.

"So you did more than brand his chest. Now all the Immortals are guilty in Xavion's dangerous nature and Jahvonis's new powers," Sarue said after wiping her tears.

"Jahvonis is Xavion's master. Does Xavion have an apprentice of his own?" Carune asked.

"I believe so, but there's something divine at work with this apprentice. She is a mortal named Alva Amott. She is an unofficial Moon Lady, but less than a year ago she was a teenager. One day she matured into a fully grown adult. Xavion and Jahvonis performed an unnatural experiment on her. She is less mortal than before. As I've been around her, I sense the powers of all nine gods, Jahvonis, Xavion, and a lunar spirit in her veins!" I stated as overwhelming fright overtook Sarue, and she snarled, "You mean to tell me there's three of these false god monstrosities in the world?"

"Watch your mouth, Sarue. Xavion and Alva have proven no threat against us, and even Jahvonis's intentions remain unclear. Jahvonis for the last eleven months has willingly saved me from harm and has never touched one hair on my head!"

"Sareyus, this lunar spirit within Alva, does it feel like Miolannis?" Carune questioned.

"Not Miolannis but someone lesser," I replied.

"One of her daughters," Lyannis said and lowered her shoulders with tension.

"It is possible that one of the eight Moon Mothers is involved in this affair. They answer only to their mother," Jado stated.

"So we have no options and nowhere to go," Sarue said in sorrow.

"The only thing I can do is trust and have faith in the love Xavion feels for me. He is the wisest, good-hearted, and the nicest man I've ever known. I believe he is more humanitarian. He took Alva as a student because he values her as a friend. Jahvonis knows Xavion and I are in love. He would never take me away from him. I will pray for Xavion to be mine regardless of how his master feels. I am confident all of this will work out for the better," I stated and returned home.

I was lying in bed when I departed, and I awoke to Xavion's hand on my stomach. He is incredibly warm and began to sweat. I removed the blankets to cool him off. I looked to the floor across the house to gaze upon Alva sleeping and Sebastian across from here. I got out of bed and walked through the house. Within the house, I felt the spiritual veil becoming thin. I wandered into Xavion's armory and forge. His Soruthian armor is on a stand, and his various weapons are displayed ornately upon the walls.

On the floor, I see the chest that stores Jahvonis within. I felt I could summon him if I come in contact with the suit. I walked closer to the chest, and it unlocked by itself! My surprise turned into intense curiosity, and I forced the lid open. The hooded mask and cowl of Jahvonis faced upward…and he stared at me.

"Good evening, Sareyus," Jahvonis spoke telepathically into my brain.

The room began to blacken. I am trapped with the light of Jahvonis's blue eyes blazing like a beacon.

"Tell me, how are you and Xavion? Have you been married yet? Have you forgotten your mission, or do you enjoy being human?" Jahvonis asked. His blue eyes reminded me of the first time I saw Xavion maskless.

"You lust more for my brother than lead him from his destiny," he said.

"I love your brother. Only love can conquer war. It commands the warriors to unclench their fists and open their arms."

"But peace cannot exist without war. Love and hate cannot exist without detachment. Your loneliness and singularity motivate you to fill the void you've had since the Cosmos Commencement. You were born with no mate of your own, and you saw an opportunity in Xavion to romance him. Xavion is designed for war. It was simple to convert the soldier into a vigilante. As beautiful as you are, you will never reforge Xavion's instincts. After all, you made Xavion and I more powerful than ever. When your reproductive instincts overpower you, Xavion and I will be gods. You will bear his seeds and give birth to the demigods to come. You have done more good than the other eight combined, and for that I respect you."

"Are you going to hurt me if you get the chance?" I asked.

"No. You are my brother's love and his future wife. You mean more to him than the world. Xavion would die for you. If you try to do away with me, I promise, you and the eight will not be safe. If I hurt you, Xavion would be a terrible foe. I love him too. I've given him more than anyone else."

"Sareyus?" Alva called from behind. "What's going on?"

I looked in her eyes, they are purple with nine pupils in each. Jahvonis has them now as I looked back at him!

Jahvonis's eyes disappeared, and Alva walked closer to me. The multiple energies and calm emotion brightened the room. She looked at the suit. She closed the chest and locked it.

"Xavion wouldn't want you to be meddling with the suit. There are things at work that only he understands," Alva said.

I remained quiet because anything I could say would be suspicious.

"Please be careful in this room," she added as we both left and returned to bed.

I noticed Alva looked alert when I got into bed with Xavion. She turned hastily and faced the wall where she lay. Toward the morning, I felt Xavion caressing my bare stomach.

In Alva's View

Sareyus had some other reason to gaze upon Xavion's suit. I hope Jahvonis did not alarm her. When I met the real Jahvonis, he had a dark aura about him but it still glimmered with light. I wonder what the relationship is between him and Mioleyis. I wonder what the story and relationship is with Mioleyis and her parents.

Mioleyis is a polite, somber, and beautiful woman. Her age is in the thousands, but she looks no more than twenty-two. So far she is an albino ghostly form with black mist for hair. When she enters my dreams, she'll appear as any ethnicity she wants. Recently, she came to me as an Ember-woman.

When we Nodinian women pray to our goddesses, the self-conscious, including me, would request they make us beautiful. The Hold of Lyannis states multiple times: *"Women of every kind are beautiful, nothing will diminish that!"*

The Hold of Miolannis states in reference to romance: *"Regardless of your features, there is someone for you. Enjoy yourself and your partner to the fullest. Be love!"*

When remembering those passages, I forget that my body has been enhanced. Xavion and Jahvonis injected me with their blood and permanently altered it. One time after Xavion was teaching me to use a sword, I asked him what he thought of my appearance.

He stated, "Alva, I know you're self-conscious. Jahvonis and I enhanced you with our blood to make you into an adult. When I freed you, you were underfed and underweight. You still had time before you were fully grown. I did not know what would happen to you with my blood. Alva, you make money to eat comfortably and I have more good news for you.

"After the injection, I used the Mourneyes to analyze you. Your vagina suffered much violent abuse from your attackers. The blood I injected into your pelvis healed the flesh back to its standard form. I examined you again when Mioleyis took you as her student. Mioleyis is a moon spirit. She controls some of your monthly menstruations. However, she is descended from Miolannis, who invented procreation. Mioleyis baptized you in lunar energy. In other words, your first-time making love will be new in every way. You're beautiful. Any man or woman will be blessed to have you. I know you are bisexual."

Xavion solidified my love for him. He knows me so much more than I know myself. I am loyal to him for all he has done for me. My views on sex are frightful because of my past. As I endure Xavion and Mioleyis's training, someday I will be brave to make love.

Right now, I am deep in the forest with Mioleyis. She is teaching me the ability to quickly teleport between areas when the moon is in the sky. When beginning the basic techniques, I had to only teleport from in front of Mioleyis to behind her. We did this from nightfall to dawn. When combined with ninjutsu, it will be useful when on missions. For now, the teleportation technique only works when the moon is visually in the sky, like night, dusk, and dawn. Further down the road, Mioleyis will teach me to do it at will to any place I can see or have been to. When Dawn came, Mioleyis returned inside me. I went to work on the ship. So far 75 percent of it is done. I also finished my Mioleyis suit. It is a white copy of Jahvonis's suit. I also made a ko katana sword.

The following night, Xavion trained me in my dreams. I suited up as Mioleyis, and I had a mission. I was to infiltrate a heavily guarded castle, assassinate the lord, steal his locked book, and free his slaves. In this dream, the lord was a slaver of fifty women. They are locked in a single building with an underground tunnel that is beneath the floorboards. But here's the problem: four guards are always patrolling the house. I'll have to kill the guards, hide the bodies, and free the women. There are more guards protecting the lord. I must climb the wall that leads to his balcony and enter his room.

The whole mission took two hours and forty-five minutes. I gave the book to Xavion. He broke the lock off and read a passage to me: "The way of the ninja is enduring and surviving. You are ready to enter the world as Mioleyis. In two days, we leave for Underground East Nodin for a mission. Congratulations, Alva!" Never have I been more tempted to kiss Xavion!

It is February 5 of the year 904. Xavion and I journey through the subterranean as Jahvonis and Mioleyis. Two people who follow one Yazjian warrior culture. Two shinobi, one black and one white. We resemble the Hongangan yin and yang. Our illuminating sights provide excellent clarity in the darkness of the earth.

Our melee weapons match our armor. I have my ko katana while Xavion has his kukri and ringed dagger. Our swords are on our left hips. Our shuriken and senbon are in our pouches. The bo shuriken are worn on the inner portion of our gauntlets (which carry six on each arm). Before we departed, Xavion forged me a ringed dagger. We both wore them on our right hips. They are double-edged with handguards. These can be thrown or used in close-quarters combat.

One thing I must make clear is that traditional ninja did not ever wear armor like this. They did not carry as much equipment as Xavion and I do because they would be highly encumbered. Due to our enhancements, we can get away with the armor and higher amounts of equipment. We were never trying to be traditional, but a true ninja adapts to the times. The conservative samurai adapt to modern warfare, if it makes sense.

On this mission, we refer to our aliases. Our mission in East Nodin is to gather intelligence on their battle strategies and anything else that is useful. East Nodin has a higher poverty rate than the West. The common and impoverished are segregated from the upper class. The wealthy and powerful live as oligarchs in a gated community. The slave camp is fenced off with only twelve guards patrolling. As expected, the slave camp and common sections are dark, dirty, unsanitary, and riddled with xenophobic propaganda. The images of the Soruthians are exaggerated with dramatic hairstyles, big lips, big noses, literal black-colored skin, oversized turbans, and apish features. The common homes are greatly damaged with excrement fouling the air and ground. The oligarchal section is elegant and plastered with blue banners and images of Aylund. In the common section, the streets are riddled with darkness. Stealth movements are easy to accomplish. The higher community is the only one with lava light. Never did this area look dreadful. We moved along the rooftops. The palace of the Vakuuttava is beneath our feet. The information on the military should be in Aylund's room.

"Why don't we kill Aylund?" I asked in Mioleyis's telepathic voice.

"If we kill him, then Johan will not come to the surface. However, we can strike terror into his nation. Follow my lead."

Aylund's room resides on the sixth floor. We climbed through his balcony into his room. The sleeping tyrant is lying in bed with the ax of Hakun on a mantle. On a dresser are Hakun's skull fragment and a bundle of Helga's hair. Across the room, Jahvonis found a locked chest. After silently picking the lock, inside are the documents of East Nodin's military records and recent information. We folded the most important documents and placed them in our pouches. Jahvonis took the skull fragment, Hakun's ax, and Helga's hair. As we climbed down the building, Jahvonis spoke to me telepathically.

"Mioleyis, go to the slave camp. Get as many people out of there as you can. There is a boulder blocking a tunnel at the back of the camp. Move the boulder aside and hide behind it. I have another matter to attend to. Leave if I am not back in one hour after you've hidden," Jahvonis said as he moved further into the gated community.

From a rooftop that overlooks the slave camp, I examined the perimeter. The guards are far apart and lazily doing their job. I crept up to each one. I severed their vocal cords from behind. My dagger is dyed with blood.

The campers were only given bedrolls. Among the one hundred slaves, only twenty are Nodinian. The rest are all Soruthian men, women, and children. They are of Ember, Bark, Sand, and Ebony lineage. I woke up the nearest man.

"I'm here to free all of you. The guards are all dead. Please wake up all you can. We're leaving tonight!"

We woke everyone up, and surprisingly, no other guards came to investigate. Are the two kingdoms this irresponsible? We all gathered by the boulder as I used my enhanced strength to move it aside and replaced it when all gathered in the tunnel. Twenty-five minutes later, Jahvonis moved the rock and we all stormed into the tunnels. There is blood on Hakun's ax.

A Short Narration

When the morning came, Aylund awoke in bed. His eyes opened to his blue-adorned room. His smug facial expression gave him empowerment. As he began to toss and turn, he felt a thickly wet and warm fluid upon his left side. He panicked as he threw the covers off. In bed, he found the severed head of the guard captain. His screaming became horrifically worse as he stared at the wall with impending doom. The wall at the foot of his bed was ironically decorated with the five severed heads of his generals. They were pinned to the wall with three above two and connected with blood streaks that formed a pentagram. These five heads all lost the same skull fragment as Hakun. Next to the outside of every head, going clockwise, are five letters: *J-O-H-A-N*.

On February 1, Jado privately met with Sareyus, Lyannis, Carune, and Sarue. Jado began. "Sareyus, we are concerned about the gravity of Xavion's military career. Before we get to business, is Xavion able to craft you a necklace?"

"What would the necklace be for?" Sareyus asked.

In Kane's View

Much has encumbered my mind during these many years. Everything changed when Xavion (under the guise of Jahvonis) crossed my path that day. I still mourn the loss of Mataraves. For years, I played the antagonist role against Xavion. His vigilante persona has been both my greatest challenge as a warrior and person.

In the years after Mataraves's death, Xavion and I waged a personal war across Ang in pursuit of the Witchfinder General. For a time, I wrongfully hated Xavion because he was a quick scapegoat for the crimes of my life—a scapegoat for my deformity, my wife's suicide, Alastair's upbringing, and the sustained life of Johan and Aylund.

Xavion represented everything I was not: heroic, selfless, and honorable. Xavion still has plenty of room for growth. Coming to him after Alastair's betrayal was the most difficult thing I've done. Cutting someone's throat was easier than asking help from my former enemy. I am grateful that Xavion did not assault me when I came to his house. He saw the honesty in my eyes. He knows I want to do good. Helping the Independents in this war is my graduation for a better life.

The Hand of Doom began to change when Jahvonis appeared. A division occurred as Alastair entered adulthood. Everything was in order until the issue of Jahvonis was mentioned. The Hand was losing its mission against the royal houses and did everything they could to stop Jahvonis. One man was more of a threat than two empires who abused their power. An army must maintain priorities in order to succeed.

The student that I dueled before the Hand's division is named *Algoth* (Al-gut), and he is now a full-fledged ninja. He admitted to me that Jahvonis and I are the finest shinobi in Nodin. He was inspired by Jahvonis to better his skills.

I arranged a strategy with General Vallen before the battle in May. The ninja would use our guerilla tactics to sabotage and infiltrate areas of West and East Nodin operations. An hour ago, we and other Independents ambushed a lesser West Nodin battalion. My force and I are camped not far from the construction. When I am gone, Algoth is in charge. We have not renamed ourselves. We are a hired but loyal hand for the Independent Party.

I am walking through the site at noon on February 14. Today is Xavion's birthday. Outside the house, Xavion is doing sword drills with Alva, the audience is Sebastian and Xavion's partner, Sareyus. Alva is using a Frankish arming sword. I can tell it is of her making. On the bottom of the blade, there is an Italese word engraved into it. The sword is named *Lunanera*. It means "Black Moon." During the drills, Xavion used his talwar.

"Remember, Alva, use your superior blade length to keep me at bay," Xavion said as she gripped with her right hand. With six evasions by Xavion, he parried Lunanera with the spine of his talwar. He locked the blades together and slid the tip close enough to Alva without harm.

"Yield," Xavion said humorously.

Sebastian and Sareyus applauded with admiration. Even I am astounded with his technique and innovation.

"Xavion," I called.

He turned his head in my direction.

"What is it, Master Kane?" he asked from his distance.

"May I speak with Alva? For a moment only?" I asked.

"Though it is not necessarily my business, what do you want to talk to her about?" he questioned.

"To apologize for what Alastair did to her," I stated as Alva gripped her sword tighter.

"What you want to say to me, you can say in front of all of us," Alva replied sternly.

Once more to show my sincerity, I removed my mask. All but Xavion mildly flinched at my deformity.

"Alva, I, Kane Beorler, apologize for the heinous crimes that my son, Alastair Beorler, has committed against you. His lust against a child and assault against you is despicable. No true warrior or person would rape someone, especially a child. His abusive treatment of you will not go unpunished," I said.

Her eyes turned purple. When she blinked, they became blue.

"Though Alastair is your son, I will kill him. With you joining our party, Alastair is now a target. He and his men will be dealt with. Do not change your mind, or you will be dealt with the same way. However, I accept your apology, Master Kane," Alva said.

I put on my mask and began to walk away.

"Kane, why don't you come inside and join us for lunch? We are celebrating my birthday," Xavion offered kindly.

For the next few hours, I enjoyed food and beverage with these people. No talking of work, only simple socializing. Xavion cooked the whole meal. It was seasoned spaghetti with chicken breasts, beef meatballs, garlic bread; and it was served with a separate spiced marinara sauce. Goodness, this man can cook. We each had three plates, and nothing went to waste.

Xavion and I would trade ideas, and he offered to remake my armor and weapons. To have anything made by Xavion is a privilege. When Xavion makes an item, he engraves his initials and an octagram into it. If we win this war with Xavion's leadership, anything he makes will be near priceless!

I will now tell of my origin. I joined the Nodinian military when I was nineteen. I had previous knowledge of warfare. In my first ten years of service, I had fought in the final stages of the Theranth Wars. I fought for the Ericsons when our families were intermarried. I was head of Aylund's personal guard when he was eighteen; I was thirty-eight. I was considered the best soldier in his army. Many times he vented his lust for my wife, *Carla Beorler*. She and I married on September 9, 872. Alastair was born the following June on the eleventh. With Aylund, I publicly threatened his life if he continued to spew heresies about Carla.

At the *Siege of Amon Brav*, I was facially struck with a fiery torch. I also had many cuts and lost much blood. During our retreat and defeat from Amon Brav, I was to have a blood replacement. The only blood available was of a Theranth prisoner. The flames on my face were extinguished. I was comatose for eleven months. I remember during my lucid dreams, there was a man with dark-blond hair and glasses looking over me. He would place his hands upon me. I remember seeing ambers upon a brass necklace.

When I awoke, I was stronger, faster, agile, and possessed immense knowledge of foreign martial arts. I assume the Theranth was a martial artist or some miracle gifted me this. By this time, East Nodin moved underground. When I came home from the doctor's, I found Carla hanging by her throat. My grief and anger became rage. Next to her body, I found a note from her admitting that Aylund raped and impregnated her. She wrote a goodbye paragraph to our son Alastair and myself. I stormed like a hurricane into Aylund's encampment and slaughtered all of his guards. Dozens more came, but I was saved by a group of masked men clothed in brown leather who fought with speed and stealth.

After the Theranth Wars, the Nodinian Hand of Doom was in its infancy. They saw from hidden areas that I fought similar to them. When we fought past the guards, Aylund fled with many soldiers, protecting his hide. The Hand and I ran. They protected me as I retrieved Carla's body and our sleeping child. We traveled through many tunnels that were seldom trodden. When we entered their hideout, I wrapped Carla in cloth and kept Alastair in my arms. I was brought before the grandmaster, a Far Eastern man with gold skin.

"Welcome, Mister Beorler. I am *Master Sun Wu.* You have entered the Nodinian chapter of the Hand of Doom," he said.

"I am grateful for your warriors that they saved my son and I. Master Sun Wu, why was I saved?" I asked.

"We keep records on all of Aylund's ranking officials. I was brought to Nodin to stop the East and West empires. My ninja knew early on of your enhancements, Kane. When we learned of the pregnancy of your wife, we knew when you awoke, you would need our help to achieve vengeance. Also, you were closest to Aylund. Kane, you are of vital importance to our cause. If you wish to protect yourself, your son and avenge Carla's suicide, then please consider my offer. I want to induct you into our ranks as my personal student. I offer you the position of shinobi in the Hand of Doom. What say you?" Sun Wu offered.

"My military career is over. I fought long and hard to ensure my people's survival, and I am repaid with my lord defiling my wife and taking hold of my stepson. If this is how a government repays its citizens, then I will aid in its destruction," I stated as Sun Wu and Alastair looked upon me.

Master Wu stepped down from his stone seat. "Without sounding arrogant, it is custom for the student to gently bow to their new master," he informed.

I bowed as instructed with Alastair in my arms. For many years, Master Wu taught me the Eastern martial arts. Ninjutsu was the primary focus when applying the arts to warfare. I trained for five years before I went on my first mission.

When I parted from Xavion's home, I was greatly tired. I was also relieved of how smoothly things went with Alva. I do wish that my past with Xavion didn't haunt me. After all the violence and pain we've dealt to each other, we still sat down, broke bread, and socialized. Xavion still granted me forgiveness when I felt I did not deserve it. I feel like weeping due to his kindness to me.

My branch of ninja began wearing the purple dodecagram on their shoulders and on their foreheads so the Independent Party can identify us from the Hand of Doom. Our job right now is to gather intelligence on East and West Nodin.

Though Alastair ruined Algoth's graduation, he is ready to go out in the field. I resumed the exam with the bokkens. What I'm looking for in Algoth is endurance, resourcefulness, surprise, and technique. All Algoth has to do is ground me and force me to yield. He passed with flying colors! He used my tiredness against me and did not fight on my terms. That is how a ninja succeeds, by controlling the terms and flow of the battle. Algoth went to bed in happiness.

In Alastair's View

I am going insane. The rest of the Hand is weakening my grip. I still beat myself up about the deep shit I have stepped in. There is no way I can bring Kane back or back down from the contract on Xavion. I've seen him fight Kane and win. He's killed Mataraves and several hundred people in these past years. No amount of prayers to the Dark Lord can save me from Xavion's wrath.

My leadership is failing. Twenty of my men have gone missing, and only forty remain. I suspect they have fled to escape the Hand's eventual downfall. The last forty and I have spread across the surface searching for any lead on Xavion. Thinking of what he could do to me brings tears to my eyes.

In Xavion's View

"Xavion," Sebastian called, "there is a host of Soruthians wanting to talk to you. They're waiting on the outside of camp."

"I'm on my way." I replied. As I stood in the house, I used a large purple and white fabric tube to wrap my head into a turban. Many cultures in the world wear these. In the back of the turban, I wore two female red-tailed hawk feathers. I wore brown knee-high moccasins and a purple-and-white sash belt. I wore a necklace made from wampum and amethysts. My jambiya is tucked into my sash upon my stomach. My talwar is in its scabbard. The scabbard is worn on my pants belt. The sword is suspended on the belt by an open leather pocket (connotatively called a "Frog"). The talwar is on my left hip.

I walked with Sebastian toward the host. "Sebastian, this group is highly sensitive. I do not know how they'll react to Nodinians. Let me talk to them."

On the outskirts of the construction site, the Soruthians and the former slave Nodinians stood as I came over the hill. There was a short moment of silence. The Barks especially looked upon my talwar and jambiya. Ten representatives came, two women and men of each ethnicity. Five women and five men stood before me with curiosity. They continued to stare at my purple eyes for a reason of their own.

"Good morning, everyone," I said politely.

An Ember woman spoke. "Are you the one they call the Mourningstar?"

"Yes. My name is Xavion Mourningstar. I am the commander of the Independent Army. We are fighting for a better Nodin to which *all* people can live freely. Since the vigilantes freed you, none of you are slaves— and you will be slaves *no more*! Though I am predominantly Soruthian, I am Nodinian and Yazjian as well. The

North is my birthplace, and I will fight for its future," I stated.

The Bark man then spoke. "I have heard horrifying tales of your talwar, Xavion, and I say your name is not common in this world. Tell us how a Soruthian became a commander in a Northern army?"

"I was a soldier-slave who fought for fifteen years under King Johan Edling. I escaped to the surface for a better chance at freedom. I knew with the Independent Party that all of you could be freed. Now, before we go on too many rabbit trails, how many people here have any military experience?" I asked.

The Ebony woman spoke. "Slow down! We can't fight without knowing what kind of government we would be fighting for. Tell us what everyone has to gain if we fight for you."

"The short way to put it is that all people, regardless of demographic, will have equal opportunity, equal demographic pay, freedom to marry, and freedom of creed and religion. All slaves will be emancipated and slavery is abolished. Everyone gets universal healthcare and free high-quality education. This is done by taxing the wealthy, large businesses and all religious institutions. All monarchies, nobility, aristocracies, feudalism, and capitalism are abolished. All citizens will have the right to bear arms. Weapon owners will receive a certification card that is valid universally in the nation where they have full citizenship. Multiple certifications will be required for multiple citizenships.

"All resources and industries are federally regulated. All Nodinian countries will have a minimum of four political parties. All judicial courts and judges will be neutral and abstain from partisan allegiance. All leaders are elected by popular majority votes. The working class controls the means of production, trade, distribution, and exchange. Lastly, various anti-corruption measures will be implemented. Any leaders who defy them will be impeached. All Nodinian national governments will be fully democratic. The political and academic institutions will be separated from religious institutions—separation of temple and government. You see that ship across the field? If we win this war, anyone can board it and go to Soruth."

The men and women looked at each other curiously with approval.

"You mean if we fight for you, we can go home to our families?" a Sand man asked.

"Yes! I was appointed to go with you to act as an intermediary for any Nodinians who wish to go south. Now, is anyone willing to fight for their freedom?" I asked nicely.

Thirty men and twenty-three women raised their hands. With those hand gestures, a small battalion of Soruthians brought their warrior heritage of women and men to the north. This image is a foreshadow of a better world where all demographics are one global community. A world I intend to be a part of.

I returned home while still in my formal attire; Sareyus had not begun her shift yet. She became lost upon me. Her eyes glistened as she blushed. She stepped toward me finding her words.

"You are beautiful! My goodness, you're lovely! How regal, charming, and colorful!" she exclaimed with joy.

"Thank you. This is my formal attire."

"Soruth would be proud! I love your turban! How your hair hangs beneath its wrapping, it's ornate. Your jambiya is divinely masculine. How…inviting…"

"My eyes are up here." I joked. She took another quick look at jambiya; the amethysts caught her glance.

"Xavion, you have many amethysts, yet you do not use them. Only your jambiya is ornamented with them. Is there a reason?"

"My Jambiya, while functional, was intended to be symbolic. The amethysts are my mineral of choice. The varying purples and lavenders humble me. I wish for the day when I no longer make arms and armor. Someday, I desire to make jewelry, instruments, and clothes."

"Xavion, would you consider making something for me?"

"That depends. What would you like?"

"I would like a necklace of spare amethysts. I would enjoy having a turtle pendant with an amethyst shell. Along the string please add eight trapezoids that fan out. Between each one, use small amethysts between silver beads."

"How stylish. With a matching gown, you will look godly. I will get to work." I smiled.

Chapter 14

<u>In Narration</u>

February ended, March went, and April arrived. The clock is running out of time. The battle for Nodin is drawing upon us. The Independent Nation still gathers support. From each country, twenty-four other cities have joined the party. The soldier numbers of the nation are now eighty thousand. Xavion's influence and charisma grow, but his modesty remains strong. Amon Brav is now occupied, and its defenses are ready. Ballistas and catapults sit high on the mountain fells.

Xavion has appointed Alva and Kane as his bodyguards. Kane put Algoth in charge of the shinobi on the day of the battle. Alva's lunar powers have grown tremendously. If the battle lasts into the night, she will be even more dangerous than Xavion!

During this time, Kane's armor was remade by Xavion. The armor is almost identical in appearance but with minor plating. Sareyus's romantic passion for Xavion holds no bounds. She is running out of time. Her future actions may be her best.

Alastair has learned that Xavion is among the Independent Party. He and all his men are planning to end Xavion before the battle. Johan and Aylund are on the move. Their armies will arrive on time. As East and West battle it out, the Independents will storm the field. The Purple will destroy the Red and Blue. It is the same tactic the Soruthians used in the three Continental Wars of the three lives.

Jahveyis, Bravious, and Tovis have awakened; and without the knowledge of Sareyus, they declared Jahvonis and Xavion as enemies of the gods. However, Jado, Lyannis, Carune, and, shockingly, Sarue, joined Sareyus's side of the debate. This gives Jahvonis another card to play.

On April 22, Sareyus returned from work; she purchased something special and hid it in tied fabric.

Xavion sat patiently waiting on their bed; Sareyus walked in on him.

"You're home early. Busy, I assume."

"I have been tinkering with repairs, yet not all crafts are intended for harm. May I give you something important?"

"You may," Sareyus said while failing to conceal her joy.

Xavion rose. From behind him, he presented the completed necklace to Sareyus. Her flattering joy cast tears down her rosy freckled cheeks. She held it in both hands; she kissed Xavion warmly.

"I have something for you. Please wait until tomorrow," Sareyus said as her heart rang like a gong.

In Sareyus's View

Today is April 23. Xavion and I continue to grow more in love. Our kissing moments increase in length and intensity. Recently, he had me sitting upon the dresser with my legs wrapped around his hips.

The ship is finally finished, and I've made enough money to live on for several months. I hear among the other workers that I am fortunate to be Xavion's partner. Yesterday I purchased a purple dress and hid it in wrapped fabric. It was excellent timing for Xavion to present my necklace. I put the dress and necklace on and walked outside. My hair is moisturized and combed. I am wearing no makeup. As I walked, I turned a few heads. The spring sun blooms my fiery orange hair and my purple attire is radiant. I understand how Xavion feels, purple clothes are rare in Nodin. Xavion is speaking to another blacksmith. I stood in Xavion's vision, and I finally caught his gaze. He finished his conversation and walked toward me. The turtle pendant almost sat in my revealed cleavage. Between my orange hair, green eyes, and purple attire, Xavion's attention is multitasking.

"The gods have blessed me today," he flirted.

"They would like to bless you further…if you allow them to," I flirted back.

He looked at me deeply and thought in great depth.

"I would be foolish to refuse their blessing," Xavion said as we held each other's hands and walked.

When we entered the house, it is empty and we locked the door. It is noon. We embraced in a warm hug.

We began to kiss and caress. My hands gently held his shoulders and loosely hung around his neck. His large broad hands are smooth and firm as he held my widthful hips and lower back.

I am submerged in his smoke. The tranquil aroma of sage, tobacco, sweetgrass, and cedar cleanses us and invokes our debut. I realize this is smudge, the medicinal smoke of the Embers!

Xavion's euphoria-inducing presence brought a ticklish excitement. The rhythm of my heart is overdriven. My blushed goosebumps are raised with anticipation. He slowly undressed me. I undressed him after.

Xavion and I began to consummate our relationship. Our debut is full of smiles, laughter, joy, exploration, peace, romance, mutual satisfaction, and fertilization.

When we finished, we lay in a lovers' embrace. We wept from happiness. Our contagious tears and gentle kissing brought tiredness upon us. Within Xavion's smoke, we saw four figures. The smoke formed four children.

They are two girls and two boys, all with purple eyes. Their mixed features brought more joyous tears to Xavion and I. The children smiled as Xavion gently held my stomach. They then turned into adults. I know now I am with children. The first Goddess to have a natural conception.

Twice a day, between April 24 and April 27, Xavion and I became intimate. Our relationship is now four-dimensional. Our Spirits, Hearts, Bodies, and Minds are bonded to each other. Two Medicine Wheels that are well-rounded.

In Narration

April 28, 904
7:30 a.m.

Final preparations have been made for the *War of Nodinian Independence*. Xavion and the majority of his material possessions have been moved into a private bunker within Amon Brav. Only his military armor and weapons remain in his home where he can quickly get to them. He changed his weapon combination. He will wear his talwar on his left hip and a tomahawk on his right. His jambiya is still worn on his stomach. He will also bear his shield. The hammer-headed tomahawk is mostly an emergency weapon and tool. The hammer portion is for breaking plate armor.

The Jahvonis suit and all other miscellaneous items are in the mountain and are under various locks and keys. For the past three days, thunder and lightning plagued the weather. Tovis is sending a message.

Alva is running her drills and hand-to-hand exercises with Xavion. She uses her superior flexibility and gymnast-like reflexes against Xavion's strength and speed. Alva is also fast in her striking but not as fast as Xavion. In a surprise grapple, Alva grounded her master and trapped him in an arm lock. The student for once beat their master!

"Excellent! Excellent! Excellent! I applaud you, Alva Amott!" Xavion exclaimed as Alva picked him up.

"Have I finally beat the great Xavion?" she joked.

"For today!" her master stated.

Sareyus and Sebastian watched as the student and master repeated with hand and sword. At noon, they ceased. Sareyus got up to hug Xavion, and they kissed. Alva felt envious. She used her Mourneyes to analyze Sareyus. She saw the children beginning to take shape.

"When are we leaving for the mountain?" Sareyus asked.

"We will leave soon, my love," Xavion replied.

"Xavion, we should resume our drills. I'll need much training if you expect me to guard you," Alva persuaded.

Sareyus ignored her words and locked her arms around Xavion. There they stayed for a few minutes. In those minutes, they were playfully waltzing in the yard with the forest around them. Alva glared as her envy turned to jealousy. She did not appreciate how Sareyus ignored her, but she is not upset with Xavion.

From across the field, Kane walked to finalize plans with Commander Xavion before he traveled to Amon Brav.

Near Xavion's home, someone is nestled in a tree. He watched from a distance of three hundred feet. Sareyus faced the direction of this person while hugging Xavion. She was in a trance of love. She heard a snapping sound of wood and the whistling wind. An arrow was fired with Xavion's head being the target. Sareyus panicked, and with lightning speed, she threw Xavion behind her. Alva screamed as the arrow pierced Sareyus from the left shoulder blade into her left bronchial tube. The citizens in the area panicked, and the guards prepared for a possible attack.

"No!" Xavion screamed with agony and despair. He caught Sareyus in his arms in a hug. She coughed her scarlet life force upon Xavion. He broke the head of the arrow and pulled the rest from her back. He laid Sareyus down. Sebastian and Alva rushed to her. The goddess lay crying and dying.

"Xavion...please do not blame yourself."

"Sareyus, don't do this to me! You can't die, I can't lose you too!" Xavion cried dolefully and sobbed.

"I could never have prevented this. I know now you are needed more than ever. You are the best man I have ever known. The gods envy your valor. They are proud of you. I bear our children," Sareyus said as Xavion was lost in her fading eyes. The goddess's eyes turned purple. "We love you, Xavion," Sareyus lamented as the last testament of her mortal life.

Xavion knelt there as history repeated. Three of his dearest friends crossed over in his arms. He gently kissed her and accidentally swallowed her blood. Her last breath was with Xavion's. She passed back into the veil with Xavion's hand being the last thing she felt. Her soul bore the children and fled back to the Gods' Hall. The pantheon sensed the death of Sareyus's vessel and gathered to meet her.

The arrow was shot by Alastair. He fled from the tree and ran. Xavion blew a blood vessel in his eyes, and he snapped. He closed the eyes of his second love. The agony of Astrid and Mataraves were alongside Sareyus. This confusion is insanity. First, Xavion makes love with Sareyus, and five days later, she is taken from him. Her sacrifice could cast Xavion into the abyss. Jahvonis looked as he was shocked at this sudden death. Sebastian guarded Sareyus's body. He brought her inside and locked the door. Sareyus lay on the bed while Sebastian guarded the door with the Mourningstar mace in his left hand.

"After him, Xavion!" Jahvonis yelled.

Xavion's anger erupted. He grasped his talwar and ran in the direction of the shooter. Alva clenched Lunanera and ran after her master. Kane stormed off in the other direction. He knew it must have been Alastair who did this.

Alastair ran frantically. Xavion and Alva are still far behind. As they reached the light-green woods, Xavion huffed and puffed as his tunnel vision blinded him. After fifteen minutes of chasing, Xavion stopped. All is quiet. The Mourneyes activated, and the Hand of Doom surrounded them. In an instant, they attacked from hiding. Fifteen men charged at Xavion and Alva. Alastair is nowhere. The clashing of swords and other metal weapons gave sound to the woods. Several minutes of parrying and striking occurred. Xavion and Alva are fighting to protect each other. They found an opening and began to cleave the Hand with their swords. The Hand of Doom attacked with the ko katana, wakizashi, and tanto dagger.

Alva engaged four men who stood taller than her. Lunanera's length is an advantage. The arming sword clashed, and it dealt significant damage. Alva sliced into the chest of the first, stabbed the stomach of the second, severed the left leg of the third, and decapitated the fourth. Xavion used his advanced saber skills to slay and parry.

The Hand of Doom continued to swarm the two of them. Another ten minutes of this ambush passed until Xavion and Alva fled further into the woods. At an opening patch, a volley of arrows came from the east. They hid behind two tree trunks. Xavion climbed the tree and soared from branch to branch. He silently dropped down behind the archery line and began cutting. Alva bolted over and individually severed the bows with Lunanera. The rest of the Hand came from the west, and minor reinforcements came from the east. They are surrounded and at the center of the horde.

From the west, a host of ninja came over the hill and are led by Kane! They are the Independent Ninja Force, and they crashed at the back of the Hand of Doom. Kane swung precisely with his dadao while Algoth attacked with his *kama* scythes. Shouting, cursing, and clashing became the *war ensemble*. Kane's twenty men are slaying their former comrades with ease.

Kane demonstrated his agility as he did a backflip to avoid an attack from in front. As he was in the air, a Hand Ninja failed an attack from behind. Kane landed a chop to his head with his dadao. Kane caught the dead ninja's sword, and he threw it into the first attacker. Kane severed the right arm of another enemy and cut his jaw off. Kane is wearing his leather armor.

Algoth used his kama to trap blades and cut into the elbows, hamstrings, and faces of the enemy. His third killing ended after pulling both kamas from the throat and skull from one of the Hand.

Alva grabbed her sword by the handle and threw Lunanera like a lance, which pierced through a man as he fell backward. One of the Hand ran to grab her sword. Alva sprang through the air with a kick. The ninja quickly leaped back up. Alva swept his legs, and he fell on the sword. The pointed octagonal pommel pierced his head through the left eye socket. Alva pulled him off with her left hand and held Lunanera in her right. She overkilled him by cutting his upper head off. His jaw was left behind.

During this battle, Xavion released bolts of lightning through a punch and sword swing. The lightning largely chained through the Hand, which killed ten of them. Parvati Kali is ornamented in blood and organic tissue. His last kill was cutting a man in half from his neck down through his groin and decapitation for overkill.

When the final Hand member was cleanly beheaded by Kane, Alastair fired three separate arrows from a tree at his father, Alva, and Xavion. He missed Alva and Xavion. Kane was hit in his bicep. He tore the arrow out and threw it into Alastair's ankle. He was pinned to the tree. Algoth tossed his right kama into Alastair's right shoulder. Alastair's weight caused him to fall from the tree in pain.

Alva ran to stab Alastair. She was stopped by Xavion.

"No, Alva!" he shouted.

"That monster raped me and killed your wife! He deserves this!" Alva screamed.

"He will suffer worse than this," Xavion whispered into her ear.

Kane walked toward the crying Alastair.

"Father, please save me!"

"You lost my love when you divided the Hand and almost killed me. You are not my son… Mataraves was *my son*!" Kane shouted as he stomped upon both of Alastair's wrists and ankles. His amount of force broke the bones in these areas.

"Take him alive! Bind him and bring him to the mountain!" Xavion ordered.

Kane hoisted Alastair over his shoulder. Alva threw a right and knocked him unconscious. Four of his teeth were knocked out. The Nodinian Hand of Doom has been defeated. The North is free from Mustasurma's hold for the time being.

As they returned to the construction site, the guards met them as they were drenched in blood.

"Lord Xavion, what happened?"

"We have captured the leader of the Hand of Doom. He will await trial for the murder of my wife! Take him to Amon Brav, strip him, and lock him up!" Xavion commanded.

The guards carried Alastair away.

Xavion and company walked toward the house. The population who surrounded the house watched the Mourningstar drip blood upon the soil and on the floor of the house. Sebastian wept as Xavion came in and walked his silent funeral march toward his wife. Though they were never married, they were spiritually betrothed. Xavion knelt down on the right side of the bed. He wept;

his tears washed the blood from his angelic face. Alva knelt beside Xavion and cried her blue eyes into the bloody lake upon the floor. Kane knelt maskless and was beside Sebastian on the left side of the bed. Jahvonis and Mioleyis's spirits stood at the bed's foot and gazed at the dead Sareyus. The rest of the ninja guarded the house.

Sareyus's funeral is underway. She is lying upon a pyre in a field outside the construction site. This field is surrounded by a forest. Sareyus was placed in another purple dress and she wears the amethyst turtle necklace that Xavion made for her. Her body is placed in a large ring of various roses, violets, cedar leaves, tobacco leaves, pine needles, sweetgrass, and sage. Her ruby ring is worn on her left index finger.

Xavion stood next to the pyre. He gazed upon the deceased beauty of Sareyus, his final love. Four hundred mourners stood in the east and south. Alva, Sebastian, Kane, Vallen, Bjorn, and Kristoff stood behind Xavion. Jahvonis invisibly stood beside Sareyus (which kept the other gods away). Mioleyis invisibly stood beside Alva. Xavion is dressed in his formal clothing. The same he wore when he met the freed Soruthians.

The Mourningstar lit the bowl of his pipe tomahawk; inside is ground tobacco. He did not smoke it but held it to his heart and prayed. Next, he held the pipe up and faced seven directions—east, south, west, north, sky, earth, and himself. The smoke with the circular rotation and seven directions invoked a presence that only Jahvonis and Mioleyis understand. Xavion lit a torch and followed the same pattern with the pipe. The hidden presence once more accepted the offering and invocation. Xavion gently placed the torch on the mound of herbs and flowers. He stepped back as the flames rose. As Sareyus was surrounded by fire, a great herd of various animals came from the north and west. Wolves, rabbits, birds, bears, horses, squirrels, foxes, deer, reptiles, and many more rested in the valley. Aapo ran and whinnied to Xavion. Cardalen and Valkoinen sat on Xavion's shoulders; and Spirit, the Kermode bear, lay next to Aapo. The people were deeply amazed at this moment. A fellowship bloomed between different life-forms. It's strange how death brings people together. All is silent. Xavion grabbed hold of a twenty-two-inch hand drum and mallet. After four-spaced honor beats, he began singing his lamentation.

> *Soaring Red Tail, Grandfather rise. Eastern Flame brighten sky. Golden rays, seventh day, my respects I will pay. Woodland realm, Great Plains grace, desert sand on my face. Lead me to the place where the horse will race.*
>> *Way hey high yah*
>> *Way hey high yah*
>> *Way hey high yah*
>> *Way hah yoway high yah*
>> *Way hey high yah*
>> *Way hey high yah*
>> *Way hey high yah*
>> *Way hah yoway high yah*
>> *Wampum sea graces me. Turquoise stone on the flute I've blown. Song of prayer, clouds I stare. North wind blows*

*through my hair. Sacred Oak, dreams,
I awoke. Cleansing ailment, smudging
smoke.*

    Way hey high yah
    Way hey high hah
    Way hey high hah
    Way hah yoway high yah
    Way hey high yah
    Way hey high yah
    Way hey high yah
    Way hah yoway high yah

    *Hail Cosmos, life restored, maker of
all welcomes you. I will pray. Red Road
ways.*

    Way hey high Yah
    Way hey high Yah
    Way hey high Yah
    Way hah yoway high yah
    Way hey high yah
    Way hey high yah
    Way hey high yah
    Way hah yoway high yah
    Way hey high yah
    Way hey high yah
    Way hey high yah
    Way hah yoway high yah
    Way hey high yah
    Way hey high yah
    Way hey high yah
    Way hah yoway high yah

Xavion composed this song. It is titled "Red Prayer." The choruses are all vocables. Xavion finished the song with four honor beats that rang through the forest. "Aho!" the Soruthians yelled. "Aho" is one of the Ember equivalents for "Amen." For the next twelve hours, Xavion sat upon the ground and watched the pyre. He realized that Sareyus, Astrid, Hakun, and Helga all had orange hair and all of them burned in fire. Tears fell from his amethyst eyes and hot steam flowed from his nostrils. He knew the attempted murder is Johan's doing. He grew angry how the king of the West has taken both of his loves away.

"She will be fine, Xavion," Jahvonis said with his left hand on Xavion's left shoulder.

Xavion returned home. Before the funeral, he cut a locket of Sareyus's hair, and he will cherish it forever. He decided that Sareyus is the last woman he falls for. In his mind, because they made love, they are espoused. No one else will have his heart or flesh. Sareyus's ring was carried by the smoke back to her in heaven.

After the pyre ceased burning, he collected a portion of ashes into a jar. As he dug through the ashes, he found her turtle amethyst necklace. He looked at it and each of the amethysts have a mild red pigment. It is slightly warm. The purple and red of the jewelry is beautiful. Xavion kept it as a memorial and ceremonial item to Sareyus. What Xavion does not know is that the red inside the amethyst is actually a portion of Sareyus's power and spirit.

The state of this necklace was a contingency plan devised by Jado and Sareyus. This was in case Sareyus's body was killed on the earth. She planted a portion of herself within it after she and Xavion consummated. With Xavion being so in love and sentimental with Sareyus, she knew he would wear the necklace proudly. After she made love with Xavion, she acquired all of his abilities. It was Xavion's inseminations that caused this.

Sareyus did not intend to absorb Xavion's abilities, but she knew what would happen if she acted on her human instinct. She remains spiritually pregnant. She needs an earthly body to give natural birth. She will endure the pregnant side effects for years.

Overall, the plan was to empower Xavion with her powers. They succeeded! When Xavion pleasured Sareyus, he absorbed her essence. Swallowing her bloody kiss also helped. The four infants inside Sareyus's womb will develop in the years to come.

Xavion slept only for three hours. He dressed in his armor and traveled to Amon Brav. As he sat upon Aapo, Cardalen and Valkoinen landed on his shoulders.

"The East will soon arrive," Cardalen said.

"The West should be here by noon," Valkoinen stated.

"Lord Xavion, if this is the last time we meet, you are the best human I have ever known," Cardalen stated with worry.

"I agree with Cardalen. You are a worthy example of a true lord. You make us proud, Xavion. You have the support of the animal kingdom." Valkoinen said.

"The free people will fight and die for you," Aapo stated.

"And you are more worthy to be king than anyone else in the north," Jahvonis complimented.

Xavion rode off through the woods. He saw the mountain as it grieved under the spring moon.

Chapter 15

In Narration

Xavion sat in his bunker staring off into space. Seven ivory-colored candles were burning as he wore Sareyus's necklace. His military armor stood on display. All of his personal weapons are here. He sat nude with his legs folded on the ground with a single candle before him. The jar of Sareyus's ashes is in front of him. His eyes are closed with his hands resting on his knees. His smudge once more flowed. The candles burned like stars and seared well into the morning.

As Xavion meditated, he viewed every important face that led up to this morning. He saw Sebastian, Johan, Astrid, Sareyus, Jahvonis, Mataraves, Kane, Alastair, and Alva. The images landed on Sareyus, and a strange moment took place. The Mourneyes activated, and hot steam flowed from his mouth. The pupils of the Mourneyes then transformed into two large octagrams. Each octagram sat upon a black outline of the medicine wheel. One pupil sat outside the octagram's north, east, south, and west points. Yellow-colored chi energy flowed with the smudge. Xavion's experience grew more psychedelic; he is not intoxicated.

His tears turned purple, but he did not sob. The flames of the candles enhanced and became larger. Ethereal flames burned on his body. They represented the seven chakras. They range from the head to the groin. In order, they are the crown, third eye, throat, heart, stomach, pelvis, and root. The flames are colored top to bottom. They are purple, indigo, blue, green, yellow, orange, and red. The flames of the seven candles reflected the chakra colors.

It did not stop there. The yellow chi, white smoke, and steam formed a circle around Xavion. The seven candles bloomed in their separate sticks. Within the circle, the four compass directions are disconnected and abstract, like four opened gates. The Circle Seven candles amalgamated with their chakra equivalents. The Creators, Cosmos, ghostly, impregnated the dense energy.

For eighty minutes this continued, and Xavion did not speak but only breathed steadily. At dawn, Xavion stood on the balcony that overlooked the battlefield. He raised Parvati Kali while facing south. The new form of the Mourneyes remained strong. He spoke an incantation into the field:

Gods of life! Grant me victory in my conquest of tyranny. Long have you waited for the war in the north to end, and it shall die today! Nodin shall be free of warring empires and will be one. Your children of the north and south are unified in this fight.

Guide us, your children and allow our hellish day to become a heavenly night!

Higher upon the mountain, Alva sat looking up at the moon and absorbed its energy. Her soulful and cold blue eyes looked down upon Xavion.

"You love him, don't you, Alva?" Mioleyis asked.

"I do…with all my heart. For all he has done to help me, he deserves to be loved and cherished. I cannot imagine my life without him now, and I would give my life to see him continue his. I don't want him to be alone for the rest of his days," Alva said with hope.

"Alva, Xavion needs a friend, and it has been only hours since Sareyus's funeral. He needs time to heal and love himself before he can move on," Mioleyis said.

"Sareyus was pregnant with their children. She would have had quadruplets. Xavion will mourn the death of his wife and their children. After Astrid and Sareyus, I don't think Xavion wants to love again, but I will continue to love him. His happiness means more than my desires," Alva replied.

Alva then unsheathed Lunanera and looked upon the engraving. "In the battle, this sword will take the lives of the Western Empire who prostituted me to pay for their war. I will inflict the wrath of the New Moon upon them," Alva stated.

Within Amon Brav, Kane is doing pushups with his feet suspended by his bed. After one hundred, he practiced his shuriken throwing. The target is a dummy with "Aylund" written across the chest. Algoth knocked on the door, and Kane opened.

"Master, a word?" Algoth asked.

"What is it, Algoth?" Kane replied.

"If this is our last day alive, I wanted to spend time with you as a friend," the young man requested.

"Of course, we can," Kane said politely.

For two hours Kane and Algoth bonded. Since Mataraves, Algoth has become Kane's favorite pupil and they have a father-son relationship. Kane also mildly felt that way about Xavion years ago, but it became final during their alliance.

Sebastian will be able to fight. He is stationed in the mountain as a reinforcement. His weapons are his bronze arm, a buckler, and Mourningstar mace. The strategy for the Independent Party is to only take up defenses when East and West fight. They will seal the gates and hide within the mountain to deceive their enemy. They need the element of surprise to catch the empires off guard. So the siege weapons will not be loaded, and no flags will be raised.

At noon, East and West arrived. The once silent field is now immersed in metallic marching, shining steel, and banners of red and blue with pentagrams and hexagrams. Johan and Aylund stood in front of their armies. Johan bore a war ax in his left hand and an arming sword on his right hip. A shield is in his right hand. Aylund has an arming sword on his left hip and a mace on his right. A shield is held in his left hand.

The majority of the snow melted, and the grass grew. For a moment, Aylund and Johan stared each other down. They slowly walked closer. Both wore crown-styled helmets, and neither man spoke. This will be difficult for both men because they have opposite dominant hands. Their weapons will be opposing mirror images.

They were fighting since childhood. Two brothers who fought for power and love. Thousands have died for both men, and now it comes down to this final bout. Red versus Blue and East versus West. Aylund made war against his own family. His jealousy and crimes corrupted Johan. Johan is the lesser of the two evils, but he murdered his own daughter for falling in love. As they walked, they drew their swords and fought.

For ten minutes, the two kings fought and their armies cheered them on.

From afar, Xavion looked through a telescope from the balcony.

"When do we charge, sir?" a soldier asked.

"Wait for my signal," Xavion said.

Many times during this duel, either man could win. The armies were getting paranoid and anxious. They hate each other as much as their kings do. The battle went on, and both armies began to rearrange. Five minutes passed, and two arrow volleys flew from both sides. The casualties began, and the red and blue charged.

Xavion enjoyed the body count beginning. After an hour, the 200,000 men on the field soon became 120,000. Carcasses decorated the field, and the violence spread into the vacant Starkstad. Two more hours passed, and Xavion looked upon the field. The horde began to dwindle. He signaled for the Independents to get ready. Yesterday, several hundred gallons of oil were poured onto the field. Ten ballistas were aimed at the field. The long arrows were dipped in oil and ignited.

"Fire!" Xavion commanded.

As the arrows soared through the air, the Independent flags danced in the wind as the field burned!

The Red and Blue panicked and continued to fight.

The catapults were loaded.

"Fire!" Xavion shouted.

Twelve large boulders rained from the sky, and by this time, the enemy numbered at sixty thousand. The gates of Amon Brav opened. The Independent infantry marched forth and was led by Bjorn. The archers were already in front, and they fired at will. After ten minutes of archery, the bowmen retreated back. Bjorn faced the infantry. He and the Theranths are giants by comparison to the other humans. Bjorn Adolf Edling spoke loud and proud.

"Women and men of Nodin! Long you have been at peace on the surface, but today, your lives and your freedom are threatened by tyrants in Red and Blue. We have worked long and hard to end a war we had no hand in before. Today is *our* day to unify the North under *one* flag and be *one* people! This is our only chance to tell the world that Nodin is for *all* people! Charge beside me! To war and the future!" Bjorn cried! Mellanöstern's blade rested flat against Bjorn's right shoulder and was held in his right hand.

They charged as their hearts quickened. They sprinted with passion and hope. The human yells and Theranth roars terrified East and West. The Purple crashed into the horde, and the Battle for Surface Independence truly began.

Bjorn and Amandus's skills in violence empowered the Independents. All of them are coated in blood. Xavion ceased the archers, ballistas, and catapults before the infantry swarmed the field. The strategy worked. The enemy is too occupied to realize a mutual threat. Already the battle is in Xavion's hands. He stood on the balcony with Kane, Sebastian, Kristoff, Vallen, and Alva. The numbers of the Independents gently lessened.

"I'm going down there. Kristoff, you're in charge if I do not return," Xavion commanded.

Alva, Vallen, Kane, and Sebastian drew their weapons. Minutes later, a second wave of infantry was released. It was a mix of Nodinians and Soruthians while also being humans and Theranths. This wave was led by Xavion! When he entered the fray, he slashed with Parvati Kali and bashed with his shield.

Xavion and Kane fought deeper to reach Johan and Aylund. This new wave proved to be the most violent. The strategy is to capture more space on the field and keep pushing the enemy back as they weaken each other.

Johan and Aylund are bruised and bloody. During this bout, Johan's armor is dented and cracked while Aylund is bleeding from the forehead. Their helmets were thrashed and lost on the battlefield. They also encountered rival opponents. Both used maces to break the lords' armors.

Alva is the most dangerous woman on the field. Among the twenty-four war maidens, Alva is a hero and a symbol for women all across the North. Lunanera's legend and prestige grew with each kill. Bjorn's immense strength and sword skill took more and made space on the field.

Sebastian rechristened the Mourningstar mace as he regained his confidence. He met General Daveth on the field, and they were locked in combat. Daveth was bloody, bruised, and groggy. His sword was broken, and his skull was crushed by Sebastian. He achieved his justice!

Amandus rallied the Theranths as they reveled in the chaos and bloodshed. The Man-Beasts were mentally lost in the battle and claimed the most lives. Vallen did not hesitate to drive his ax into his foes. He slew three generals from West Nodin. He fought for the best future of Nodin, and battling his former comrades is a small price to pay.

Another half hour passed, Aylund and Johan are completely separated. A sea of warriors is between them. As Aylund fought the soldiers of two armies, he saw an armored man covered in blood... Kane!

Johan is surrounded by his men who were attacked by the Independents. When the western sun shined on him, he saw the man behind this attack: Xavion Mourningstar! The Independent commander began torturing Johan with slashing humiliation. The quick cuts with Parvati Kali began to immobilize the king.

Kane was following the same technique. Five more minutes passed. Aylund went for a strike with both hands on his mace. Kane clenched the dadao and severed both of the Vakuutava's hands. Aylund screamed as he fell to both knees. Kane stood over him. "For Carla," he said and swung his sword downward and severed half of Aylund's head. With a rightward horizontal cut, he removed the rest of Aylund's head. Kane continued to fight. His mission is accomplished.

During this time, Xavion continued to cut Johan as hot steam flared from his nostrils and mouth. The commander used his curved talwar to counter Johan. The king's sword was parried by the back of the talwar. The blades were locked. The talwar was twisted and thrust into Johan's throat! The king stared into the purple eyes of Xavion.

"For Astrid," Xavion said. The new Mourneyes activated as the talwar was removed. Xavion opened his mouth as a ball of fire began to build. The octagram on his chest gave more power. A bright flash of light illuminated the field. A colossal fire blast incinerated the bodies of Johan, Aylund, and eight hundred more enemies. Xavion gained this ability from Sareyus. The blast ranged for one mile east. All not caught in the blast looked in awe. When it ceased, the survivors of East and West fled the field. The Independents cheered in victorious glee. The Battle for Surface Independence was won.

The Independents ran to their commander. They chanted his name as they walked with him to Amon Brav.

"Xavion! Xavion! Xavion!"

In the mountain, the soldiers and civilians cheered and celebrated. There was no counterattack from East or West Nodin.

Two days after the battle, a large gathering was held in Starkstad. This is the trial of Alastair. On a large wooden stage in the center of the city, our heroes and a headsman stood off to the side.

"Alastair Beorler, you stand guilty for the crimes of assault, murder, conspiracy, and rape. We have four witnesses to your heinous acts. The people of Nodin demand your execution. Do you confess?" Kristoff announced.

Alastair spat in Kristoff's face as he was held up by the guards. Kristoff elbowed his face. The impact was amplified by his bloody broken nose. Alastair was tied down to a table and is nude.

Xavion stood silently as he wore his formal Soruthian clothing, Sareyus's amethyst, and Mataraves's knife. He drew the knife and slowly stepped toward Alastair's right side. He began to whimper. "May Hamish and my wife rejoice as the wicked fall to ruin." Xavion said as his eyes shined in ominous violet. Xavion gripped Alastair's dark-blond hair in his left hand. He initiated a slow scalping. Alastair screamed and whined like a child. The bloody and fleshy top of his skull stung as air flowed within. Xavion then moved behind Alastair's head with his hairy scalp in hand. He handed the knife to the headsman.

The headsman gripped the shaft of the ax and moved into position. Alastair looked on with fearful tears. The headsman held the ax in their left hand. They are adorned in a black cloth robe and hooded mask. They used their right hand to remove the hooded mask. Underneath is Alva Amott!

She put the ax aside and began the vile, sweet, and vengeful torture of her attacker. She made an incision on his scrotum and yanked his testicles from his pelvis. She then sawed through his penis at the base. The three organs that defiled and impregnated her will do harm no more. With the ax, she chopped off his extremities. The ax came down below his knees and removed his legs. The pitch and volume of his screams continued to rise.

His hands were next, the tools that beat her and gripped her private areas are broken and destroyed. She took both of his arms off by cutting through the elbows. The blood that stained the wood is putrefaction. Alva and Xavion looked upon Alastair with the Mourneyes. The ax came down across his throat before he died from exsanguination. His decapitation was the end of the Nodinian Hand of Doom. His remains were burned.

The rest of the day was a vast feast and memorial for those who died in the name of freedom. Through that time, Alva was laughing in happiness for she gifted herself a good future. Kane did not mourn Alastair but did mourn for his past with the Hand of Doom.

Xavion became the most popular attendee at this party. Hundreds gathered around him to hear his stories with the military. When he and Alva were together, they gave hugs as a sign of close friendship.

On May 20, a public gathering was arranged. A celebration for the surfacers achieving independence. Xavion received many gifts that day. The simple gifts were amethysts. People now believe Xavion is divine. The purple stones are offerings to him. Soldiers did their best to appeal to Xavion.

Blacksmiths gifted their finest weapons and armors. Purple cloaks, blankets, and many other clothes were made for him. The Barks made a long hooded purple robe with a large white octagram on the torso. They also gave him leather sandals. There were Theranthium weapons gifted to Xavion.

The Ebonies gifted Xavion a few items. The first was a traditional short spear known as the *iklwa (eek-wa)*. With the help of a bladesmith, the second gift was a saber-sickle sword known as the *shotel (show-tell)*. The Sands followed the same idea and granted Xavion a weapon, a club-sword known as the *macuahuitl (ma-qwah-wheat)*.

The Embers crafted a metallic version of their *gunstock war club*. It is shaped like a rifle. On the outer curve of the club, there is a blade that allowed the club to slash and chop like a saber. There is also a decent-sized cross guard. With this club, Xavion has a lot of versatility. The images of chopping, slashing, and bludgeoning made him grin. This was his favorite gift alongside the macuahuitl. The inner curve was tapered enough to focus the blunt force on narrower areas that will increase damage. This club can be used single-handed or doublehanded. The Embers also had one of the ball-headed clubs made for Xavion. Sheaths were designed for the edged weapons.

As Xavion and company sat at a large table within Starkstad, he prepared his words for a public announcement. He tapped a spoon against his amethyst-adorned bronze goblet.

"Everyone! Everyone, please gather around so you can hear me!" he asked.

All in the distance gathered at his front and sides.

"I wanted to say thank you all so much for your gifts. I will treasure them forever. We have defeated the Underground Kingdoms, and without their leaders, they will request to be a part of the improved Nodin. Please do not discriminate against them. Respect your differences and work toward a better future.

"While for now we can celebrate, but we have one more threat to extinguish—the dragon Kuolemajää! As he sits atop Vuorijää, he plans his conquest of the north.

We are the best defense against this beast. We must prepare an assault so that our freedom as Theranths and humans is assured!" Xavion exclaimed.

"How do we know the dragon is hostile? What proof have thee, Xavion?" Amandus questioned as he stood up from the table.

"Amandus, during the siege of Vuorijää, did you find Kuolemajää beneath the mountain?" Xavion questioned back.

Amandus remembered it was Kuolemajää who commanded the Theranths in their conflict against the humans. If Amandus lies, the reputation of the Theranth military becomes negative.

"Yes. It was Kuolemajää who commanded us Theranths against the humans. We deserted his leadership after our mission was complete. Remember, we Theranths were created to be weapons. We fought to become people!" Amandus stated with truth and honesty.

"And is your allegiance to the Independent Party?" Xavion asked.

"To the Independents and to the Mourningstar!" Amandus stated while looking Xavion in the eye.

"I make a motion for Xavion to lead us on our next campaign!" Bjorn stated.

"Motion seconded," Kristoff said.

"All those in favor?" Kane shouted.

The crowd cheered with approval.

"All those opposed?" Kane added.

The crowd was silent.

"I accept my nomination!" Xavion shouted.

The crowd cheered. Through the gleeful cheering, the ears of the Theranths picked up a shrill cry from the north. A cold, windy blizzard stormed upon the town. A white ray of ice and frost was spewed. Kuolemajää had attacked.

In an array of panicking swarms, the citizens screamed as forty of them were frozen in an icy block of quick death. The archer guards fired at will. Kuolemajää regained his white fur and feathers. His scales are at full strength. Kuolemajää's visible weakness is the skin upon the inside of his wings. A large puncture or cut could render him flightless. He circled around Starkstad and trapped the town in a ring of ice. Several thousand arrows continued to hit him, but they were microscopic in damage.

Kuolemajää summoned another blizzard. From the sky, thousands of razor-sharp ice spikes rained and killed hundreds. The dragon landed on the longhouse and crushed it. With one swing of his front forearm, he sent dozens flying into the air.

In the fray, Xavion activated the second-level Mourneyes. Hot steam flowed from his breath, and electricity formed in his hands. He fired his bolts and spewed his flames. The white dragon felt the searing shocks. His green eyes looked upon Xavion's. Kuolemajää knows this is the gods' son. As he glared upon our hero, Xavion is prepared to give his life for Nodin. As the snow continued to blow, lightning and thunder broke the sky. Tovis cast his bolts down upon the dragon. Kuolemajää took flight and retreated back to Vuorijää.

Five hundred casualties were claimed by the dragon. None of our main characters were lost; but Xavion, Kane, and Bjorn were injured from ice spikes. The blizzard and thunderstorm ended. The ring of ice began to melt. From heaven, Sareyus accelerated the heat in Starkstad, the ice melted quicker. Those who were injured were treated after the town was evacuated. The water in the ice healed Xavion as it melted. Kane had a spike in his calf, but his high pain threshold kept him calm. Bjorn was punctured in his left tricep; his wound had to be cauterized.

A mass funeral was held that day. The bodies of the deceased were separated by gender and buried in a large grave. Xavion gathered his company, the jarls, and the Theranth Chiefs of the Independents. They had a meeting in the field where Sareyus's pyre was held.

"The Dragon of the Northern Winters has made his move. When do we make ours?" Alva asked the men.

"We know where to find him, but how do we defeat Kuolemajää?" Amandus questioned.

"You are the only one here who worked with Kuolemajää. Do you have any information we can analyze?" Kristoff inquired to Amandus.

"In the Theranth Wars, Kuolemajää taught us to fight with sophistication. The guerilla tactics we learned from the Soruthian Theranths. Kuolemajää knew how we were transformed and abused. He used our anger and weakness against us. The dragon's plan was to use us to conquer Nodin. After we defeated the humans, we discarded Kuolemajää for he was in no position to control us. The only viable weakness we found was that his snout is less scaled. From our records, his scales are as hard as steel. Our Theranthium is much harder and can penetrate it. The skin on his wings can be torn, but even arrows did little damage against them," Amandus informed.

"A spear, an ax, or my greatsword could cut through his wings. But we'll need a whole army and siege weapons to slay him. If his snout is the only viable weakness, someone will have to get close to cut him. If we can damage his nose, his breathing will be negatively altered. If the dragon cannot breathe, then he'll be vulnerable," Bjorn said.

The other advantages the Independents have are Alva and Xavion. All of Starkstad saw Xavion cast lightning and breathe fire. While Jahveyis and Bravious still see Xavion as a threat, Tovis saw an opening to strike Kuolemajää.

"We have no choice. Vuorijää must be assailed, and the white dragon slain. I propose in two days, we march on the mountain. All in favor?" Xavion asked.

All raised their hands.

That night as Xavion slept, he strayed into a dream. He dreamt of hugging Sareyus. Little did he know that in this dream, Sareyus cast her previous image into his subconscious. Xavion was wearing her amethyst necklace. Sareyus can use this gem as a secondary window through Xavion's first-person view. The same ability can be achieved by seeing through his eyes (like Miolannis and Jahveyis). After four hours of reliving his time with Sareyus, Xavion fell into another dream, this time with Jahvonis.

"I have to talk to you," Jahvonis said.

"About Kuolemajää?" Xavion replied.

"Yes. I have some experience fighting dragons."

"What was your battle with Mustasurma like?" Xavion asked.

"It was the hardest battle I've ever fought. It was I who lost in the end. Granted it was Jahveyis who slew me. The dragons can shape-shift into humans and Theranths. Avgrund is the only one who can turn into an Aquranth. Mustasurma was in his human form when we fought. He wore armor. This battle occurred during the Second Armageddon. Jahveyis interfered. I don't see Kuolemajää fighting in any mortal form," Jahvonis stated. He summoned a mass of black mist in his right hand. What he summoned was the Hellhammer mace. Xavion knew this is the mace of the Dark Lord.

"This is what you need to defeat Kuolemajää. His scales are no match for this mace. When you wake up, this will be at your side. There is a thunderstorm outside, inhale as much of it as possible. Your powers and Hellhammer are your best weapons against the dragon. Another thunderstorm will take place when you face Kuolemajää. His size will attract more lightning when he's airborne," Jahvonis said.

Xavion grasped Hellhammer in his right. The eight flanges on the Yazjian-style mace are large. The mace is twenty-four inches long. It is entirely black. "Thank you," Xavion said calmly.

When he woke, Hellhammer was in his right hand. Jahvonis altered the mace's energy to accommodate Xavion's powers. Jahvonis, since acquiring Hellhammer, has greatly lessened Jahveyis's connection to it. Jahveyis can no longer summon the mace. Hellhammer now fully belongs to the Black Paladin.

Xavion entered the wilderness. He saw Alva inhaling the electricity. She sat with the unsheathed Lunanera in her hands. The blade sparked with static. Xavion lightly breathed flame onto the mace head, and electricity enhanced the weapon's magic.

The following morning, Starkstad was approached by several thousand men who were armored. These are the surviving warriors of the recent battle at Amon Brav. They came not bearing the red and blue colors. They were met by the Independents. This turned into a full surrender from the Underground Kingdoms. The representatives of the Red and Blue signed a treaty and contract to relinquish their governmental power, to hand over their records and resources, free all slaves, and all current soldiers are to be enlisted under Commander Mourningstar and the jarls of Nodin. They signed their names and stamped a bloody thumbprint. The soldiers of the purple party now number approximately 180,000.

The following morning, half of the army marched north to Vuorijää. This host contained Alva, Kane, Bjorn, Vallen, Sebastian, Kristoff, Amandus, and Xavion. The strategy is to ground Kuolemajää and damage his wings and snout. The Theranths and Bjorn, with their Theranthium weapons, will damage the dragon's scales. The archers are vital. If they can shoot his wings or eyes, then the dragon is more vulnerable. The remaining soldiers stayed behind to protect civilians.

On August 8 of 904 in the Third Life, the ninety thousand men and women stood across the valley from

Vuorijää. It is winter in this region. The sky is dark, and the mountain stood tall and white. Alva prayed, for she and Mioleyis could sense the goddess within the ice. Xavion stood at the front with his friends. The entrance to the mountain is barred by an iron gate. This was made by the Theranths many years ago. The entrance is too small for Kuolemajää. It's unlikely he's hiding inside. A thunderstorm began. Tovis is striking the mountain to draw the dragon out.

From the tip of the mount, Kuolemajää shouted as he entered the electric sky, "Thunder god! You dare trifle with the White Lord of the North!"

As he looked southward at the army, he flew upon them as arrows and spears began to fly. Those with melee weapons waited until the dragon landed. It is sunset, and the new moon rose. Tovis increased the lightning velocity. Kuolemajää's wings are severely pierced by arrows. For twenty minutes the lightning kept the frost breath at bay. Sareyus greatly increased the heat in the sky, which harmed Kuolemajää's cold-based power.

The new moon powered Alva. She took a deep breath, drew Lunanera, and teleported onto Kuolemajää's right wing! His flapping almost shook her loose, but she gripped her sword by the handle and thrust deep through the other side. She used her weight to drag the sword down through the wing. Kuolemajää screamed as a bolt struck his snout and momentarily paralyzed him. As he fell to the ground, Alva teleported back to the ground. The Independents swarmed, and the dragon scales began to wither and tear.

Mellanöstern was thrust deep into the flesh. Bjorn and the Theranths created many entry wounds. Xavion struck the front arm with Hellhammer. He fractured Kuolemajää's right wrist. The dragon quickly regained his mobility. He began swinging and sending soldiers high into the air. Xavion jumped in front of Kuolemajää and spat a large fireball into his face. Our hero began electrocuting as Tovis threw another bolt to the dragon's spine. The soldiers attacked again. Alva (being smart) tossed a long spear into the dragon's left eye! Sareyus drastically increased the heat around the dragon.

Kuolemajää is running out of options. When the paralysis faded, he fought back with a vengeance. He stood upright on his hind legs, and with his wings, he flapped a typhoon that sent hundreds flying east. The flapping widened the tear that Alva caused. He breathed frost into the sky, and once again, thousands of ice spikes rained. Bjorn blew a horn, and from the southwest, a flaming boulder soared. It exploded on the back of the dragon's head. The boulder was fired from a catapult.

Bjorn sprinted as the beast was groggy. He jumped forward at Kuolemajää's left heel. Mellanöstern cut through a weak spot and severed the heel tendon. Kuolemajää fell on his stomach as the army continued to pummel away at his body. Hellhammer broke Kuolemajää's right hand.

Meanwhile, under Vuorijää, Miolannis stood frozen in ice. She is conscious but still unharmed. Her cell is still frostbitten. In these past months, Miolannis wondered long if anyone would come to save her. Her spirit is trapped in the ice with her body. Her soul is ripe with despair. Many times she felt she should die and forsake her divine identity. She looked back on her history with Kuolemajää, Jahvonis, and her eight daughters. She looked back on her experience with Sareyus. If Miolannis is ever saved, she will be a better goddess and person. The one thing she regrets is not being a better mother to Jahvonis.

The Dark Lord Jahveyis saw his one chance to free Miolannis. In his hellish black armor, he used Bravious's war hammer to viciously break away the ice that imprisoned his beloved. He began when the Independents arrived in the valley. He is nearly done, soon the Courtship will reunite. Jahveyis intelligently used his energy to great effect. The war hammer crushed the ice. The Dark Lord used both hands on the hammer. It will take a long while before he's finished. He also magically bent the ice away. He could do this after attaining Miolannis's powers from their marriage.

The Independents continued to harm Kuolemajää. The thousands who stabbed, bashed, and cut into his skin were horrific acupuncture. In a last burst of adrenaline, he spun around and took Xavion in his left hand. When he spun, many soldiers were either crushed or flew in the wind. On his good leg, he hopped into the air and flew back to the mountain.

"*Xavion!*" Alva cried.

"Follow him! Rescue Xavion!" Kane shouted.

The Independents ran violently after the dragon to no avail. Xavion's hands were still free as he bashed the left hand of the dragon. Tovis is now in a dilemma. Xavion's death leaves Jahvonis without a host, but Kuolemajää's death can lead to the defeat of the other dragons. In a hasty move, he shot another bolt to the neck of the white dragon. Kuolemajää began to nosedive and crashed landed on the mountaintop. He dropped Xavion in a loose patch of snow. The ground crumbled in an avalanche. The Mourningstar fell deeper into the mountain.

Three hours passed as Xavion lay in the snow underneath Vuorijää. Sareyus kept him warm and secure from the intense cold. Xavion rested, but he is in pain from the long fall. Hellhammer is close to his side. He breathed heavily, for he was losing his breath. Being in the dragon's grip was the most frightening experience he's ever had. The amethyst necklace changed into a magenta color. Sareyus kept Xavion in comfortable warmth. This reminded Xavion of the day they lay together. Xavion fell asleep. In his dream, Sareyus lay on top of him and they kissed. As they kissed, they both held onto the amethyst necklace.

"Awake, my love. It is not your time yet. We all believe in you. I love you, Xavion," Sareyus said and disappeared.

Xavion awoke sore and warm. He took off his helmet to breathe. He looked up at the ceiling and saw the hole that he fell through. He prays that Kuolemajää hasn't slain his comrades.

"Xavion," said a voice.

He looked upward to his left and saw the black ghostly form of Jahvonis.

"You are not finished yet, brother. There is more fight in you, enough to finish Kuolemajää. You can do this, Xavion. It is your destiny!" Jahvonis said as he faded.

The quake of the dragon's fall cracked Miolannis's prison. The Independents could find no way into the mountain; they had to wait. The snow that surrounded Xavion melted. He drank the water to heal his wounds. From across the room, he saw a shining object poking out of the snow. He cautiously stumbled to the item. When Xavion came upon it, he saw a long maple shaft. He pulled it out from the loose snow. It is a battle-ax. On the langets, it reads, "*Giljotin.*" The great ax of Leif Edling III. Xavion grabbed hold of the rusted weapon. He used his earth powers to bend the rust off. He journeyed to the top of Vuorijää. The trip took several hours.

At dawn, Xavion stood within the Chamber of the Dark Lord and the Moon Mistress. Kuolemajää lay motionless but alive. Xavion used his stealth walking. He planned to chop into the beast's remaining eye. Valkoinen sat on the icy spire of the mountain. Xavion is close, in an instant, Kuolemajää, spewed a blast of ice. Xavion saw his life flash before his eyes. His instincts activated his fire breath. The second-level Mourneyes, the octagram, and Sareyus's amethyst all powered simultaneously. The blast of fire was eight stories tall. Within the flame, Sareyus cast an ethereal self-image breathing fire. Kuolemajää is defenseless.

When the blast was finished, Kuolemajää's white color was burned black. Not wasting a moment, Xavion chopped repeatedly at the dragon's snout. The long rest Kuolemajää had helped him gather energy. He once again used his right leg to hop into the air.

During this bout, Jahveyis finally freed Miolannis. She fell into his arms. She is icy cold.

"I knew you would find me," she said in a faint voice.

"No one will take you from me ever again!" the Dark Lord swore as he removed his helmet.

They kissed with reunification.

"Jahveyis, if Kuolemajää could accomplish my kidnapping, what could the other dragons do?" Miolannis asked.

"My love, do not worry about them. They cannot harm us and they never will," Jahveyis replied.

"It does not matter. It has been proven they can escape. We must show them that rebellion will not be tolerated. I will return, my business is not finished," she said as she faded into a snowy breeze.

Miolannis soon stood above the chamber of the Courtship. She looked down at Xavion and up at Kuolemajää as he flew above the spire. Tovis threw one last bolt at the heart of the dragon. He fell as his heart stopped beating. Miolannis greatly erected the ice spire. Kuolemajää's impalement was his doom. Nodin is saved.

Miolannis and Jahveyis traveled back to heaven. Kuolemajää's blood soaked the ice and snow. Xavion collected the dragon's blood in his canteen. It would take him twenty-four hours to get back to ground level. On the way down, he ingested the dragon's blood.

The soldiers waited long hours for some sign of Kuolemajää or Xavion. On the morning of August 10, the soldiers began to leave for there is yet no sign of their commander. They assumed his death.

"Hello, everyone!" they heard from atop of the iron gate. They looked up, and there was Xavion.

"Sensei!" Alva cried in joy.

"Xavion!" Kane said softly.

The commander slid down with Giljotin in hand.

"Did you kill Kuolemajää?" the army asked.

"We *all* killed Kuolemajää!" Xavion said humbly.

The journey home was long with glee and laughter.

That night, Xavion returned Hellhammer to Jahvonis. Xavion felt that the mace is too special to use heavily or extensively. This would allow Jahvonis to further experiment on it.

Another celebration was held in Starkstad to honor the fallen and embrace those who survived. Xavion gifted Giljotin to Vallen and Bjorn as an heirloom of the Edlings. While Astrid and Johan were the last of the royal house, small bands of the Edlings still live underground and on the surface.

Alva approached Xavion with a hug that night.

"I was so worried about you," she said.

"I never gave up," Xavion replied.

"I was scared to face the world without you," Alva admitted.

"Everything worked out. Please do not worry," Xavion said.

Nodin is in its happiest generation. No empires, no dragons, and no wars. Between November and March, Nodin's laws were altered and rewritten. Nodin became a progressive democracy.

At that time, the Soruthians, Xavion, Alva, Sebastian, Kane, and a portion of the ninja were packing their possessions. All were met with much endearment and valuable offerings. On March 8 of 905, the *Freedom* ship is ready to be boarded.

"Are you sure you wish not to stay?" Bjorn asked Xavion.

"Yes, Bjorn, I am sure. We have done all we can to help Nodin. We have succeeded. My Soruthian family wishes to return to the Motherland and I owe them that," Xavion said.

"You and the Soruthians are part of our family. Should you need us, we will come to your aid. This is our last gift to you and your captains," Kristoff said.

Four men brought out four large chests of gold coins. They were accepted gratefully.

Kane approached Bjorn. "Bjorn, I know the story with Alastair and Aylund is sad, but I see you as a better man than them and myself. I trust you, Vallen, and Kristoff as you sit in the Nodinian Congress. I'm sorry that I cannot be here to see you grow, but I have too many bad memories here."

"I know how you feel, Master Kane, but I see you as my father if no one else. I forgive you and your past. I wish you a good future." Bjorn said. The giant hugged Kane and picked him up in the air.

Out of the fifty Ninja, five stayed behind to teach ninjutsu to any students. The shinobi will once more make their mark on the world. The remaining Soruthians and Nodinian immigrants boarded the ship. Kane helped an elderly man with a walking staff to travel the ramp to the deck.

"Thank you for your help, my good man. We are fortunate that Nodin is at peace. As I say, *the reputation of a thousand years may be determined by the conduct of one hour*," the elder stated.

"All is as you predicted, Master Wu," Kane replied to this grandmaster.

Xavion was last to board. He took Aapo and Cardalen with him. As the vessel floated down the large southern river, a crowd of thousands bid their farewells with cheering. The sea is a great vast blue haven of Carune with a blue cloudless sky to match. The water is calm and clear.

Xavion is at the wheel and is the captain. Sareyus only made the heat mild. Lyannis made the sunlight bright but not overbearing. Many women watched Xavion's beauty and powerful stance. The men watched him and admired his reputation and modesty.

On June 1, Xavion looked through his telescope in the southern direction. He saw a large island as they sailed down from the north. He saw a shipping port. There is a flag that is colored red, yellow, white, and black. At the center of the colors, he saw a great seal. It reads, *"The Seal of the United Ember Nations."* He saw a host of Ember warriors amassing. Their war chief is a man with a roached haircut, tattoos, and scars. He bore a tomahawk, knife, bow, and an arrow quiver on his back.

Meanwhile, in heaven, the gods told Miolannis what occurred in her absence. They sat in a great debate over Kuolemajää's death, Jahvonis's infiltration, Xavion's progress, and Sareyus's pregnancy.

"The death of Kuolemajää is the beginning of something large. Jahvonis's assault shows that he has hostility. Yet his theft of Hellhammer proved to be a blessing in disguise. While Jahvonis and Mioleyis are my children, I will not work against them if they mean to do good.

Jahvonis may not like his father and I, but he unintentionally helped save me. Mioleyis only joined Xavion's group to save me, and they passed with flying colors. I applaud Sareyus for finding love and her future as a mother. While Xavion is our son, he is not Sareyus's son," Miolannis stated.

"It is true. I made love with Xavion, and I bear our children. I do not regret my choices or my time being human. I am proud to have experienced mortality. For now, all that matters to me is rebuilding my body, having my children, reuniting with Xavion, and making sure none of the other dragons escape," Sareyus stated.

The gods sat in awkward silence, little did they know they are being watched. Through Sareyus's eyes, there is a watcher in another realm.

"Excellent," Jahvonis said.

To be continued in
The Mourners:
Books 4–6 of Xavion & Sareyus

About the Author

As a teenager, I intended Xavion & Sareyus to be my first novel. I began experimenting with writing at ten and took it seriously at fifteen. My first story was a teen and young adult romance, which greatly inspired this story. Alongside my writing, I play the guitar, bass guitar, and several Native American-style flutes and drums. I love studying history. My ancestry is amalgamated between Moorish, Indigenous American, and European. My full tribal name is *Sleeping Turtle the Laughing Hawk Straight Arrow*, but I personally prefer *Sleeping Turtle* as my tribal name.

www.ingramcontent.com/pod-product-compliance
Lightning Source LLC
Chambersburg PA
CBHW030349030726
47497CB00002B/248